DATE DUE		
12-12-99		
	JUL 23 1999	

BRANCH

SOLAR
ECLIPSE

BY JOHN FARRIS
FROM TOM DOHERTY ASSOCIATES

SOLAR ECLIPSE

JOHN FARRIS

A TOM DOHERTY
ASSOCIATES BOOK

NEW YORK

SOLAR ECLIPSE

A Forge Book
Published by Tom Doherty Associates, LLC
175 Fifth Avenue
New York, NY 10010

Forge® is a registered trademark of Tom Doherty Associates, LLC

Designed by Lisa Pifher

Library of Congress Cataloging-in-Publication Data

Farris, John.
    Solar eclipse / John Farris.—1st ed.
      p.   cm.
    "A Forge book."
    ISBN 0-312-85072-7 (alk. paper)
    I. Title.
    PS3556.A777S58   1999
    813'.54—dc21   99-26074
                                                   CIP

First Edition: July 1999

Printed in the United States of America

0 9 8 7 6 5 4 3 2 1

ACKNOWLEDGMENTS

"Cheerfulness keeps up a kind of daylight in the mind." Forgetful Rosalind is quoting, on page 162, Joseph Addison (*The Spectator*, May 17, 1712). On page 193, "Heaven's awful rainbow" belongs to John Keats. On 308, "Perked up in a glist'ring grief . . ." is adapted from Shakespeare—*Henry VIII*, Act Two, Scene Three. The line Ros quotes on page 317 is from Jimmy Rodgers's *The Brakeman's Blues* (*Yodeling the Blues Away*).

I owe Sheriff Glenwood Humphries (ret.) of Washington County, Utah, a great debt for his generosity in taking time to answer my many questions about law enforcement within his jurisdiction. Mike Dee, curator of big cats at the Los Angeles Zoo, contributed valuable information about the personalities and habits of South American jaguars.

I.

WHAT WE ALL WANT IS SAVAGE DELIGHT.

—JAMES DICKEY
SORTIES

1 BONNER WAS OKAY UNTIL the shooting started. Then the sight of the sedan careening through the hotel's parking lot while gunmen with automatic weapons opened up got to be too much for him. The sedan crashed into a pickup truck, putting an end to the action. Doc Scanlan's new wife Katy, who was twenty-five years younger than Doc and pretty impressed with the movie stuff, looked around at Bonner as he got to his feet and excused himself.

As he walked away from their table in the Galaxy Room, he heard Doc say, "Honey, you don't know what the man's been through."

Doc came into the men's lounge while Bonner was splashing cold water on his face. They'd known each other since El Paso, kept in touch after they left the DEA, a year apart. Doc was one of those rare men over fifty who looked good with a crew cut. He did the weights and swam a lot and had a bronze desert tan. Bonner looked at his own face through blurry eyes and thought that he probably didn't get out enough any more.

"Okay?" Doc asked him.

"Yeah. Sorry." Bonner accepted a hand towel from the lounge attendant, who was dressed like a character from *Star Trek*. The hotel, thirty-five hundred rooms at the south end of the ever-expanding Strip, was called the Space Odyssey.

They went back to their table. Choice view from a sixth-floor terrace of the Strip and the monster hotels, now known as "destination resorts," on either side. Doc was the chief investigator for the

Nevada Gaming Commission, and he got celebrity treatment at all of the hotels. Katy, who had been a dancer at the Luxor before becoming the third Mrs. Scanlan, smiled at them and said, "They're getting ready to do a stunt next."

Because movies seemed to be her major interest, Bonner said, "They shot some of *Butch Cassidy and the Sundance Kid* in my country."

Katy said, frowning, "I don't believe I've seen that one."

Doc said, "Before your time, honey," and he and Bonner exchanged looks, Doc with a trace of a wry smile.

"Thinking about getting married again, Tobin?" Doc asked him. "The deputy, what was her name?"

"Luz. I don't know. Maybe we're too comfortable to get that serious right now."

He worked on his salad, glancing from time to time at the parking lot. A stunt woman was getting into pads before going to work. Knees, elbows, hips, kidneys. She also was wearing a complicated orthopedic brace on her right knee. Good-looking, from what he could tell at a distance. A lot like Demi Moore, whom she was doubling for. Tall and athletic—but they all had to be athletes in that business.

Katy said, "That's the same one. This afternoon she jumped out of a helicopter onto the roof of a van? A good twenty feet, and they were traveling in opposite directions. I majored in circus at Florida State, but I wouldn't have the nerve to try that."

Doc glanced at his pager, took out his cellular phone. Bonner watched him, thinking that it must be a pretty good life. Bonner was in Vegas for a deposition, and Doc had already hinted that he could get Bonner into a top security job at one of the new resorts under construction nearby. Not a hard life at all, dealing mostly with drunks, card and slot cheats, petty thieves and scammers. Six figures annually.

The steaks in the Galaxy Room were as good as the steaks at the El Cortez downtown, but since his trip to the men's room to collect himself, Bonner had concentrated on the wine, and his appetite wasn't there anymore.

The movie people were rehearsing, getting the timing of the stunt down. Katy said that movie stunts were called "gags." The gag that was coming up required a stunt driver to accelerate, then stop his vehicle within three feet of the woman who was doubling for Demi. Simultaneously she was catapulted with enough force to roll the entire length of the car and drop off the trunk. She did a trial run for timing, padding across the hood of the car, then they were ready to film the gag, cameras placed so it would look as if she were really getting smacked by the speeding car.

Some way to earn a living, Bonner thought. But he admired the way she controlled her body to minimize the risk.

After the print take she came up, limping in spite of the knee brace. But she pumped a fist in the air, and the crew applauded. Demi ran out and hugged her. The stunt player took off the wig she'd been wearing and shook out her own hair, as dark as Demi's but curly. An assistant director called for a meal break and everybody headed for the catering truck.

Bonner and Doc talked about how the War on Drugs was going. Bonner thought it was interesting how disaffected they both had become, given enough time and distance from their involvement with a cause as hopeless as Prohibition.

"Get a lot of traffic up your way?" Doc asked.

"Sure. Tons of stuff pass through every week. Unless they're so stupid they beg to get arrested, we don't bother with it."

"No?"

"Drug interdiction on a county level? What it amounts to is law enforcement for profit. We have a couple of commissioners who are hot for it. Enhanced revenue, no tax increases. I'd need three times the manpower I have now, because most of my deps would be spending their time in court proving legal stops. I'd need a new jail—which God knows we could use. The trouble is, you can't define when abuses of search and seizure turn into corruption. The only thing you can be sure of, it *will* happen."

"Power corrupts, but absolute power is kind of neat," Katy said. She had a pretty good sense of humor, Bonner thought. Doc had done all right for himself.

"How's the election look?" Doc asked.

"According to the polls my opponent pays for, I'm down two to one."

"Who's the competition?"

"Looks good wearing a pair of six-shooters. Owns a car dealership."

"You know I can get you fixed up in Vegas."

"So can I," Katy said, with a well-meaning smile.

Bonner smiled back, thinking of the stunt woman in the parking lot, getting up off the deck with a bad knee, then pumping that fist with the enthusiasm of a high-school quarterback. It occurred to him that in spite of her pain she was probably having fun.

He saw her again in the Space Odyssey's casino. She was playing roulette with a group of friends from the production, which had wrapped for the night. Doc and Bonner were at one of the circular bars on the perimeter, looking down on a neoned nightmare of video poker hands, slot machines tolling like the bells of an evil religion, and craps table frenzies. It wasn't strictly Doc's business, but a team of scammers working high-limit blackjack tables had been blitzing a few of the better hotel casinos. Doc was keeping track of a well-dressed woman who had won forty thousand at the Mirage the night before. Whoever she was, she was new to the Strip and not on the computer net maintained by the hotels.

The chief of security at the Space Odyssey stopped by to chat.

"There're at least six of them," he said. "Probably more. Never the same team two nights in a row."

"What are they doing, counting cards?" Bonner asked.

"That's a load of bullshit, another myth about 'winning systems.' Try keeping track of the cards in a four-deck shoe. In a single-deck game, our dealers shuffle after every hand, but it's not really necessary. Let 'em count. House breaks them all, sooner or later. No, when we have big losses, either it's a player who is having the streak of his life, or the dealer. A really good mechanic, top-card peeker and second-card dealer, is just about impossible to spot. The dealer we're watching has been with us four years. Vito's one of our best. Never any problems."

Doc said, "But it's a boring job. They have too much time to think about how easy it is to cheat."

After the security guy moved on, Bonner asked, "How do they handle a cheating dealer if they can't prove anything?"

"They work him over with a big bonus, then put him on ice until the whales come to town. The Arab and Asian billionaires who don't care if they drop ten million in a week, as long as they're having a good time. The casinos, even the most respectable, are happy to use mechanics like Vito to increase their take. In Vegas, everybody cheats. Take a look around. The overhead in this pleasure dome is higher than the gross national product of Ecuador. Damn right they cheat. They have to keep the stockholders happy."

"And silent partners like the Sinaloa Family?"

"That's only a rumor. I have no comment." Doc finished off his scotch, his sixth of the night. Some redness had crept into his eyes, and he tended to squint when the booze was getting to him. He smiled. "But there would seem to be a certain irony involved here."

"Considering what we used to do for a living." Bonner shrugged, not in a mood to pursue the irony, if that's what it was. Psychological benders came out of nowhere, and getting buried alive in the glooms was the last thing he needed.

"Want another, Tobe?"

The movie people were splitting up, and Bonner watched the stunt woman walk away, slowly, stifling a yawn, favoring that right leg. It was five after one in the morning. She had no chips to cash in.

"Time for me to hit the sack, I guess. Deposition's at nine sharp. With luck I'll still get in a day's fishing before I go back to work."

"We don't see enough of each other, and that's a fact. You like Katy?"

"You're a lucky man, Doc." Bonner thought he meant it. But he'd already decided, in spite of his difficulties at home and the prospect of a cushy job, that he would be too far off his range. His mother, who had taught American Lit at the college level, had summed up Vegas after her only visit by paraphrasing Melville: "In no world but a fallen one could such pleasures exist."

He thanked Scanlan for his hospitality. Katy was headed toward them, with a fistful of dollars from playing the quarter slots. Bonner kissed her cheek and gave her shoulder a squeeze, then made his way through the crowds, between tables, and past the prestige baccarat room, down aisles of slots to the arcade of shops and quick-stop cafés. At the Space Odyssey you had to negotiate a hell of a lot of temptation to get from the reception desk to the elevators in the arcade wing. Like a minefield where the only thing that blew up was the guests' better judgment.

The stunt woman was waiting for an elevator. She was wearing glasses, round lenses lightly tinted, gold wire frames. Bonner looked at her in the mirrored facing of the elevator bank and saw her eyes shift, meeting his.

"That knee must be giving you fits," Bonner said.

"I'm getting some twinges," she said, with a smile calibrated to discourage the interest of outsiders.

Bonner was used to people who didn't want to talk to him. "I was watching from the Galaxy Room. I really don't know how you do that stuff."

She had looked away with the smile still there. The elevator doors didn't open. She blinked and turned her face to Bonner, game to pass a few more seconds in trivial conversation.

"It's timing, mostly. Reflexes, coordination."

"How long have you been at it?"

"Oh, a lot of years. Are you a doctor? What's that convention they're having here, some speciality I can't remember the name of?"

"Me either. I'm just a county sheriff." Having said it, he regretted the *just*.

She nodded, but didn't say anything. Maybe she was mildly disappointed that he wasn't in the medical profession.

The elevator arrived. Bonner got on behind a couple of other guests and lost track of the stunt woman. A skinny guy in a photographer's vest had claimed her attention. She glanced at the elevator as the doors were closing, clearly wanting to escape, but the guy had the self-important pesky look of a minor functionary in the movie crew, someone whom she couldn't afford to blow off.

Twenty minutes later, lying down after a small scotch, he was still thinking about her, rolling across that car, getting up to pump her fist in the air. She had looks that stuck with you, but it was the wild exuberance he remembered best, with a certain longing and wistfulness.

North of Las Vegas on Interstate 15, grueling sun and dry blue weather gave way to an overcast sky. Soon the wind picked up from the east and was blowing tumbleweeds across the empty, high desert stretch of roadway. Speed limit seventy-five. Shay Waco figured the highway patrol wouldn't pull her over for doing eighty. At that speed her three-year-old Chevy Tahoe was rocked from time to time by strong gusts, but there were no handling problems. With the Tahoe.

"When do I get to listen to what *I* want to listen to?" Pepper said, bleakness and animosity in her face. An expression the Irish do particularly well, Shay thought.

"The deal was, one of my CDs, then one of yours."

"*Yours* has been going on forever." They were well into one of those weeks of not agreeing on much of anything—music, food, spending money—and Pepper was still nursing a deep grudge. She'd wanted to start her summer vacation with her father in New Guinea, where Liam was photographing the new movie of a talented director who had the soul of a crocodile. Malarial downpours, heat that turned brains to oil slicks: not the ideal environment for an easily bored eleven-year-old with her father's fair and sensitive skin. Shay didn't know how Liam would survive without going heavily in debt to the bottle again, but that was his problem. He knew the risks and had been only halfhearted with his offer to take Pepper for a few weeks. But Pepper, as always, read her father poorly and was in a rage for two days when Shay stood firm. The apple of her eye. Green apple, for most of this trip.

"I wish you'd let me have headphones. Then I could listen to what I want when I want."

"And lose twenty-percent of your hearing before you're twenty-one. Uh-uh."

"No way! Liam gave me a hundred dollars before he left, and said I could spend it on anything I wanted!"

"As long as you cleared it with me first."

Pepper slumped in the right-hand seat with her arms folded and her fists clenched. Thrift was one of the hard lessons of life they were both still learning. Pepper wore her latest indulgence, one of the generic T-shirts (T-SHIRT printed in block letters across her chest) she'd had made up in Vegas after Shay had earned a sizable paycheck for three days' work on the Demi Moore flick. The stunt coordinator an old buddy of hers.

Before leaving Vegas she'd visited a chiropractor and doubled up on the Naprosyn so her knee wouldn't swell to twice its normal size. But after eighty miles of driving through the parched landscape, Shay was now having sharp pain in her right leg from an irritated sciatic nerve.

"Listening to Connie Francis," Pepper complained with a sideways grimace of despair, "is giving me ear cancer."

"It's probably wax. Would you like a Q-Tip?" Pepper squirmed and narrowed her eyes. "Then hush."

"Well, how much more do I have to *endure?*"

A few raindrops appeared on the windshield as they drove toward Mesquite, on the Arizona border, a tab version of Glitter Gulch. Palm trees, waterfalls, acres of tinted glass to tone down the brutal sun. Player's Island was advertising an all-you-can-eat buffet special, $7.99.

"Hungry?" Shay asked. It was a quarter past seven. They'd had a late lunch at the Hard Rock.

Pepper stirred fretfully again. "I don't want to eat in a casino."

"Food's usually good."

Pepper decided to make her main point.

"Liam said to keep you out of casinos," she said, as if it were almost too heavy a duty to bear.

"Oh, he did?" Shay had already slowed for the exit. She smiled ironically.

"Mom, could we keep driving? I'm not hungry and I don't need to go. Let's just get there. Wherever *that* is."

"Spanish Wells." Shay speeded up again, a nettlesome something tossing in the chambers of her heart. Past the new hotels the town of Mesquite appeared on their right—riverbank strip of green, the rest of the valley being gobbled up by housing for casino workers. Low-hanging clouds that obscured the mountains ahead, pale dust from newly scraped and leveled land blowing hard beneath the threatening clouds.

"Utah? That sign says 'Welcome to Arizona.'"

"We have to go through a corner of Arizona, but we're almost there."

"How long since you've been home?" Pepper asked, yawning.

"I never really thought of it as home. Once I left. I guess it's been—twenty-two years."

Connie Francis finished singing "Breakin' in a Brand-New Broken Heart."

Pepper sat up suddenly, her face glistening by stormlight, and reached for her CD carrier. "Yes!"

Shay smiled halfheartedly and retrieved ear plugs from the breast pocket of her Western-style shirt. Pepper responded with a small hectoring grin as she removed Francis and popped in a bootleg *Rage Against the Machine* album. More rain splattered the dusty windshield in spaced drops. The speed limit in Arizona was sixty-five. The fuzz-buster began beeping. Shay kept it at seventy and saw a couple of state cops side by side on the wide median, setting up shop for the evening. Blow your wages in Mesquite, have a few beers, hit ninety on the straightaway to the Virgin River Gorge on your way home to Utah, get ticketed for another bundle. Arizona didn't need casinos.

By the time they reached the gorge, it was raining as if the sea were coming back to those ancient vertical cliffs. The Tahoe's head-lights were on. Shay passed a truck with two trailers laboring on the incline. Light beams of other cars like ricochets through the torrent. The deluge and the curving way up from the bottom of the deep gorge gave Shay the crawly sensation of somehow being reborn.

Pepper had asked why they were going, and Shay hadn't had a good answer, not wanting to say Because I hope he's changed. Pepper had no predjudices against her paternal grandfather, whom she'd never met; she had dutifully written her thank you's to Silverwhip Jack for the birthday and Christmas savings bonds that already had provided her with a substantial college fund, and the framed one-sheet from his heyday as a B-movie cowboy star which Pepper had kept in her room for a while. As far as Shay knew her mother, secure in the life she'd made for herself after they'd packed up and left Silverwhip Jack, had never bad-mouthed Jack in Pepper's hearing.

It was all bygones with Shay too, or at least she'd tried to convince herself this was true. The old Silverwhip sometimes rampaged in her dreams, and she'd wake up quaking from anger or dread. During her early childhood Jack was long out of the movies and barely earning their meals with small-time rodeos and his own unlucrative business ventures: some men just had a seam of hard luck buried in them, as deep as their genes. He was still good-looking in those days, with a full head of gray-white hair and the nightmare eyes of a rogue malamute. He had his old movie horse, and that one-of-a-kind bull-whip—valuable, but never for sale.

The shooting she infrequently recalled as if it were a scene from a horror film she'd seen at an impressionable age. Not something that had involved her personally.

2 THE RAIN EASED UP for a couple of minutes as they came within sight of the lights of Spanish Wells on the Utah side of the gorge. On her cellphone Shay tried the number Jack had given her, heard, after four rings, the answering machine kick in with a few bars of cut-to-the-chase music. Then:

"This's Jack. Reckon I'm out for a while and don't know when I'll be back; but I keep up with my messages, so when you hear the crack of the old silverwhip, talk all you like. If it's the one about the space alien and the church lady, I heard it already. Ciao."

Shay decided against leaving a message; she had a hand-drawn map he'd supplied.

"Could we get a diet Coke or something?" Pepper asked.

"Sure." They pulled off at the exit south of town and Shay parked at a handy McDonald's.

Inside her mother used the bathroom while Pepper bought drinks and fries.

Pepper had worn her Angels cap and shades inside, put on a Universal Tours sweatshirt, knowing it would be chilly. It was a McDonald's, but not quite like the Mickey D's on Moorpark near their home in North Hollywood. Subtle differences in the shadowless decor, as mind-numbing as a visual chant. The lights bright enough for surgical procedures. Unfamiliar teenagers behind the counter in perky caps and team colors, newly inducted into the workforce. They were, Pepper noted, in a different time zone. She'd been out of pager range of her friends for two days. This caused a deep tremor of concern,

made worse by the fact that she didn't know exactly where she would
be sleeping tonight. She had both of her pillows and several stuffed
animals with her, but had neglected to smuggle one into the alien
McDonald's. The food looked and smelled the same, but Pepper was
wary. She adapted by going into hiding behind dark glasses. A small
earring in each lobe, sweatbands on her wrists, appliqué tattoos, gold
ankle chains almost as fine as human hair. She was loaded with pre-
teen cachet.

Catching sight of Pepper, huddled in the oversize sweatshirt at a
corner table beneath a planter brimming with plastic fern and scru-
pulously biting her french fries in half, Shay wondered how her
daughter would have coped in New Guinea. A whole new world of
trappings and taboo, intoxicating currents of magic and superstition.

At their table Shay studied the map. Thunder shook the plateglass
of the drive-in. She looked up to see herself in the watery window,
her mother's face—Roman, classical, something heavy in each round,
dark eye, like a burden of history. Her mother had emigrated just
after World War Two. Thirteen years old, distant relatives in the ports
and vineyards of Northern California.

"How old is Granpa?" Pepper asked, carefully dipping the bitten
ends of a fry into a little pond of catsup.

"I think about seventy-three. He never liked to tell his age."

"Does he still ride?"

"I don't know."

"How come you haven't seen him for so long?"

"I didn't like him much."

"Have you changed your mind? I mean, because he has so much
money."

Shay gave her a look, low-voltage displeasure.

"I don't know what he's worth, Pepper, and I don't care."

Pepper twisted insecurely in her seat and changed the subject.

"I wonder if he'll like me."

"He'll adore you. Everybody does. Eventually."

Pepper responded to Shay's sly smile with a stuck-out tongue.

"Does he know I can do a twenty-foot fall?"

"I think you told him that in one of your letters." Shay folded
the map reluctantly, cleaned her glasses on a paper napkin and looked
at a Hispanic family in a nearby booth, kids plowing through Big
Macs, their solemn carmelized faces like dipped apples at Halloween.
Shay thought about the Mexican girl who had been her best friend,

those years before the shooting, and wondered if Lucy was still in Solar County.

"Finished?" she asked Pepper. "Well, I guess we can find his place okay."

"Is it where you used to live?"

"No. That was up around the park, where Jack had his western town and rodeo. He doesn't do that stuff any more, not that it was such a great living to begin with. Did you drink all of that Coke? Better visit the bathroom before we leave."

●

They drove up West Valley Boulevard, which Shay barely recognized. New shopping centers, cute restaurants with names like the Peekin' Duck, tiers of pricey homes and condominiums on streets cut into the claret-red clay of the mesa on the other side of the boulevard, all the way to the airport and runway on the south end of the high bluff. Spanish Wells had been founded and laid out by Mormon settlers, the original town in a strict grid pattern, their streets, each exactly 132 feet wide, shaded by ash and locust trees. It had been a part of the Prophet Smith's grand design for all Latter-day Saints to have a house in town as well as a farm outside of town. Now the Wells was a snowbird and retirement community, fiercely hot in summer but with a milder winter climate than the rest of the state. Golf all year, serpentine emerald courses amid the riddled sandstone cliffs, ancient even by geological time.

Tonight, beneath a stark dangle of lightning, runoff flowed like a new river down the glistening four-lane blacktop. The part of the late evening sky that wasn't black with clouds was a deep indigo. Shay wondered what sort of road wound through the cottonwoods beside the Aquiles River to the spread Silverwhip Jack had managed to acquire, but she felt secure with her 4WD Tahoe. He hadn't mentioned a wife in his letters of the past year, but Jack, even at his age, was unlikely to be without a female companion, maybe even a new brood.

Shay turned left where the green highway sign pointed the way to the community of Windbow; she drew a heavy breath knowing, now that she couldn't gracefully retreat, how much she didn't want to be here, feeling condemned by some obscure failure of hers. In spite of the increasingly explicit notes of loneliness and a desire for reconciliation in his recent messages, it might be best just to leave Jack alone. You didn't kick an old rattler off his sunning rock if you had good sense.

West of Windbow they crossed part of the Paiute Indian Reservation and, according to Silverwhip Jack's scrawled directions, turned north to follow the Aquiles River upland, Shay watching the miles click by on the odometer until the highway bridged the river, *Rage Against the Machine* about to give her a raging headache. Maybe headphones might not be such a bad idea. Pepper chewed gum obliviously, the atmosphere around her head one of artificial spearmint. Gum was one of the few treats Shay allowed. McDonald's once in a while. They were both allergic to most food additives. Shay ran the juicer often at home and kept charts in the kitchen of what they were eating. So protective; but, as Liam had pointed out, she'd let Pepper have a dirt bike, and had taken their daughter tandem skydiving on her tenth birthday. Shay preferred the obvious but—to her mind—controllable risks in life.

The rain had slackened for five minutes; then there was a new cloudburst to contend with, like driving through an endless waterfall. Visibility was down to a couple of hundred feet, but there was almost no other traffic on the road. The landscape, what she could see of it, seemed equally empty until they reached the Desert Rose exit.

Desert Rose had a spa and a golf course on the flank of an extinct volcano. Past the golf course they ran out of paved road, which had been as lumpy as wiring wrapped with electrician's tape. Two gravel roads branched off like filaments into sagebrush. *Take the left fork,* Jack had written. *Cross the iron bridge. Go left again.* Then it was to be one and sixth-tenths of a mile along the north bank of the river to his gate.

Jack probably hadn't taken the unseasonably heavy rain into account. The Aquiles was already overflowing, flooding the small bridge.

"Uh-oh," Pepper said anxiously. "Can we get through?"

"Yeah."

"Maybe we should go back. It looks deep."

"We'll be all right."

Shay eased the Tahoe across the bridge. The water flooding over the plank floor of the bridge was only a couple of inches deep. The road on the other side had been built up with riprap, and the flood-waters hadn't erased it. They were quickly on higher ground. The road made several turns through what looked like orchards planted close on both sides; the roof rack of the Tahoe brushed against a couple of rain-glazed boughs laden with ripe apricots.

"There's a gate," Pepper said. And a drive hedged with eight-foot oleanders, but the signpost, when Shay put her side-mounted spotlight on it, read SIMBA SPRING RANCH.

"I don't think that's it."

"This really sucks," Pepper complained. "Aren't we going *up?* We were supposed to turn left across the bridge."

"The river was over the bank on the left," Shay said irritably. "Or didn't you notice?"

"You don't have to be sarcastic. I think we're going the wrong way, we should—"

"There's no place to turn around yet," Shay said, modifying her tone.

The road was only wide enough for a vehicle and a half. Shay went to four-wheel-drive as the incline became steeper and the footing slick. Lightning exploded in their faces. Trees had become scarce on this rocky slope, well removed from the aquifer of the valley below.

The road made an abrupt ninety-degree turn, and Shay slowed down.

There was a rusted barely legible sign on a long low, iron gate across the road. Something *dam* something *no entry.* But the gate was standing open. Below and to their right, lightning glared on the choppy surface of a rock-lined, man-made lake, beaches with red sand, coves of cottonwoods and globe willow. To their left was a sixty-degree slope down to a finger cove of the broader valley they had left behind.

"What's this?" Pepper said.

"Looks like a reservoir."

"Can we go across?"

"We'll have to. The road probably winds back down to the valley on the other side."

"We're lost. I *hate* this. I wish it w-would stop r-raining."

"We'll be okay."

Shay drove slowly across the graveled top of the dam, unable to see, even with high beams, the other end of it. They were totally exposed here, and the gusting wind hit the Tahoe hard. Pepper's wad of gum was like a skin-covered walnut on one side of her jaw. Her mouth may have been too dry for her to chew anymore. Her fits of nerves always manifested in a slight popping of her hazel eyes and a heart-wrenching stammer. Shay took her right hand off the wheel long enough to clasp Pepper's cold hand.

"Just w-watch where you're g-g-going, *please.*"

A sandstone cliff, looming left. Something parked there, a piece of yellow road machinery or a large backhoe on treads; Shay pulled toward the reservoir side, trying to locate a continuing track where the earthen dam ended.

The other vehicle came around the base of the cliff that overhung the road so fast she barely had time to register what it might be—a large pickup, Prospector or Silverado—before racked lights on the cab roof blinded them. Shay was already spinning the wheel hard left, with nowhere to go except head-on into the partly raised bucket of the backhoe, when the SUV was struck violently on the right side, just behind Pepper's seat.

Windows blew out like a hailstorm and the mashed Tahoe was spun half around, slewing off the gravel and down the steep slope. As they slid the front end tilted up, tires unable to bite and hold on what was mostly dirt-covered shale beneath columbine and rabbit-bush. Shay had been taught recovery techniques by a couple of the best stunt drivers in her business, Ron Rondell and Bobby Bass. But this was no carefully controlled movie gag that took into account everything about the vehicles involved, exact speed, angle of inci-dence, and precise point of impact.

Her head bounced up and off the rearview, the blow driving the wire rims of her glasses into the flesh of her brows and cheeks. There was nothing she could do, and

We're going to roll! Shay thought, knowing that once they did, continuing to roll and then dropping nearly straight down to the big rocks piled up at the base of the dam, there wouldn't be much hope for either of them. She abandoned the useless steering wheel, man-aged to turn off the engine, and reached for her screaming child.

The Tahoe crunched down on its roof, which held because of the rollbar Shay had installed. As more glass shattered, the Tahoe rolled upright and came to a jolting stop twenty feet down the slope, tipped at a drastic downward angle on Shay's side, caught in the lean of a white pine tree not much thicker than a fence post. The cracked windshield was littered with dry pine needles. Through straggly branches Shay saw only rain and darkness, the high beams illuminating the crowns of other trees, piñons or juniper, that were almost directly below them. Either they were small slow-growth trees, or they were frighteningly far away.

Shay hugged Pepper tightly to quiet her, not wanting to breathe herself. She knew a lot about fear and how to control it; panic was a different sort of animal. Born in a flash, it consumed all of your energy while clawing you to death from the inside out.

"What happened? What happened?"

"Don't. Don't shake us. We're hung up, but I don't know for how long."

"We've got to get out!"

"Wait. Don't move." Shay stroked Pepper's head gently, running her fingers through the red-gold curls, looking for injury. Trembling, harsh breathing—but the girl didn't appear to be hurt. Blood was running down the inside of Shay's nose to a corner of her mouth; her glasses were twisted on her face. She couldn't focus through the skewed lenses. She reached up slowly with her left hand and took the glasses off, trying to remember where she'd stored her rec specs.

"What are we going to do?"

"Don't hyperventilate, Pepper. You're breathing too hard, slow down! There's somebody up there. I think they stopped. They'll help us." *Unless,* she thought, with a rush of fury, *they're too goddamn drunk to do us any good.*

Anger gave her strength. Still keeping a calming hand on her daughter, Shay looked back and up through a half-demolished tailgate window, the glass like a billow of frozen lace. A blaze of running lights from the pickup truck, which she couldn't see, illuminated the downpour. So the driver *had* stopped after running her off the top of the dam, but where was he?

Shay had more pressing concerns. Water was pouring into the Tahoe through a broken offside window, not just rain but a steady stream from the cliff face above them. And if it wasn't draining out again, then the Tahoe was getting heavier.

"Pepper?"

"Yeah, Mom?"

"I think my rec specs are in the compartment on your side? I

can't see very well; my glasses are broken. Could you reach—
carefully—in there and get the specs for me?"

"Okay."

Shay wiped blood from her cheek and pressed two fingers against
the cut between her eyebrows.

"Do you remember which duffel we packed our biking helmets
in?"

"Uh, the red one."

"Okay."

"Why do we n-need—" Pepper stared at her. *"Are we going to
fall?"*

"I don't know what's going to happen, but—"

"Why can't they come and g-get us *out* of here!"

"That's no good, Pepper. Be calm and we'll be all right."

Shay decided to ease out of her shoulder harness. She unlocked
it, turned carefully in the seat, reaching behind her through the
stream of water falling into the Tahoe. She brushed spray from her
eyes and squinted, trying to see who might be up there.

A single blurred figure. Probably a man, judging from size and
shape. He wore a black slicker or rain suit and a black rancher's hat,
brim low over his face like the broken wing of a raven. He had
stepped into the rain-streaky glare behind the parked backhoe, and
was looking down at the wrecked sport-ute, taillights in the air, the
right rear tire well off the slope.

"Hey!" Shay yelled at him, as lightning cracked overhead, turning the sky to wet gossamer. *"Help!* Get us out of here!"

She rubbed more water from her eyes, and when she looked again
he was gone.

As Shay felt around on the middle seat where they had left the
duffels, the Tahoe slid perceptibly, an inch or more, as if the weight
of it had begun to uproot the Rocky Mountain white pine.

Pepper's terror expanded, burning up the air they both breathed.

"Mom! Ohmigod, we're going to—"

"Get my specs, Pepper." Shay found the leather handles of a
soaked duffel and pulled it slowly into the front seat with her. "We'll
have to get ourselves out."

Pepper's stunned face was like blue ice in the glow from a bolt
striking the cliff above them. Some rocks came bounding down toward them, clattering over the roof, and the Tahoe teetered a little.
Pepper screamed.

Shay began pawing through the duffel. Bicycle helmets, bungee cord. Good so far. She heard the roar of a big engine on top of the dam, as if the wheels of the truck were spinning for traction. Running away? She had no time to think about the asshole who had run them down. With their combined weight and that of the engine block, plus the water they were taking on, the Tahoe was nose-heavy, putting a lot of stress on the single tree that somehow kept them pinned to the sixty-degree slope. But its root system could give way any moment.

"Going out the back, Pepper. Put your helmet on. And where are my *glasses?*"

While Pepper leaned forward against her harness to open the dash compartment, Shay, puzzled by the continued revving of the truck engine, looked up again through smashed glass and driving rain, now illuminated from a different angle by the lights above the windshield of the unseen truck.

What she could make out, even without specs, was the yellow bulk of the backhoe moving slowly sideways toward the edge, twenty feet above them.

For a few seconds she couldn't accept what he obviously was up to.

"M-mom, here! What's wrong now?"

Shay turned her head slowly to stare at Pepper. She couldn't find words to describe their predicament. She took the rec specs and slipped the elastic band over her head, looked again and saw that the backhoe was tilting slightly as the driver of the pickup used all the power he could squeeze from his engine to push it down on top of them.

And he was doing it just right, bumper against the rear of the treads, taking advantage of the displaced center of gravity with the front-end bucket raised. Probably on a dry, paved surface he couldn't have budged it; the treads would have had too much drag. Now they were piling up mud and gravel, a slow bulging wave that crested then slid down the slope toward the Tahoe, the corrugated roof of the small cab visible as the downhill tilt of the earthmover became more pronounced.

Shay heard a strangled cry from Pepper and got busy.

She clapped a bike helmet on Pepper's head, then bound one wrist with the elastic cord, making a loop for Pepper to slip over her other hand when the time came.

"What are you—"

"So you don't lose your grip on me. We have to jump."

"Jump—*where?*"

Shay put on her own helmet, then reached under her seat for the Alpine ax she kept there, along with a holstered Beretta Cougar. Too much gun to fit inside a boot, and nowhere else to put it on her person. She regretfully left the Baretta where it was and bashed out the window on her side with the ax. Pepper wasn't watching; she couldn't take her eyes off the moving backhoe.

"*It's going to fall on us!*"

"Let's go!"

"Mommmmm mmm m!!"

"Pepper, you can't be afraid; you have to do just what I say!"

The driver's side spotlight was still working; Shay clicked it on and aimed it at the trees growing in a tight vee of canyon below, between the dam embankment and the cliff face, trying to get some idea of how far they would have to jump—*call it what it is,* Shay thought angrily, *a free fall.* But at least as long as the spotlight remained steady she had a ghostly target area in the downpour. From this distance the wet gray-green boughs of the piñon looked deceptively like one of the safety piles used in high-fall gags on the movie sets. She knew better. The needles were springy, not sharp, but the nestled cones of the piñon could cut like razor blades. The trick was not to bounce off the compact branches of the conical tree and go flying into the rocks even farther down the slope.

"Now!"

Shay freed Pepper from the seat harness and climbed out through the window space, reaching for a handhold on the roof rack as the Tahoe rocked a little; she heard a dry cracking sound almost like lightning, and it froze her blood as she clung precariously to the vehicle, one foot on the windowsill, reaching down for Pepper.

"Climb up over me! Hold onto my back and tie your wrists together!"

"Oh God. NO mother—!"

"That backhoe is going to crush us flat. We have to *GO,* Pepper! You've been jumping with me since you were three years old; it's just like a parachute jump!"

"No, it's not!"

"*Now!* Hurry!"

Shay half-dragged Pepper, five-four and nearly a hundred pounds, up through the window space. The girl clawing for a handhold on her shoulder, throwing her right arm desperately around Shay, across her breasts. Shay grabbed her by the beaded belt of her jeans and held on as Pepper bound her wrists together and clenched her arms more tightly around her mother.

Too much weight, Shay thought, terrified of slipping or turning over in the air as they fell and crushing Pepper beneath her. *Jesus, Jesus, Jesus*—in a flash of lightning she saw the backhoe topple and come crashing down the slope toward the sport-ute.

Shay turned awkwardly with Pepper's face pressed between her shoulder blades, legs dangling. "*Mount up!*" she screamed, felt Pepper's thin legs wrap around her waist, let go with her left hand, and, with as much action as she could get from her weakening knees, pushed off from the sill and launched them both into the track of the spotlight. Just behind them the backhoe hit the Chevy with an impact Shay felt rather than heard, destroying it like a junkyard compactor.

Then the light vanished, like the sudden end of a dream.

3 FALLING WAS NOTHING NEW to Shay: it was both a job and a pastime. She was preparing for the impact even as they plummeted toward the wet treetops (barely seeable now in a mild flash across the torrent sky), calculating probabilities by the split second. *"Hang on tight!"* she screamed at Pepper, but the girl's fingernails were digging in below her collarbones; no need to remind her.

It took them a little more than three seconds to reach the highest piñon, Shay thrusting out both hands at the last instant, tucking in her chin.

The impact was worse than she had imagined, and there was nothing much to hold onto, slippery boughs sliding through her arms as she tried frantically to brake, her legs thrashing as they slid off the first piñon and fell a short distance to another—but more slowly, and this time she was able to grab a branch with a numbed hand and hold on momentarily, feet dangling until she kicked out and lodged one boot in the crook of a bough. Her exposed skin felt flayed; the palm of her other hand was bleeding from a gash, slippery when she tried to secure themselves more firmly to the swaying tree.

"We're okay, we're okay!"

Pepper was crying. They were both hurt, Shay realized, no way to know yet how badly. The trick now was to get them both on the ground. What had happened to her sport-ute and the backhoe? The Tahoe's lights were out. It was dark where they clung to the underside of the piñon. That was good. She didn't want to be seen. But she thought she heard the sound of the pickup truck's engine, fading, lost altogether as thunder rumbled.

Yes, go away, go away—but someday I'll find out who you are. You miserable son of a—

"Mom, I'm slipping! Something's stuck in my knee; it hurts!"

Slender supple branches holding their weight. Shay pressed in close to the trunk, rain streaming down her face, and, feeling for handholds, gradually took them down the rest of the way. Lightning. She glimpsed the crushed remains of her sport-ute, on the rocks a dozen feet away from the stand of piñons and juniper, smelled hot oil in spite of the rain. The backhoe lay bent and upside down nearly on top of the Chevy, bucket teeth upthrust and gleaming like the teeth of a dinosaur mired in tar.

Pepper quaked in her arms, collapsed with a sob when she tried to put weight on her left leg.

"I can't. I can't. It really hurts!"

She jumped and moaned when Shay touched her knee. Left hand. Shay already knew that at least two fingers of her right hand were broken, the little finger bent at an extreme angle from the palm. Pepper flinched. Blood, and a broken-off branch lodged beneath Pepper's kneecap.

Hospital, Shay thought dizzily, rocking a little on her own lacerated knees. It hurt her to take more than shallow breaths. Pepper would have to be carried. But where was she supposed to go from here?

"I'm c-cold," Pepper said in a voice so faint Shay suspected she might be going into shock. "C-can't we get out of the damn rain?"

Shay looked around again as the sky flickered with light. And thought she saw, partway up a canyon, a blunt stone chimney and part of a steep shake roof, only a glimpse through the cottonwoods that followed the winding of the full river to the southwest.

"I saw something—might be a house. I'm going to put you on my back again, Pepper. Hold on to me."

Pepper groaned slightly but didn't say anything. Using only her left hand, the broken fingers of her right hand slipped inside her partly unbuttoned shirt, Shay loaded the girl up, gritting her teeth against the pain from her injured rib cage. And got moving, stumbling progress along the boulder-size riprap at the base of the dam, sloshing through the overflow from the swift river to the modest embankment held in place by the roots of cottonwoods and locust trees. Anxious for Pepper, whose grip on her was weak, but thinking now, as she swallowed blood from a cut inside her mouth, about the man in the pickup truck that had rammed them. The trouble he'd gone to, dumping the backhoe down the slope of the dam.

Wanting to kill them. No other explanation would do—but *why?*

The house toward which she struggled seemed, as Shay got closer, to be inhabited, though no lights were on. There were a couple of walled lots, odd-sized, one an oval, like a corral, the other nearly triangular, enclosing a black mesh satellite dish and nothing else. The house, as best Shay could tell by brief moments of stormlight, was of native sandstone. Two low wings with overhanging roofs, a second story in the middle. There was a sport-ute and a Cadillac, one of the old showboat models, parked in the river stone driveway. Wild growth, cactus and manzanita, up to the partly covered front porch. Cut stone floor, wood table and chairs, a couple of Mormon rockers, stone planters filled with yellow-starred euryops and fan palms, the blades dripping in the rain. There were also a child's pink Big Wheel and a yellow plastic sandbox with a raked awning, a touch of tot circus in one corner of the porch.

Lights came on around the front of the house when she approached within fifteen feet of the porch, lugging Pepper on her back. Shay saw their helmeted reflections in the Thermopane porch door as she eased Pepper down into one of the rocking chairs, out of the rain. Lights, but no alarms. No hostile dogs streaking out of the dark. No one looked out.

"Where are we?" Pepper muttered.

"I don't know if anyone's home. I'll break in if I have to to use the phone."

Pepper clutched at a sodden sleeve of Shay's western shirt.

"Are you all right?" Pepper said in an exhausted voice.

"Yeah, sure I am."

"Why are you holding your hand like that?"

"It's nothing. I busted a couple of fingers grabbing at branches."

"How far . . . did we fall?"

"I'm not sure."

"More than twenty feet?"

"Sixty, almost seventy feet would be more like it, from the time it took. And we were falling through some wet heavy air."

"Hey," Pepper said with wan enthusiasm. "Beat my record."

"Sure did." Hurting, still tense with rage, Shay felt like she was going to start bawling. "You're terrific, Pepper."

"I'm thirsty. My knee hurts like hell. It won't bend. Is it broken?"

"Don't know, darlin'. Just don't touch or try to move it. I'm going to try to raise someone now. You sit tight, why don't you?"

There was an old-fashioned iron bell with a clapper by the door in the alcove entranceway. Shay rang the bell ferociously, as if announcing the arrival of plague, then pulled open the porch door and banged with the heel of her less-injured hand on the mahogany front door.

"Help! Somebody! Please open up. We've been in an accident and my daughter's hurt!"

Impatient, shuddering, she turned the knob and, as she had expected, in spite of the presence of a deadbolt lock, she found the house open.

"Hello?"

A TV was on, somewhere in the house. The whitebread American game-show host was saying, "Gary is a professional house-sitter, and his hobby is building ultralight airplanes."

Foyer about fifteen feet square, wide satin-finish Ponderosa pine planks, Navaho throw rugs, staircase. Below the staircase, a grandfather clock with a jolly man-in-the-moon face. The time was 9:34. Dinner was in the air, overcooked it seemed to Shay.

The motion-detecting lights outside switched off, leaving Shay in the dark.

"Mom?"

"Hold on," she called, and located the light switch next to the door with her left hand.

By the light of the overhead fixture in the foyer she found her way back to the kitchen. Beyond the kitchen, a round table in a dining nook, five places, five people at or near the table, stiff, wordless, as if they were a little miffed that Shay was joining them late.

Lightning.

The glass doors behind the table were shattered. It was raining in.

Most of the blood had already washed off the shards of glass that remained in the panes. The strongest odor in the rain-laden air was that of burned meat in a smoking oven.

Shay groped numbly for another light switch. Three of the faces became, suddenly, too clear.

Corpulent older man, balding, but with thick, dark sideburns, leaning back at the head of the table, one arm hooked over the back of his chair, head cocked at an angle toward the doorway, dark eyes open. Two puckers in the forehead, an inch apart, and a throat wound, his shirt front drenched in blood that had only begun to darken.

"Yes," Pat Sajak said, "there are two Ms."

Heavy woman in the chair at his right hand, streaks of gray in her shiny black hair, an ear like a blood spider, cheekbone exploded. Her face was down next to her plate, in the crook of a plump bare arm. Gold glittered on her wrist.

Across from her, overturned chair, a body sideways on the floor. Female. Short skirt hiked above her youthful thighs, pink crescents of panties. A spilled bowl of saffron rice near her outstretched hands.

Two kids—*kids!*—a boy and a girl, she may have been a year older than Pepper. Both shot to death where they sat, petrified by the sight of the intruder—or intruders—with the cold nerve and technician's touch.

There were red-and-blue parrots in a cage near the blown-out doors. Unharmed. Side-stepping on perches, making those little vexed head motions, not talking. Thick medieval-looking yellow candles on the table, extinguished, by the rainy breeze or burst of violence, snuffing gunfire. A religious woodcut on one wall. Beneath it, a well-used white guitar leaned with Latin panache. Some after-dinner music from *papi,* possibly a family tradition. There was a high chair in one corner, opposite the parrots. Unoccupied. No sign of an infant, unless one had fallen, dead, from someone's lap, and was lying under the table. Shay chose not to look beneath the draped tablecloth.

She turned and walked back through the kitchen, pausing to turn off the wall oven that was leaking smoke. Not soon enough. A smoke detector had gone off. Shay inhaled at the wrong time and reacted by throwing up on the tile floor.

Pat Sajak said, from the eerie nowhere of gameshow land, "Spin or solve the puzzle?"

So now she knew what it was about. The guy in the pickup. The backhoe, as if she could have seen him well enough to do any fucking good.

"Mom? Where are you?"

No, Pepper. No, no, no, for God's sake don't come in here!

Her mouth was clogged with vomit. She ran water in the steel sink, drank from the tap, rinsed, spat it out. Otherwise left things the way they were, wine bottle uncorked on a sink counter, the smoke alarm shrilling, what was she supposed to do with five dead people anyway?

One of the parrots suddenly squawked in Spanish. Shay nearly screamed.

Heart fumbling, she returned to the foyer. Where Pepper waited in the doorway, looking past her, trying to make out something at the top of the stairs.

The bright object came whizzing and bumping down the stairs toward Shay's feet; she did a hysterical sort of dance trying to get out of the way until she identified the object as a toy car. Pepper, standing on her good leg, stooped painfully to retrieve it. A red light was flashing on top of the car; there was a tinny winding-down siren.

Pepper pointed up the stairs. The back of Shay's neck, already clammy, froze solid. Her impulse was to scoop her daughter up and run like hell from that house.

Instead, because there was no fear in Pepper's eyes, Shay held on and looked up too.

She saw a toddler in pajamas belly down on the top step, hanging there, looking over his or her shoulder—hair just long enough, in thick curls, to disguise the gender—reaching down cautiously with a chubby foot for the next step. Made it, and continued to come down, looking at them, making breathy sounds of exertion, saying a few words that must have been Spanish.

When the baby reached the next to last step before the foyer, she—a pink hairbow that had gone unnoticed before was Shay's clue—sat down as if tired and held out a hand to Pepper.

"Es mio," she said stuffily. The baby's nose was red and runny.

Pepper put the toy police car on the floor and sent it skidding back to her.

The baby laughed. Shay went over and put her arms around Pepper, who was trembling.

"I'm sorry. But I want you to go back outside. Wait for me."

"What's that noise?"

"Smoke alarm. It's okay, just something—in the oven. In the oven. I need to find a phone. There's probably a playpen for—now *go outside.*"

Shay felt as if her face were about to twitch out of control. Pepper's fingers tightened on her uninjured left hand.

"What's wrong?"

"Some people have been shot. I don't want you to see it." Now her eyes were filling up. It was already hard enough for her to see through the misted rec specs. She kissed Pepper. They were shaking. In the kitchen one of the parrots screeched. "I don't think he's still around. He wouldn't come back. We'll be all right. Just do what I say."

Pepper clung to her, and Shay gasped at the strain on her ribs. Pepper made a sound that was between laughter and a scream.

"And you said I couldn't go to New Guinea because it was too *dangerous?*"

4 TOBIN BONNER GOT OUT of his car, the Crown Vic Police Interceptor model, businessman brown, in front of the Santero house at 12:15 in the morning. The early season monsoon had moved on to Nevada, stones of the driveway still wet with a hard glitter like the starry sky. Peeper frogs by the billions along the purling river a hundred yards downhill. He joined his chief investigator, who was outside on the porch having a smoke. The only four hearses available in Solar County were lined up to receive the bodies of the Santero family, once Bonner had his look at the murder scene.

Inside the house a baby was crying.

"How was Vegas?" Lucy Ruiz said.

"Those bright lights hurt my eyes."

"Sorry you didn't get some time off."

"Yeah, the fish were just starting to bite when you called. Maybe I'll get back up to the lake in a couple of weeks."

Lucy shook her head and turned toward the house.

"I don't think so. This one's bad."

Lucy had a lush brown-toned beauty but a poor body—short in the leg, shoulders like a man. The standard khaki uniform, high boots and laden gun belt didn't flatter her. She liked wearing her uniform anyway, although he'd told her more than once she didn't have to. Maybe it was because she preferred to carry a major handgun, .44-quad Mag-na-port with a five-inch bull barrel, a Big Slam if there ever was one.

A van from the local bureau of a Salt Lake TV station was crunching toward them on the drive. One of Bonner's deputies flagged the van thirty yards from the house.

"What's the name again?" Bonner asked Lucy, taking a drag from her cigarette and giving it back. The baby inside was still crying.

"Santero." She glanced at her notebook. "Gustavo and family. From Mexico, Guanajuato. Permanent resident status, according to papers in his office. They've lived here about thirteen months. Bought the house from the McCovey estate, says Johnny Mack Broone." Broone was the deputy for the sector in which the house was located. "He didn't know them too well. The Santeros kept to themselves. The older kids attended the consolidated in Windbow."

"What did Santero do for a living?"

"Investments of some kind, the impression I had from a quick look around his office. They must have been pretty well off." Lucy nodded toward the house. "Broone says the estate was asking one ninety-five. Three acres on the river." Lucy finished her cigarette, dropped the butt on the stone-flagged porch, and squashed it with a bootheel. Then she put the remnant in a baggie. "I don't know what his business was, but he liked high-tech security stuff. The office is full of surveillance and eavesdropping devices, most of it illegal for civilians to own. He had good cameras, tape recorders, night-vision goggles, and a scanner for picking up cell-phone frequencies."

"Professional snoop?"

"If he wasn't, then he had an expensive hobby. A hobby that might have been embarrassing to the neighbors, if they knew."

The bureau chief for the TV station, whose name was Richards, walked up the drive with his cameraman.

"Don't turn that on yet," Bonner advised him. They weren't on good terms. Bonner considered all media people adversarial, and Richards biased in favor of whoever came along to run against him every four years.

"What's up, Tobe? I heard four or five dead."

"I just got here myself. Give me half an hour."

"I heard execution-style."

Bonner looked up as a hawk tipped its wing to the crescent moon.

"I'll have something to say when I have something to say."

Bonner put on latex gloves he'd taken from a carton in his car and went inside, Lucy behind him.

"Is the kid hungry? Wet?"

"Could be both. I saw some formula in the fridge. I'll take care of her until somebody from Child and Family Services shows up."

"How old?"

"Little girl. Precious. I'd say twenty months, from her tooth count and vocabulary."

"The sole survivor. Who found the bodies?"

"I'll get into that. The weirdest coincidence. Why don't you have a look, so Caswell can start moving the bodies? I'll warm up some formula."

Two more investigators were in the kitchen and the dining nook, tape measuring and drawing diagrams. They nodded to the boss. Everyone seemed constrained, including Lucy, in the presence of massive death. Walking on eggs. All the lights were on. They had put down butcher paper in places on the terra-cotta floor. Dark blood stains near the table were marked in chalk. The Solar County coroner, whose day job was pharmacist, stood by with his arms folded. There was a collection of brass casings in a Ziploc bag on the tiled counter that partly separated the dining nook from the kitchen.

"Gold Dot hollow points," said Caswell, a hunter and gun hobbyist. "Nine millimeter. Total of nine shots fired, from what I can tell."

One of the caged parrots cracked a sunflower seed in its beak.

Bonner looked carefully at each body, touching two of them: the woman and the older girl, on the floor. Rolling their heads a little, flexing a livid hand. The adolescent boy and girl, seated at the table, had each been shot over the ear. The older girl through the heart and the bridge of her nose. Gustavo Santero had collected three bullets, as if he had been the first target and the shooter—assuming a lone gunman—needed to settle down before turning his weapon on the other victims. Only the girl on the floor had made it to her feet, or had been standing and serving. From the position of her chair in relation to the table, and from the way she lay twisted on the tiles, a large blue-handled spoon clutched in her right hand, that seemed the most likely possibility.

Lucy took up a position between the counter and the wall, pointed.

"The shooter stood here, from all indications—where we found the casings, the panes that are broken out. The head shots to Mama and Papa all left exit wounds."

"The sequence may have been, bang-bang-bang to Papa, bang-

bang to the girl on the floor as she turned at the sound of the shots or saw him shot, then Mama, then the kids. Real quick. What do you think, Cas?"

The coroner fingered his sunken, pursed mouth as if it hurt him to speak. He had a small hard hairless dome and skin like moccasin leather. Caswell looked as if he might once have been captured by headhunters but had talked his way out before the shrinking process could be completed.

"Savvy with guns. A lot of practice. Six, seven seconds to do them all."

"They knew the shooter," Lucy said, going back to the stove where she was heating formula in a pan. The baby continued to fuss unhappily, upstairs somewhere. "He walked in, I'd guess, while they were at supper. Hiya, don't let me interrupt anything, Papa didn't even have a chance to offer him a seat. Thanks, this won't take a minute. I'll stand. Then the gun came out, *hasta luego.*"

Cas said, "Even if they were acquainted with the shooter, don't people panic and try to run when there's a gun firing at them?"

Bonner shook his head. "To give you an example from my shooting war, your reflexes have to be conditioned. Those kids sitting there, three or four quick shots. If silenced, there's only a whisper. They see holes opening up in Papa's face, his head blowing up as panes of glass break; they see their sister, if that's who she was, turn and scream just as she's nailed and goes sprawling. Then they turn in their chairs the way they are now; they freeze and pucker and die."

His recitation depressed everybody, including Bonner. Five bodies. At least double the normal annual homicide rate for Solar County.

"All right," Bonner said. He was beginning to find it hard to talk from outrage. "Now who found them, and when?" LEFT

Lucy took her time. "The shooter must have by the way he came in, front door. We've got some mud scrapings, but they won't tell us much. So he walked outside in the rain and got into his pickup—"

"How do you know what he was driving?"

"And took the short way out of here, up by the dam, where he nearly collided head-on with another vehicle, driver lost and just wandering around. A three-year old Chevy Tahoe owned by Shay Waco of North Hollywood, California. What's left of it is below the dam."

"Rolled?"

"Yeah."

"Waco? Any relation?"

"Silverwhip Jack's daughter. Here's what I meant by coincidence. Shay and I were buds growing up, over by the park."

"How about that? She's still alive? Do we have a description of the shooter?"

"Not that lucky. She saw a pickup. Shay is positive that's what he was driving. Came at her around the base of the cliff at the west end of the dam, big crunch and over they went."

"They?"

"Her daughter's traveling with her. Says the same thing, blue pickup truck."

"How bad did they get hurt?"

"Bad enough so I sent them to the Med right away. But that isn't all. After they get hit the first time, the SUV is hung up above the ravine where the dam abuts the cliff, so the driver of the pickup, our suspect, takes a look, gets back into his vehicle and proceeds to shove a backhoe down on top of them."

"Went to a lot of trouble, didn't he? But Miss Waco claimed she never saw the guy."

"Only a glimpse. Couldn't describe him. He wore a slicker and a Stetson. Shay doesn't know if he was alone in the pickup. You want to hear the incredible part? When she realized the guy was trying to kill them, Shay jumped from the Tahoe with her daughter hanging on to her back, jumped close to seventy feet and went crashing down into some piñons. That probably saved their lives. I forgot to mention what she does for a living. Stunts. In the movies. Shay Waco was Fontana McCall's stunt double for three years. If she didn't have the training, Shay and her daughter—" The look on Bonner's face stopped her. "What?"

"Tall, curly dark hair, wears glasses?"

"Her hair was a mess, but, yeah. Why?"

"Nothing, really. I may have met her, I mean she was in Vegas jumping out of helicopters for a movie. It was one of those starting-a-conversation-while-you're-waiting-for-an-elevator things."

"Oh. Well, that's quite a coincidence." Lucy took the bottle she'd been warming from the boiling water and shook a couple of drops of formula onto the back of one wrist, then tasted with the tip of her tongue.

"Where did you learn to do that?" Bonner asked her.

"Are you kidding? My mom raised nine kids. Some of them I was actually related to."

Lucy passed Johnny Mack Broone on her way out of the kitchen.

"Checking the neighbors," Broone advised the sheriff.

"Who's closest?"

"Guy and Pam Baker. Simba Spring Ranch."

"Haven't seen Guy and Pammy since their tiger was snatched a few months ago. Are they home now?"

"With a dozen other big cats. Also that grizzly, the one that's been in movies? Tame, supposedly, although I'd sure give it a wide berth."

"They didn't hear or see anything?"

Broone shook his head, took a kitchen match from his shirt pocket, and began chewing lightly on the wood, as if in the throes of a tender craving.

"How well did they know the Santeros?" Bonner asked him.

"By sight, except the young ones. They swam in the river all the time. Kids spoke some English, Mrs. Baker said, but they tended to be shy. She let them hang around the ranch sometimes; they liked to bottle-feed the cubs."

"Who else?"

Broone rubbed the back of his lined neck and tried not to stare at the bodies. He was a big man, retired from Fish and Game. Except for a pale stripe near the hairline, Broone had the sun-cured, precancerous look of the lifelong western outdoorsman. The flesh of his face was so complexly folded and creased and loose, it looked as if it had been carelessly stapled to his skull.

"Next to Simba Spring there's the place owned by a man named Gehrin. He's one of those global businessmen, resident status, owns homes in three or four countries. I know they've got two million sunk in their property here, but he's not around much. His wife seems to like Utah—climate's good for her allergies or something. She is sure enough a looker, although she has a little bit of a weight problem. The caretaker said she's home right now, but he hasn't seen the Mister for three or four weeks. Then on down the road where the river makes a wide loop is Jack Waco's ranch. He wasn't home neither."

"Did the river flood tonight?"

"Yes, sir. It don't take much, you know, for the Aquiles to get over its banks when the washes are running full. The road's passable now. Some rain we had. I can't remember the monsoon ever being this early. What you want me to do now, Tobe?"

"Give Cas a hand with the bodies."

Broone worked his matchstick between his teeth. He was particularly interested in the girl on the floor, her good legs.

"Do you have any notion, Sheriff?"

"Do you? Seen anything, anybody hanging around?"

"Well, you know, there's always campers on the river. Up at the reservoir. I just make sure they understand and follow the rules."

"Did the Santeros employ someone on the place?"

"I couldn't say. I didn't come around all that much; there wasn't a need to, and I've got some miles to cover." His tone made it a complaint, which Bonner ignored.

"What was a backhoe doing up on the dam?"

"Belongs, I guess I should say what's left belongs to Jed Weeks, he was doing some work for the state. You'd have to ask Jed."

"Doesn't matter. Is there a storage shed or some kind of outbuilding on the place here?"

"Horse stalls. Couple of workaday saddle broncs and a pony. Storage shed behind the stalls. Lucy looked in there already. But I don't know what she was looking for."

Bonner knew. Quantities of iodine, for one thing. Certain paraphernalia. Lucy Ruiz had studied the murder scene and come to the same conclusion, after dismissing other possibilities.

With the increase in retirees in Solar County, death had become a cottage industry. Death by accustomed means: disease, the failure of vital organs, general decrepitude. The bodies in the Santero house suggested that someone had been in haste to fill a quota. But not the work of a footloose psycho. The job looked at least semiprofessional, no slapdash element, spur-of-the-moment slaughter.

Contract work then, a payday, a payoff. Gustavo Santero, formerly of Mexico, diamond rings on his pale furry fingers. Sullied Spanish lineage; definitely not an aristocrat. The house, antique furnishings and paintings, an obviously new, custom kitchen: everything had a monied look. Right away Lucy would've been thinking drugs. A meth lab, maybe, not in the house of course because they stank, but nearby. Santero crowding in on an already overcrowded business in Solar County.

Find out why he had left Mexico and under what circumstances.

Then Bonner had another flash.

"Cas?"

"Yeah."

"When you autopsy, I mean Papa and Mama particularly, look for signs of recent plastic surgery."

"I should call in Marc Grenfell for that. What's on your mind, Tobe?"

Tobin Bonner smiled slightly, then whistled between his teeth and kept his counsel. As did Gustavo Santero, short, muscular arm over the back of his chair, head almost resting on the shoulder, the look in his still-hard coffee-bean eyes one of distant disdain. The eyes, undistorted by cranial pressure, but then two-thirds of the back of his skull was all over the French doors and outside on the patio. Dark, sensual lips, trimmed mustache, two-inch scar curving toward his broad nose across a cheekbone, much black chest hair, matted with blood: Bonner sensed, even in death, a tough guy.

Lucy Ruiz came down the stairs as Bonner was leaving. She carried the feeding infant in the crook of one arm. Lucy's face intent, her focus on the nuturing chore. The little girl smelled powdery and looked snug, growing sleepy.

"She has a fever and her nose is running. Could be why she wasn't in her high chair with the rest of the family."

The little girl's round dark eyes were fixed hazily on Bonner as she sucked on the bottle, pausing to breathe through a corner of her mouth. She let the nipple slip, beginning to nod off. Lucy held her a little more closely.

"So what do you want to do with her?" Bonner asked.

"I'd feel better if she was in the hospital. I'll take her myself when I'm finished here."

"Luz, daylight, see if there's any paint traces on that backhoe. Tire tracks up there; that part of the dam road is mostly dirt. Am I going to learn anything from Shay Waco?"

"There could be something she didn't remember when I talked to her. She was upset about her daughter. The girl had kind of an ugly knee wound."

Enough media people had found their way to the Santero house to be a public nuisance. Local paper, Phoenix and Vegas print and

TV journalists. Bright lights. Bonner's deputies were mum, so the VJs were interviewing hearse drivers or picking each other's brains. Bonner headed for his car.

"Sheriff!"

"Sheriff, over here!"

Bonner paused for a few seconds near the media bullpen deputies had made with yellow crime scene tape.

"I'll have a statement, nine-thirty in the morning, my office."

"Who was taken to the hospital? Are there survivors?"

"How many victims?"

"How were they killed?"

"I heard a baby crying! Is the baby all right?"

"Did somebody see it? Sheriff, do you have an eyewitness?"

Bonner said to his chief deputy, a former defensive tackle at Brigham Young University and with the Calgary CFL team, "I don't want company going into town, so keep them occupied. Give them something for the early news. In exchange for no names until next of kin have been notified, the usual courtesy we expect of responsible journalists."

"Okay. What do I say?"

"Five persons, we assume all from the same family, shot to death while at dinner, approximate time of death not fixed; but we should know more about that as our investigation continues. The victims appear to have died almost instantly. No sign of forced entry, no indication of a struggle, no one tried to run. Our assumption is the perpetrator was known to the family. Did you shave today, Del?"

The big deputy rubbed his jaw. "Yes, sir, but it was early this morning."

"Always carry a shaver in your car, Del, you never know when they're going to shove a Betacam in your face."

Del Cothern couldn't tell if he was serious. Bonner often had the grin and whimsical thought processes of a man with a wry approach to life.

"Couldn't you do this, Tobe? I'm just not comfortable with those news people."

"I'm an elected official of the county. I never go on camera wearing a fishing vest, sucking on a breath mint. The voters will think I've been loafing on the job."

Bonner winked at the chief deputy and made his getaway.

5 SHAY WACO, DRAPED IN a blanket, was dozing in a padded chair beside Pepper's bed, her bootless feet up on the seat of an identical chair, when she heard the door open. Her eyes, closed, still reacted to the influx of brighter light from the hospital's corridor. Her face twitched a little in annoyance.

"Sorry to bother you after what you've been through."

Then don't, Shay thought, but she looked at him anyway, tense until she saw the gold shield in the leather holder he had in one hand. He was big, with kind of a forward lean to him, one shoulder slightly advanced, you'd have to say hulking. He should be watching his weight. Hairline receding. He hadn't used a comb lately but there wasn't much more hair than the nap on a new tennis ball. Taut jaw, amused-looking mouth, bright eyes. Something about him seemed familiar, but she was too exhausted to work on it.

He left the door open a few inches, standing where his profile glowed slightly to Shay's fuming eyes, revealing a dent the size of a dime in one cheekbone.

"Tobin Bonner," he said. "I believe we met last night at the Space Odyssey. We were waiting for an elevator."

"Oh. The sheriff. You mean this is *your* county?"

"Until August, anyway." He looked in a couple of pockets of his vest, came up with a handful of bright thistlelike flies, put those away and found a dog-eared business card, which he handed to her. Shay couldn't read it without her glasses or contacts.

She looked to see if Pepper had been disturbed, but the girl was dead asleep on her back, a lot of painkiller, her injured knee in a nest of ice packs and pillows. Pepper was partly covered with a folded blanket, and she wore a hospital gown. Loopy Lou, one of her stuffed animals, retrieved from the wreck of the Tahoe along with some of their other belongings by a couple of considerate deputies, was clutched in the crook of Pepper's right arm.

"How's she doing?" Bonner asked.

"They're going to do an MRI . . . in the morning. The knee will require surgery."

"How about yourself? I see you broke some fingers."

"Pulled a muscle in my side. Bit my lip. Cracked a toof. Tooth. Sorry . . . I'm just out of it."

"I went up to the dam to have a look. I still don't know how you pulled it off."

"Lucky," Shay said, feeling only a small twinge of anxiety as she remembered and thought again about how easily the jump could have gone disastrously wrong. She yawned. "I'm awfully tired, and there's . . . nothing else I can add to what I've already." Long pause. "Told your deputies."

"I didn't see Silverwhip Jack in the lounge out there. Has he made it in to visit you?"

"No. He hasn't. He's not home yet. Or not answering his phone. Do you know my . . ."

"Everybody knows Jack. Does a lot of charity work, shows for kids. He's still a winner with that bullwhip." Bonner looked at the sleeping girl. "What's your daughter's name?"

"Laurel Cloud." Shay gave a small shrug and winced. "I was twenty-one when she was born. Sort of a belated . . . flower child. Her father and I both thought the name was . . . awesomely cool. He's Irish. I don't remember who started calling her Pepper. But that's what she goes by now." Shay wondered why she was talking so much when it felt as if each word were coming to her tongue by slow elevator. Bonner had a habit of stroking his lower lip with a thumbnail while focusing on her, as if her rambling had spiritual import.

"You're divorced?"

Shay glanced at her own ringless left hand.

"I never married him."

"Oh. Why not?"

Shay took a shallow but penetratingly painful breath, and wondered if she was going to get any benefit other than stupor from the Darvons she'd swallowed after her broken fingers had been set and splinted. The leg she had hurt the night before in Vegas was throbbing. Maybe she ought to have asked for Demmy and Flexeril. Like any stunt player in films, she was an authority on pain pills and anti-inflammation drugs, although her threshhold was high and she was wary of dependency.

"We both knew . . . it would be a mess," she said. "What happens in August?"

"Excuse me?"

"You said you'd be sheriff until August."

"Oh. August is primary month. My opponent's a car dealer and a Bircher who's been running an honest-to-God campaign. Radio spots every hour. Four Caravans on the street with his face all over them. Patterson's got money to spend; I don't. My campaign is, I put my name on the ballot. Right now it looks to be I'm down about two to one."

"What's . . . a Bircher?"

"John Birch Society. Ultraconservative, which is pretty much the temper of the entire state. Tell me about the pickup that hit you."

"Again?"

"If you wouldn't mind. Do me the favor, and I could fix you up with a cold beer."

"Ohmigod, a cold beer!"

"I was on a two-day fishing break. Still have a few cans in the cooler in the back of my car. I'll smuggle one up to you."

"I'm not registered . . . to vote in Utah."

"Pity," he said, with a quick grin. "You can have the beer anyway."

Shay felt too weary to smile back at him. "The pickup. Okay. What I know. Big job. Pretty sure it was a blue Silverado. The 350 . . . from the sound of it. Hit me on the right side. Good whack, so . . . there has to be collateral damage to his left front . . . fender. May have knocked out the headlight and . . . running lights. But he had a roof rack of halogens. I could see them . . . shining through the rain while he was putting the . . . muscle to that backhoe."

"You can't recall much about how he looked? Height estimate?"

"Oh—six feet. At least. The hat."

"A Stetson?"

"Or Resistol. Black. The shape was cutting-horse style. Front brim down."

"Uh-huh," Bonner said, and waited. Shay's head drooped inattentively to one side, eyelids closed over her dreamy burning eyes.

She asked in a small voice, "Is that worth a beer?"

He hadn't heard a lot, but what there was wasn't unhelpful. "You bet. Back in a minute."

Shay used the bathroom while he was gone, a little wobbly, winking and blinking, unable to see herself well in the lavatory mirror, and just as well. Two butterfly bandages closing cuts on her face, hair matted beyond a reasonable hope of brushing it out without washing first. Hey, come back sometime when I'm lookin' good, Shurf. But she wannted that beer. The roof of her mouth was parched. She'd only had two Darvon, a few sips of beer couldn't hurt. She soaked a washcloth in tepid water and wrung it out, sponged Pepper's face. The girl groaned softly in her sleep.

Bonner returned looking surreptitious, two cans of beer bulging in cargo pockets of the tatty vest. One can was his.

"Will you get him?" Shay asked, remembering what they'd been talking about.

"While I was downstairs I put your description of the vehicle on the computer. It could be in any of four states by now. Or dropped off a cliff ten miles from here, which is more likely."

"Sheriff. Who were they?"

"The family's name was Santero. Hadn't been living here very long."

"It was so evil. All of them, helpless. Those children."

"We don't see that kind of violence around here. I haven't, not since I've been sheriff. Before that I saw plenty."

He was silent, idly scraping his lower lip with his thumbnail, doing an impressive job of crushing his already-empty beer can with the other hand. Shay watch him hazily.

"Before you were sheriff?"

"I was with the DEA."

"Drug Enforcement Agency?"

"Administration. Everyone makes that mistake."

"Where?"

"South America, Miami, then El Paso. Then I got shot and eventually I came home."

"Who shot you?"

"Wouldn't I like to know? Who did it doesn't matter; it's who ordered it done. I've had a few suspicions over the years." He looked around the hospital room. "Are you covered for all this? MRI, private room."

"I wasn't hurt on the job, so the Screen Actors Guild pays. Stunt people have separate coverage for work-related injuries."

"That's good. Medical bills can kill you quicker than the injury. In my case, government coverage was excellent, but the benefits ran out after a few years."

"Are you still being treated?"

"No. My son is. For the rest of his life. He was two at the time, about the same age as the Santero infant."

Shay studied him. "Your son was with you when you were shot?"

"My son, my wife. There were forty-two bullet holes in the car. I was covering Vida, trying to protect him, trying to get my gun out. Pretty hopeless. They pinned us down from both sides of the car." He was telling it like an old war story he wished he hadn't started. Flat tone, hurrying a little to get the facts in, as if an occasional telling was like massaging a still-unbearable ache. "Connie died right away. I took seven hits. One of them passed through my upper right arm and got Vida in the head. The bullet's still there, so that's why—"

His pager buzzed him; he looked a little startled, recalled from the past. He took a cell phone from one of the many pockets of the vest and dialed a number after glancing at the pager message.

"It's me. Yeah. Not much. You are? Okay. Meet you downstairs in ten minutes."

He folded the phone but kept it in his hand. "Lucy Ruiz," he said. "She's bringing the Santero infant here. The Med has good child care, as good as any in the state."

"What's wrong?"

"She has a fever. Probably a summer cold. But there's nobody else, as far as we know now, to take care of her."

"It makes my heart ache," Shay said, glancing at her own child.

Bonner put his folded beer can into a cargo pocket, and found half of a roll of Certs in another.

"I'll let you get some rest. Probably want to talk to you again."

"Sure. Okay. But I don't know much." Shay looked at her splinted fingers and bandaged cuts. "Do you think—?"

Bonner paused at the door, looking over his shoulder at her.

"When he knows I'm still alive . . . what he might do. He went to a lot of trouble with the backhoe. Didn't want to leave witnesses. He probably thinks I saw more of him than I could have. I don't want to be all over TV, Sheriff. Unless I get my own show." She smiled tensely.

"We'll try to prevent that. But you're news. I wish I could say my department is leak proof. If one of the VJs gets on to you while you're here or out of Jack's place, the best policy would be to say you were blinded by the lights; you didn't see a thing."

"My real concern is my daughter's safety."

"I understand. I'll do my best. You have my card. If you recall anything else, even if it seems trivial, page me. I'll get right back to you."

Shay had no rest for a while. Three A.M., BP and temperature check for Pepper, who half woke up and was surly for a few minutes until she drifted away again into what must have been chaotic dreamland, from her occasional mutterings and twitches. Shay looked out the single sealed window of the small room, weight on the leg that wasn't hurting, tongue passing again and again over the raggedness of a chipped front tooth. She had a good view of the Mormon temple, wedding-cake white and bathed to the highest cupola in floods. Temple and flowery grounds took up a fenced city block across from the medical center complex. She had gone to school and played with Mormon children, tolerated because of her riding ability but never close to any of them. Nor had she ever set foot inside the temple, the part that was open to gentiles. In a state and community where religion was the iron fist in a velvet glove, unique in the present-day American landscape, Silverwhip Jack had been contemptuous, not of the Mormons' piety, zeal, and work ethic, but of their founder, whom he described as a con man. Jack wasn't shy about airing his views (he enjoyed pulling his dusty Stetson down over his face and mumbling poorly remembered passages from the Bible into the crown), but as far as Shay knew no Mormon had bothered to rebuke him for his attitude or his manners. No one used an automatic nailer on the truck tires, threw rocks, tried to burn the house down. Perhaps a religious community needed a fool and a heretic in its midst to confirm its sanctity. Or the saints might have been too busy in their own striving for exaltation to take much notice of a hopeless case like Jack. Why he had stayed on in Utah, when he often complained that it was difficult to get four other men together for a smoke-filled poker night, and how he had prospered in a business environment no less rife with intrigue and sharp dealing than a Levantine bazaar, was a mystery to Shay equal to the mysteries within the imposing Mormon temple.

She wondered why, since he had been expecting them, he hadn't stuck around the home place until they arrived. But that was Jack, the way he'd always been. Right now she didn't feel like dealing with him. Tomorrow she'd rent something and drive out to the ranch. Probably find him sleeping off a drunk. In that case he was not going to meet his granddaughter after all. Homecoming was already a disaster she would never be able to get out of her mind, her Tahoe smashed to hell and Pepper lying there hurt. Just let Jack get on the wrong side of her by word or action; then, bad as Pepper's knee might be, Shay vowed to bundle her daughter up and drive them back to California. Accepting another defeat, however unwitting, from her father.

First light, Tobin Bonner turning into his driveway, headlights flushing some Gambel's quail from the blackbrush growing on his side of the wash at the south boundary of his property. A red-headed male and two females, all with the distinctive plume flaring goofily from the tops of their heads. They flew toward the mesa, still dark but with a defining streak of pale sunrise beginning to erase the stars above.

Halfway to the house he saw the snake, hanging by its rattles from a low limb of a mulberry tree, one of several he had planted for shade a decade ago. He stopped and got out of his car. Almost a month since the last one had been left there. A Great Basin rattler with dark brown blotches on its tawny, glistening back, maybe five feet in length. Shot in the head with a small-caliber weapon. Wired to the branch. Mouth propped open with a stick so the fangs showed in scary fashion. Same MO every time, if you wanted to put it that way. Three dead rattlesnakes. He wondered what the significance was, if whoever was leaving them for him to find was ever going to explain what appeared to be an element of ritual. Maybe he was supposed to know already and tremble at the sight. What the fuck. It went with the job, sometimes, along with rabid, ignorant hate mail, bad press, and anonymous death threats.

Alma Darke was in the kitchen, making coffee for Bonner, herbal tea for herself. The most devout among the Latter-day Saints never touched a beverage with caffeine or alcohol, never used tobacco, and consequently had the best set of health statistics of any group in the country. Alma was a husky seventy-year-old LPN, born in Brighton, England, orphaned during the Battle of Britain, and adopted by a Mormon family. She was just beginning to show streaks of white in her coarse dark brown hair, which she did up in a French knot. She wore a bathrobe over her nightgown. Alma was a light sleeper, sometimes in a rocker in Vida's bedroom on those occasions when Bonner was out of town or burning the midnight oil at the jail.

"I heard your car. You're back early."

"There was a problem. Did you hear any other vehicles last night?"

"On your drive? No."

"Some jerk's been TP'ing my trees with dead rattlesnakes."

"Oh, my," Alma said. "How atrocious. Why, do you suppose?"

Bonner shrugged. "Whatever the point is, I'm sure not getting it."

"Would you like for me to prepare breakfast now?"

"Breakfast sounds good. I have to shower and shave and get to the office by eight. How's Vida?"

"Back from his morning run. No difficulties, I'm happy to say. One of the dear little guppies has died, but he took it rather well, though I daresay it may have been a favorite. We had a proper funeral and all."

The original house had been small, one story, two bedrooms, native sandstone with a shake roof. Over the years Bonner had indulged his bent for construction, enlarging kitchens and bathrooms, doubling the size of Vida's bedroom to allow for the marine life that absorbed him for half of his wakeful hours, adding a shady screened patio on the two sides that had the best views of spectacular canyon walls colored as vividly as a nosebleed, and the Virgin River, which ran less than fifty yards behind the house.

Bonner knocked on his son's door, then let himself in.

The room was humid from evaporation of the saltwater in the

two fifty-five gallon semireef tropical fish tanks, and smelled faintly of the seacoast from which Vida had come. Air and water pumps whispered, bubbles streamed upward through water lit by actinic blue fluorescent bulbs, populated with purple anemone, golden seahorses, blue and red discus, a tomato clown, starfish, and peppermint shrimp.

Vida was hunched over the drawing table he had made himself, naked except for ragged denim shorts and red running shoes. He had the build of a light-heavyweight boxer: long arms and back and a small waist, low body fat, abs like shock absorbers beneath the skin, which had the sheen of a black pearl in the soft light from the artist's lamp clamped to one side of the tilted white table. Watercolor was Vida's medium. He washed and reshaped his brush with his fingertips, looked around at Bonner with a welcoming smile.

Bonner hugged him, holding Vida's head against his chest. The boy's hair, close to the skull and no thicker than a caterpillar's pelt, was missing in places where scars like seams of coal remained from four critical operations. He'd had drains in his head until he reached adolescence. The right eye was opaque, like a mildewed black cherry. Vida had never spoken and never would. He could copy any passage from any book and write his own name in finely crafted script, but he could read little of what he put down with his artist's hand.

His hair was still a little misty from the shower he'd taken, skin with a fragrance of soap and lotion. He had grown a goatee, in emulation of one of the rappers he'd seen on MTV. Bonner stroked it with a finger, still holding him, and Vida shrugged, grinning.

"How many miles today?" Bonner asked him. Vida seldom missed a day of running, before dawn or during the long dusks of summer, after the sun was behind the mesas to the west and no longer a threat to him. Five to seven miles along the river, into the canyon where the park began. He had the appetite, energy, and restless nature of any athletic nineteen-year-old, and further conditioned himself by doing huge numbers of sit-ups and push-ups, often for an hour at a time on the patio.

Before the expense had become too much for him, Bonner had owned horses. Didn't miss them particularly. What he missed were the early morning rides with Vida. Bonner had taught his son to drive, and Vida knew what the road signs meant. But he could never pass the written test to obtain his license. Also there was no time of day or night when he would be safe on the roads. He enjoyed football and slapstick comedy on TV. The Three Stooges, Laurel and Hardy,

Wile E. Coyote. That old British vaudevillian Benny Hill. He liked the cooking and home improvement shows, and was already as good a carpenter as his old man, doing all the household chores Bonner didn't have time for. Because he slept days and was awake at night, Vida fixed most of his own meals, preferring pasta and stir-fry entrees. He wore a watch and could tell time. Although his IQ was well above average, Vida had never attended school. He had never met a girl his own age. But he was always occupied with something that interested him, and happy. He had his tropical fish, and his father's love, and Alma Darke to watch over him. Either Bonner or Alma provided, on a strict schedule, the medications necessary to prevent a catastrophic seizure. In spite of the heavy dosage, there had been occasional crises. Vida would never outgrow them.

Bonner noticed a troubled expression in Vida's sighted eye.

"What's bothering you?"

Vida reached for a pencil and sketchpad of newsprint and swiftly drew the likeness of a hanging rattlesnake.

"You saw it too?" Bonner let Vida go and took the drawing, then crumpled it in his fist with a little grimace and tapped the side of his head with a forefinger. Vida caught on and nodded. Bonner threw the ball of paper into the wastebasket beside Vida's drawing table and looked at one of the big tanks that lined a windowless wall of the bedroom.

"Somebody died, Alma said." Bonner bowed his head, his hands together as if he were praying.

Vida nodded again, got down from his stool and walked over to the bookcase where he filed all of the notebooks he'd been keeping since he was ten years old. Hundreds of drawing pads, uncountable sketches and full-page watercolors of tropical fish. Every fish he'd ever owned. He chose a recent pad and flipped through the pages until he came to renderings of a fish with spotted dorsal fins like the wings of a butterfly. Some of the drawings resembled cartouches, a record of the life of the fish in Vida's own symbolic language.

He showed Bonner the page and tapped the face of his wristwatch several times.

"So he was one of your old-timers. Old like me."

Vida shook his head, amused. He took the drawing pad back and replaced it carefully on the shelf.

"Breakfast!" Alma called from the kitchen.

"Put a shirt on and let's go eat," Bonner said.

Vida made a broad gesture that meant, Are you staying home today?

"Wish I could. But I'm working on a big case. Shootings. Tell you about it later." He hadn't done enough of that lately, Bonner realized. Just sat and talked about what was on his mind, having a couple of beers, reminiscing sometimes, telling Vida about Connie, whom he probably couldn't remember. Never knowing just how much Vida really took in. He was easily able to relate emotions to words, but ideas, concepts that required a comprehensive language, Bonner had no way to know.

After breakfast, before getting cleaned up to face what promised to be a long day and with no hope of much more than a catnap during the next twenty-four hours, Bonner rubbed the stubble beneath his lower lip with a thumbnail, working up to something. He said to Alma, "Well, I think we should—we need to talk about—"

"Oh, if it's the money, you're not to worry."

"You know I haven't been able to pay you for a month."

"Well, I understand perfectly. I'm fine, really."

"The fact is, I had the house appraised and I'll get word this week about that equity loan."

"Oh," Alma said, watching Vida put dishes away, her fair brow creasing. "I thought you had already approached the bank, and they—wasn't it a problem because of the second mortgage?"

"This is a private lender. I'm sure I'll get the money."

"That's wonderful news. But as I say, you need never feel harassed where I'm concerned should you find yourself a bit in arrears." She looked fondly at Vida. "Mr. Darke, as you know, was a stickler when it came to the monthly annuity payments, so as long as my needs are modest I shall always be comfortable."

"You're a blessing, Alma. Where would we be without you?"

6 BONNER HAD A LOOK at the assembled media on the flagstone patio in front of the three-story brick building that housed the county courts, sheriff's office, and jail, three vans with satellite dishes in the parking lot below the bluff at the upper end of Hamblin Boulevard. He drove around to the gated entrance to the overcrowded jail and parked in his slot.

There was a highway patrol car next to the sally-port door, the trooper unloading a couple of bearded ramblers he'd picked up on the Interstate. Undernourished, sunburnt, bloodshot, like walkouts from Hades. Their shapeless boots and clothing on the verge of wearing out; and they smelled.

"What have you got there, Matt?" Bonner said, displeased.

"Possession."

"Crack?"

"Weed. I'd say about sixteen ounces."

"Sheriff," one of the vagrants said in a voice of high tragedy, "them joints was in the bedroll I borrowed off my brother-in-law, so's I could get myself up to Idyho and visit my old mother, who's dying of a thrombosis? Sir, I never knowed they was there! Sir, I have been clean of drugs for six year with the Lord's help, and that ain't no word of a lie. Do you think you could help us out, Sheriff?"

Bonner shook his head. "It's not my beef, fellas. Sorry." Under his breath he said to the trooper, "Matt, I don't have any use for this shit. I'm overbooked as it is, and from the condition they're in they're going to need medical; we won't make a dime off either one of them."

"Tourist season, Tobe. I get my ass eat out from Salt Lake if I let bums like these two pass by."

"Yeah, yeah."

"When did the circus hit town?"

"This morning, I guess."

"How does it look? Pro?"

"We don't know a thing about it yet."

"I heard a rumor. The Feds are coming down."

Bonner gave the trooper a fast look as he was going in the door.

"You know more than I do, then."

The phone was ringing in his office. Mary Lynn, who had been with him for twelve years, was also waiting, with coffee, messages, two days' worth of mail. Mary Lynn was four feet nine-and-a-half inches tall in high heels, with a gray crew cut, a cherub's merry face, a somewhat cynical tilt to her full lips, and an always-unflappable manner.

Bonner pawed around in his middle desk drawer.

"Mary Lynn, where's my goddamn Advil?"

"Probably used it all up. How about generic ibuprofen?"

"Anything. Order of importance?"

"Eula Clawson has called *nine* times, count 'em, about the travel agency that sent her a certificate in the mail, then swindled her out of, she says, another two thousand dollars."

"I told Eula not to take the trip. She took that trip?"

"Yes. The airplane sat on the ground for nine hours being repaired, the tour guide was a drunk who made passes at two of the women, and the accommodations were, direct quote, 'a hellhole.' "

"She was asking for it. If it sounds too good to be true, et cetera. Tell Eula to leave me alone."

"Excuse me, I thought there was a primary coming up? Eula's been recording secretary of the Coalition for Community Action since memory runneth not to the contrary. The old gal is connected, in other words."

"Tell her I'm appalled, my condolences, they can't do that to one of my constituents, and the rascals had better watch out. Who else?"

"Your brother called."

"Birdie."

"Neal says he wants to give you some help on your campaign, and that you would undoubtedly benefit from the expertise he's accumulated in his failed bids for three different elective offices. That last observation is entirely my own."

"Birdie, Birdie, I don't have time for Neal's power of positive networking, or whatever he calls it."

Mary Lynn made a modest kissing sound, grinned when Bonner scowled, and consulted her notes. "Stuart Bliss in the governor's office, expressing his shock and concern and offering the full cooperation of the state patrol in solving these murders. Also reminding you that it's prime tourist season in southern Utah, and massacred families are not the kind of image our law-abiding state seeks to project."

"Multiple Birdies for that evil son of a bitch." Bonner was slitting open envelopes. He glanced across the desk at Mary Lynn with a painfully furrowed forehead. "What else?"

"Better read the lead item in yesterday's *Enterprise*," Mary Lynn said, and left his office.

Bonner put down the letter opener and unfolded the newspaper.

The three-column head of the story she'd referred to read "Patterson Calls for Audit of Jail Finances." Bonner took a breath, then dumped the paper into the wastebasket, picked up a polished orange rock from the Virgin River he used as a paperweight, and chunked it against a cushion on the couch to the right of his desk, beneath a paneled wall hung with columns of framed citations and photographs. The rock bounced off and fell to the carpet.

He yelled through the closed door at Mary Lynn, "I want Lucy, Del, and Coroner Cas in here at eight-thirty!"

"Did you get any sleep last night?" Mary Lynn yelled back.

"Hell, no! Where's my ibuprofen?"

"Coming up!"

"What time is my appointment with—?"

Mary Lynn opened the door. "I can *hear* you. Stop *shout*ing. Why don't you use the intercom, that's why we put in all the expensive phone equipment? All your appointments are tomorrow, not today." She handed him his painkiller. "You're back a day early, remember?"

"Uh, yeah. Right. What about court dates?"

"Not until next Monday."

"Okay. Would you get me Shay Waco at the Med?"

"Yes, sir, how do you spell that?"

Bonner explained about Shay Waco, then shook two tablets out of the plastic bottle and swallowed them with warm black coffee. He looked down at the clutter on his desk blotter. Some photographs were visible in the ten-by-thirteen-inch manila envelope he'd opened last. The envelope had been addressed with letters cut from a magazine. Not the first time he'd received anonymous mail addressed in that fashion. There was a woman in town who periodically sent him photographs of herself in the beefy buff, face carefully blacked out, erotic come-on prose snipped from *Penthouse* and *Hustler* pasted on the reverse sides. But those were tacky self-portraits, snapshots made, he guessed, with a camera that had a timer on it. The photos he slid from the envelope were eight-by-ten glossies, probably taken by a hobbyist with his own darkroom.

Six color photos, all of them of Bonner's son, Vida.

He looked through them slowly, feeling a twinge of dismay.

All the photos had been made with one or more extension lenses, at least five-hundred millimeter, at some point where Vida's runs along the Virgin River had taken him into the canyon just before the entrance to the park. He'd been photographed on at least three different occasions, under mediocre light conditions. But there was no mistaking who the subject was.

In the sixth photograph, Vida was standing, not running, partly obscured by the branch of a tree. He had pulled his flimsy running shorts down and was holding his cock.

From the high angle of the shot you could assume almost anything: that he was showing it off, pumping it, or just taking a leak along his usual route.

Bonner's big chest lifted and for a few moments he didn't breathe as he considered the indignity, the fact that someone with a camera had been spying on his son and wanted Bonner to know. Then, the blood beginning to pound in his already aching head, he slowly turned the photo over and saw a message in tightly coiled handwriting.

> The black spawn of the
> devil lusts after our
> sacred daughters

He put the photographs together and replaced them in the envelope, then sat back in his swivel chair, thinking about the night he had pulled the infant Vida out of a crack house in Miami, ill and malnourished, lice population like rice dust in his dirty hair, and taken him home to childless Connie. He thought about the red-tape night-mare of adoption, against all well-meant advice, and the struggle and heartache since then. The only thing he and Connie had been able to learn about Vida's origins was that his parents were probably Hai-tian boat people.

Current population of Solar County, Utah, 53,720, not counting an estimated 2,000 AIs, or alien illegals, all of them Hispanic. The permanent Indian population numbered fewer than 400. Bonner's adopted son was the only black. This was well-known, although not that many people had actually seen Vida all the while he was growing up. Probably the reason for Vida's apparent reclusiveness was not so well-known, since it really wasn't anyone's business. Gossip, whatever gossip there still was, dismissed him as profoundly retarded.

Bonner put the envelope with the photos in a file drawer of his desk and sat back again, staring at a fluorescent ceiling light that had dimmed to a burnt yellow glow.

All right.

All right, that's the end of it.

But if I hear from you again, if you ever get closer than five-hundred-millimeter camera range of my son, then by God you nig-ger-hating nutbar, you loathsome religious crackpot, you gob of shit a dung beetle wouldn't touch, then I'll make it my business to find you and I will fucking rejoice to string you up in a barbed-wire cage hung from the loneliest tree I can find in the remotest canyon that exists in my county!

Mary Lynn said over the intercom, "Miz Waco on two, boss."

Bonner sat very still for five seconds, until the ugly, muddy tur-bulence flooding his mind receded; then he picked up the phone.

"Hello, good morning."

"Good morning, Sheriff."

"I called to see how your daughter was."

"That's very thoughtful. She ate a good breakfast, and she's go-ing for her MRI in a few minutes."

"Did you get hold of Jack yet?"

"No," Shay said, a note of asperity in her voice. "I was thinking of renting a car in a little while and driving over there. What's going to happen with my Tahoe?"

"We'll get a tow truck out that way sometime this morning and see if they can move it from under the backhoe. We'll keep the wreck here for a while. You can pass that on to the claims adjustor."

"Thank you. Sheriff, I think you ought to know, I keep a Beretta in a holster under the front seat. It's probably still there."

"Appreciate you telling me. Of course, as a law-abiding person you have a carry permit from the state of California, but as long as you're visiting us up here in the Beehive state, maybe we'd better keep it for you."

"Whatever you say. Do you know more about the—"

"I wish I had some encouraging news. Why don't you give me a call when you've seen Jack?"

"Why?"

"I assumed you'll be staying out there, at least for a few days until your daughter's out of the hospital."

"I hadn't thought—I probably will."

"Just so I know where to find you."

"Okay, Sheriff. Thanks for keeping in touch."

Bonner hung up, thinking about Shay. Now there was a quality woman. Good cheekbones, a Roman nose, and an olive complexion. Nearly done in from her ordeal when he saw her, but she'd kept her eyes on him and hadn't whined about any of it. Life with Silverwhip Jack, however long she'd been in his raising, must have had its trials. Shay had learned a few things about survival. A stunt woman in the movies. Hollywood made a lot of movies in his scenic county. Because his department was responsible for issuing permits, Bonner had met many of the players. He'd detained a few who didn't know how to behave with the local women or had other felonious habits. None of the stars had particularly impressed him. Shay Waco was different.

Now what are you thinking, Bonner? Your life isn't complicated enough already? Back to work.

"Mary Lynn," he said, "Get me Broone. On the telephone. Tell him landline please."

When the deputy called in, Bonner said, "Drive over to Silverwhip Jack's place and see if there's a pickup truck missing. The last time I ran into Jack in town, he was driving that old Silverado he'd had overhauled and spruced up. Said something to me about how much he liked his new Toyota Tacoma, but the Toyota just didn't fit his ruts."

"I know the pickup you mean. It's tan, isn't it?"

"No. When I saw Jack, he'd just had the 'Rado repainted. It was royal blue. And he'd added some fancy lights. I remember thinking, man, that is a real good-looking job."

7 THE DOCTOR IN CHARGE of the orthopedic service at the Solar County Medical Center broke the news to Shay that Pepper was going to need surgery to repair a severed patella tendon and a torn meniscus. She would be on crutches for several weeks. The doctor, whose name was Verger, looked young to Shay. She wondered out loud if Pepper might not be better off at a Los Angeles hospital, UCLA or Cedars, to have the surgery done.

Verger took her reservations with good grace.

"This is ski country," he said. "I guess I've done about four hundred tendon and ligament jobs, some knees in worse shape than Pepper's. But if you'd feel more secure about having it done back home, I'll be happy to refer you. I was in residence at Cedars for three years. I'm not practicing in LA because I like the air up here better, and my wife was breaking out in hives like jelly beans waiting for the next quake to happen."

Shay called the chief of orthopedics at Cedars, who had done some work on her left shoulder after she'd fallen badly from a horse in a TV western. He gave Verger's skills an A-plus rating.

They scheduled Pepper for 7:00 A.M. the next morning. In the meantime she was able to get around the pediatrics floor on crutches, wearing her emergency room brace, and play Ping-Pong in the game room with a boy her age who was recovering from blood poisoning.

Shay took a taxi to the airport on the other side of town and rented a Windstar from Avis. Then she retraced the route she'd followed the night before until the flooding of the Aquiles River had caused her detour to the top of the dam. Across the iron bridge she hesitated, thinking about driving up there and seeing, in daylight, the place where she'd almost lost both their lives, shuddered, and thought better of it.

The unpaved but graveled and graded road that stayed on the north side of the river still had water standing in low spots. The road took her past Simba Spring Ranch, portions of which were enclosed by a high fence posted with DANGER—WILD ANIMALS signs, and one that really spelled it out for the incautious: TRESPASSERS MAY BE KILLED AND EATEN.

Next to Simba Spring was a more tailored property, also fenced, with a gate like the façade of a Spanish colonial church in tan adobe. Beyond that, a broad lawn, brilliantly green and swept by morning sprinklers. The lawn looked as if it had been imported, like an exotic carpet, from a rainier land. The driveway was crushed red volcanic rock. The house, resembling a flattop adobe pyramid, was half-hidden from the road. The gates stood open, and Shay saw gardeners inside.

Another three-quarters of a mile, and Shay came to Jack's spread. Unmistakable, because there was Jack on a twelve-foot-high billboard, in his flat-crowned black hat and western movie duds, bullwhip with the plaited silver grip in one hand. In his other hand he held the reins of a piebald stallion, rearing and pawing the wind. The horse, named Lucky, had carried Jack through forty-three features and a short-lived TV series in the late 1940's and early fifties. Lucky was long gone, but Jack, obviously in a nostalgic mood, had named the place after his old horse. LUCKY ORCHARDS was spelled out in an arch constructed from bleached deer antlers over the drive that passed through acres of trees brimming with apricots and peaches.

Pickers could be seen on ladders down the neat rows of trees as Shay followed the drive to the house. Other men dumped their long sacks of fruit into a trailer behind a John Deere tractor. A truck with the inscription LUCKY ORCHARDS—100% ORGANICALLY GROWN FRUIT passed her on its way to the co-op, or wherever Jack did his marketing.

Farm buildings, an air-conditioned horse barn, then a long dim

shed filled with women washing, sorting, and packing fruit for ship-
ment. A foreman's cottage, housing units reminiscent of a thirties-
style motel, each unit with a tiny front porch. They were paint-shy,
but there were climbing roses around the newel porch posts. Wash
hung on lines, sheets swelling in a nice breeze. Then specimen silk
trees with pink flowers, clumps of blooming oleander, some yellow-
tinted locust trees, and a couple of Southern magnolias shading a log
ranch house with a deep front porch that overlooked a pond, probably spring fed.

Good God, where had all of it come from? Silverwhip Jack had
always been a poor businessman and a worse gambler. Degenerate,
in Shay's memory. But twelve-step programs and reformed sinners
were everywhere; it could even have happened to Jack.

A deputy was lounging against a front fender of the police-model
Ford Explorer SUV that seemed to be standard equipment in the
Solar County Sheriff's Department. He was talking to a slender man
in denims and a rancher's straw hat. Shay remembered the deputy's
face—he'd been first on the scene after her call from the Santero
house—but not his name. Skin loose and crinkly on his long face,
like a one-size-fits-all Halloween mask. Brunner? Broom?

"Morning," the deputy said, a forefinger to the brim of his law-
dog brown Stetson as Shay got out of the rented Windstar. "Pleased
to see you're up and around."

"Hello, Deputy. You were very kind to us last night. I'm sorry,
I don't remember your name, things were—"

"It's Mack Broone, Miss Waco." He had a matchstick habit,
switching it from one corner of his mouth to the other. "How's your
daughter?"

"Looks like surgery, I'm afraid."

"Damn shame. On the other hand—"

The man he'd been talking to interrupted Broone.

"Miss Waco? Shay? Excuse me, I'm Tom Leucadio. I manage
Lucky Orchards for your father. It's a real pleasure to meet you at
long last. From what Mack had to say, we have God to thank for a
miracle that you're even here."

"Miraculous may be the word," Shay said, unwilling to make that
much of it and dismissing hers and Pepper's escape with a quick shrug
that hurt her ribs. She briefly shook Leucadio's hand with her left
hand.

He looked to be about thirty. No trace of an accent, probably at least third-generation Hispanic in the U.S. He had an abundance of black mustache, ostentatious with his small features, and calculating, confident eyes, contradicting what might be a habitually pious attitude. Prominent gold cross and an equally prominent gold Rolex. College ring. Phi Beta key. With jeans? His jeans looked tailored, his cowboy boots handmade.

"Mr. Leucadio, is Jack here? I haven't been able to reach him. I only have the one number. Does he have a cell phone?"

"Please, call me Tom. I've tried the cell phone number and his pager. But he might be out of range."

"Why, do you know where he went?"

"No, I'm not sure."

"When did you see him last?"

"Yesterday morning, Shay, just after breakfast. He said something about—I'm sorry, *esta in su casa*, we don't have to stand outside talking! Have you eaten? How about coffee? Mack, what else can I do for you this morning?"

Broone glanced at Shay and said, "That's about it."

Shay said, "What's going on here? Has Jack disappeared?"

"Oh, no," Leucadio said, "that's not at all likely. But Jack does get the itch to go off by himself from time to time, and he may forget to let me or K. T. know where he's headed."

"Didn't he tell you Pepper and I were coming?"

"He did. And he was very excited, as emotional, I might say, as I've seen him. K. T.—that's K. T. Brancas, our foreman—K. T. said to me yesterday afternoon that Jack was making big plans for a trail ride and a barbecue to introduce his granddaughter to some young people who live around here. He was hoping the two of you would spend the summer."

Shay nodded, looking at the deputy's face, but he was rubbing his jaw, rearranging the loose folds of skin, and it wasn't possible to tell what was on his mind. She felt suddenly light-headed, standing there in the sun, and her heart was beating too fast, not out of concern for her father—no news to her that he was the rambling kind—but from accumulated tension. "I would like some coffee," she said finally.

"Maybe I'll use the telephone in your office, Tom?" Broone said, again with the merest glance at Shay. "I needed to check in half an hour ago, but I had that flat to fix."

"Help yourself, Mack. Shay, after you. By the way, if there's anything I can do for you at the hospital—does your daughter have a private room?"

"Yes, she does, thanks."

"And don't worry about the expense."

"I haven't. Insurance should cover everything."

"I'm just speaking for Jack, in his absence. Have you eaten?"

"I nibbled some cinnamon toast this morning; Pepper didn't want it."

"How about a Denver omelet? Maybe some stewed fruit?"

"I don't know. Some coffee first."

They crossed the wide porch and entered the house, Broone just tagging along behind them. His continuing presence bothered her. Something going on; a lot of eye-contact between the two men. Was Jack in trouble with the law?

From outside the log house hadn't seemed like much, but across the threshhold it opened up. The center portion was spacious, probably forty feet square, plenty of elbow room, paintings of cattle drives and Indian fighters. A bearskin-on-the-wall, whoop-and-holler sort of room. The floor was travertine beneath an exposed structural shell composed of cedar beams with a central skylight. There was a gallery on one side overlooking furniture groupings covered in Navaho-patterned fabric or various leathers, including Appaloosa hide and thong-stitched buckskin, and a hearth of uncemented river stones on the other side, adjacent to the open kitchen area. Undressed floor-to-beam solar-gain windows faced the pond. Beyond that, to the west, cloud shadow lay like a birthmark on the brow of a mountain. The deep roof overhang moderated the power of the summer sun. The house was air-conditioned and the air dustless, smelling pleasantly of cedar, oiled leather, a pie in the oven.

"Jack kept the façade the way it was, those great old hand-hewn logs, but completely gutted the interior, added two wings, a sprinkler system. Which, if you're going to live in a log house—Felicita!" A slight young woman with bangs and braids looked up from dough she was rolling out in the kitchen. *"Café para la senorita Waco, por favor."*

"How long has Jack had this place?" Shay asked, when they were settled down by the hearth.

"Well, it wasn't all of a piece in the beginning. The house and about twenty acres, Jack bought, I think it was in eighty-two. Then we added acreage as it became available, and the business prospered.

There're seventy-eight acres now, and we employ at least twenty-eight part-time workers during picking seasons."

Shay wondered about the implied partnership, his smiling confidence as he regarded her. Lustrous eyes that widened and narrowed subtly as he breathed. He had active hands. When he wasn't touching something of value on his person—an earring, the band of his Rolex, a turquoise-studded belt buckle—his fingers dangled on his crotch or poised below his lower lip, which looked as hard as a scar. It was the hand signals that tipped Shay off. No matter how polite his manner and conversation—or how married he might be—he was one of those men who were always thinking about pussy and how to get it.

Probably she ought to be flattered, knowing herself to be a wreck today. But Shay had already decided she didn't like Tom Leucadio.

"So Jack went off, and nobody has a clue," Shay said, as Felicita served them coffee.

"Well, I wouldn't say I don't have a clue," Leucadio replied with an indulgent smile.

"Meaning?"

Leucadio shrugged slightly. "Jack still has a fondness for a good time. And the ladies. You know."

"He has a girlfriend somewhere?"

"Two or three times a month he'll be gone overnight, maybe for a day or two."

"But you don't know who she is?"

"There could be more than one," Leucadio said, with that shrug again. "Jack mentions some names from time to time. They call him here."

Shay studied a painted Hopi carving, glowering from a tabletop like a stolen god.

"In spite of his age, he's still considered to be a catch."

"Oh, yes. Do you take sugar?"

"No, thank you."

Shay settled back with cup and saucer in her lap, feeling weary. She still wondered why Jack, if he had been looking forward to their visit, had picked their day of arrival to answer the call of the wild.

"I called the airport this morning," Leucadio said, "to see if Jack was using one of our planes."

"One of—how many planes does Jack own?"

"Three. Nothing fancy, hobby-type aircraft. There's an old D-model P-51 he had reconditioned when he was still going to air shows, and an AN-2 Flying Truck we use to service some accounts overnight. He's probably had the Truck for twenty years. And there's a twin-engine executive Cessna—for putting on the dog, as Jack says. But all the planes are accounted for. Don't worry, he'll come strolling in any time now."

"I need to get back to the hospital, so that's where he can find me when he does come home."

"Shay, if you don't mind my saying, you look as if you could use some sleep. I've heard what you and your daughter went through last night. What a terrible ordeal; it still shows in your eyes. And finding those people murdered—"

"How well did you know the Santeros?"

"I didn't know them at all. The house isn't actually on our road, it's partway up that little box canyon near the dam, half a mile north of Simba Spring. I knew someone had bought the McCovey place, and I probably should have stopped by to say hello, but I don't live here, at the Lucky. My work day is so crowded"—he looked discreetly at his watch—"there isn't a lot of time just to be neighborly."

"A lot of people around here must be scared."

He nodded slowly. "Word gets around. Felicita is the only one who showed up for work at the house this morning. Usually there are three girls. And I saw Mrs. Gehrin with a pistol on her hip, while she was out for her morning ride."

"Mrs. Gehrin?"

"Signe. She's German, or Swiss. The Gehrins live directly east of us; you must have seen their place driving in. That adobe monstrosity, if you'll pardon me. Maybe in Arizona it would work. No one's quite sure of *his* origins. He probably has more than one valid passport. I've heard that Gehrin is one of those speculators who makes an enormous fortune, loses it, makes another just in time to save his neck. More coffee?"

"No, this was fine; it bucked me up. I'd better be going. Pepper gets anxious, and she has a lot of pain even though she won't admit it."

Leucadio made a *simpatico* face.

"The guest suite has been ready for days. If there's anything more I can do to help—" He took out a business card. "Here're my numbers, day and night. And the minute Jack comes home—"

"Thanks. How long have you been working for my father?"

"I was picking apricots for Jack the first year he owned the Lucky.

Barefoot, hair down to my shoulders, ten bucks a day. I must have impressed him, somehow. He sent me to school. Stanford. As soon as I had my M.A. in Business I took over as manager; the other guy was, you know, just an old crony of Jack's who could barely read and write. In the last eight years we've seen major improvements in the profit picture."

His smile was full and satisfied—he loved saying it—*profit picture.* No animosity showing, but Shay got this message too, as clearly as if there had been another movie-style billboard outside the gate of Lucky Orchards, one that featured Tom Leucadio full-length, a gold-and-leather grandee. He didn't just have designs on Silverwhip Jack's profitable business, he already had his hooks in it.

Shay had only a glimpse of the dog running into the road and little time to react; as she swerved, thinking dimly *not again,* the low front end of the Windstar thumped solidly against the animal and she saw it tumble into some ornamental plants growing outside the massive adobe-and-wrought iron gate of the Gehrin place.

The dog hadn't made a sound as it was struck. Shay pulled into the crushed-rock drive and got out, trembling, looking at the still form cushioned in dusty spurge. Black dog, male, probably a Rot-weiler. As she approached she saw that he wore a chain choke collar with the remains of a chewed leather leash attached.

The dog's eyes were closed, his muzzle and blunt massive head covered in blood. His chest heaved convulsively a couple of times, a hind leg twitched. Then he was still.

I didn't mean to, Shay thought, lower lip between her teeth, bit-ing back tears. She looked down the drive toward the house with the shape of a flat-topped pyramid. The gardeners she had seen earlier were gone; the sprinklers had been turned off. Half a dozen black-and-white magpies were on the lawn, bathing in the cool, soaked grass. She looked helplessly at the dog again.

Shay left the van in front of the gate and trudged down the drive toward the house to tell somebody about the accident.

Before she reached the front door she heard voices from behind the house and took a privet-lined terra-cotta path instead. It led to an avenue of tall blue cypress and, at the end, a white gazebo above a free-form swimming pool like a rock grotto. A waterfall dropped several feet into the shady part of the pool from beneath the gazebo.

A man and a woman were having brunch there, presumably after their morning swim: they were both bare to the waist. Shay stopped twenty yards away behind a large urn of cacti. There was a good breeze blowing off the river, cooling her sweaty face; the tips of the cypresses swayed and touched gracefully beneath the flawless sky.

The man rose from his seat and leaned across the table to give the woman a kiss. He was completely nude. His sizable scrotum swung out as he leaned, like a ship's anchor headed for the deep, and his balls squatted momentarily on a fruit plate beside a wedge of orange-fleshed melon. It looked like a surreal still life from where Shay stood, but neither of the lovers appeared to notice. So they had been skinny-dipping. And weren't expecting company. The kiss was a long one, and he was lazily erect when he sat down again. Considerable length, but narrow as a broomstick, Shay noted.

The woman smiled blissfully. She seemed older than he, ample, not fat but with the beginning of a double chin. A motherly, nurturing bosom looked untouched by the sun. She raised a stemmed glass of juice to her lips.

"How can you be sure they weren't Mexican?" the man asked.

"The accent, Neal. I know my Latin accents. My father was ambassador to Colombia and then to Venezuela. I grew up in South America. Colombians, they speak with *cumba*, like the Argentines, who act very Italian. No, I never mistook the Santeros for Mexicans."

"What's *cumba?*" the man asked, taking the silver lid off a chafing dish that sat on the sideboard of a copper-and-chrome outdoor grill that looked as if a team of horses would be needed to move it. He helped himself to poached eggs. His slicked-back blond hair was drying in the breeze, and strands of it fell across his brow.

The woman demonstrated with an airy dancing rhythm of her small hands. Her own accent was German, to Shay's ears. "A sensual, flirty lilt. A sugary tone. They sound like crème Brûlée tastes. The Mexicans speak textbook Spanish, no lisping or slurring. The most awful Spanish is Cuban. Cubans grate on the ear. Naturally they are not the best lovers among Latinos. They don't have the time; they would rather be making money."

"Excuse me," Shay said, raising her voice to be heard over the steady swish of breeze and the splash of falling water, "but I'm afraid I've run over your dog."

They both looked at her, the man called Neal more startled than the woman. He jumped a hand toward the Remington Stackbarrel twelve-gauge parked across the seat of the chair next to him. Then he relaxed with a slight shudder as the woman smiled calmingly at him and called off the alert with a little flourish of her fingers. He reached for a flowery napkin and arranged it over his private parts as if he were putting an infant to bed.

"My name is Shay Waco. I think he must have chewed through his leash. I wasn't going that fast, but he just ran in front of me."

"Oh, God," the woman said, putting a palm to her forehead as if bracing herself. "What a tragedy—"

"I'm very sorry. What do you want me to—"

The woman laughed unexpectedly, her bosom jiggling. "I can hardly wait to tell Wolfie! I knew it was bound to happen. There's no worse pest than an untrained dog. How many of my flower beds has Tito dug up? We're well rid of him." She looked keenly at Shay, the hand now across her brows to shade her eyes. "But are you sure he's dead?"

"I liked Tito," the man said.

"I'm afraid so," Shay said.

"Well, don't worry. We don't blame you."

"Did you say Waco?" the man asked.

"Shay Waco."

"Related to Jack?"

"I'm his daughter."

"How delightful to meet you! I'm Signe. And this is our good friend Neal. As long as nothing can be done about Tito, why don't you join us?"

"Well, I—"

"Wolfgang should have given Tito to me," the man said. "I would have trained him."

"Nonsense, Neal, the dog was a horror. That breed will turn on you and tear your throat out while you sleep. I wouldn't allow Tito in the house with us," she said, in an aside to Shay.

"I'm very good with dogs," Neal said stubbornly.

"What do you want, acclaim? Put on your robe; I'm afraid Shay feels a little awkward." The woman made no move to put on her own robe, which was draped over the back of her chair.

"My daughter's in the hospital, and I—"

"Oh! You must be the one. I should have guessed. That maniac almost killed you too, or so I heard. Come, come and talk to us. I want to hear all about the dreadful thing. Neal!"

Neal scooted his chair around and picked up a flimsy kimono, silk with painted storks and bamboo, and wriggled into it without showing any more skin to Shay. Signe continued to sit, perfectly at ease, unabashedly naked, plucking at the tufted white fur of a Persian cat spread over her thighs. She gestured with her other hand, bringing Shay up to the gazebo like an acolyte to an altar.

It was apparent that Signe Gehrin hadn't done any swimming. Her flapperish helmet of black hair had a single artful pig's tail curl on her forehead, with tiny turquoise-beaded braids over each bangled ear. Her brown eyes were fully made up, wicked dark slashes at the corners, as if applied by a charred brand. It was a face that captivated without being beautiful. Wide at the temples, giving her the appearance of being brainier than most mortals, and always two moves ahead in every situation. Bold cheek and jawbones; nothing soft except for the fatted bulge of underchin. Her aureole and nipples were the size of sink stoppers; one of them was pierced by a gold ring with a jade inlay. She was as stark and earthy as a cave painting.

"Oh, you certainly *did* have a rough time of it," Signe said, observing her limp as Shay mounted four steps to the floor of the gazebo, then looking over Shay's patched and bruised face. "And your daughter's at the Med?"

"Her knee was ripped by the stub of a branch when we jumped."

"That's an amazing story," the man said, glancing at Signe to see if she'd heard it. He was reddish blond and probably shaved his body; it couldn't be that hairless past adolescence. From a distance Shay had calculated he would be in his midthirties. Seeing him point-blank she added a decade. He had a good width of shoulder and stayed in shape, but his long nose was fiery, his lips sore-looking from fierce weather. His eyes were pale gray, slightly pinked by sun or pool water, and set deep in his skull. Familiar eyes to Shay, as if she'd seen him elsewhere—a slight registration, in passing, on her subconscious. His smile was unaffectedly boyish, but today he had the vague daze and wince of a stubborn hangover.

"We were lucky," Shay said, seating herself because there wasn't much else she could do at the moment, watching Signe pour tea into an untouched cup. Bare feet and knees and thighs everywhere under the glass-topped table, she kept her own legs tucked close to the chair. "I really don't want to intrude. And I'm sick about the dog. Someone needs to—"

"Neal will take care of Tito, won't you, Neal? On your way out."

"I suppose so." His eyes were on Shay. Shifting a little in his chair, he placed a knee softly against hers. "Can you talk about it?"

"Have I seen you somewhere before? You look—"

Neal seemed to back off for a couple of moments, at least mentally, before smiling. The intrusive knee stayed where it was.

"Family resemblance. You must have met my brother by now. Older brother. He's the sheriff."

"Oh. Yes, he did come to see me. In the middle of the night. I barely remember what we talked about. He brought me a beer; that was sweet of him."

"I guess Tobin does have his moments," Neal conceded. "I tried calling him earlier this morning, find out what news. Everybody's in a state of shock." He glanced at the twelve-gauge shotgun on the chair next to him. "Something new for us folks. Urban terror comes to Solar County." The knee again, chummily. Shay drew hers away. "How exactly did you get mixed up in this nasty business?"

"I'm not mixed up in anything. All I know is, we got lost while I was trying to find another way over here. The river was flooded. We were plowed by a pickup truck. I wouldn't know it again if I saw it. Then our SUV rolled over the edge of the dam, and I—got us out of there. We had to free-fall into some pine trees; that's how Pepper was hurt."

"Is that where all those cuts came from?" Signe asked sympathetically. "But how did you *ever* find the courage to do such a thing?"

"It was instinct. Training. I do stunts, in the movies. Falls are my speciality."

"Orange hibiscus," Signe said, setting the teacup and saucer in front of Shay. Shay fidgeted on the yellow cushion of the iron chair.

"I want to apologize for—you know," Neal Bonner said, totally focused on her, going into a kind of cruise-control sincerity mode as he held his kimono loosely together with one hand. She kept her eyes on his face and her expression blank. "Of course we weren't expecting anyone to drop by."

The gold of Neal Bonner's wide wedding band flashed a little in a ray of sun. The same sun, shot through viney latticework overhead, touched Signe's brow, and she adjusted her own chair minutely to avoid it. The lap cat looked up with slitted blue eyes, then put its head down and nuzzled Signe where her abdomen creased below her pouty navel. The activity gave Signe visible goose bumps. She purred back at her kitty.

Shay said, "I spend a lot of my time on movie back lots. You see everything, eventually."

"Movies," Neal Bonner mused. "I had some money in a film a few years ago. Shot locally. It was an independent production. Never realized a dime on my investment. I don't know what happened, except the producer was a thief and I think the distributor kept two sets of books. Anyway, it was an interesting experience. I'm always looking for new ventures. And I did meet a lot of starlets."

"You dog," Signe chided him.

"I didn't mean that the way it sounded," Neal said, his brow puckered in consternation; but there was a hint of guilty glee when he smiled.

"Yes, you did."

"Signe and I have been close friends since the Gehrins came to Utah," Neal explained.

"Shay is a grown-up and the situation is rather obvious, so stop your groveling for approval. We are *lovers*. Wolfgang knows."

"And doesn't care."

What about your wife? Shay thought, profoundly bored with him, the charm that had begun to peel in middle age like a bad sunburn. She drank half of her tea while Neal Bonner asked if there had been rape and pillage in addition to the brutal murders in the Santero house. Shay said she didn't know; she was out of there in too much of a hurry.

"Oh, leave her alone, Neal," Signe protested, briefly touching fingernails to Shay's forearm. "Can't you see she doesn't want to think about it? How would *you* feel?"

"Maybe you'd like to take a swim?" Neal asked Shay, as if offering aquatic balm by way of apology. "The pool is fresh artesian water, no chemicals to sting those cuts."

"A lovely suggestion," Signe said. "I might even go in myself." Another aside to Shay, amusement in her dark eyes. "But only to the belly button; I've never learned to swim a stroke."

"No, thanks," Shay said, getting the prickly feeling that she was being manipulated by a couple of pros at erotic gamesmanship; no, make that semipro. She was from Hollywood, and there was nothing anywhere to match the level of competition on those playgrounds of Sodom. Wasn't much to Neal Bonner, as far as she'd been able to tell, except for his considerable tackle, some boyish moves, and a predictable story line. Signe Gehrin was a different matter—she could raise a sensual chill the way a full moon raised the yowl in cats. You felt a need to step cautiously in her vicinity, not knowing what might spring at you. "But I really do feel I'm intruding. There's a dead dog by the road, if anyone cares. My daughter probably misses me, and I should be going. I'm sorry about the circumstances, but it was pleasant meeting both of you."

8 THE VOICE ON THE telephone says, "I checked with Panama. My money hasn't been deposited."

Enrico Sinaloa sits back on the cream-colored leather sofa in his office on the forty-second floor overlooking Biscayne Bay, a choppy peasoup green this morning as storm clouds move in off the Atlantic. He wears his usual navy business suit, Armani, and a blue-striped shirt with French cuffs. His gout, the Epicurean's disease, is acting up today, and he has removed his tasseled black loafers to relieve some of the throbbing pressure in his toes.

Ricky says, "There seems to have been a misunderstanding of the terms."

"I don't think so. It was done. The news is out. No names yet. But you know the names. The true names. Do you want me to repeat them for you?"

"It won't be necessary. I'm aware that five birds fell from the branch. However. There is a sixth, still peeping in the nest."

Silence. Ricky adjusts his headset slightly, then reaches down and slowly slips a black silk sock from his most painful foot, looking in dismay at the swollen red joints. So much pain from his latest indulgence, only one celebratory glass—although a very full glass—from the bottle of Canaiolo nero flown in from his newly acquired winery in Tuscany's Carmignano district. As the sock drops to the carpet, Enrico's assistant Analita comes in through double walnut doors with his medication and an ice pack on a gold tray. She kneels and applies the ice pack tenderly to his outstretched foot, while Ricky winces and waits for the inevitable reaction at the other end of the line.

"What is this shit?" says the voice on the telephone.

"What do you suppose?"

"Nothing was ever said about a chick in the nest. You can't ask me—"

"I ask nothing. A proposal was made to me. The terms were acceptable. I understood that you would perform to the letter. I am ready to fulfill my obligation. When you have fulfilled yours."

"Sweet Jesus, how much revenge will it take to satisfy your fucking blood lust! Five birds on the ground; that isn't enough?"

Silence, this time on Ricky's part. Analita looks into his eyes, looks away instantly, rises and walks to the refrigerator concealed in an old Spanish armoire. She takes out a bottle of sparkling water and pours a glassful.

"I can't do that," the voice on the telephone says, trying for a reasonable tone, emotion pulsing across the distance like a small tsunami. Wrath, and bad blood. "It was lousy, last night. Those two kids—but a baby, shit, man."

"Enough," Enrico says harshly, "or I will not continue this conversation. Let me remind you, the matter of your fee is in the balance."

Analita brings the water to Ricky and takes the cap off his gout medicine for him.

"The least I deserve," says the voice on the telephone, "is half now. The other half when—are you prepared to be reasonable, *señor?*"

Ricky swallows his pills; he has an easily triggered gag reflex and taking any kind of medication is difficult for him. He presses the heel of one hand against his sternum, massaging, coaxing the pills to go down.

"*Nada,*" he says, when he can speak. "You will receive *nothing* until the chick is out of the nest. I know where she is now. You have made things unnecessarily difficult for yourself, but that is your problem. *Claro?* I advise you to keep your end of the bargain without delay. I will know when it is done. It will not be necessary for you to contact me again, ever."

When the connection is broken, Ricky removes the headset and places it on the sofa beside him. Analita is down on one knee again, tenderly holding his swollen foot.

"The ice is too painful," he says to her. *"Estoy sufriendo.* Take it away."

Enrico begins to tremble, although not from the touch of the ice. His clumsy-looking red face is frightening. The flesh looks as if it has gone through a Cuisinart, then has been patted imperfectly back together. He bursts into sobs.

"Oh, my brother! Why did you do this to us? How could you believe that you would get away with betraying us?"

He places a hand on Analita's ash-blonde head, fingers groping through her coif until he grips her shapely skull. It is as pleasurable to both of them as if he holds her breast instead of the bones of her head. Analita raises his bare foot to her lips and caresses it as if she has given herself over to rapture in a reliquary. She continues the caressing for the next quarter hour while Ricky tries, and fails, to get his rampant emotions under control.

●

Lucy Ruiz pulled into the driveway of the Santero house, greeting the man on duty in the shade of a massive old sycamore. He was a reserve deputy, using his own car: the Solar County Sheriff's Department was stretched thin today. The ASPCA also had a truck there, two members looking after the Santero horses.

She parked behind the Expedition SUV that had been sealed with crime scene tape preliminary to being towed to impoundment at the jail and went into the house. The air-conditioner was on. Except for scuff marks and dried mud on the Ponderosa pine boards of the foyer, everything looked tidy.

Master bedroom in one wing downstairs, three bedrooms upstairs. Boy-girl-infant. The baby's name was Cymbeline. Crib in there, which she had learned to climb out of, the usual brightly colored mobile hanging above it. Changing table, circus-wagon toy chest, chest-of-drawers. Lucy opened the closet door, found a diaper bag and a quilted zippered traveling case for Cymbeline.

She packed several changes of clothes for the baby in the traveling case and went downstairs again, leaving the case at the foot of the stairs. She went into the master bedroom, stood inside the door for a couple of minutes just looking around. Four-poster queen-size bed, a prie-dieu at the foot of the bed, religious paintings and icons on the four walls.

Now somewhere in the house, you'd think, they would at least have an album of family photos, if not portraits of all their good-looking kids. So far Lucy hadn't been able to find anything except a few dozen Polaroids, taken inside and in the vicinity of the house they had moved to thirteen months ago. No past history in photographs. Unless Gustavo Santero had kept them locked up in the safe in his office.

Need to find that combination, Lucy thought, somewhat edgy in the stillness of the house. She had a feeling she could always count on, like spiderwebs brushing the back of her neck, that something important or valuable was at her fingertips.

She was booting up the computer on Santero's desk when she heard a couple of cars on the river-rock drive outside, doors slamming.

They came right into the house. They seemed to know where they wanted to go first. Lucy looked up from the computer screen when they entered the office.

"What are you doing in here, Deputy?" one of the men, a real squirt, asked.

"I'm Lucy Ruiz. Chief Investigator for the Solar County Sheriff's Department. What do think *you're* doing? This is a crime scene and posted off-limits to all but Sheriff's Department personnel."

The woman with them said, "We're taking over this investigation, beginning now."

"The fuck you are. By what authority?"

From the flicker in the eyes of the two men with her Lucy knew that she was the authority, or part of it, even before she showed her ID: photo and thumbprint on one side of a leather folder, U.S. government seal on the other. Lucy caught part of her name, KATHARINE something, and the words SUBCOMMITTEE ON INVESTIGATIONS—OFFICE OF THE DIRECTOR, before she closed the folder and put it away in her sensible purse.

"What subcommittee?"

"Senate Governmental Affairs, Deputy Ruiz," the woman said, taking a step closer to read the nameplate on Lucy's uniform blouse. As if she thought that Luz might have given her an alias.

"And I didn't catch *your* name."

"I'm Katharine Harsha. This is Ted Wyrick, and Tony Sweets."

Sweets—it sounded to Lucy like a Mafia nickname—was the little guy. He had the expression of a man with a stealthy mind. Wyrick was sporting one of those mini beards that made his cleft chin look like a pussy. The two men nodded, their eyes roving around the office of the late Gustavo Santero. They were all dressed like morticians, grays and blacks, although Katharine Harsha also wore with her extremely sincere pin-striped suit a yellow-and-blue scarf that might have been from Hermes. She had a plain bony Scots face, with a faint map of veins beneath milky skin and shoulder-length auburn hair, her best feature. Permafrost blue eyes and a haughty upper lip. Her fair skin was going to burn up in this climate, Lucy thought. The high bridge of Harsha's nose already was bright red from limited exposure to the sun.

Lucy said, "I think I should call Sheriff Bonner. Right away."

"By all means. More of our people, and a couple of federal marshals, are arriving at his office just about now."

"More of you? I don't get it. What is your interest in the Santero killings?"

"You don't have to get it, Deputy," the squirt named Sweets said, with a dismissive smile. He went to the computer and turned it off, turned it around, studied it, then opened a small tool case he had with him. He began to remove the computer's hard drive.

"We'll want everything you've taken from this room," Katharine Harsha said to Lucy.

"I haven't taken anything out of here."

"No software?" Harsha asked.

"Like I said. Nothing."

"All right. Thank you, Deputy Ruiz. If we need you, we know where to find you."

"I suppose you'll want to read my crime scene report. My laptop is in my—"

"For now we're not that interested in the progress of your investigation, Deputy Ruiz. Who killed the Santero family is not as critical for us as finding out—other things that we believe may have a connection to the murders."

"You can call me Luz, if I can call you Kate," Lucy said; she went simmering outside to her Explorer to phone Tobin Bonner.

"Chinga, who do they think they are?"

"Take it easy, Luz. There's nothing we can do. I've seen the paperwork already. It's theirs, for now."

"This pisses me *so bad*—"

"Have a little tranquility; we'll talk about it later. I've got company. More expected."

"*Puñeta!*" Loud enough for a double echo up the canyon. A small flock of purple-striped swallows took off from under the eaves of a pump house where they had built their seasonal nests and went skyward like F-16s.

"Luz, remember what happened the last time you got this nuts? Get a hold of yourself, I don't like it any better than you."

"Yeah. Yeah," Lucy said, stomping the heel of a booted foot into the driveway rocks. The last time she'd thrown a wingding, she'd inadvertantly slammed a car door on her hand. "I'll see you then."

"If they want anything, try to cooperate; otherwise you're off the clock now."

"And off the case? You, too?"

"We'll talk about it," Bonner said, having lowered his voice. "But you know me, Luz."

"Yeah," she said, and was able to smile slightly as the connection broke.

●

Tobin Bonner looked at the man from the U.S. Marshal's Office and said, "How many other 'protected witnesses' have the feds located in my county without telling me anything about it?"

"Well, that's the point of it, Tobe," said Bobby Polikarski. He was a full-gutted man with a westerner's drooping mustache. "They *are* protected; and it's a matter of need-to-know, which is *never* when it comes down to local law forcement."

"Yeah, so we're a dumping ground for garbage you need to get rid of after DOJ puts them through the mill, never mind that some of them may be former hit men or rapists with recidivist tendencies."

Polikarski looked at some of the framed citations on Bonner's paneled wall and didn't comment. Bonner leaned back in his noisy chair. "Want to tell me who put them here, and why?"

Polikarski shrugged.

"Okay," Bonner said, "here's what I came up with last night and this morning—after Marc Grenfell confirmed that the two adults had had plastic surgery. Santero, or whatever his name is, is a member of an important family in the drug trade, one of the newer families doing business in Peru, Colombia, probably Mexico, too. Nobody I'd know. They're all new to the cartels since I was forcibly retired. Either the DEA stung Santero and had enough to put him away forever, or Santero went to them for sanctuary, to protect himself from his own breed. Maybe he was losing out in a power play, or maybe he was just greedy and not satisfied with his arrangement. Whatever. He ratted out somebody important, in exchange for the Witness Protection Program, was allowed to keep part of his stash in Panama or Zurich, and retired to a life of leisure in Solar County. How am I doing so far?"

Polikarski worked his brush cut over with his fingernails, said, "I tried that new stuff they sent me as a sample in the mail, but I guess I should go back to Head & Shoulders."

"It always works best for me."

Polikarski buffed some dandruff off his nails, using the lapel of his blazer, and said, "Crest. I have great checkups with Crest. How about you?"

"My dentist has me on Mentadent. Too much plaque, she says. But I've always been a lazy brusher. I don't like spending a lot of time in the bathroom. How much did the DEA leave Santero with?"

"What do you think?"

"I think they took two-thirds of everything he owned up to having stashed. It went straight into the black-money drop. That's what we used to do."

"You're too good for the job you're in, Tobe."

"Yeah, well, I probably won't have it after August the tenth."

"Competition this go-round?"

"Archer Patterson Jr."

Polikarski nodded, picturing the man. "I went hunting with him once. He gut-shot a buck, then wouldn't track it through some heavy brush."

"That's Archer. He wants an audit of jail finances. You believe that?"

"Pissing in the holy of holies."

"How does he think county sheriffs plan their retirements anyway? On our salaries?"

Polikarski grinned. "I would've thought your brother had you in high cotton by now."

"Fifteen thousand I sunk into that caffeine-free, root-beer franchise on Neal's advice. It was impeccable, he said. That was Neal's word for it. He had great partners, he said. Impeccable partners. Root beer and chicken-fried steak. Jesus, what an ugly combination. Closed in three months. Great location, though. Maybe we could've got a Burger King or something for that location, but the lease was faulty. I said to Neal, 'You must've spent your entire three years in law school moonlighting on your meat flute'. Now what I was thinking, Santero wasn't killed because somebody wanted to grab the rest of his money. That would have required other measures. Like carving up one of his children in front of his eyes, but even then he probably loved money more than a kid or two. No, they found out where he was and sent somebody to do the job. But I saw a lot of get-backs in Cali and South Florida. You couldn't walk inside the room for the gore. This was no tooted-up homicidal maniac last night, taking Polaroids after, FedExing body parts back home."

Three more men walked into Bonner's office without knocking. Bonner sat up suddenly, eyes narrowing to specks of flint.

"Speaking of the DEA," he said.

"Hello, Tobin. Long time."

"Hello, Dale," Bonner said to the Alpha male of the group. "How you doing?"

"Just hangin' in like Gunga Din. But I'm not with the DEA anymore."

Bonner peered at some papers on his cluttered desk blotter.

"Senate Governmental Affairs Committee, the Permanent Subcommittee on Investigations, Level Two. What's Level Two represent?"

"Federal Interdiction, Anti-Terrorism. FIAT."

"You're the director? Finally playing up there in the Show, Dale?"

"It means a certain level of autonomy, yeah."

"Congratulations, I guess," Bonner said. He folded his hands, looking at Stearman with a faint smile, nodding to the federal marshal.

"Bobby Polikarski, Dale Stearman. We worked El Paso together, assigned to EPIC." Bonner looked at the other men, no real status in their manner, and dismissed them as handlers for Stearman. They stayed well to the front of the office.

"So you're taking over the Santero case? How many on your team? I probably don't have room for all of you here. We're busting at the seams as it is. County commissioner's turned me down twice on a proposal for a new facility and a bigger jail."

"No problem, Tobe. We took some rooms at the Ramada."

"Anything else I can do for you, give me a holler. How's Edie?"

"Old news, but you wouldn't have heard."

"Sorry."

"Well, it's the nature of the game. Some wives don't have the staying power. We're not home that much, are we? It got worse when I transferred to Washington; she hates the climate. Mind if I sit a spell?"

"Hell no, where are my manners."

Dale Stearman was a tall man with a bit of a stoop. He looked at the available chair at one corner of Bonner's desk as if he were thinking of dusting the seat, but sat anyway. He was, give or take a year, Bonner's age, but he had retained most of his muddy red hair, which he wore brushed back with a pale part on the left. Probably he was coloring it by now, Bonner thought. Stearman was still having trouble with a cowlick. His was an all-American kind of homeliness, the lines of his forehead cut as deeply as endearments on the trunk of a lover's lane oak. Pontillist's array of freckles that from a distance merged into a deep tan complexion. Large brackets around a mouth with only a thin slice of upper lip. He chewed gum ruminatively, and had the habitual smile of a man making love in his dreams. But often, Bonner remembered, there had been something angry brewing in Stearman's dark eyes, as if so much of what he saw or heard disgusted him. Not surprising, considering his occupation.

"How's your boy?" he said to Bonner. "I understand you had to have him institutionalized."

"Yeah, well, that was a long time ago, and only for a few months while I was handling some problems of my own."

"I heard." Stearman tried but managed not to appear sympathetic; the contraction of crooked lines in his forehead giving the impression of a hostile spider. "I would have come to see you, Tobin, but I was in Thailand around that time."

"I appreciate the thought," Bonner said, a visceral clenching almost like a cramp below his navel. "So what can you tell me?"

Stearman was one of those men who shrug only one shoulder. "What we're doing here?"

"For a start."

"Checking out some information that came our way."

"Pertaining to Gustavo Santero? You don't mind my asking a few questions, do you, Dale? Seeing as how we go way back."

Stearman had a curious way of sitting, half-slumped, feet on the floor, long, freckled, tangerine-colored hands hanging limply beside the chair, his jaw working leisurely on the wad of gum while he stared at Bonner.

"I don't suppose there can be any harm in letting you know, but it's not for public consumption. He is, or was, Gabriel Sinaloa, one of the four Sinaloa brothers. The oldest, but not the wisest. You know of the family?"

"I've heard the name."

"They came into power in South America after the decline of the Medellin and Cali cartels, the most profitable criminal conspiracies in history. The Colombian government finally brought some heat to bear, long after we were rotated out of there. Rodriguez Gacha was killed by government troops in eighty-nine, Ochoa turned himself in after extracting a promise of no extradition to the States, and you know what happened to Pablo Escobar."

"Arrested, escaped, shot by police."

"As for the Cali cartel, it was supposedly smashed with the arrest of the Rodriguez brothers."

"Uh-huh. A twenty-five-billion-dollar-a-year business."

Stearman nodded. "The Sinaloa brothers took over the trade, operating out of Cartagena, Curaçao, Guadalajara, San Pedro Sula, and Miami. There are four of them, as I said. Gabriel was the oldest, the least educated, a throwback to the days of Escobar; a cocaine terrorist who gave a lot of money to the church, who liked having gangs of little kids follow him in the streets when he came to town, handing out wads of pesos while they pelted him with flowers, kissed his hands as if he were the pope."

Bonner thought about the corpse he'd seen, the arrogance in the swarthy face no amount of plastic surgery could remove. The eyes gone stale in death, pupils dusting over as if with the residue of thoughts interrupted by a bullet.

"It was Gabriel's money that sent the others to good schools in the States. Enrico Sinaloa, who's based in Miami, went to Choate and Dartmouth. He's an investment banker, keeps his plate as clean as a dog's dish, and DOJ still doesn't have a thing on him. The others in the triumvirate, Roque and Innocencio, are just as smart. Since Gabriel defected a year and a half ago, Roque maintains the alliances with the Mexican brethren. Innocencio was running the day-to-day until Gabriel spilled; he had to get out of Colombia. Interpol believes he was at the poppy conference in Milan about six weeks ago."

"Broadening the family interests?"

Stearman closed his eyes, his face sagging a little from the weight of his fatigue.

"We're not sure. Coke is still the drug of choice in this country, but maybe they're looking to the future. Anything portable and profitable. The world is a wide-open bazaar nowadays. Stuff a lot more lethal than sniffy and smack is moving south and west through the old CIA pipelines."

"For instance?"

"Not relevant to this discussion."

"So what did Gabriel Sinaloa do?"

"Became an embarrassment to the others. You know these old-timers: *plato o plomo*. Silver in your hand or a bullet in your head muthafuckah. A federal *bicho grande* Gabriel was bribing to cut down on hijacking losses on the border offended him by paying lewd attention to Gabriel's oldest daughter. Gabriel had him capped. Breaches of etiquette all around. The *judiciale* had ties by marriage to the Chihuahua organization, which we know so well. Considerable tribute was in order, and *muy pronto*. Enrico suggested ten million to the *padrino* in Ciudad Juárez." Stearman saw one of Bonner's eyebrows twitch. "Oh yeah, it's still Jaime Loza. Our old bud, Steel Arm Jimmy."

Hearing the name, after not having thought about Loza for at least a couple of months, Bonner felt the hard pain again, under his navel, and deep, like something coming to life inside a cyst.

"Gabriel paid five and refused an act of contrition, thereby seriously screwing up his family's relations with all four of the Mexican organizations. Without them, of course, eighty percent of the coke the Sinaloas were moving into this country on a daily basis would just sit in those big warehouses down south. To make matters worse, within a week the Mexican government issued a deportation order for Gabriel. Gabe said fuckem, he was the one who had been wronged. The *judiciale* had stolen his daughter's virginity and left her pregnant, and what was Steel Arm Jimmy going to do about *Gabriel's* honor? Death threats were issued on both sides. Two *machos* hefting their balls at each other. Eat this, *pendejo*. You have to wonder. Has any of this shit changed in ten thousand years? Anyway, Ricky Sinaloa stepped in again and finally negotiated a settlement, but the other boys had had enough of Gabriel's posturing. They removed him from the board; full share, of course, but no further voice, and Roque's oldest son, Javier, took over as liason with the Mexican organizations.

"Maybe it would have ended there, in spite of Gabriel's hurt pride. He'd always resented Enrico, who was closest to him in age, being the spokesman, you know, the final authority. Then somebody blew up Gabriel in his stretch Mercedes. Bad job. He came out of it with a limp, second-degree burns, and the suspicion that his brothers had engineered the hit. Twenty hours later, the DEA had Gabriel and his family under wraps in Houston."

"Singing the pure gospel. Hasn't amounted to a hell of a lot, if Enrico is still unindicted and operating out of Miami."

"Probably three-quarters of their business is legitimate, swallowing all that narco money. Mining interests in Peru and Chile, oil exploration, banks, wineries, golf resorts, a soccer team, hotels. A casino in Vegas and two down south in Mississippi, honeychile."

"I'd heard the Sinaloas have a Vegas connection."

"Settled in two years ago, after reaching an accommodation with the Chicago mob. They own twenty-eight percent of the Vaquero. As for how the money moves, Gabriel didn't have an inkling. The actual procedures. In the old days there was better organization in a pile of puke, but they've learned. Ricky is deft, you have to give him that."

Bonner sat back, balancing his letter opener by the point on an outstretched index finger, flipping it into the air, catching it by the handle. He looked from Stearman to Bobby Polikarski.

"So the remaining Sinaloa brothers signed off on Gabriel after he took up residence here. Blood atonement, down to the last drop. I assume you have an interest in learning how that came about."

Polikarski said, "If there was a sellout, it wasn't someone at WPP."

"No offense, but you're top man in this district, Bobby. Who was running Gabriel?"

"I was."

"DOJ wasn't through with him then."

"No."

"So what are we talking about, half a dozen need-to-knows?"

"Four, counting myself. All platinum security clearances."

Bonner looked at Stearman, who shook his head.

"I didn't know Gabriel's whereabouts until three o'clock this morning."

Bonner thought that was probably a lie. He said irritably, "But you had an interest in him. Since when does the United States Senate have such an abiding interest in a spick drug dealer? Someone big in Washington get his fist caught in the Colombians' cookie jar?"

"Better for you to stay in your corner, Tobe. Don't answer the bell."

"What's that, a warning?"

"Come on," Stearman coaxed. "Why do you want to work so hard?"

Bonner's skin crawled. "Because they were killed in Solar County. Because I smell something bigger than a blood atonement. When was the last time you saw Gabriel Sinaloa, Bobby?"

"Can't answer that, Tobe."

"He was still in business, wasn't he? What, the same old business? I haven't spotted a big increase in the local traffic, and you have to admit, I'm adept. Our major problem is meth, but it's mostly kids and AIs who are using it. So what was Gabriel's new business?"

Stearman raised his right shoulder slowly, as he'd always done when challenged or annoyed. It was a minor comfort to Bonner, knowing how little he'd changed. Dale Stearman looked like a hick, but he was a man who moved through labyrinths few other men knew existed, leaving virtually no traces of his passage or his dealings.

"I honestly don't know, Tobin. We're here to comb through Gabriel's computer files. Do some asking around. As for who killed him—well, we know that already, don't we? Who set it up. The technician, what difference does it make? He'll never be found. The way it happened with you, Tobin. No doubt about who set it up. No way we could ever hope to nail him for Consuela's murder."

Bonner sat with his head tilted back, eyes searching distantly for something, jaw clamping and unclamping. It looked as if he were having a mild seizure.

Stearman glanced at Polikarski and got to his feet.

Polikarski said gently, "I'll need the autopsy reports when you get them, Tobe."

"Yeah. Sure."

"Family gets the bodies back. After we formally notify them. I suppose closed coffins, so nobody in the family has to look at Gabriel's face again. Withered flowers on the coffins, dog shit mixed with the grave dirt, no mourners, no priest, isn't that how it's done?"

"Yeah. That's how it's done."

"I'll be seeing you," Stearman told Bonner.

"Yeah. Anytime. You've got my home number. Keep me advised."

Mary Lynn came in a few minutes later and found Bonner with his head on his arms on the desk.

"Boss?"

"What?"

"Roy Lee Sumtree called in, said he didn't want to use the radio, but it's very important. Line two."

Bonner sat up, squinting the cobwebs from his eyes, and took the call.

"Big R, what's happening?"

"I'm outside Dry Bones Canyon, just east of Caballo Rojo. Couple of hikers with me. They found a blue Silverado 350 pickup way back up the canyon, smashed all to hell like it was driven off the cliff. Didn't know if you wanted me to run the plate."

"No, I don't want an inquiry on the computer just yet, anyway I have a good idea whose Silverado it is. Hikers say anything about a body in the cab?"

"No, sir. Hold on a second." Bonner could hear him asking questions; a female voice answered him. The deputy came back on. "They're saying the condition it was in, you couldn't get a door open to look inside. But there wasn't, you know, the flies or buzzards you'd expect."

"Okay. Coming at you, Big R. Twenty minutes."

On his way to the interstate Bonner used the drive-thru at the Burger King on Division Boulevard to pick up a cheeseburger, Coke, and fries. Burger King was humming, parking lot full at two in the afternoon, three cars ahead of him. They should have had a Burger King, he thought. Instead they had Rooty Chick'n. A shoo-in for the Business Fiasco Hall of Fame. How he had let Neal talk him into that one, a mystery for the ages.

After he paid for his lunch, Bonner had a five-dollar bill left in his wallet. Three blocks east he hit the interstate and headed north, winding the Crown Vic up to ninety. The soft bun of the cheeseburger had a tendency to wad against his palate. Bonner wondered how much longer the IRS was going to lay off him.

Never go into business with your relatives.

9 DR. VERGER, THE ORTHOPEDIC surgeon, visited Pepper on the Pediatrics floor, bringing with him his anesthesiologist, a Native-American doctor named Tonya. He also had a teaching model of the human knee. The two doctors devoted twenty minutes to show-and-tell for Pepper's benefit, which relieved some of her anxiety about the upcoming surgery. Pepper appeared to like Tonya, who would be putting her to sleep and waking her up when it was over. She didn't like the idea of being on crutches for the rest of the summer.

"I can't ride a horse, can't ride a bike, do *any*thing."

"Pepper, I know," Shay said. "I can't tell you how many times I've been hobbled, when I should have been earning a living. Six weeks isn't so bad."

"It's just the whole stinking summer! And do I have to stay in the hospital after the operation?"

"You're better off here, since I'm in a motel."

"Godddd! Why can't we stay with Granpa?"

"Because Granpa has chosen to be unavailable right now, and I don't feel good about moving in out there until he comes home."

"Godddd!"

"Pepper, will you ease up on me? I don't know what else to do, and I'm dead on my feet. Now let's stop the whining; it's time you had your bath."

Two of them in the small bathroom was a crowd, and Pepper was furtive, perhaps hostile about being naked with her. Pepper had been wearing jogging bras for several months, not saying anything to her mother, but Shay realized now there was a definite need; Pepper's breasts *were* rising, like biscuits beginning to take the heat of the oven. A gingery puff of hair had appeared above the tight purse of pudenda, and her hips seemed to have flared since the last time Shay had taken her shopping for clothes. So soon, she marveled; but of course Pepper would be twelve at the end of October. Too soon anyway, this physiological ripening, the body's creative burst into puberty. *No fair,* Shay thought, half-seriously. She wanted her baby for a while longer, if only to insulate herself from the inevitable encroachment of her own obsolescence.

Pepper wore a neoprene sleeve brace on her knee. They had only a shower to work with, and Pepper's hair needed washing. She kept her back to her mother, gripping one of the vertical bars in the stall. Shay maintained a trickle from the showerhead so as not to get soaked herself.

"You're growing up," Shay said, lathering, as if Pepper needed assurance or approval of the perplexing surge within and without; her words only made the girl tense and uncommunicative, except to bark criticism of Shay's efforts, and curtly refuse, after the shampoo, a cream rinse to free up a few tangles.

"I can do the rest myself," Pepper insisted, snatching a washcloth from Shay's hand. Still unwilling to look at her mother, as if she felt oppressed by Shay's uncommunicable yearning to be needed and appreciated.

After Pepper had put on clean sweats and was drying her hair, she seemed to ignore the painful throbbing of her knee. Her previous edginess vanished, to be replaced by the vivid Irishness that was the other side of her nature. In an upwelling of good spirits, she became talkative, clinging affectionately to her mother as if they were about to jump off, again, into another, more distant but exhilarating unknown. Shay felt magically restored in all this dazzle to whatever status she had fallen from and wasn't able to refuse the treat when Pepper proposed that they go to the lounge for a Coke.

"They have diet cherry," she said, asserting responsibility. At UCLA Shay had been warned of possible hereditary complications because Liam's side of the family was riddled with diabetes, but Pepper radiated good health, and there was no point in worrying about what she was consuming while she was in the hospital.

They passed the nursery on their way to the lounge. Wide, undraped windows offered a full view from the corridor of the pink-and-lemon walls, decorated with cardboard characters from *Winnie-the-Pooh*. Amid scattered childsize furniture of molded plastic, Lucy Ruiz sat rocking Cymbeline. She wore a white lab coat over her khaki uniform and gun belt; a surgical mask covered her nose and mouth. The only other patient in the nursery was a two-year-old boy who had had an operation to correct a defective hip joint that prevented him from standing or walking. Cymbeline had nearly fallen asleep in Lucy's arms, a pacifier slipping from one corner of her bubble-flecked mouth.

Five minutes later Lucy joined Shay and Pepper in the lounge.

"How're you doing?"

"Hi, Luz."

"They're putting my knee back together in the morning," Pepper announced. "How's Cym? They won't let me go in there to see her."

"A little cranky. She has a cold and she's cutting a couple of opposing molars; her gums are about to pop like boils." Lucy got a can of grape soda from the machine and sat down with them, black leather creaking, the butt of the big revolver she wore rapping lightly against the back of the chair. It was still a novelty, something of an astonishment, for Shay to see her childhood friend like this, remembering mostly skinned-up legs, tattered shorts, hand-me-down T-shirts that never quite covered her belly below the navel. Clean, though, body and clothing always washed, her thick mop of hair gleaming in the sun like wet licorice.

"She misses her family," Lucy continued. "She's named them all for me. We think now the oldest girl was her mother, but I wasn't able to locate a birth certificate."

"Where's her father then?" Shay asked.

"Who knows?"

"Are you getting anywhere?"

"No," Lucy said darkly. "We were run off the case today, so I don't know what my status is right now."

"Run off?"

"Girl, you can hardly keep your eyes open. When are you going to get some rest? I mean a bunch from D.C. is in town, National Security Directive empowerment; they're all over the Santero house. It's something big. How's Jack? Tell him hello when you see him.

He used to scare the pee-yooey out of me when I was over at your place, walking around half-bagged in his longjohns, cracking that old blacksnake."

Pepper said, "Granpa?"

Lucy smiled, and Shay thought how fortunate she was that all of her best features had stayed with her as she matured, the beautiful teeth and dimples like pips of ice in her dusky cheeks. Too bad she was so stocky; that smile belonged in pictures.

"He's changed a lot now that he's older," Lucy said to Pepper. "He reads a lot of books and he's turned into something of a philosopher. When I take my breaks at the Short Wolf, I always look in the windows first to make sure Jack's not around. He'll latch on to you over a cup of coffee and leave your ears in tatters before he's done. Leave you in stitches, too, if he's in a jolly mood."

Shay said, "Jack hasn't been seen, Luz, since yesterday morning, according to his people out at the ranch."

"That so? He was expecting you, wasn't he?"

"I thought he was."

"Leave you a note or anything?"

"Huh-uh. He's seventy-three, of course; he could've got his days mixed up, although Tom Leucadio didn't think so."

"Tom doesn't know where he went?"

"No." Shay looked sideways at Pepper, a look Lucy picked up on. She smiled slightly. "So you're not worried."

"I guess not," Shay said, putting both hands to her face.

"Shay, if you don't stop yawning, you'll have me doing it, too."

"Sorry," Shay muttered.

"What did you and Mom do when you were kids?" Pepper asked Lucy.

"Oh, got into messes. It was usually us against the Mormon kids, neither of us being Mormons."

"Why not?"

"*Soy Catolico.* Shay will have to speak for herself."

"I was interested. I read the *Book of Mormon* and *Doctrine and Covenants,* and I went to Sunday school a few times, until they started insisting I be baptized right away. You know how they are about baptisms."

"Around the clock nowadays," Lucy said. "The temple over there is a baptismal factory, from what I hear. Apparently we're near the end of the Dispensation of the Fulness of Times, as the LDS call it.

They're trying to get as many souls as they can through the veil and into the Kingdom before Endtimes."

"Maybe I would have joined because I hated being an outsider, but it was around that time we headed for California, without Jack."

"I never heard the full story," Lucy said, with an interested lifting of her thick, tapered eyebrows. "Jack obviously couldn't walk very well for a couple of weeks afterward."

"What happened?" Pepper asked, getting big-eyed.

"Not now, please. Luz, I think you're right. I'm going to fall over if I don't put in some sacktime."

"Where're you staying?"

"Comfort Inn, a few blocks down the street."

"Give you a lift?"

"Thanks. I've got a rental in the lot."

Lucy's radio came to life. Police code, something about the national park. Lucy acknowledged the call.

"I was about to knock off myself," she said regretfully, "but a hiker's fallen from a trail in the park, possible fatality, so I have to look into it."

"Why?"

"It's government land, but the sheriff's office has jurisdiction up there. Only four of the park rangers have law-enforcement powers. We get half a dozen bad falls a season. Usually it's hikers who don't pay attention to the warning signs, and they climb where they shouldn't. Occasionally some poor soul gets pushed. It must look like an easy way to get out of a bad marriage. Tough to prove. Pepper, I'll look in on you tomorrow after your surgery. I want to bring a few toys for Cymbeline, if the feds will let me back in the house."

"What's going to happen to Cym?" Pepper asked.

Lucy paused on her way out.

"I'm going to adopt her," she said. She smiled, shaking her head vigorously, proudly, at the wonder of it, love at first sight, and left Shay and Pepper looking at each other.

●

When the alarm of her travel clock went off at six-thirty, Shay, in sleep as remote from time and the world as if she'd been sealed in a mine shaft, barely heard it. Otherwise she might have slept on through the night and Pepper's surgery early the next morning. She dragged herself slowly from bed and stripped, went into a cold shower, and gritted her teeth until she was certain she was going to stay awake, if a little muzzy, until Pepper got her ten o'clock meds and was ready to sleep herself.

As if she didn't feel terrible enough already, Shay found when she toweled herself off that she was bleeding, which explained the gassy bulge of her abdomen and the overall feeling that she had spent her dream time on the rack. She thought about Pepper, how soon it would be coming for her, and fought down a bluesy impulse to weep, tears of love and inadequacy. Looking disconsolately at her nude self, presented in three different aspects in several mirrors while she used a blow-dryer, Shay dwelled on new bruises and scrapes. She was accustomed to a few old scars like slices of tallow on her tanned skin, didn't really notice those anymore. But she'd seldom seen herself in such battered shape, and her weak, twinging right knee had her concerned. Not much cartilage left there. Better get out the orthopedic brace. Anyway, thirty-two wasn't the boneyard. She could still be proud of her breasts and legs. Unlike some of the screen queens she doubled for, she didn't have a bad angle anywhere. A really *great* ass, pardner. Slowly getting the best of her downer mood through meticulous inventory. Dark-brown curls, each the size of a baby's fist, sprang back with the heat. Never fucked anyone for a job, even if she happened to like the stunt coordinator. Who was it who'd said the first two skills an aspiring actress needed to learn were crying on cue and fellatio? Probably a casting director. She always delivered the gag, not blowjobs, and the top coordinators respected her. Hang on to your self-respect; fate will sort out everything else for you. Shay's morale level crept up as she brushed her hair, but she had a long-lasting cramp, she was hungry, she wanted to talk to somebody; a dog with a kind face would do. She used the emergency tampon in her makeup kit, found clean khakis with an elastic waistband, leg room for the knee brace. As she was about to leave the motel room she picked up her rumpled photographer's vest. Not unexpectedly, she found a cell phone in one of the cargo pockets. Shay had five of them, all over the place, and several pagers. In her hit-or-miss existence, she never knew when a job would come up.

There was a Mickey D's nearby, the same one she and Pepper had stopped at the night before after arriving from Nevada. Across the street, next to another motel, was a more conventional restaurant, not part of a chain. Weathered board siding, an old ship's anchor on a concrete pedestal, fake portholes, a mock gangplank over a goldfish pond to the entrance. Judging from the cars in the parking lot, their customer base was good. So okay, seafood tonight.

At seven-fifteen the late sun still had some sting to it as Shay walked to the restaurant. The hinge on her bulky knee brace was not articulating smoothly, and the day's lingering heat felt as thick and sticky as orange Jell-O.

The hostess was a tall girl of about eighteen, wearing a full-length denim skirt. She had blonde hair, a do that puffed out from the back of her head like exploded rope.

"Hi, my name is Sarah. Welcome to the Captain's Table. How many in your party tonight?"

"By myself, unfortunately."

"Oh, you're traveling alone?" Shay nodded. "Where're you from?"

"Los Angeles. We were in an accident nearby; my daughter's in the hospital."

"Oh, no!" Sarah sucked in her breath, preparing for the worst. "I hope she isn't—"

"Banged-up knee. She'll be okay."

"Bless the Lord. I know you'll appreciate some peace and quiet while you eat. Let's see. The Cockleshell Room isn't open tonight, but since I'm the assistant manager, I guess I could seat you in there. You'll have a TV or I can find you a paper to read."

"That sounds great, Sarah. My name's Shay."

"I go on break in a few minutes," Sarah said, leading Shay to what amounted to an alcove of the restaurant, separated from the bar by latticework draped with shell-encrusted fishnet. "If you want somebody to talk to. I mean, I know how it is, being alone and away from home."

"You're not from Utah?"

"Yes, I am. I was born here. Not in Spanish Wells. A little place, New Hebron, seventy miles east. But I haven't been back lately. Would you like a booth, Shay?"

"Thanks."

"Here's your menu. How about something to drink while you're deciding? The only thing that's for sure not on the menu tonight is the grilled swordfish."

"Iced tea, please, unsweet."

"I'll find out which of the girls has the lightest workload and send her right in."

Shay glanced at the chalkboard menu, chose a broiled fisherman's platter, glanced at the baseball game on the television mounted below the ceiling in one corner, smelled beer and wished she had ordered one, then gazed through the small tinted window at traffic along the interstate two blocks away. The waitress bustled in, gray hair, a bull-dog's bow-legged width and overshot lower teeth. She took the order. Shay looked out the window again, smothering yawns.

A silver-gray Cadillac, looking new but with a film of dust, had pulled into the parking lot. Darkly tinted windows. It stopped parallel to the anchor chain that marked off the lot in wide scallops from pylon to concrete pylon, stradling three diagonal spaces. No one seemed in a hurry to get out.

Sarah rejoined her, bringing Shay's tea and a cup of coffee for herself.

"Good to get a load off. I had to work lunch today, too, trading off with Beck. She had a date to go windsurfing in the sandhills."

"I've never tried it myself. I've done just about everything else."

"Bungee jump?"

"Four or five times. But I like to get paid for it."

"You do? How?"

"Stunt player."

"In the *movies?* Holy crow. I wish I had the nerve. I ski, but I'm a SPORE. That's a Spastic Person on Rental Equipment. How many movies have you been in?"

"Maybe forty. Twice that many television shows."

"I guess I wouldn't recognize you if I saw any of them. You do look kind of like, what's her name; she won the Oscar a couple of years ago?"

"Fontana McCall. I usually double for Tana, but she got bit by a funnelweb spider on a location in Australia and hasn't been able to work."

Sarah shuddered. "Oh, yeah, there was something about that in the *Enquirer,* I think. I don't read it, but one of my roommates at college buys those things; she eats up all the gossip. Do those big stars really fool around all that much?"

"Not with me. I'm way down the pecking order, so to speak. Mel Gibson sends me gag gifts when he sees me on one of his sets. That's about all the action I ever get. Where do you go to school, Sarah?"

"Utah State. I'll be a sophomore, that is, if I can get the money together." She looked anxious about the task, compressing her lips, perhaps compulsively adding up anticipated costs. Sarah was pale for this part of the country, anemic paleness, as if her youthful engine was forever running a pint or two low on blood. Her blue eyes, a watered-down blue, had white arcs of sclera beneath them, giving the impression that her pupils were about to float up faintly and be lost beneath her lids, in a kind of mediumistic trance. "I'm working two jobs this summer, four nights a week at Belle Meade, that's a retirement home. I just make myself useful, sort of a candy striper you'd call it."

Shay was aware of the Cadillac opening up suddenly, three doors at once. A very large man, at least six-seven and more than three hundred pounds, stepped out first. He wore new-looking overalls and a camouflage T-shirt. The remarkable thing about him was his pure white hair, neatly trimmed in bangs across his sun-darkened forehead, and a thick half-moon of beard, also trimmed, completing a full circle around his face, doubling the size of his head, hiding his ears. All of this abundant hair rippled in the fading reddish sunlight like a field of ripe grain in the wind, never losing its shape as he walked away from the Caddy, a shuffling walk, as if he found it a little difficult to move all that bulk.

Another man, not even half the size of the first one, got out of the backseat. Rancher's twill suit, white cowboy hat, way too much hat for his narrow head. He scurried, if you can scurry in pointy-toe boots, to catch up with the bearded man. The third man took his time getting out of the Cadillac. Tall and craggy, dark gray business suit. Hair thin and patchy on his crown, as if he had mange, but long in back and gathered into a queue *fourché*.

The first two came across the lot to the restaurant. The third man remained beside the Cadillac, chin lifted, gazing at a single-engine plane coming in for a landing to the airport on the bluff. He was smoking a cigarette in a holder. Shay thought there was something

European about him. The cut and drape of the suit maybe, or the way he held his cigarette holder. He didn't seem to belong with the other two men, and in fact had distanced himself by refusing, with a curt annoyed shake of his head, to join them in the Captain's Table.

"Have you done any acting?" Sarah asked.

"I've done a few bits, on *Renegade* once and in direct-to-video flicks. But I'm still looking for my big break."

"I don't know what I want to do, really," Sarah said, looking down at her clenched hands and bloodless nails. "The idea was just to get an education, I haven't decided on a major yet. I'm good with computers. My best girlfriend—"

The bulldog waitress brought hot rolls and a cup of clam chowder for Shay, who offered the basket of rolls to Sarah. She broke one and buttered a piece lightly. "I only eat one meal a day, usually lunch," Sarah said. "I'm just a poor eater, I'd probably feel better if I liked food more. Do you know karate, martial arts?"

"Sure. I'm no Michelle Yeoh, but half the work I get is fight scenes."

"My best girlfriend," Sarah said again, a touch of warmth creeping into her cool features, "is an intercollegiate judo champ. Her name is Dally. She's from Toole—"

Sarah stiffened, a hand going to her throat as if she'd half swallowed a sharp bone. But it was something in her ears, not her throat: the voice of one of the men Shay had noticed in the parking lot, harsh and rumbly, a voice that could have used a muffler.

"Oh, God, no," Sarah whispered fervently, crumbling the portion of roll she had in her right hand. "Don't do this to me."

Shay glanced at the restaurant entrance, where sunlight flooded through the open door. The bearded man had to stoop considerably as he came in.

"What's wrong?"

"It's—it's—oh, please, *don't* let him see me! I have to get out of here." But she continued to sit there, agonized and unable to move, staring past Shay in ambushed terror.

"Who are you afraid of, Sarah?"

"It's my—father."

The word fell from her lips so freighted with despair that Shay didn't need to ask anything else. She reached into a pocket of her vest for the card key to her motel room, pushed it across the lacquered plank table, and under Sarah's left hand.

"Comfort Inn, Room 202. It's my room. If you need a place to go, for a little while."

Sarah's hand closed on the plastic card. Her eyes drifted to Shay's face.

"Well, scoot," Shay urged her. "I'll tell you about *my* daddy, sometime."

Sarah nodded, startled, then with a flash of gratitude in her eyes. She rose to leave the booth but froze again. The stumpy man with too much cowboy hat, like Yosemite Sam in a Warner Brothers' cartoon, had spotted her and was coming through the nearly empty bar to the Cockleshell Room, the sounds of his hard heels echoing slightly.

"Sarah Dubray! Now just a minute, Sarah! Don't run off again. Honey, we need to have us a serious talk."

Sarah's face changed as if his tone, genial enough but with that male inflection of petty authority, had poisoned her to the roots of her heart. Her mouth twisted savagely.

"Who's this?" Shay whispered, and Sarah said, just able to get her mouth open, eyes only half visible beneath their lids, "The man I'm bidden to marry."

She sat down again, more or less collapsing, and moved to the wall, hands knotted, face averted against disaster.

Shay looked at the small man in the butterscotch-colored rancher's suit and bolo tie. Hard to tell his age. He had severely popped eyes and bags piled upon bags beneath those eyes, so much dark purple color that at a glance his eyes seemed to be half-drowning in ink. His lower lip was popped as well, pendulous. He wore a trimmed sandy mustache. He was all eyes for the reluctant Sarah, barely offering Shay a glance as he attempted to slide into the booth.

Shay propped her left foot on the seat opposite her before he could sit down. He gave the intrusive foot a perplexed look, devoted a little more study to Shay's face and manner, and remained uncertainly standing beside the booth, looking back for reinforcement.

"How old are you, Sarah?" Shay asked her.

"N-nineteen. I'll be twenty in September."

"Would you pass me the pepper? My chowder's cooling; I'd like to get started." Though she kept a friendly eye on the girl, her peripheral vision was taken up by the approach of Sarah's father. The pip-squeak she'd fenced off didn't worry her for a second, but the large, bearded man obviously was going to be the problem. "Some crackers too, please, Sarah." Shay, reaching for the pepper shaker, briefly closed her own hand reassuringly on Sarah's thin hand. She felt shockingly cold.

"Who in the blue-eyed world are *you?*" the man in the white cowboy hat said, trying to make it sound indulgent and humorous.

"My name is Shay. I'm here to have dinner, as you can see. Sarah is on her break, and we were having a nice talk. Which we'd like to continue, if you would do us the courtesy."

The bearded man had pulled up six feet away from the booth and just stood there taking this in with his hands at his sides, head tilted a little, pursing his red lips within the puffy doughnut of white hair. Nothing Santa Claus-y about him; his was a ruthless face with jet black brows, unplucked, and the small, riled eyes of a bull elephant. He had a decided quiver about him, the blackly haired left hand, the huge head. Perhaps it was from the onset of Parkinson's; or he might have been like a boiler with a faulty thermostat, on the threshhold of overload. No way to get around it, he was a scary presence. With all those robust daddy genes in the draw, Shay wondered why Sarah was so fragile and peakèd. In appearance only, however. Although the girl had withdrawn for now, Shay had glimpsed in Sarah a hard center, some deep-down fire and resolve.

The pip-squeak turned slowly and exaggeratedly to Sarah's father, eyes as round as old-fashioned ivory doorknobs. "Did you hear *that?*"

Sarah's father, except for the quivering and a slight wheeze while he breathed, failed to react. He was a man who understood the power of his silences.

"I don't want to lose my job," Sarah said, speaking up with some strength in her voice. "I have to go back to work in a few minutes. There's nothing, I've tried to make it plain, *nothing* to talk about. Could you leave me alone now?" She still wasn't looking at either of them; her eyes were focused bitterly on the backs of her smooth, joined hands.

Instead of addressing his daughter, the bearded man looked long and curiously at Shay, who passed a few moments of his scrutiny by dipping into her chowder. They made good clam chowder at the Captain's Table.

"My name is Rhondo Dubray," he said finally. "And, as you already know, Sarah is a daughter of mine. Not my youngest, nor my oldest. I have seventeen daughters and twenty-one sons. Only one of them has ever broken a covenant with me or with the Brightly Shining."

Sarah made a soft sound, her faded blue eyes telling of psychic exhaustion.

Rhondo Dubray said, still speaking to Shay, "Please accept my apology for interrupting your supper. Whatever you're having tonight, it's on me. Now if you wouldn't mind finding another place to sit, we'd like to have some privacy while we prayerfully meet with our disfellowshipped daughter and together seek the guidance of the Lord in removing the stain of sin from her heart."

He was hard to place. Overalls with a buckaroo roll over his scuffed, cheap, cowboy boots, but an educated if pedantic tone. Shay said, her own voice firm but not disrespectful, "Sarah's of age. I'm sure you realize she doesn't have to talk to you if she doesn't want to."

Sarah spoke up with a steely passion. "I have never broken a covenant with *the Lord*. And I know *the Lord* will not turn his back on me because I won't marry a man who already has four wives, one of them barely fifteen."

The designated husband said in exasperation, "There's just no talking to her, Rhondo. Now I think what Sarah needs is—"

Rhondo Dubray held up a hand to stifle him, looking at Shay, who had put the soupspoon down and taken out her cell phone. She found the card she was looking for in her wallet and began to punch in the number.

"Who do you think you're calling?" the pip-squeak asked her.

"Sheriff Bonner."

The pip-squeak laughed and looked at Dubray, who shrugged. The pip-squeak suddenly turned ugly, yanking the phone out of Shay's hands.

"Talk to him all you want," he said, "as soon as we leave with Sarah. Tobe Bonner knows a sight better than to interfere with the Brightly Shining." He had a grin that was mostly gums, very small teeth. "That's a fact, Rhondo? When was the last time we saw Tobin Bonner in New Hebron? He knows not to come around." The pip-squeak returned to Shay. "Now this is a *family* matter that don't concern you, and Sarah is coming with us. Right this minute. Because I, for one, have had all I can stand of her rebellious attitude."

He took his eyes off Shay and reached out, fingers tightening on Sarah's arm above the elbow, pulling her toward him. Sarah reacted with hysterical impetus, hitting him with her other hand, knocking his hat to the floor. He was, predictably, half-bald. Sarah gave him a hard shove away from the booth, trampled on his hat, but failed to break his grip. They went round and round in a struggle Rhondo Dubray stepped away from, hands still at his sides.

"No discipline here," he rumbled warningly at the pip-squeak.

The kid who was working the bar and the girl who had taken over as hostess looked in at the sounds of struggle, shocked by Sarah's increasingly ferocious efforts to kick and claw her way free, her face distorted by anger and hatred. The pip-squeak, smiling grimly, kept his head cocked back and his eyes out of the way of her fingernails while he one-handedly manuevered Sarah like a fish he'd caught, knocking over chairs, banging her into tables, forcing her toward the door.

Rhondo Dubray patted his beard as if it were the family cat.

Shay came up out of the booth, not seeming in a hurry but moving fluidly toward the strugglers, pausing until the pip-squeak's head came around to her as he evaded a flurry of slaps. Then Shay unloaded a handful of pepper directly into his bulging eyes and followed with a quick left-footed sidekick, the heel of her boot connecting with his chin. His head rocked back, spit flying, and he hit the floor on his shoulders, rolled, hands going to his face and peppered eyes, as Sarah ran crying from the room.

Shay turned to Rhondo Dubray and said, "Don't even think about going after her."

Dubray lowered his lightly quaking hand, palm out to Shay, gesture of peace or deference.

"You do have tricks up your sleeve. What did you say your name was?"

"Shay Waco."

"Oh." He pondered the name. "Not one of Jack's brats?"

"Get me some water!" the pip-squeak cried. There was a bloody piece of broken tooth caught in a crease of his lower lip. "My eyes, the fucking little bitch blinded me!"

"I'm nobody's brat. Don't get any ideas about me, Mr. Dubray. I can hurt you." It was pure bravado. In spite of her skills, she had doubt. He was huge.

"I don't want to get hurt," he said mildly. He looked at the pip-squeak on the floor. "Frenchie, get up. It's only pepper. And mind your mouth. Such language is an affront to the ears of the Lord."

He took a step sideways, reached down with one hand, caught the pip-squeak by his collar, and set him on his feet. Showing off for Shay how easy it was. Frenchie tried to find a handkerchief to blot his scarlet, streaming eyes. Now he was sneezing uncontrollably, snot going everywhere. Dubray grimaced and handed him a napkin from one of the tables, then walked him out.

Near the bar in the other room Dubray turned, as if he'd remembered something vital.

"Tell Jack hello for me. We used to do some business together. You might say I made him a rich man, but he's been slow to demonstrate his gratitude. Well, good night. Sorry again for the interruption. Don't worry about Sarah. She'll soon accept her discipline and will recognize that the fellowship of the Brightly Shining is all that truly matters in this life."

10

TOBIN BONNER LEFT THE office at seven-twenty after a meeting with a rookie deputy who had been overzealous about busting AIs at a construction site. It turned out that one of the six had a green card, and, shortly after he was jailed, an ACLU lawyer promptly filed suit against the sheriff's department for wrongful arrest and as many other charges as he could think up.

Bonner drove west on Division Boulevard, coming up behind a new Dodge Caravan with Archer Patterson's campaign posters on the sides. At West Valley Boulevard he pulled up alongside the Caravan, which had stopped for the light. As luck would have it, Patterson himself was driving. Bonner touched off the second phase of the siren, *whoop whoop*, to get his rival's attention, and put the window down on the shotgun side of his Crown Vic.

"Hey, Arch, you selling many vans nowadays?"

Patterson was one of those men who spend a lot of time with a hair dryer in the morning. He had a high forehead and scrunched-together features below thick, dark eyebrows, a face that looked as if it had been squeezed into a bottle. He looked warily at Bonner.

"Business couldn't be better, Tobe. Why?"

"I see so many on the street with your posters all over 'em, I figured you didn't have any better use for them."

"Looking at our best month since we bought the dealership."

"How about we go *mano a mano* at the Rotary lunch Thursday? Exchange some views on law enforcement?"

"Well, that sounds like a good idea, but I have to skip the Rotary this week; business in Salt Lake."

"Oh, yeah, gotcha. The Fourth's coming up. How would you feel about getting it on at the VFW clambake?"

"Fourth of July? See, I don't have my scheduler handy, but—do you think that's an appropriate place for a political debate?"

"Always has been," Bonner said genially. "The VFW gives me a chance to wear my Silver Star clusters. And you can show off your award-winning dealership plaques. Now there's a picture I'd like to see on the front page of the *Enterprise*. Of course, your brother-in-law wouldn't print it. He's fonder of allegations about how I run my fuckin' jail."

Horns were honking behind them. Archer Patterson smiled edgily. "Holding up traffic, here, Tobe."

"Let 'em wait. Archer, I'd like to leave you with a couple of hard facts, not bullshit allegations."

"What do you mean?"

"A gut-shot deer can survive maybe two or three days in the wild, Arch. I know about getting shot. I know what the pain is like, no matter how much morphine they give you to try to ease it. Think about that buck, Arch. That buck didn't have no fuckin' morphine. He's the reason why I'm going to get up off my butt now and concentrate on whipping yours in the primary."

Bonner hit the clear-out phase of his electronic siren and the flasher lights behind the grill of his Crown Vic, pulled out and around Archer Patterson's Dodge, and went hotdogging up West Valley Boulevard in a fit of sheer exuberance.

Lucy Ruiz, wearing a tank top and panties, stirred on the sagging mattress of the brass bed when she heard, in spite of the noisy air conditioner in her small bedroom, Bonner come in. Only his weight could make the floorboards creak just so. She sighed and let go of the handgun beneath her pillow.

It wasn't dark yet; the sun on one plain wall opposite her bed lit the crucifixion, His pierced flesh like immortal gold. She closed her eyes again, sat up long enough to strip off her top and remove the panties, then she lay back, hearing Bonner get undressed.

"Brought you a beer," he said, easing down on the mattress beside her.

She was thirsty. She drank half, and when he tugged at the bottle to get it away from her some of the beer dribbled between her breasts and ran in an amber foamy stream toward her tight navel, where Bonner intercepted it with a lick.

Lucy shuddered. *More.* Goose bumps.

"I'm pretty whacked tonight," he said, crouching over her, the old mattress sagging even farther.

"Umm."

Lucy took the bottle back and drank again, meanwhile working with her other hand on his sometimes reluctant cock; but this evening everything was highly satisfactory. She finished the beer, and it was time. She relaxed, looking at him now, smiling. Knees apart, lightly haired pelvis lifted, letting go of his cock when it was seated, sliding down on the bed to accommodate him better, back rounded, taking him by the balls now, pleasantly drowsy but able to be aroused, playing his balls like fleshy musical spheres while he fucked her in his slow absorbed comfy manner, breaking a sweat and beginning to grimace, ummm-ummm, Lucy feeling it more urgently now: keep it keep it coming don't stop oh *fuck* me, watching his intent face until her orgasm made her gasp and clench the back of his head with both hands, drawing him down to a lingering kiss, *te adoro mi tesoro.*

Spanish is a loving tongue.

The things you think about: Lucy was glad she'd changed the sheets before piling in for her nap. He deserved the best her modest home had to offer. She wondered about the freshness of the eggs in the refrigerator. He would be hungry.

The things you think about: a deer with its guts half-exposed, lying on its side in the woods, trying to breathe. The flies storming.

"How I'm doing?" Bonner asked.

"Oh, man."

"Seriously, Luz."

"In bed, you mean."

"Uh-huh."

"You should change your last name, spell it with one 'n'."

"I could take that two ways, of course."

"Take it as a compliment."

"You want to go back to sleep?"

"I want to fix you a Spanish omelet. After we have our shower."

While they were soaping, Bonner said, "The guy's name is Dale Stearman. We worked together in Peru, then met again in El Paso at the DEA's Intelligence Center there. He was above me, by then. Now he's with some hush-hush Senate-sanctioned group in Washington. By the way, Santero's real name was Gabriel Sinaloa, one of the big narcotics dynasties down south. He was dropped in our midst courtesy of the Witness Protection Program."

"I kind of had an idea. Why are the feds here?"

"Because, I assume, Sinaloa knew something that was of great interest to the U.S. Senate, as well as Justice. Why Stearman and not the FBI? Maybe he outranks them, but what do I know?"

"Well, you know that Sinaloa probably wasn't back in the drug business, using his home computer to establish routes and sales. We'd have been aware of activity in our area. Who had him hit?"

"Probably his own brothers, after he ratted them out to the DEA. Damn."

"What's the matter?"

"Soap in my eye."

Lucy handed him a washcloth.

"How many are there? Stearman's group? What do they call themselves?"

"FIAT. Federal Interdiction, Anti-Terrorism. *Fiat*, I think, means 'absolute authority.' There're eight of them on hand, that I know of."

"Then they aren't just here to crack a safe or some computer code. Funny we never heard of them before."

"These groups, and subgroups, get set up at the request of some very big people for specific tasks that don't quite fall within the parameters of DOJ, Military Intelligence, or the CIA. They have the initiative to draw personnel from anywhere, as the need arises. The money's always available for one more clandestine organization. And it's generally unaccounted for. Now Dale, I have reason to believe he's a very rich man, on a government salary."

"Wash my back? You mean he's always been on the take?"

"Yes. But it's never been only a matter of money. Greed is not Dale's true nature. Treachery is. His come is to play the bad guys off against each other, walking away laughing to himself just before the blowup. If some good guys happen to be in the line of fire, those are the breaks. Dale came along in the wrong century. He should have been a feudal lord."

"What else don't you like about him?"

"I've always suspected he was the finger man down there in El Paso. I'm pretty sure of what his reasons were. Forty-two bullets in the car, Luz. Twenty of them went through Connie. Her head, her heart, nothing left of her heart at all. She was buried without a heart."

"*Hijole!* Tobin, no! Stop it! You don't know for sure. Don't even *think* about—"

Bonner lifted his soaked head from the focused spray of the shower and blinked at her.

"Think about what? Did I say anything, Luz?"

"You don't have to say—"

"There are no coincidences in life. That's my firm belief. I've used the last fifteen years of my vacations, I even took three months' leave a few years ago. I spent all that time in El Paso, Juárez, in Chihuahua state. I never got near the top trafficker, Jaime Loza. But I talked to some of his close associates. I don't believe there's a man alive who can resist opening his heart to you when you're taking his fingers off, one by one. It was kind of grim work. But you know what? In the course of it, God revealed Himself to me."

"*Dios mio!*"

"And I put it together. Purely circumstantial evidence. Dale could laugh me off in a court of law. But I'm satisfied. One day soon we'll get together, Dale and me, over a couple of beers. I want him to know none of it matters now. His national security directives, his exalted position with You Ess Guv. He made the bad mistake of coming to my state, my county, my *home,* where I live, with my crippled nineteen-year-old son."

Lucy had her arms around him, the top of her head pressing hard against his sternum.

"*Càllate!* I won't listen!"

He stroked her wet shoulders, played with a tendril of wiry hair that was sticking out from under the elastic edge of her pink shower cap. He kissed a soapy ear, whispering, "Luz, Luz. Treachery is an art any man can learn. If he hates long enough, and hard enough."

Pepper nodded off early, and Shay returned to her room at the Comfort Inn at a quarter past ten, having stopped at a Smith's food market in the shopping center up the street to load up on dried fruit, juices, organic tea, liquid yogurt, a couple of frozen gourmet dinners, a bottle of Napa Valley cabernet, picnic plates, and plastic cutlery. In addition to the whirlpool tub, the room had a small refrigerator, coffeemaker, and a microwave oven.

The TV was on when she opened the door with the spare card key. A rerun of *Happy Days*. Shay recalled her crush on Ron Howard when she was Pepper's age. Now he was directing. She'd worked a couple of days on one of his pictures, and was bashful around him because he still had the fresh teen face she'd adored. But only half his hair.

Sarah Dubray was stretched out in her denim skirt on one of the queen-size beds and didn't wake up or budge in her sleep. Shay smiled and walked around quietly storing the groceries, put two of the frozen dinners in the microwave—she was still trying to sit down to her first square meal of the day, having completely lost her appetite after the altercation at the Captain's Table—then went into the bathroom to change underwear and tampons. She swallowed a Midol with apple juice and looked longingly at her own unmade bed. The microwave beeped. Sarah sat up with drowned-looking eyes. Shay smiled at her, noticing that Sarah's left wrist and forearm had been bruised and scratched by the fingernails of the heinous little bastard who had tried to drag her from the restaurant.

"Hi."

"Hi," Sarah said weakly. "What time is it?"

"Ten twenty-seven."

"Oh. I fell asleep. What's that smell?"

"Beef tenderloin tips, scalloped potatoes, herb dressing, new peas in butter sauce. You hungry?"

"I don't know. I guess so." She coughed harshly, as if trying to bring up some lung butter, her cheeks pinking. "Could I use the bathroom?"

"Sure."

While she was in there, Shay set the small table and brought out the microwave dishes, opened the bottle of cabernet. Sarah returned, looked at the food, sat down opposite Shay, and droopily picked up a fork.

"I honestly don't know if I can."

"It's all right. Have a glass of wine."

"Wine?"

"Do you drink?"

"Alcohol? No. Never."

Sarah looked at the bottle and at the plastic cup, then with an expression of misgiving poured a couple of ounces. She raised the cup, sipped a little. She didn't know if she liked the taste. A second sip persuaded her. When she had finished the wine, she started in on the potatoes.

"I already ate once today, I think. But these are *so* good."

She looked at the wine bottle again. This time Shay poured for her.

"What's it all about, Sarah? Nobody can force you to marry that man. Particularly if he already has a couple of wives. He ought to be in jail."

Sarah said in a weak voice, "You don't understand."

"Let me give it a try. The Brightly Shining is one of those LDS splinter groups that have always been around. Like the Lafferty Brothers, the Leaping Longos, or the Lambs of God. Fundamentalists, and usually polygs. Your father's one, for sure. How many wives does he have?"

"Six, right now. That I know of. There may be others in Mexico. My own mother died when I was three. I was raised by . . . one of the others."

"Married to your father?"

"Yes." Sarah drank half of the wine Shay had poured for her. "It's so *warming*. I never knew that. Spirits are supposed to be evil; that's what I was taught. Poison. Spirits makes you drunk, and then the devil gets hold of you." Her expression clouded. "Although I know for sure some of my brothers have been drunk, and they seemed the same to me after."

"Who is Frenchie?"

"Papa's second cousin. He hates to be called 'Frenchie,' but everybody does. His name is T. Frenchman Dobie. I don't know what the *T* stands for." Sarah hiccuped and looked startled. "He's Papa's accountant. Keeps all the books. We're all supposed to turn over the money we make working in the Wells or at the casinos in Nevada to Mr. Dobie. I didn't, though. I mean I didn't give him all of it because I wanted to go to college. I've had up to three jobs at once. But I only told Mr. Dobie about one of them. He got suspicious, though. There wasn't anything he could do, I guess, until Papa came back a few months ago."

"Came back from where?"

"He was in prison for three years. In Mexico. It cost him a lot of money to finally get out. I heard more than three million dollars."

"What kind of trouble did he get into down there?"

"I don't know," Sarah said, with enough body language to indicate she didn't want to talk about it. "But I know he's worried about money now. It has to do with the EndTimes and the need to finish the work of the Brightly Shining. In Papa's Apocalyptic Revelation, I was about ten years old when it came to him, he saw the creation of the Brightly Shining. The Creation, he said to us, was going to be very expensive. We were all bidden to go out into the gentile world and make as much money as we could to further the work of the Creation, which in its glorious brightness will defeat the legions of the evil Dark One who has already been born and will walk the earth before the Second Coming of Jesus, and who will lead those Saints not devoured at the Gathering by the Dark Ones into bondage and eternal damnation instead of to the restored City of Enoch." The rush of words ended until she had gulped a couple of deep breaths. "Thus did God reveal directly to Rhondo Dubray his Plan for a cleansed and chastened world, which was then told to us, amen."

Shay cut into some beef tenderloin with the inadequate little saw-toothed picnic knife, not wanting to look at Sarah just then or think about the apocalyptic vision whirling in the girl's head like some sort of out-of-control theological thrill ride.

"Maybe I shouldn't have told you all that," Sarah said, clenching and unclenching one hand, a little vertical groove having appeared between her thin eyebrows.

"Oh, don't worry," Shay said cheerily. God's missions on earth, she thought, always involved the credulous and devout. They also frequently seemed to be covert, as secretive as espionage. "How did you manage three jobs? When did you sleep?"

"Oh, I didn't," Sarah said, her normal voice restored, although she had given herself a slight case of the hiccups. "Hardly at all—for months and months. But it was so important for me—'scuse me—

to save enough to go to college. I had such a great time there. I made new friends. Like Dally. I never really—darn, there I go again—had friends in New Hebron; I mean, it's like we're all related, one big family."

Sarah reached confidently for the wine. Shay started to caution her, then let her pour. Soon she'd sleep again, which was probably the best thing. Sarah Dubray was down to a nub of nerve after the ugly scene with Papa and Frenchie, possibly close to a severe breakdown. If it was reasonable to judge from her recent outpouring of babble.

"How many are you? In the Brightly Shining?"

"Oh—I'm not sure. New families come to town all the time. Maybe a thousand in New Hebron. Mexico, I couldn't say."

"You need to eat something with all that wine, Sarah."

"I *am*. See, almost all of my potatoes. I never have cared much for meat. But it's all delicious. I can't thank you enough, Shay. And for everything you did. You stood up for me." Something like a smirk settled on Sarah's lightly perspiring face, as if she were picturing Frenchie as he hit the deck, his eyes clogged with black pepper. "Dally would've, too. She's good at Judo, I think—I told you. Man, she would've cleaned his *hic!* Well, shit. Plow."

Sarah's expression changed from vengeful to morose as she continued to drink. "I really miss Dally. I've never been able to tell her about me. Her grandfather's an elder of the First Quorum, her family would be horrified to know—everything there is to know about me. They'd forbid Dally to room with me. I think I'd—kill myself if that happened." Her lower lip trembled, and both eyes were magnified by globes of unshed tears like morning glorys dripping dew.

"I'm excommunicated," she said. "We all are. But I pretend like it's not true. I just lie to everybody, and it's—*killing* me."

"Sarah, you're a good person, stuck in a terrible situation. You're doing the best you can. Don't be hard on yourself."

"Mr. Dobie would come around, while Papa was away, and say to me, 'Sarahhhh,' like that: '*Sarah*, it's time.' Time to have his *babies* is what he meant. For the good of the Brightly Shining. He said Papa had betrothed me to him when I was twelve years old. Huh. Of course, Papa tells all the girls who they're going to marry, and they just *do* it. I said, 'I want to hear it from Papa.' I was stalling. I never could stand his big ol' buggly eyes." She looked at the marks on her wrist. "Couldn't stand him touching me. His fingers sliding up and down my arm, fooling with my hair. He gave me little kisses on the neck." Sarah crashed a fist on the table, lower lip protruding wrathfully. "He had no *right*."

"Where do you stay in town, Sarah?"

The question made her apprehensive. "Oh, I'm in a house with some other girls from New Hebron. Mr. Dobie likes having us all *together;* makes it easier for *him* when he comes around to collect the *money* every week." She progressed, by degrees marked by sips of wine, from apprehensive to alarmed. "But I can't go back there! He'll have somebody watching for me."

"I wasn't going to toss you out, Sarah. What we want to do is guarantee you some official protection. You sure don't owe anyone the rest of your life. There's no action your father can take against you, short of kidnapping. And that will land him up to his armpits in a stinking shit pile."

Sarah giggled, coughed, changed color, and sat with both hands lightly clenched at her throat, trying to get herself under control. She looked steadfastly with dazed red-rimmed eyes at Shay.

"You're being such a good friend. Felt that, first time I saw you. Here's someone could be my friend."

"I don't want to see you get pushed around."

"I feel so warm."

"I think you've had enough to drink."

"Maybe we could go to bed now."

"Turn in whenever you're ready."

Sarah got up a little unsteadily, leaned on the table, moved her face slowly toward Shay's and kissed her on the lips, her own lips primly together. She tasted, a little sourly, of the wine she'd drunk.

"There," she said, as if she'd completed an exercise at charm school.

Shay said, with no show of discomfort, "What was that for?"

"You can undress me now," Sarah said, straightening up, almost losing her balance as blood rolled through her in a slow wave.

"You've got the wrong idea, Sarah."

"Why? It's wha' girlfriends do. Dally told me. They make each other feel good. Don't be shame; nobody gets hurt." Sarah smiled dolefully, massaging her unsteady head with the palm of one hand.

"Oh, honey. Even if I were gay I wouldn't take advantage of

you. I just want to help, however I can. And most girlfriends don't sleep together."

"They don't?"

"Take my word for it."

Sarah nodded, unsure but obedient. "I feel *awful* buzzy. Would you least tuck me in?"

"That I can do. I've got a spare sleep shirt for you. Go and change. We'll talk more in the morning."

Sarah said, "Sometimes I wake up in the night when I'm alone. I hear a voice saying, *God isn't; I am.* Then I see his face, and I know who he is. What he wants. And he is coming! Not even Pappa can stop him. *He is coming for me.*" Sarah lowered her head, eyes squeezed shut in misery and terror. She trembled. "That's why I need to sleep with you. When I'm warm enough, when I'm happy—then I don't hear the Dark One's voice."

Shay was dozing off on her side of the motel room when the phone rang. She looked at the dashed red numerals on the face of her travel clock. Eleven-forty. Now what the hell?

Sarah slept on her right side, breathing slowly and sibilantly through her mouth, only the back of her blonde head and her frazzy ponytail visible. One shoulder was canted high, and outflung arm and lax hand across another pillow, as if in sleep she'd thrown something away.

"Hello."

"Shay, it's Tobin Bonner. Sorry to be calling so late."

Shay cleared her throat. "No problem." She waited. His voice had sounded hollow and distanced, as if he was on a speaker phone. Did the man ever sleep?

"I'm having a press conference at nine in the morning, but I wanted to tell you before you heard it from the media."

Shay sat up. "Tell me what?"

"Late this afternoon we found a wrecked Silverado pickup truck way back in a canyon in Caballo Rojo State Park. The truck was Silverwhip Jack's."

"Yeah? Wrecked, how do you mean—"

"It was driven or pushed off the canyon rim, dropped about two hundred fifty feet and rolled another fifty downhill. No way we'll ever get it out of—"

"Was Jack—?"

"No, no, there wasn't anyone in the truck. No sign of Jack anywhere. I wondered if he'd been in touch."

"No. I haven't heard from him."

"I see."

During the ensuing silence and while her brain slowly unclouded, Shay realized where Bonner was going with this.

"Do you think—are you trying to make a connection between Jack's Silverado and—what happened last night?"

"Blue Silverado 350. Roof rack of halogen lights. That's what you described to us."

"Yes, well—there must be a lot of—was the pickup you found dam—that's dumb, of course it was damaged; it fell off a cliff."

"I'll have a forensic team up there at first light, looking for traces of paint off your Tahoe."

"But this is—Jack? *Wait* a minute."

"Nobody's accusing him of anything yet, Shay."

"You're not?"

"No."

"What's the press conference about then?"

"We'll keep the ownership of that Silverado to ourselves for now."

"For Jack's sake, I hope so."

"I wish he'd turn up, Shay, that's all."

"Yes. So do I. Now I'm really worried."

"We'll proceed cautiously on this."

"With a press conference, bright and early."

He was slow to reply. She closed her eyes, removed the receiver of the telephone an inch or so from her ear, listening instead to the zingy whine of 18-wheelers on the interstate close by, the scraping footsteps of someone on the stairs near her door, a man and woman quarreling in monotones.

"Shay, as long as the media's in town, I might as well use them."

She rested her face against the endpieces of the receiver. "Use the media for *what?*"

"I think I mentioned, I'm in kind of a tough campaign for reelection? Five murders. We've never seen anything like it in Solar County. People are nervous; they look to me for reassurance. Even though I don't know a hell of a lot to tell them, still I look pretty good on the tube."

"Thanks for sharing that with me."

After a few moments Bonner said with a rueful chuckle, "I deserved that. Man, my face is red. Shay, it's only politics. I just didn't want you to get the wrong idea. We're mum on Jack; you have my word. Nobody knows he's missing yet." There was another pause, and she heard a crackling sound, like stars frying briskly in heaven or tires passing over gravel. "How's your daughter? Tomorrow's the day?"

"For surgery, yes."

"What sort of music does she listen to?"

"Oh, MTV stuff. You don't need to—"

"My pleasure. Well, good night. I'll probably see you tomorrow."

"I'll be at the hospital all day," Shay said. "Good night, Sheriff."

"Just call me Tobe," he said genially, his voice shrinking, becoming toneless and tiny as if it were being sealed in a time capsule. "Everybody . . ."

Shay waited again, politely, heard no more from him, and reached out to hang up. Then she lay back, now too jumpily awake with images and premonitions to close her eyes. From the spray of light on the roughly textured ceiling, seeping from the gallery outside through imperfectly joined curtains, she conjured a glare of headlights, a glimpse of a windshield coated with rain like a layer of dripped wax. The driver inside the cab was as vague as a long-interred notable in a coffin with a tarnished viewing window. Only that fleet second of visibility, but could it have been Jack driving?

No, she wasn't going to believe that. When she'd had her last look at the driver in the rain, he was wearing the hat and a black slicker, but he was too tall, with high shoulders. She hadn't seen her father in many years, but Jack was only about five-eight, and his shoulders sloped. In recent photos of himself, age seventy or so, that he'd sent to Pepper, Jack was still able to wear the double-breasted cowboy shirts and tight pants that had been his costume in Saturday matinee programmers like *Six-Gun Showdown* and *Law of the Silver Whip*. Lean, mean, and vain, that was Silverwhip Jack Waco.

But his truck had been dumped into a remote canyon, either to hide it or smash it so badly the experts would have difficulty connecting it with the truck that had totaled her Tahoe.

Whatever had happened to Jack, or his truck, she could be certain of one thing: Jack hadn't walked into the Santero house and shot five people in cold blood. He'd worn an ivory-handled Colt Peacemaker .45 in his movies but seldom drawn it, handling the bad guys with his fists and trademark bullwhip. The only gun he'd ever had around when Shay lived with him was a fifty-year-old double-barreled Merkel shotgun, a presentation piece that had been neglected in its custom leather case until the night Shay took it from the closet and, trembling, hearing her mother crying in pain, loaded the gun with birdshot shells from a dilapidated old box on the back of the shelf. The truth was, Jack not only didn't like guns, he was afraid of them.

A wonder that, when she fired both barrels at him, the dirty old shotgun with cobweb in the bores hadn't blown up in her face.

Bonner clicked off the car phone after talking to Shay and, yawning, made the turn into his driveway. Home at long last.

He was halfway up the drive when he saw the runner leave the shadows of the locust trees on the east side of the house, cross the stony yard with something like a Camcorder in one hand, and jump into an ATV beside the waiting driver. The headlights of the all-terrain vehicle came on, and it went snarling away toward the Virgin River, weaving and dodging the boulders and patches of desert growth that took up two-thirds of Bonner's property.

Without a thought he turned off the driveway, not following the ATV but going another way toward the river, where there was a rutted road, soft dirt and sand through a shallow ravine. Nothing in the way that could tear the differential or oil pan out of his Crown Vic.

He turned his spotlight on as the ground slanted down to the river, operating it with his left hand while the car slewed toward the neon-bright ribbon of water. But they were thirty yards ahead of him on the red ATV, flying across sand and gravel bars, doughnut tires sending up plumes of water as they headed north toward the park. In the long focused throw of the spotlight Bonner identified without recognizing the pair: the head of the driver bald and deeply tanned, her head nearly shaved except for dark spikes of topknots, gala loops hanging from her earlobes.

Both riders looked back as the spotlight beam grazed them. He was wearing shades. The girl merrily gave Bonner the finger.

Bonner put on the brakes as the road changed from dirt to river rocks and turned off the spotlight, hearing the sound of the ATV's engine fading to the level of a bee's hum.

Fucking ABs and their Ironhead cunts! They'd been multiplying like rabbits in his county during the past couple of years.

Then his anger became a chill and he thought, *Vida*.

He backed up the narrow road almost as fast as he'd come down it, found a place to turn, and went jolting back to the house.

Vida was in the kitchen baking cupcakes. He looked up as Bonner walked in and smiled. Apparently the intruders hadn't harassed him. Maybe he didn't even know the Ironhead pair had been around. What they wanted at his house was unclear to Bonner, but he'd find out and damned soon.

He made himself relax and picked up one of the cupcakes, still hot from the oven, no icing yet. He peeled off the paper holder and ate it in three bites. Apple and spice, delicately flavored. Vida had a knack for so many things.

"These are great." He gave his son a hug. Vida looked at the kitchen clock, then at Bonner, who was rubbing his eyes. Bonner poured a cup from the coffeemaker Alma Darke kept on for him most of the day and night, and carried it back to Vida's room. He didn't feel like looking around outside for dead rattlesnakes tonight. There wasn't going to be anymore of that, anyway, because the Aryan Brotherhood had officially given notice that they wanted to be run the hell out of Solar County. And he wouldn't be in the mood to hear any shit about their civil rights after he did it

●

From Vida's collection of videos he selected one of Elvis's live performances and sat in the rocking chair watching the King in his starburst planet suit with matching cape and a gold belt buckle the size of a license plate. He sipped black coffee, waiting for Vida to finish up in the kitchen. Vida was good about not leaving messes for Alma to deal with in the morning.

In spite of the caffeine Bonner went to sleep first, still rocking, the empty cup and saucer in his lap. Vida came in and looked at him a little sadly, then carefully tried to take away the cup Bonner was gripping with thumb and forefinger. Bonner woke up anyway, for a few moments; he looked at Vida as if the boy had asked a question, and he was groping for an answer.

"Gabriel Sinaloa knew who his killer was. It wasn't some spic button guy he'd never seen before. Or one of his brothers. Otherwise Gabriel would have reacted, scrambled to protect his wife and children. He was a hard-nosed son of a bitch. But no, he sat there as if they were making small talk. So the shooter probably had to be a local. Somebody he saw a lot of, who had learned what Gabriel's real identity was, then contacted Enrico Sinaloa to make arrangements. Okay, but how would the shooter know to do that unless he'd been in the business himself? Beats me. But it was somebody from around here who needed a big payday. Had to have the money."

Vida nodded patiently, as if he understood.

"Needed the money," Bonner said, his moments of focus and clarity waning. His eyelids fluttered.

Vida reached out and cupped a hand on Bonner's forehead. The fluttering ceased, his eyes closed, he breathed harshly twice, chest heaving, then his brow smoothed out as he relaxed into sleep.

Vida went to the closet and got a blanket down from the shelf, draped it around his sleeping father. Then he turned his rapt attention to the fish, brilliant as hovering angels in their shimmering tropical pools.

11

THE TWO MEN HAD spent all night beneath the highway bridge, gagged and bound so securely back-to-back they had no hope of wriggling together along the dry wash and out into the open, where they might have been noticed in spite of light traffic on the road to the Jasper National Forest. At first light a brace of Walker hounds belonging to a landscape artist named Hallendale, who was squatting on government land in an old Airstream trailer, came across the hapless pair and made enough of a ruckus to alert their owner. Hallandale got on his old Indian motorcycle to investigate, then had to backtrack a mile to fetch his skinning knife because the knots in their rawhide bonds had been soaked in water and couldn't be untied. He also called the law.

Tobin Bonner was alerted at 7:45, and drove halfway across the county from Trampas to Simba Spring Ranch, where he found Guy Baker with badly chafed wrists, aching muscles and a surly mood. He was drinking Irish whiskey in his coffee.

"Bloody hell, Tobe, this is the second time in six months! What are you going to do about it, is what I'm asking."

They were on a covered patio of the Bakers' rustic one-story house. Doors to every room in the house opened onto the patio, which had a lot of hanging baskets and copper tubs filled with sprays of dried sage, roses, and sunflowers. The furniture was the kind of sturdy hand-hewn stuff, Mennonite and Mormon, that was practical in a household where a couple of chimpanzees, a year-old lioness, and a nine-foot-tall grizzly wandered in and out. Right now the grizzly was off in a corner of the patio, banished with a favorite toy. He wasn't paying attention to anything but his gold-painted basketball; but whenever Bonner considered the proximity of the unchained bear, a mountain of glossy fur, his balls shrank a little. The purring honey-eyed lionness he could live with; she was out of sight for now, which helped his concentration.

"What kind of loss are you looking at?" Bonner asked.

"In strictly financial terms, it's no big loss for us; Marco Polo's insured for fifty large. Of course we're losing the fee for the movie he was going to be in, that was fifteen hundred a day, and a two-week guarantee."

Bonner whistled. "For a black jaguar?"

"Certainly. Black jags aren't particularly rare in captivity, but for one that has been highly trained—no mean feat—we can almost name our price. Forget about the potential loss of income. It ain't the fuckin' money, dearie." He shifted his weight uncomfortably on a striped pillow; a night spent sitting on hard ground had caused his hemorrhoids to flare up. "I came across Marco Polo in the Mato Grosso when he was only hours old and separated from his mother by poachers. Hundreds of hours of care and attention were devoted to his raising. That's what hurts so terribly. It's no different than having the snatch put on one of your kids."

"Think it's a ransom deal?"

Baker shook his head. "It wasn't on the last occasion. We never heard a word from the buggers. There's no legit resale prospects for either cat; their ears were tattooed for insurance purposes. Poobah's in some billionaire Asian's private zoo, or else he was shot dead by hunters paying upwards of twenty thou a day for the privilege of tracking and killing a Sumatran tiger."

Pam Baker raised her sorrowing blue eyes. "Fewer than fifty of them are left, you know, in the wild."

Guy reached for her hand and held it. He was a stocky man with shoulder-length hair, lank and untrimmed, and stubble like a bed of nails. His wife, a large-animal veterinarian, was twenty years younger than Guy. She had a shaggy mop of prematurely graying hair and a low-cal body, nose and legs like a flamingo's. Her tanned hands and bare arms were laced with the scars of her occupation. She was missing the first joint of her left thumb, bitten off by a bad-tempered lemur.

"Who else on the ranch knew your travel plans besides Kit Eddington?" Bonner asked.

"After our other lorry, with Poobah in it, was taken, I've been extremely cautious. I never dreamt there'd be another occurrence—" Guy's normally ruddy complexion darkened further. "But you're not thinking that Kit—he's been with me longer than Pamela, actually, and he owns a piece of the operation! I would trust Kit with my life, have done as a matter of fact, that time in Kenya when—"

The cell phone on the table beside a cleaned-up platter of pork cutlets and *huevos rancheros* rang and Guy scooped it up. A lengthy harangue began immediately, Guy with the production manager of the film being shot in the Jasper National Forest. He got up and wandered around the patio as he talked. Pam looked at Bonner, shaking her head resolutely.

"Guy is absolutely correct; it's absurd to suspect Kit. He is above suspicion. After all, he *was* bound hand-and-foot with Guy all night long."

"I'm only asking questions, Pam, feeling my way here. What are your ideas?"

She shrugged helplessly. "Well—it's someone who knows a choice animal, that's a given. Also, I'm sure, he knows his way around big cats. Although Marco Polo was relatively predictable with us in controlled situations, one mistake and our thief could be clawed to ribbons. Marco *is* capable of working himself into an ugly humor very quickly if he doesn't receive his vittles bang on schedule."

"How much does he eat?"

"Seven to eight pounds of Nebraska Feline Mix, six days a week. Half-ration on Wednesdays, bones on Sunday, and live chicks on occasion when he needs extra vitamins or meds that he might sniff out if they were mixed with his regular fare. All cats are finicky that way, so we simply inject the chicks with whatever we need to give him, and he bolts them right down."

Bonner glanced at his watch, then at the grizzly sitting and bouncing his gold basketball off the wall of the house, catching it with a paw the size of a baseball glove. Then he looked out across the ranch yard. Near an oversized barn Lucy Ruiz was talking with Kit Eddington, a tall Aussie who wore an Anzac hat. An ostrich strutted gimpily by the patio like a mad old duffer looking for a bone to pick. There were flocks of birds on the extensive tree-shaded grounds pecking morsels from piles of animal dung. The grizzly put down his basketball and dropped to all fours, lumbered over to Pam's side of the table and put his head in her lap, making a noise like a motorboat.

"Sweet old Dovey," Pam crooned, reaching for an apple in a basket. "Nobody's going to take *you* if I have anything to say. Now go outside to eat this; *go* on, there's a dear boy."

Bonner looked at Guy, who was trying to straighten out the PMs dilemma by suggesting where he might rent another jaguar for the Stephen King horror movie that was filming in the forest.

"Guy spend a lot of time on the phone?"

"A fair amount, I'd say."

"*That* phone?"

"Well, yes, I reckon; Guy is always on the go during the day. A portable blower is more a necessity than a convenience for the two of us."

Guy no sooner had hung up than the phone rang again. This time it was for Pam, the vet, someone with a sick llama needing a diagnosis. Pam went into her office to consult her computer files. Guy sat slumped in his chair. Bonner switched on his tape recorder again.

"What time did you leave yesterday?" Bonner asked.

"Kit and I loaded Marco Polo into the five-ton, which is a traveling cage, you see, climate-controlled, all the comforts he's accustomed to at home. We must have started for the location about eight o'clock."

"Where did you stop?"

"In Desert Rose, at the Shell Mart."

"Did you notice them while you were gassing up?"

"No, nothing registered at the time. There were half a dozen vehicles at the pumps and in front of the convenience, perhaps two or three more pulling in off the road while I filled the tank. Kit went inside to take a whiz and buy some beef jerky, which he's constantly nibbling on; Kit has made a valiant effort to give up gaspers since they found a tumor the size of a pear in his brother's remaining lung."

"About what time did you leave Desert Rose?"

"Must've been half past. The light was still good."

"Didn't notice anyone following?"

"Yeah, I did notice then, because the road is so empty along that stretch going north. Two of them, side by side on bikes. The headlamps on. Not in a hurry because Kit was doing only around sixty Ks, a little less, for the comfort of the animal. They stayed back there, oh, it must have been for ten kilometers, then suddenly came blazing toward us. Kit remarked on the fact as we were being rapidly overtaken, just before the Shining Butte turnoff. They timed it well. Each rider wore one of those dink black helmets with chin straps, and red ski masks. They made rather a devilish appearance. They each had a gun, nasty little machine pistols of a type I'm not familiar with. They came roaring up on either side of us, and the one on Kit's side fired across our bow, so to speak. Of course we got the message."

"Anything unusual about their motorcycles?"

"I seldom pay attention to the damned things. Big ones, of course, a lot of chrome. Let me think. Utah license plates, but the numbers were a blur to me, it happened so quickly."

"Physical description?"

"Oh, come on, Tobin. They were both of medium height; they wore biker clothing. The one waiting for us beside the Shining Butte Road, where we were forced to turn off, was a woman. Taller than either of the men, rather a decent bod, but she wore the same getup as the other two. Neither Kit nor I were allowed to gawk at her. She took the wheel of the truck straightaway and drove off with Marco Polo."

"In what direction?"

"Toward Shining Butte State Park. And there is nothing else I can tell you. It was dusk; the road was empty. No one saw us hijacked, and we spent a fucking long and dismal night lashed together under that bridge. Fortunately it didn't rain, or we might well have drowned when the wash filled up."

Guy rubbed his stubble with the knuckles of one hand, staring disconsolately at Bonner.

"Any notion of how to proceed?"

"We have a description of your truck on the net already."

"Oh, well, it could be in Mexico by now. That would be my guess."

"Why?"

"One of the shooting parks I mentioned is located down there, in Chihuahua. Owned by a notorious drug lord, who relaxes with his cronies and invited big shots by bagging great cats you seldom encounter anymore, even in their natural habitat. What stinking arrogance! Never a thought to the consequences of callously dispatching animals that may be only memories a hundred years from now."

"Would you be talking about Steel Arm Jimmy Loza?"

"Loza, yes, I believe that's the name. Steel Arm?"

"He used to pitch both games of doubleheaders with a Mexican League team back in the fifties."

"As to his current activities, I'm sure he's protected by his government, the old *mordida,* and if it *is* Loza who's been rustling my animals, how could we ever hope to prove it?"

"I don't know," Bonner said, "but it's a place to start. I need to get rolling, Guy; that other matter up the canyon behind your place—"

"Yes, good Lord, what a terrible shock! Puts our hijacking into perspective, I suppose. Those children. Pam and I were acquainted with the children, you know. They'd come around, fascinated with our menagerie." He looked up as Pam came out of the house, carrying the cell phone and a video cassette. "What were their names again, puss?"

"The Santero kids? Edgardo and Consuela."

"My wife's name was Consuela," Bonner said. "What about the kids' parents? Did you see much of them?"

"No, very little. I was up there on two occasions that had to do with their horses. Removed rather a large splinter from the cheek of the big sorrel; he kept rubbing out the stitches in his stall, and the wound abscessed."

"Did they ride a lot?"

"The oldest girl—hard to tell her age, I'd say late teens, but very mature-looking—she often rode with her father. Occasionally I'd see her with her boyfriend."

"She had a boyfriend?"

"Fiancé, perhaps. They were certainly at the heavy petting stage—" Pam's cheeks glowed. "I'm *not* a snoop, you know. I saw them at it only once, from a distance. In a very heavy clinch on a blanket, in that lovely little copse where the Aquiles is deep enough for swimming."

"Recognize him?"

"No. But you can get a look at both of them, if you'd like." Pam held up the cassette. "This is a tape we made several months ago while Kit was putting Marco Polo through his paces for a film. I

wanted you to see what he looks like. The girl—I believe her name
was . . . Graciela." She looked at Guy, who shrugged. "Yes, that's it.
Graciela. Anyhow, they were on horseback outside the fence, watching, so they're in the background of some of the shots. But not in
very good focus, of course."

"Let's have a look," Bonner said.

They went into the shuttered living room, still cool from the
night, and Pam put the cassette into the VCR. The TV was a sixty-
inch projection model.

"How do you train the big cats?" Bonner asked, watching Kit's
efforts to get Marco Polo to spring from the limb of a dead tree onto
a well-padded Guy Baker. No onlookers in the background yet.

"Dominance training is for circus-type acts," Guy said. "Meat
training for the movie actors. For dominance we use a whip, a prod,
anything that establishes authority. The cats must believe one has
control over them at all times. They know better, of course, and so
do we; but it's a game I reckon they find amusing. Movie cats do
their thing for food. They'll only work when they're hungry. One
must always be aware of a cat's threshhold of displeasure. Marky,
when merely annoyed, could take half of one's face off with a swipe
of his paw. Should a trainer seriously annoy a big cat, he would be a
goner."

"Freeze, Pammy?" Bonner said. With a change in camera angle,
two horses and riders, stationary, had appeared on the tape.

Bonner studied the big screen. As Pam had told him, the riders
were out of focus, too far away to tell much about them. Graciela
had shoulder-length dark hair. Her companion, behind her and to
her left, was tall in the saddle, wore a short-sleeve yellow Polo shirt
and sunglasses. He had a lean aspect, scattered hair from riding hard,
probably blond. She rode a roan Appaloosa; his big horse was a chestnut, with a white forehead.

"Does it get any better? I mean, the background?"

"I'm afraid not," Pam said.

"Okay. Well, thanks. I'd like to borrow the tape for a few days,
see what can be done with it."

"You're curious about him?"

"We don't have much to go on. Can you guys give me any help?"

Pam handed Bonner the tape and they walked outside. Guy said,
"We didn't socialize with the adult Santeros."

"There was the language barrier," Pam said. "Mrs. Santero spoke not a word of English."

"How was his English?"

"I'd say he spoke it well enough to have a social life independent of the family."

"How do you mean, Pammy?"

"Oh, I'd see him round and about, with one woman or another. One in particular he seemed to fancy."

"Do you know who she was?"

"I can't recall the name, but she was spectacular. A head taller than Mr. Santero. Close-cropped, dyed red hair, fiercely made up eyes, the dress and style of a biker chick—but no, she would be the leader of her own pack. Mr. Santero had a certain swagger and ruthless appeal of his own, but I'd say it was ill met by moonlight with this dolly. As the vet on call, I happened to be in close proximity to the two of them at the Memorial Day Rodeo. She was entered in the barrel race, on rather a nifty bay filly that seemed to have received excellent care. I can't fault her horsemanship. Otherwise, I found her to be a boisterous bragging bitch. Also—disturbing. How can I explain? There was an eerie psychic tone to her that rubbed my skin the wrong way."

Pam reached out and tapped Bonner on the shoulder; his mind seemed to be wandering.

"Would you happen to know who I'm talking about, Tobin?"

"Her name's Ros. Rosalind Dubray."

"*Those* Dubrays? Oh, my."

"I missed the rodeo but I'd heard Ros was back. I busted her a few times when she was just a kid. Shoplifting at first, then prostitution, badger games, felony assault: Ros beat the living shit out of three older boys with a bicycle chain. One of them was in a coma for three months. Ros skipped a stay at the state juvy by pleading mental and went through counseling. At the same time she took up with a retired anthropologist, whose thirst for knowledge was overmatched with his thirst for scotch. Maybe he was studying Ros. We think she did him in with a shovel for a handful of savings bonds, turned the back of his skull to mush, but the DA didn't have enough on her to go to trial. I drove Ros down to the Nevada line in handcuffs, unlocked the cuffs, and pointed her in the direction of Vegas. She said she'd cut my nuts off someday, and went laughing through the mesquite to seek her destiny. She was, at that time, two months shy of her fifteenth birthday."

"Is that cult still in business?" Guy asked. "The Brightly Shining?"

"Yeah. Thriving. Amazing how many people will buy into schizoid Armageddon bunk like Rhondo Dubray is peddling. On the other hand, consider what the citizens of this country buy into whenever it's time to elect a president."

"They're polygamists, aren't they? I've often wondered why the lot of them aren't in jail."

"Times have changed; morals have changed. The legal situation is complex. The U.S. government has more politically tasty fish to fry. Nobody in county or state government is much interested in spending the time or money needed to bring charges of bigamy, or open and notorious cohabitation, or whatever, because even if they win the case, the penalty is likely to be a year's probation. The real problem isn't plural marriages; it's white slavery. There are never enough young girls to go around. When they reach sexual maturity polyg women are condemned to one pregnancy after another. The young men are encouraged to leave and find employment, and wives, on the outside. The elders don't want competition from young bucks for the available virgins. Rhondo Dubray and the other cult leaders will go to war to protect their fiefdoms; it's happened before. If I went down to New Hebron and started making arrests for statutory rape and child abuse, which is what their culture is really based on, every elected official in Solar County would wake up to pipe bombs on their porches and in their mailboxes. When it comes to zealots, there are only two choices: leave them alone, or be prepared to kill them."

Lucy Ruiz walked up to the patio with a Burmese python draped around her shoulders.

"Isn't he cunning? They named him Embraceable Hugh."

Bonner frowned at her for being unprofessional on the job; she pretended not to notice as she handed the snake, its chocolate body divided into yellow-edged squares, back to Kit Eddington. From the way he smiled with his horsey teeth, the animal trainer had taken a liking to her. Bonner looked at his watch again.

"Lucy, follow me over to the Santero place? I need to stop in for a minute."

The driveway to the house was blocked by sawhorses, so they left their rides down by the river. There were three vehicles parked close to the house, a couple of rental cars and a gunmetal gray van with no markings and a federal government license plate. Lab van. Bonner wondered where it had come from. Overnight from Los Angeles?

They leaned against a fender of Lucy's SUV and she smoked a Marlboro. The morning breeze swept through ash and cottonwood trees along the low riverbank. Sunlight danced over the current of the shallow river.

"What about Eddington?" Bonner asked her.

"If he's guilty of anything, he's a wonderful actor."

"Yeah, I don't think it was an inside job. Remember what you were telling me about Santero's hobbies?"

"The surveillance equipment? Is that what we're here for? The feds wouldn't let us touch it, if they haven't packed everything up already."

"You said he had a scanner he could use to pick up cell phone conversations."

"Right."

"I think Gustavo Gabriel Santero Sinaloa tuned in to what was happening at Simba Spring Ranch, for amusement or possibly profit, taping Guy's conversations with movie people who wanted to rent an animal or two. He easily could have known about Guy's plans to transport Marco Polo to the location in the Jasper."

"How could he be a catnapper? He was dead yesterday."

"Gabriel would already have set it up. A hands-off deal for him, anyway. Just something to while away the time and make a nice profit on his hobby. Gabriel was an accomplished thief at the age of six. From what I hear, by the time he was ten he was doing assassinations for the drug cartel he and his brothers eventually ruled. Knowing a little something about his personality, I can understand why he would be fascinated with Rosalind Dubray."

"You think Ros is involved in this?"

"Guy gave me a sketchy description of the perpetrator who drove off with the truck. A head taller than the two men; 'rather a decent bod' is the way he put it."

"I expect that's an understatement. She was six feet when she was fourteen but I think she's grown a couple of inches since then. She does have a bod, all right; knows how to show it off."

"Where did you see Rosalind?"

"Here and there, on her bike, in town. She pulled up beside me on division not long ago. Doing that thing with the hand throttle, revving, *arummmmm-rrummm,* looking over at me. Smiling. God, but she has a creepy smile."

"She remembered you?"

"Ought to. I jerked the snot out of little Ros that time I caught her taking money at knifepoint from boys she'd lured under the bleachers at football games to grope her. She couldn't have been older than twelve, but way big for her age, and strong. She got in a couple of good shots; my left ear was twice normal size for a week. There was something so elemental and heartless about her, even at that age. What would she be now, twenty-four?" Bonner nodded. "So what do you want to do?"

"Pay Ros a visit. She shouldn't be hard to find."

"You or me?"

"Better let me take this one, Luz."

They heard the sounds of horses moving upstream and saw, through the boughs that hung like pale green clouds over the sun-struck river, an Arab gelding and a chestnut mare coming toward them. Signe Gehrin, on the mare, wore cowgirl-style clothes: a fringed antelope jacket with a long, flowing kerchief and a cream-colored Resistol. Her husband had on a tweed cap and jacket with whipcord jodhpurs. He was using an English saddle.

"Who are they?" Lucy asked.

"The Gehrins. Wolfgang and Signe."

"Damn fine-looking Arabian. Where do you know them from?"

"One of Neal's parties I got dragged to. I had the impression that Neal was cultivating Wolfgang, who is some kind of entrepreneur, and screwing his wife on the side. Not what I'd call sound business judgment, but you know Neal."

"How many kids do Neal and Poppy have now?"

"Three at college, three at home. The brood's occupied Poppy, but Neal's never been able to keep his zipper closed."

"Good morning, Sheriff!" Signe called, when they were fifty feet away.

"Good morning."

"Is anything the matter? I mean, anything else?"

"One of the Simba Springs menagerie was taken last night; we've been investigating."

The Gehrins stopped their horses near the bank, where they were eye level with Bonner and Lucy Ruiz. "Which of their animals was it?" Wolfgang asked, as if he was personally acquainted with them all.

"A black jaguar named Marco Polo."

"Valuable, I should think. And not the first time this has happened, I seem to recall."

A fly buzzing around the Arab's nostrils caused the horse to shake his head and sidestep into a backwater of the river, where he faltered and nearly sat down on his gorgeous tail. Wolfgang handled the Arab expertly until he had good footing again. The horse trembled slightly, then raised his tail and dropped a couple of steaming muffins.

Bonner said, "A few months back the Bakers also lost a tiger they were transporting to California. The thief drove off with their truck while the driver was having dinner."

"We hear the animals at night, sometimes," Signe offered. "The horses bang around in their stalls when those lions are doing that peculiar cough of theirs. It's exciting, actually; gets the blood going, doesn't it, Wolfie?"

She seemed to be taunting him, but there was no measurable reaction. Wolfgang had the laid-back flattened crown and jutting, hard-bitten profile of a bird of prey, but his eyes were narrow and lightless; it was difficult to make contact with them. One of those men who, even when they seemed to be looking at and listening to you, might be looking behind you instead, or thinking about something else. International businessman Neal Bonner had done some fawning at the party. A high-flyer, impressive jet-lag credentials. There was an ironic chill about Wolfgang, all that altitude maybe, the subsonic vaulting over continents.

Signe reached out and brushed a fly away from the divided queue that was crooked over the back of his collar. Wolfgang shrugged reflexively. He was looking at the Santero house, a hundred yards uphill at the front of a box canyon.

"Quite a lot of activity this morning," he said. "Do you know why the Santeros were murdered?"

Bonner was going to say nothing, then changed his mind.

"For money."

"Robbery was the motive?"

"No. That isn't what I meant."

Signe appeared to flick a little dust from the sleeve of her husband's hacking jacket.

"They were Colombian, darling. Didn't I mention it?"

Wolfgang said to Bonner, "Santero was being protected by your government?"

"Wolf-ie," Signe said, low in her throat, as if she were disappointed in him.

Bonner looked at her with an encouraging smile.

"You seem to have figured out quite a lot about your neighbors. How did you know Santero was Colombian?"

"The accent, Sheriff."

"*Habla usted Español?*" Lucy asked her.

"*Sì, hablo bien.*"

"How well did you know them?" Bonner said.

"The oldest girl—her name was Graciela—rode often, by herself. We would meet here and there, exchange a few words. I found it difficult to know her; she seemed shadowed by a tragedy that had all of her attention. Occasionally I would see her by the river with the little girl."

"Cymbeline," Lucy said. "*Pobrecita.*"

Signe nodded in her direction. "Adorable. But was she—?"

"No, she was spared."

"God's blessing."

Wolfgang seemed impatient to be on his way. They were one of those couples, Bonner noted, who are always exchanging meaningful looks, part of a complex code of signals evolved from a marriage that survived on the thrills to be had from sexual warfare. One of the Gehrins might end up shooting the other, but in the meantime they would seldom be bored.

"Did you know Gustavo Santero?" Bonner asked Wolfgang.

"I only saw him from a distance, on a few occasions. I don't spend a great deal of time here, not as much as I'd like. My businesses take me all over the world. As a matter of fact, I flew in just yesterday afternoon."

"What's your line of work, Mr. Gehrin?"

"I buy, merge, and sell. Small- and medium-size companies."

"Do you ever get down to Mexico?"

"Now and then. Why?"

"Business or pleasure?"

"My business *is* my pleasure," Wolfgang said. "Am I being interrogated, Sheriff?"

"No. But I do have to warn you."

Wolfgang made his Arab dance. "Excuse me, please?"

"There's a state law about walking horses in our streams. Water's one of our precious resources; we never seem to have enough of it. Horses can't help themselves, but they pollute the water. The fine is five hundred dollars."

"I was unaware of this law, Sheriff. Are you citing me?"

"No, not this time. As a man who's careful in his business dealings, you must take pains to make yourself aware of the laws of the countries where you do business. And I'm sure, since you spend as much of your free time as possible in Solar County, that you'll want to help us preserve the beauty and integrity of the environment that attracted you in the first place."

"Yes, I do. Your concerns are mine, Sheriff. Signe?"

They turned their horses and guided them to the south bank, where there was a trail around deadwood, through chokecherry and monkshood growing in damp places amid the standing trees. The morning, already powerfully alight and resonating with insect and birdlife, had begun to take on heat. The river in its divided course rippled clearly over smooth, brown rocks.

Lucy said in a low voice, "You don't like him either."

"He'd be a tough man to play poker with."

"And she has the smile of a blood drinker. What was that about Mexico?"

"Hell, I don't know. An idle question."

Lucy lit another Marlboro, eyes closing for a moment as she dragged on the filter. "You don't ask idle questions. I was watching her. She was a little tense. Her eyes seemed to pull back in her head."

"Just amazing, isn't it? How many people might have known that good neighbor Santero was from Colombia, while the poor dumb son-of-a-bitch sheriff didn't know dick. Now I wonder who also knew he used to be big in the narcotics business and had a price on his head. Give me a puff."

Lucy handed him her cigarette and looked at the Santero house. Dale Stearman and Katharine Harsha, deep in conversation, were walking slowly around the front porch.

"There's our competition."

"They aren't competition," Bonner said. "They're just in the way. Maybe we can scope out what it is Stearman's after. If Santero was important to them, it's even money he was fulfilling part of his obligation to WPP by informing on somebody. Which may be the best explanation for all of the surveillance gear. Probably enjoying the game, setting up a game or two of his own on the side, although with Dale Stearman that's asking for real heartache."

"Now *wait* a minute," Lucy said.

Bonner laughed at her expression.

"No, I don't know that Stearman had Santero killed, but it's not beyond the realm of possibility. Let's go fire a couple of wild shots and see who flinches."

"Sometimes you scare me, Tobin. That's not a lie. These are U.S. government *bichos,* with God knows what powers of detainment, should they choose to exercise them."

"Birdie."

"Damn you," she said, frustrated but amused. And to herself: "*Y qué?* What's the worst can happen to you, Luz, you don't get to change your underwear for two weeks?" She looked at Bonner. "What about your press conference?"

"The media will wait. They don't have a hell of a lot else to do."

●

Dale Stearman and Katharine Harsha took in the approach of the local law with no show of enthusiam.

"Morning, Dale," Bonner said. "They treating you okay at the Ramada?"

"I slept all right. What brings you out this way, Tobe?"

Lucy stared at Katharine Harsha, who looked coolly away after a few moments.

"There've been a couple of problems, animals stolen from the menagerie at the Simba Spring Ranch, which is just across the river there."

"That so? What kind of animals?"

"A Sumatran tiger and a black jaguar. The tiger's on the endangered list. The pair worth, say, a hundred thousand. They were trained to do movie work."

"Respectable money," Stearman said, looking mildly impressed. He took a pack of spearmint gum from his blazer pocket and offered it around, then unwrapped a stick for himself, looking at Bonner as if knowing there had to be more on his mind.

Bonner could see and hear, from where he and Lucy stood at the edge of the porch, that walls were being ripped out inside the Santero house.

"Redecorating the place, Dale? By the way, this is my chief investigator, Lucy Ruiz." Stearman nodded cordially. "And I haven't met—"

"Katharine Harsha," she said, introducing herself and offering her hand. "Nice to meet you, Sheriff."

"I'd say you're about a fifty," Bonner remarked.

She looked confused. "How's that?"

"Fifty SPF, the most sunblock you can buy. Otherwise skin like yours will burn badly, even if you stay away from direct contact with the sun. We call it a sky burn out here. Reflected ultraviolet rays. I mention that because your nose, if you'll pardon my saying, looks a little sore already."

Harsha smiled slightly. "Thanks, it is."

Bonner twinkled at her, and Lucy wanted to kick him.

Dale Stearman said, "Can I do anything for you, Tobe?"

"No. Probably not. Because what I'm needing, you haven't found either. And you won't."

"What d'you mean?"

"The surveillance tapes Santero made but never turned over to Bobby Polikarski. If they weren't in the safe—and it's an easy guess you didn't find them there, otherwise you wouldn't be ripping the house apart—then somebody else took them. The shooter, for instance."

Temperament was suddenly in the air, like a new strain of virus in flu season.

Katharine Harsha gave Lucy a look and said, "How long were you in the house yesterday, Deputy? Before we arrived."

"What does it matter? I was here the night before, too, but I didn't remove or cause to have anything removed from the house. Except dead people."

Bonner shrugged. "You're welcome to have a look at our evidence log, Dale."

"Yes, I know. But why do you think there were surveillance tapes? Who would Gabriel have been surveilling?"

"Oh, anybody and everybody, Dale. He was such a big shot, the humdrum life of a protected witness couldn't have appealed much to Gabriel. So to help pass the time he worked up a hobby or two. Getting to know the neighbors without them knowing a damn thing about him. Sparsely settled out here, though. Let's see, there're the Bakers, from whom he might've learned when valuable animals were being trucked to movie locations; the Gehrins; Jack Waco, of course. A few other mostly marginal-income families."

"Or maybe it wasn't a hobby," Lucy said, watching Katharine Harsha closely.

"What's that, Luz?" Bonner said. "Oh, I see what you're getting at. Because the federal government already had somebody on the local scene, even somebody as treacherous and undependable as an ex-drug lord, it made sense to them to provide the late severely perforated Gabriel Sinaloa with some snooper devices not available over-the-counter so he could feed back information about one of his neighbors. That's real smart of you, Luz; no wonder I made you the chief investigator for the Solar County Sheriff's Department."

"I try to be worthy," Lucy said, with only a small twitch at one corner of her mouth to betray the deadpan effect.

Stearman said, in a bored voice, "You always liked to show off, Tobin. It wasn't a good idea then. It's not a good idea now."

Bonner cocked an ear and said, "There it is. That hint of official sanctity. Events in motion, complex and unlikely alliances, layers of intrigue surrounding a mission. If it goes on long enough, the center shifts, and shifts again, until no one can find it anymore. The original purpose disappears at some point; then the whole thing becomes beside the point: but the intrigue continues, spreads, deepens, demands input, sacrifices, funding. Massive funding. We know it's out there; we can feel the heat it gives off. We just can't make out what it's supposed to be."

Stearman's thin mouth had a look of mean amusement. "Our purposes are legitimate and urgent, Tobin. Anything else we can do for you today?"

"What have you done for me so far?" Bonner asked, with a look of astonishment.

"Or anything you feel you ought to share with me?" Stearman said, staring for a few moments at the river bottom where Bonner had been talking to the Gehrins.

Wyrick, the one with the droll chin whiskers and short-but-Sweets strolled out of the house and stood near Katharine Harsha. She said to Stearman, "I'd better be going." She shifted her gaze cordially to Bonner. "Is it much of a drive to New Hebron?"

"About seventy miles," Bonner said. "Have a nice day. Dale, see you around. Luz?"

They walked back to where they had left their vehicles.

"Smart-looking woman," Bonner said. "Nice coloring. Somehow you get the impression her pussy is as gray as a ghost."

"You'd better not be planning to confirm that. What do you think she wants in New Hebron?"

"They've made a connection, or they already had one, between Rhondo Dubray and Gabriel Sinaloa. Pam Baker told me she saw Gabriel with Ros Dubray at the Memorial Day Rodeo."

"She and her daddy are mortal enemies, or at least they used to be. If he was ever scared of anything, it was *that* bitch. All those obedient, docile daughters, and somewhere in the midst of his brood up pops Rosalind. Right string, baby, but the wrong yo-yo. Rhondo must have thought one of his wives was entertaining the devil when he wasn't around."

"He and Ros might have had a reconciliation," Bonner suggested.

"When donkeys fuck. Now what am I going to do about Marco Polo?"

"The animal might have been driven to Mexico. Border patrol, federal police. Call Grange Kilbuck or Larry Cave at the DEA in El Paso, see what they might know about a hunting preserve Steel Arm Jimmy Loza supposedly maintains in Chihuahua. I'd also like to know if Loza was blood-related to the *judiciale* Gabriel had offed down there for getting his daughter with child, or if the hombre was just on Steel Arm's payroll. By the way, I forgot to mention, the autopsy showed Graciela had had a C-section about a year and a half ago."

"Confirming what we suspected."

"Luz, while you're calling around, get hold of Leland Burling at Las Vegas Metro and find out if they have anything in their files on Rosalind. Vegas would have been her first stop after I kicked her out of Solar County. Might as well query California and the Mexicans, too. One more thing. Isn't Logan McAfee's kid a stockbroker in New York?"

"Investment banker. He's no kid, Kyle's my age. Doing very well, I hear. Why?"

"We want anything he can dig up for us on Wolfgang Gehrin. What the hell, try the FBI and Interpol too. Also, Wolfgang said he flew in here yesterday afternoon. Let's confirm that, and find out where his flight originated. Having fun?"

"Man, you know I love it."

Mary Lynn followed Bonner into his office.

"The VJs and hot media babes are clamoring for you outside."

"Five minutes. Do I have a tie somewhere?"

"If not, I'll borrow one from one of the guys."

Bonner handed her Pam Baker's videotape. "Express this to the lab we use in Salt Lake. We're interested in the pair on horseback. She's one of the murder victims. Enhance as much as possible, I want to know who Graciella's lover was."

"Yes, sir."

"I learned something fascinating this morning, Mary Lynn."

"Yeah, what?"

"During intercourse, the male rhinoceros ejaculates nearly once a minute for an hour and a half . . ."

"I'll bet I know who we have to thank for that information."

". . . Then at least ten years go by before he even wants to look at a female rhinoceros again."

Mary Lynn giggled and said, "Messages."

"Not now."

"Just one, Emory insisted. Those vagrants the highway patrol dumped on us yesterday morning?"

"Uh-huh."

"Both HIV-positive. Emory took them out of the population."

"That's great. HIV-positive."

"Their names are Hanratty and Mizell."

"So what?"

"Hanratty says he wants to talk to you."

"I don't want to talk to him."

"Claims he saw somebody being buried a couple of nights ago. In a plain pine box, by the light of the moon. The mourners, or undertakers maybe they were, wore old-fashioned black frock coats, the kind that button all the way to the knees? It was along about two in the morning."

Bonner was in his bathroom splashing water on his face. He looked around at Mary Lynn.

"In a ghost town cemetery," Mary Lynn concluded.

"Did he also say he was there when they nailed up Jesus?"

"I don't think so. You're dripping on your shirt."

"Stop pestering, Mary Lynn, and find me that necktie." Bonner reached for a towel. "By the way, what music does your fourteen-year-old listen to nowadays?"

"To name a few, Barenaked Ladies, Smashing Pumpkins, Butt-hole Surfers."

"Butthole Surfers! The very name sets your toes to tapping. See if you can find time today to pick up a couple of those Pumpkin CDs at Wal-Mart. Take it out of petty cash, put in my IOU."

12 SHAY WAS READING in a chair beside the bed of her sleeping daughter when Tobin Bonner pushed opened the heavy door and looked in.

"Hi," he whispered. "How did the surgery go?"

"Dr. Verger said it went very well, no complications. Come on in. What time is it getting to be?"

"Quarter to one." He took off his hat and joined Shay by the bed. "What are you reading?"

"Philip Roth."

"Any good?"

"I never can get enough of the sexual angst of middle-aged Jewish men."

Bonner took a Wal-Mart sack from his suit coat pocket. "Couple of CDs Pepper might not have."

"Thank you. Smashing Pumpkins. She'll love these. I promised her headphones, against my better judgement. Kids wear them everywhere. That's the problem; they look to me like a race of little drones."

"I thought, instead of flowers—she's probably not old enough to appreciate flowers the way most women seem to." He looked at the bare windowsill. No flowers there. A thin line of outdoor light glowed like radium around the drawn-down blackout shade. A rectangle of softer fluorescent light was flush with the wall beside the hospital bed; seen against it, Shay's curly dark head and paler, healing face resembled a painted Roman bust on display in an intimate mu-

seum. She was wearing pale yellow coveralls over a blue T-shirt and
was barefoot, which excited him in a complex way that didn't have
everything to do with sex. Small, straight feet, actual little toes, not
puny nailess vestiges from being crammed for years into unwearable
shoes. Bonner had always liked watching Consuela care for her own
feet: the lotions, the pedicure, the nail gloss. He felt a bloom of heat
in his scarred chest, an unexpected drop of rich blood from one of
the sealed-off streams of his life.

"Nothing from Jack?" Bonner asked.

"Your guess is as good as mine. Or have you found out something?"

"About the truck? We're assuming for now it was stolen. Where
and when, Jack would have to tell us."

"If he's able," Shay said grimly.

"I don't think we need to make that conjecture at this time."

"When *will* be the right time? Tomorrow, the next day? His truck
was stolen, for God's sake, probably by the one who committed those
murders."

Pepper took a deep, dry-sounding breath and then coughed, her
eyelids trembling. She was sleeping off what was left of the anesthetic
in her system, her head and shoulders and the wrapped knee both
elevated. Shay wrung out a cloth in a stainless steel bowl of water
and held it on Pepper's forehead. Pepper lifted her head from the
pillow, turned her face down and retched some ropey, clear vomit
into the cloth that Shay placed under her chin. Pepper cleared her
throat and spoke in a broken monotone about something Bonner
didn't catch. Shay answered her affirmatively, then offered a glass of
soda, coaxing Pepper to sip through a straw. She didn't want much
of it and subsided into twilight again, drops of liquid from the post-
op IV sliding down a transparent tube into a vein on the back of her
right hand.

Shay asked, "Are you trying to find him, Sheriff?"

"Tobin. Since the truck, yeah; now we're trying to find him."

The door opened again and Sarah Dubray walked in, carrying two
pungent sacks of take-out from Jack-in-the-Box.

"I went ahead and got some fries for Pepper because she might—"

Sarah looked from Shay's face to Bonner's as he turned. Her face
changed in an instant, from mild exuberance to startlement and fear.
She seemed to flatten as if she'd turned a corner into a hurricane
wind or run into something unholy in a dark churchyard, her mouth

stretching across her face in a rictus, eyes squinching almost shut. Then she dropped both fat sacks of burgers and fled.

Bonner said, "Hey!" and was almost unbalanced as Shay bolted past him on her way to the door. He was nearly as surprised by Shay's quickness as he had been by the girl's reaction to his presence in the hospital room.

He followed Shay out into the hall in the aftermath of a cry from Sarah Dubray as piercing as the yowl from a run-over cat. She staggered a little near the nursing station, having attracted the attention of everyone on the floor. Shay caught up and put an arm around Sarah, guided her into a bathroom with a quick backward glance at Bonner.

Bonner returned to the room, picked up the sacks from the floor, put them on the swing-out tray attached to the bed, and waited, wondering if he'd ever seen the girl before. He couldn't be sure; at that age so many of them looked alike.

A nurse he did know, daughter of one of his father's old hunting buddies, came in to check on Pepper's vital signs. On the small side, jaunty, hair the color of rusted baling wire. She looked at him for an explanation of the little drama in the hall; he shrugged.

"Your dad doing all right?" she asked, fitting a blood pressure cuff around Pepper's lax arm, pumping it up.

"Four years now, no recurrence."

"That's good. Was it his thyroid gland?"

"Yeah. Haven't seen you in a while. Justine, isn't it?"

"Right. Well, I got married, and we moved to Portland for a couple years. Now I'm back, but *he's* still in Portland." The blood pressure cuff made a sticky, ripping sound as she took it off. Pepper half opened her eyes, smiling dazedly. "Are you going to win the primary, Sheriff?" the nurse asked Bonner.

"I always do."

Nowadays it only took a second to get a temperature readout from the ear. Justine put the Thermoscan back into the holder she wore at her waist like a pager, jotted the number down on the chart on her small clipboard. "Well, good luck."

Probably ten minutes had passed; Bonner felt a little awkward, hanging around, but he was curious about what was going on with the kid who had run from him. Pepper seemed to be okay, so he left the room and walked down the hall toward the nursery. Cymbeline, the newly orphaned granddaughter of Gabriel Sinaloa, was inside playing with a pediatrics volunteer, a plump teenager in a pink jumper.

Shay Waco was in the lounge with a calmer Sarah Dubray, who managed to look at him without flinching when he walked in. She was drinking from a can of ginger ale.

Bonner smiled at them.

"What was it, my bloodshot eyes or my sulfurous breath?"

Shay smiled and glanced at Sarah; she was holding tightly to the girl's free hand. To Bonner the girl appeared to be in the kind of daze that follows a sharp shock. Her eyes were as pale as watermarks, without spiritual charge; they merely existed in her face, like souls adrift in limbo.

"Sarah had kind of a rough experience yesterday, Tobin. We both did. She thought we might be in trouble."

Bonner shrugged. "Not with me. Why don't you tell me about it, Sarah—Sarah what?"

"Dubray."

Bonner nodded, as if her last name could be a partial explanation in itself, and waited. Shay gave the girl's hand a little squeeze.

"My father's back," Sarah said. "I guess you know."

"They had him in a federal jail in Mexico, is what I heard. Charged with statuatory rape."

"I don't know what he was charged with," she said, with a faint grimace of distaste. "While he was gone, I got a GED because, you know, the school in New Hebron isn't recognized by the state. Because we're all—anyway, I made good grades on my SATs and passed some other tests and I was able to get into Utah State."

"Good for you," Bonner said. "I assume you didn't feel that you were ready for one of those patriarch-arranged marriages."

"I'll *never* be ready for life in the Principle," Sarah said, her eyes quickening.

"But Rhondo has other ideas. He pledged you to somebody, when you were younger?"

"Yes. I haven't been home in a while. I've been working as an assistant manager at the Captain's Table. They came yesterday evening. My father and Mr. Dobie."

Shay picked up the story. "This Dobie character got rough with Sarah. Do you know him?"

"Oh, yeah. Frenchie Dobie. He's Rhondo's top man in the inner circle of the Brightly Shining."

"He tried to literally drag her out of the restaurant. Sarah and I were sitting there talking, minding our own business. I wasn't going to let it happen, so I—stopped him."

"Uh-huh," Bonner said, looking at her in admiration. "We've got your *pistola*, so I assume Dobie is still walking around and not leaking from a couple of brand-new buttonholes."

Shay wasn't sure she appreciated the teasing. "I didn't do all that much. I think he broke a tooth."

"What did you hit him with?"

"She kicked him in the chin!" Sarah said, spots of triumphant red in her ivory cheeks. "It was the neatest thing I ever saw. Shay knows judo."

"Tae kwon do," Shay amended, looking at Bonner. "I suppose he could get me arrested for what I did."

"Misdemeanor battery? Five hundred dollar bond. Sounds as if you had cause. My guess is the magistrate would toss it out." He shifted his attention to Sarah and said pleasantly, "So that's why you got scared when you saw me?"

"Yes, sir."

"You thought sure I was going to arrest you and maybe turn you over to Rhondo?"

Sarah nodded.

Bonner nodded too, watching her with a casualness Shay found deceptive. She pressed Sarah's hand again, and Sarah gave her a quick, puzzled look.

"Sarah, you're over eighteen, aren't you?" Bonner asked.

"Yes."

"Then you don't have to talk to either your father or to Mr. Frenchie Dobie should you choose not to do so."

"That's what I told her," Shay said.

"If either of them persists, if they come around to where you live or even to the restaurant, which I believe your daddy owns a majority interest in—"

"I know that."

"There are laws on the books that can be enforced. Laws against stalking. Does that make you feel any better?"

Sarah looked down. "I guess so," she said, barely audible.

Bonner went through his routine of searching for a business card, then sat down at one of the tables and wrote on the back for half a minute, handed the card to Sarah.

"Want to read it to me?"

Sarah bit her lower lip, concentrating on his Rx-style handwriting, and stumbled through the message.

" 'To whom—it may concern: should the—rights of Sarah Dubray, a vested citizen of the state of Utah, be vi——violated, I will take a personal interest in the per—prosecution of the violator. Tobin T. Bonner.' "

"You don't have to be afraid of them. If either man comes up to you again, anywhere, just hand over my card."

"Well—I don't think my father will like that very much."

"I doubt if he liked that Mexican jailhouse well enough to want to repeat the experience. Now, maybe you can do something for me, Sarah."

She drew back just a little. "What?"

"I'm looking for your sister Ros."

Sarah took in a shocked breath. "But I don't know—I certainly don't have anything to do with *her*."

"When was the last time you saw Rosalind?"

"Oh—well—I don't even *know*."

"You have no idea where she might be living?"

"Of course not! Why would I? She's—the most hateful person I've ever known in my life. Worse than hateful. Evil." Sarah took another big breath, shoulders quaking. "What—what did she do this time?"

"I just want to ask her a few questions. But you can't remember when you saw her last."

"I'm not sure. She was gone for a long time. I think she was in Mexico. We never had anything to do with each other, after—"

"After?"

Sarah pulled her hand away from Shay's, clenched both hands in her lap.

"I don't want to say. It was personal. Degrading. I told you Ros was hateful."

"Were you afraid of Ros? When you were younger?"

"A lot of us were," she said, her blue eyes doing a slow remembering drift upward until they were only half-visible beneath the tweaking lashes.

"Would any of your sisters know where I could find her?"

"I don't think so. We never talk about her."

"Do you girls all live together in town?"

"Yes. But I'm not going there any more. I keep all of my valuable stuff—my cameras, my traveler's checks, a bracelet my best girlfriend gave me—in a locker at the airport. Shay said I could stay out at her father's ranch until I—decide what I'm going to do."

Bonner handed her his pen with another business card.

"Why don't you write down where you were living, and the names of a couple of your sisters I could talk to? One of them just might have some information about Ros that would be helpful to me."

Sarah's hands clenched tighter. She had gradually scooted around on the seat of her chair until she was nearly sideways to Bonner. She inhaled, so deeply and powerfully it was as if she were trying to levitate. She seemed to be appealing to Shay for something ungiveable, like the meaning of her life.

"I think it would be all right," Shay said gently.

Sarah trembled, then turned back to Bonner suddenly and, almost rudely, snatched pen and business card from him, folded her lips tightly against her teeth, and wrote, like some left-handers, with her hand warped oddly and secretively around the pen. She took her time.

"Here," she said, having finished. "But I'm sure they don't want to be bothered either with anything that has to do with Rosalind."

Bonner thanked her and tucked the card away.

"Shay, would you mind walking out with me?"

Shay glanced at Sarah, who said, "I'll stay with Pepper. Those burgers must be cold by now."

"There's a microwave in the nurses' lounge they'll probably let us borrow. Go ahead and eat something, Sarah, I won't be long."

She walked with Bonner down three floors from Pediatrics and out into a courtyard, the heat and glare like a blast furnace beyond the tree-shaded perimeter. Shay winced and shielded her eyes; she was wearing untinted contacts. Bonner offered her his sunglasses.

"Must be a hundred and two this afternoon," he said. "I've lived here a good part of my life; I'm used to it." He motioned to a bench. "Want to sit a minute? I won't keep you, busy day for me."

"There's something you didn't want to tell me upstairs?" Shay asked.

"Not in front of Sarah. I thought you ought to know more about Rhondo Dubray and the Brightly Shining."

"I think I know enough."

"You may not have grasped just how powerful the cult is, powerful in numbers and their fidelity to the creed. There may be five thousand of them in southern Utah alone, although the government has never attempted a census. Most of the Brightly Shining have been excommunicated by the Elders at One Temple Square for adhering to the Principle, which means polygamous marriages. But because Rhondo has his followers convinced that he is the one true Revelator, chosen and guided by Heavenly Father and Mother, they aren't suffering spiritually. Or materially. It's a rich cult. An estimate I heard recently was sixty million net worth. I don't have cause to doubt that. The Brightly Shining, through a complex of corporations, has large interests in or owns outright ranchland, nursing homes, construction companies, orchards, trucking concerns, and a couple of banks. Those are his legal activities. He was involved in wire fraud once, but beat the rap. For enough cash he'll break any law, being a law unto himself. Rhondo also has a history of ruthlessness—as many as twenty blood atonements during his power struggles with family members or rival sects, several of which he incorporated into the Brightly Shining. They own an entire town, New Hebron, which is down the road on the Arizona border, with the Grand Canyon in front of it and some impenetrable canyon-land behind. There are caves in those canyons I've only heard about, man-made caves for an underground fortress like NORAD in Colorado. On a smaller scale, of course; but it's also come to my ears that Rhondo has over twice the net worth of all his corporations invested in that Armageddon hidey-hole, which is still under construction. According to Rhondo's teachings, his town is to be the site of the new Zion, prophesized in Genesis and also the Book of Mormon, where there's going to be a final gathering of saints after various unpleasantness pertaining to the millennium is out of the way. Whatever that is, Rhondo is personally going to handle it, so I guess he bribed his way out of that Mexican prison just in time. By the way, according to sources I consider reliable, it cost Rhondo eight million in U.S. dollars to duck a kidnapping conviction that would have seen him hung for cohabitating in his Mexican enclave with the fourteen-year-old daughter of a PRI official. And another five million to get a twenty-year sentence for statuatory rape reduced to something over three on a lesser contributing-to-the-deliquency charge, which doesn't count for a hell of a lot in Mexico."

"Why should I care about Rhondo Dubray's problems?"

Bonner turned his lightly perspiring face into a breeze that swept through the sycamore and catalpa trees. He looked thoughtful but relaxed, pleased with himself somehow, taking pleasure in her company.

"I thought you'd find it interesting. Rhondo obviously has an ongoing need for cash. Bales of cash, because the millennium, as we know, is just around the corner, and his work probably is far from done. He's had a flock of marriageable girls like Sarah working to fill the coffers instead of making babies, but on the scale we're talking about their contributions don't amount to much. My guess is he's making arrangements to run dope again."

"Again?"

"He tried it before, but his distribution was lousy on this end—I mean it was one screwup after another. They made money for a while; you have to be terminally stupid or unlucky not to, unless you give the stuff away. But two of his sons were killed in Salt Lake, and one of the Brightly Shining's inner circle was busted in a sting operation down in Sonora. Amateurs, all of them. I called in somebody I had reason to suspect was in charge of Rhondo's air force, another amateur, and had a heart-to-heart talk with him. Maybe I saved his life, I don't know. I didn't owe him a damn thing, but I felt kind of bad for him. Life hadn't been treating him too well, since his heyday. Couldn't make ends meet; his wife and kid left him. I'm happy to say he did get himself straightened out after that. Now I only hope he's not mixed up in some other sorry business of Rhondo Dubray's."

Her expression was suddenly drab and he felt a little heartless for going about it this way.

"Oh, God. You're talking about—my father."

"The one and only Silverwhip. Shay, there were bloodstains on the seat of his truck. Don't know yet if the blood is animal or human. But they were recent."

"Oh, damn it," Shay said, with a lowering of her curly head. The nape of her neck looked bare and hot. She took off the sparkly brazen sunglasses Bonner had loaned her and cupped her eyes with one hand, fingertips digging into her brows, dislodging one of the butterfly bandages over the thin black half-inch of a healing cut. It was in this moment of her revealed vulnerability in the pitilessly bright day that he felt the full numbing sensation of love for Shay Waco. It felt exactly like loading up on three quick scotches. Double scotches. Not tipsy with desire, but heartily, sweetly drunk with love. It was a sensation he planned to cherish, even though he knew there was nothing he could or ever would do about it.

When he got back to the office, Bonner caught up on some business with the DA's office over the phone, then took from his desk drawer the envelope with the photos of Vida he had received in the mail. He turned over the one with the message on the back, took out the card he'd had Sarah Dubray inscribe for him, and looked at the handwriting for a couple of minutes before calling in his resident graphologist.

"I'm not sure, but I think these were written by the same person. She was trying to disguise her handwriting when she put these names on the back of my card. See what you think."

Mary Lynn pulled up a chair to a corner of his desk and angled the lamp closer while she studied the handwriting samples.

"Ugly sentiment," she commented, not turning over the photograph.

Bonner nodded, looked up a number, and called his bank. The vice president he wanted to talk to was away from his desk. Harry Rosser took one afternoon a week for golf and two hours of another afternoon to attend to his mistress. Bonner couldn't remember which day this was, tee-up or fuck. He made an appointment for the following morning. One more day probably wouldn't matter; he was already deep in default on the mortgage.

Mary Lynn made some notes on a legal pad, frowning.

Bonner went through a stack of memos. Another one from Emory, who was in charge of the twenty-two-deputy force at the overcrowded Solar County jail. The name Hanratty had come up again. Bonner remembered him. A few ounces of marijuana in a bedroll, something like that. Emory seemed to think the vagrant was worth talking to. Bonner checked his watch and decided against it; he'd send Del Cothern, once court adjourned for the day.

The button representing his private line lit up on the telephone console.

"Hey, Tobe."

"What's up, Neal?"

"Poppy said to me this morning, seems like a month of Sundays since we had Tobin over for dinner; doesn't he like us any more?"

"Did she? That was thoughtful of Poppy, but it probably hasn't been all that long."

"How about tonight?"

Bonner had already decided he was taking Shay Waco to dinner.

"I've made plans. Thank Poppy for me."

"Tomorrow night then." When he didn't hear an immediate objection Neal hastened to firm up the invitation. "Listen, we'll count on it. Seven-thirty? Been awhile since you and I have had a chance just to sit around and talk."

"Sure. Looking forward to it. Gotta go, Neal."

When he looked up after a few seconds of blank-faced contemplation, Mary Lynn was watching him.

"What's the matter?" she asked.

"I don't know. There are nuances that creep into Neal's voice. I could almost hear him cracking his knuckles over the phone. Maybe it's nothing."

She nodded, looked down at the handwriting samples.

"What d'you think?" Bonner asked.

"I'm eighty percent certain they were written by the same hand. The attempts to disguise weren't really worthwhile. Total inconsistency from one loop or *t* crossing to the next."

"She was trying to do it under my nose. I'd already scared the bejesus out of her, not intentionally. Her reaction was out of proportion when she laid eyes on me. As if she'd been anticipating I'd turn up."

"Guilty conscience, you mean? Anyway, she compresses the loops of her *e*'s and *s*'s, typically anal; the slant of both samples is nearly the same, the dots on the *i*'s miss by a letter or so, and on and on. The handwriting is generally immature, I might even say indicative of a highly repressed nature. You also have these little telltale smudges left-handers often leave, the edge of the palm rubbing across words before the ink is dry. What does she feel guilty about, Tobin?"

"Have a look at the photos."

Mary Lynn turned each one over, studied them quietly, read the inscription again, half aloud. " '*The black spawn of the devil lusts after our sacred daughters.*' " She looked up with a squeamish shrug. "Somebody, in my opinion, has severe emotional and sexual problems."

"I think the girl's hobby is photography. At least she mentioned stashing cameras for safekeeping in a locker at the airport."

"What's she like? On the surface."

"She has that anemic, blonde, teen-model appearance. Tall, small-boned. Kind of weepy, daze-y, pale blue eyes; they don't seem to express much of a solid personality. I might think drugs, but the ego is there. She keeps herself up. Hair and nails immaculate. When I cornered her into writing on the back of my card, something else popped out. Just briefly. Like a badger from its den, all tooth and claw. Matter of fact, I saw it twice. Before she turned tail and ran when we first bumped into each other. If she'd had a knife in her hand, I think instead of running she might have gone for my throat. A purely atavistic thing. I've seen it maybe three times in twenty-six years of law enforcement."

"From docile to homicidal quicker than you can swallow your spit. Uh-huh. I saw it too, when I was in psychiatric nursing. Before it turned out I had a screw loose myself."

"Extreme postpartum depression doesn't qualify as—"

"Crazy is as crazy does, so I was crazy," Mary Lynn said, with her lop-sided cynical smile. "Anyway, take some good advice and handle this one with care. That 'black spawn of the devil' crap is—"

"Maybe," Bonner said, "she was only writing what someone else made her write. Did I tell you her name? Sarah Dubray."

"Oh my God," Mary Lynn said. "*Another* one?"

"Yeah. The problem is, young Sarah has apparently become real close to a good friend of mine. Hey, I had this dream last night? You like hearing my dreams, don't you, Mary Lynn?"

"Wouldn't miss one for the world."

"It was a campaigning-for-office dream. Parade, or something. Anyway, there were mobs of people, all familiar faces, I guess everybody who's ever voted for me in the past. Family, friends, people I've known for years, who I'm comfortable with. I can't describe how secure I felt. Almost to the point of tears from happiness as I went around handing out my flyers, accepting congratulations as if I'd already won. Then I saw they were all puppets. Jaws clacking up and down, puppet eyes rolling, grinning puppet grins. They made a kind of roaring noise, like incoming rockets. There was a lot of puppet string all braided into one thick rope, which went into a tunnel under the middle of the street. I knew there must be a maze of tunnels, although I hadn't known about them before, and that something way down there in the dark was controlling all the puppets. I was afraid to look. I didn't want to be sheriff anymore. I took off my badge and my gun and my medals, and I walked away. The puppets were just lying around lifelessly all over town. The sun was blinding me. I looked at my feet, and they were puppet feet flopping a couple of inches off the ground, not touching. I felt a tug on the string that was attached to the back of my neck and fell backward into the tunnel. I woke up in a sweat in a rocking chair in my son's room, goggle-eyed fish swimming all around. I had bitten my tongue; it's still pretty damn sore. What do you think? Is that one in your book of dreams?"

Mary Lynn said, after a few seconds, "It's probably the feds; they have you frustrated."

"Yeah, I guess so."

"And maybe you simply want to change your life."

"Maybe I do. Part of it, anyway. Make a reservation for two tonight at L'Cerbiàttolo. Eight o'clock. And since I'm a little short this week, tell Dominic to bill the department."

13

THE SALOON WAS ALWAYS known as the Crystal Chandelier. During its heyday, lasting until the late sixties, there was a bar fight every afternoon at three-thirty, followed by a shoot-out in the street at four. The sound of the six-shooters, firing blanks but still noisy, so disturbed the hens on the chicken farm across the road from Silverwhip Jack Waco's western town and rodeo that they all went berserk and died. A lawsuit was filed, but by then Jack's town was closed, his wild west show defunct, Jack himself nearly bankrupt. There was a war on, a war that had provoked social revolution, and campy western Americana was passé. In 1978, a landslide from the mountain behind the town buried half of it under rubble and slabs of rock the size of house trailers. The Crystal Chandelier went untouched, although Jack's infirm movie horse Lucky, thirty-two years of age, was wiped out while nose down in a feedbag.

A year later Rhondo Dubray bought the property cheap, but made no effort to redevelop it.

Ros has redecorated since moving into the Crystal Chandelier, throwing out the musty mooseheads and whatever furnishings remained, shoring up the second-floor gallery, restoring the curved mahogany bar, and replacing shards of backbar mirrors with new stained glass, a motif of white tigers and black leopards in green jungle. She rewired the drafty building herself, installed heating and air-conditioning and plantation shutters on the Palladian windows, at the staircase landing and over the saloon's entrance doors.

But she can't seem to be rid of the flies, or find out how they are getting in. She has made the refurbished Crystal Chandelier as snug as a bank vault. But the flies keep coming. Right now she is distracted by flies like floating bullets within a slanted pillar of white sunlight and two more of them, oily, electric green, crawling across the face of her sixty-inch TV, in a corner below the staircase where the player piano used to be.

In exasperation Ros puts the tape she's watching on hold and gets up from her hammock to fetch another Dos Equis from the refrigerator behind the bar.

Frozen on the screen is the reverse of a cameo: that richly black, Nubian face in a nimbus of tropical waters. The patient, peering eyes, Priapian temple bones that seem to Ros, after repeated viewings, about to bring forth horns.

Ros sprinkles a little more sugar water on the square of flypaper she has hoped will attract the monsters, and returns to her wide, woven macramé hammock with the Dos Equis. Some fly spray would do the trick, but Ros is brutally allergic. She stretches out long legs in the hammock. Her legs have a smooth, honeyed glaze; her toes, each with three knuckles, are as long as her fingers. She sips beer and restarts the tape.

The Camcorder is a good one, automatically compensating for the hand tremors of the youthful operator Ros dispatched to the sheriff's house the night before. There is a blurred vertical window-pane to one side of the frame, but the images of Vida, captured through a bedroom window, are rock steady.

That beautiful black body: the mesmerizing menace of major muscle groups in play. Ros scratches a nipple, thoughtfully, through the fabric of the tank top she's wearing, then suddenly bears down, pinching herself hard. Her eyes are in reverie, betraying no pain. She freezes the tape again. This time the view is of Vida's rippling back, arrested in midstride.

Charmaine, handing over the Camcorder, had said to Ros, "Watching him walking around in his Jockey shorts, I swear I had all I could do to keep my other hand off my pussy."

Ros said, "Charmaine, you hate boons. That's why you left Bogalusa."

And Charmaine said, "Yeah, but I always wanted to get fucked by one. Just before I blew his nigger brains out."

Not this one, Ros thinks, although she's more or less in agreement with Charmaine's visceral reaction. *I need him.*

From what she has seen of Vida so far, he's not a retard. There is intelligence in Vida's rapt face. He sketches incessantly. Yet Ros already knows that he lives a near-monastic existence, only leaving the house to jog along the Virgin River, always deep into the purple twilights of the painted canyonland.

The shaft of dizzying sun that slants down through a round skylight Ros put in while having the old tinderbox shake roof replaced makes the normal midafternoon dimness of a shuttered place seem sepulchral by contrast. The slowly shifting brightness has begun to interfere with her viewing of the tape, which she's already seen four times. She shuts off the VCR and yawns. There is a black stone vase, lyre shaped, atop the massive TV, white roses in the vase. Touched by the sun, they look incandescent.

Rosalind's cell phone rings.

"Yeah?" She listens, frowning slightly. "Tell him he has to wait a few minutes; I just got up."

Up on the gallery, KayCee leans toward the light with half-closed eyes as if she is about to drink from a waterfall. She has pulled on an extra large Rahowa T-shirt after rolling out of bed; it drapes her past the knees. Rahowa, for RAcial HOly WAr. Like all the girls in Rosalind's orbit she has affected a short hair style. KayCee's is dyed lavender, with a single black streak of lightning across the top of her head.

"Dads is coming out of it," she says.

Ros turns off the TV, finishes her beer, and goes upstairs.

Silverwhip Jack Waco is sitting on the edge of the bed in one of the plainly furnished rooms, holding his head. He is naked. His knees are apart. A limp condom with its plummet of semen hangs from the end of his cock.

"Oh, Jesus," he says softly, repeating it three or four times. His eyes are closed. KayCee hops on the bed beside him and snuggles a breast up into his sweatily matted gray armpit. Jack winces.

"Somebody tell me where I am."

"You're home, Jack," Ros says. "The Crystal Chandelier. Remember the Crystal Chandelier?"

"Oh, Jesus. What happened to me?"

"You got drunk, Jack. Tied one on in a biker bar outside of Renaldo Springs."

"The Mesquiteer?"

"You bet."

Jack turns his head, the back of his neck cracking audibly.

"Ros? Is that you, Ros?"

"Get his eyes open, KayCee. One eye anyway."

KayCee pries apart sticky pink lids with the thumb and forefinger of one hand.

"Who are you?" Jack says to her, beginning to quake.

"KayCee."

"How *old* are you?"

"Old enough to know better; too young to give a shit," KayCee says merrily.

"Oh, Jesus."

"You going to live, Jack?" Rosalind asks.

"I hope not. How did I get here?"

"McMurtry gave me a holler when you started getting belligerant and driving his customers away. You're way past the legal age limit for getting the shit stomped out of you in the parking lot."

"I don't remember." Jack begins to cough, wrapping his arms around himself. "How long've I—"

"Two days."

"Honey," Jack says to KayCee, "don't lean on me; that's a good girl."

KayCee pinches his stubbly cheek and says, "You old fucker." She bounces off the bed and winks at Rosalind. Ros thumbs her from the room and leans against the doorjamb, arms folded high, her head in profile like that of a mute, avid lioness. Her hair is as red as Raggedy Ann's, but neater.

Jack is coughing again.

"There's a pan under the bed. Don't get sick on my floor; I don't want to clean up after you."

Jack runs fingers through his full floaty head of hair, which in spite of not having been washed for three days is like soft down from a pillow. He sags back slowly, breathing in broken-down rhythms. Except for the gray pelvic smudge like ashes from a long-dead fire and gnarly chest hair, he has the lean, toned body of a much younger man. Ros didn't have to promise KayCee the moon to sleep with him.

"Why'd you do it, Jack?"

"Do what?"

"Go on a bender."

His mouth fumbles for justification. One ice-blue eye wanders, hauntingly.

"I didn't mean. Hell, maybe I did. My daughter's coming. It's been, I don't know. Twenty years. All of a sudden I got cold feet or something. What day is it?"

"Thursday."

"Thursday! No. Christ! She's *here* already. My granddaughter, too."

"I believe they are. Ran into a little difficulty is what I heard."

Jack tries to lift his head, but can't keep it off the mattress for more than a couple of seconds. The pounding in his temples is excruciating. "What d'you mean, Ros?"

"Oh, you'll find out. Want coffee?"

"Hell's fire. I *really* want some coffee."

"Take it easy. I'll send KayCee up."

"That girlie? Ros? Did we—"

"From the looks of things."

"But she's a kid."

"So what? You had fun, and KayCee doesn't mind. I guess you're still quite a stud, even with all that bourbon in you. This is the second time I've looked out for you, Whip-man. You know I always keep book. So right now you owe me a couple, huh, Jack?"

Jack gets his head and shoulders up, the cords of his runneled throat standing out.

"What do you mean? What do you want from me, Ros?" His croaky voice is in a depth beyond desperate.

"I was going to do Jimmy a favor, but he decided to send his own team. So you're off the hook for now, I guess; but sober up, who knows when I'll give you a call. You can still fly, can't you, Jack?"

"Hell, yes, I can fly."

"So drink your coffee, use the spa I put in, hang around until your head feels better. Then I'll have one of the ironheads call Tom Leucadio to pick you up."

"Tom? I don't want him to know that you and me—"

"Oh, shit, Jack. You'd be surprised what Tom knows. We'll leave you off down the road then. Hitch a ride home, if you want to."

"I can drive myself home."

Ros looks back at him as she is closing the door.

"Forgot to tell you. Somebody took your truck while you were boozing it at the Mesquiteer. Used the Silverado in the commission of a crime. Five killings. No problem for you, though. You have one of those ironclad alibis, as they're called. You were doing bourbon, cocaine, and pussy-wussy with a fifteen-year-old runaway from Michigan City, Indiana. Man, don't that turn back the clock. See ya, Jack."

Rosalind is halfway along the gallery toward the stairs when she hears Jack throwing up violently. But from the sound of it he has managed to get the pan out from under the bed in time. Ros grins. Thoughtful of Jack, but they have always, with a few lapses here and there, enjoyed that kind of relationship.

●

Ros is on the roofed porch of the Crystal Chandelier nursing another half-frozen Dos Equis and taking in the view north to the high red walls of the national park, only a mile on up the road. Over the looping razor wire that tops an eight-foot stockade fence surrounding Silverwhip Jack's western town she can see the traffic, almost bumper-to-bumper, and a lot of it RVs or trailers behind pickup trucks, all of the vehicles burdened with bicycles, kayaks, trail bikes, towed compact cars, or ATVs. Tourists winding their way along the last mile of blacktop to the national park's southern port of entry, where, by 9:00 A.M. on a summer's morning there already is no room for them.

The Easterners drive up from the high-security gate, park near the hitching post and concrete water trough, which is full to overflowing, and get out of the rental sedan. They get out and seem immediately to wilt a little in the intense heat. She's wearing wraparound sunglasses, a head scarf, and zinc oxide on her nose.

Rosalind lifts a hand in lazy greeting.

"Come on up. Set a spell, neighbors."

Katharine Harsha walks up the steps to the porch, with Dale Stearman behind her.

"Dale? Gimme kiss," Ros commands, sitting up in her rocker and tilting her face toward him.

His lips brush her cheek; he squeezes a collarbone lightly.

"Long time, man. Who's this?"

"Katharine Harsha. I'm a government investigator."

"I didn't think your occupation was 'spouse,' " Rosalind says. "Could you guys cozy up to a brew?"

"Yes," Dale says, fervently.

"Katharine, there's a refrigerator behind the bar inside. And use my bathroom downstairs if you need to freshen up."

"Thank you," Katharine says, after a long moment and a glance at Stearman behind her dark glasses. He shrugs with his right shoulder. Katharine goes inside.

"Where'd you get *her*, man?" Ros asks idly, recrossing her booted feet on the railing in front of her.

"DIA loan-out. She came highly recommended."

"Clothes are dusty. Looks a little frazzled."

"They had an accident on the way to New Hebron this morning."

"Don't tell me!"

"Falling rock. One of the rocks took out the front end of the car they were driving. Right up to the firewall."

"It's been known to happen. Falling rock. In a particular canyon I'm thinking about. Haven't been down that way in years myself. But you know, the approach is posted. Used to be a big sign. English and Spanitch: 'Y'all stop here, call ahead for an escort.' Otherwise, rocks have a way of falling on the unwary or the uninvited."

"Now we know."

"Too bad they never made it into town. I don't suppose it's changed very much, except Pappy's spent years lining all those caves with concrete. I hear the womenfolk still wear the ankle-length calico skirts I had to wear when I was a kid. Try taking a pee in a hurry when you're wearing one of those. Sunbonnets, shit. Quaint as a curtsy."

"You still have a way about you, Ros."

She shows him a genial face. Dark Elysia of her eyes, the jutting prognathic grin.

" 'Always the dullness of the fool is the whetstone of the wits.' Which play's that from? For each wrong answer, two points will be deducted from your IQ."

"I don't know."

"*As You Like It.* I'm named after her, I mean Rosalind from the play. It's the only thing my mother ever did right. My IQ's one-eighty-five. Not bad, for a seventh-grade education. I can read three thousand words a minute. I'm also polyglot: Spanish, Japanese, Far-see, Greek—I learned each language in a few months, depending on who I was hanging out with. I took that MENSA test, which is how I found out how smart I really am. Certified fucking intellectual. I'm what you call an autodidact. Self-educated. I'm also a self-fashioner. I evolve through sensation, the more intense the better. Have you read Michel Foucault? Never mind, you're probably too political and repressive to get any of his philosophy."

"I hear Jimmy reads a lot now."

"Yeah, he does. I turned him onto books, just another way of getting him through the night when he couldn't crank it up any more. Steel Arm, Jell-O dick. It happens when they start thinking about their mortality, and the Last Judgment. Speaking of sex, I gave Jimmy his first blow job. Some men are squeamish about that. Did it bother you to have yours between these teeth of mine? Must have, for all the results we got. My gnathic index is only one-oh-five. That's way below average for *Australopithecus afarensis.* For example. I could have it fixed, but I like my scary grin. You look down in the dumps, Dale. Cheerfulness keeps up a kind of daylight in the mind. I forget who said it. Let's get something out of the way, all right? I didn't kill them. I'm not into offing people, particularly little kids; besides, I kind of liked Gabriel. He told me once he had some gypsy blood in him. That gave me palpitations, for some reason."

"Do you know who killed them?" Katharine Harsha asks, coming out of the saloon with three cold beers.

"Hey, you look perkier there, Katharine. But stay out of the sun with that camellialike complexion. My other words of advice, don't go near my apocalyptic Pappy. That stretch in jail did in what was left of his rational mind. He's paranoid about the government as it is. More than rocks could fall on your head. A beer for me, how thoughtful. Now don't annoy me, Kate, the prettiest Kate in Christendom. I'm talking to Dale here because he's an old friend, and Dale *only.* Maybe you and I can hook up later, when you're off the clock. Have some laughs, get loose and dirty with each other, scratch where it itches."

Katharine smiles, a lips-together smile fixed to her face like a leech.

Ros links an arm with Stearman's.

"Come on. I'll show you around the place."

There is a rumbly murmur on the road, powerful engines in barely moving traffic toward the national park. Some vehicles coming back, southbound. No room. The visitors will be waved through or turned away. Eventually the vibrations from the road will bring down another chunk of red cliff that looms over Silverwhip Jack's old town.

"How long have you been back?" Stearman asks as he and Rosalind walk with their beers, seeking the shade from false-front buildings labeled DRY GOODS and STAGE LINE and ROOMS TO LET. There's a tiny church and a fake graveyard and a rebuilt stable. On the front wall of the stable, over the wide entrance, is a faded, chalk-pale painting of Jack in full cowboy-hero dress, ten feet tall, lashing out at an unseen 'dog heavy.' Two kids with bald, sweaty heads, wearing AB hate broadsides in tattoo form—dozens of intricate tattoos—are working on the disassembled engine of a motorcycle in front of the stable. They give Stearman looks.

"About six months."

"What brings you home?"

"I don't know, really. Acting on some kind of migratory impulse, I guess. No motive. No plans."

"Yeah? Have you seen much of Rhondo?"

"He just got out, what, three months ago? No, I haven't seen much of him."

"You arranged it, though. You and Jimmy."

"Humanitarian impulse," Ros says with a hard grin. "Pappy's bearings were burned out. He's got a terminal case of the shakes. He's afraid he won't make it to Endtimes. Well, isn't that sad. What's Pappy got to do with your interests?"

"What do you think?"

"Pappy's version of Endtimes? I've been hearing about it for years. It won't happen."

"It's a lot easier these days than we let on to the general public."

"Man, you are really scaring me."

"Good. You should be scared."

Ros tilts her bottle of Dos Equis way back, staring at him as she drinks.

"I still don't get your interest in all this."

"I'm a guvmint employee. Occasionally we guvmint employees need to do a little work to justify our bloated budgets."

Ros is tickled. "Jimmy says you're a government all to yourself. What's the catchphrase? No accountability. That's Never-Never Land, practically. Even Jimmy is a little scared of you. No, I take it back. The only thing that scares Jimmy is the Great Hereafter. Isn't that sick-making?"

"I guess Steel Arm's last checkup didn't let a lot of daylight into his mind."

"He never said. But you could see his brain turning to shit. He's begun to sense that he's led a deeply flawed life. He sees priests. He's no fun anymore. I try to give him a lift once in a while. Send him four-footed presents. He calls me up, two or three nights a week, three in the morning; we talk until dawn. You can see I'm a wreck from lack of sleep."

Rosalind suddenly takes Stearman by his free hand and tugs him gaily toward an air-conditioned steel utility building sitting by itself inside a separate electrified fence. There are two German shepherds on guard duty. Ros opens the gate with a card key.

"I kind of like your little gal-pally from Defense Intelligence. But if you've got designs, I'll leave her be."

"Don't let me stand in your way, Ros. So you wandered home from Mexico, leaving a grieving Jimmy behind."

"Mexico's too damn full of Mexicans to suit me."

"How long were you with Jimmy?"

"Oh, that's sweet. 'With' Jimmy. That's adorable. Since I met him in Vegas, more or less."

"Did Jimmy post the D and B on Gabriel Sinaloa?"

"Not a chance. As I said, he's been preoccupied. That thing he's growing in the middle of his brain may turn out to be a conscience, before it kills him."

"But of course he knew where Gabe was."

"Sure."

"You told him."

"Sure. When I found out Gabe's true identity."

"How?"

"He talks in his sleep, asshole, what'ya think. Give me a hand with this door?"

Together they roll the steel door, a little wider than the trailer of an 18-wheeler, aside. The shaded lights overhead are muted. In the middle of the cool utility building, taking up two-thirds of the concrete floor area, is a five-ton customized truck with the Simba Spring Ranch logo on it: the lithe body of a black jungle cat in full eclipsing leap across a big red sun. In a corner of the building is a small cage filled with baby chicks.

Stearman can tell from the odor what's in the truck before he sees it. He's not sure he wants to see it, but what the hell; he's already seen the stolen truck.

Ros turns to him with an engaging grin, finger to her lips.

"Thanks, Ros, now I'm an accessory. It won't look good on my year-end review."

"I just wanted to show him to you. God, but he's beautiful."

"Time you got over your Siegfried and Roy phase."

"I'll always be an animal lover."

"You send them to Jimmy."

"Jimmy's an animal lover, too. He's scrupulous about how he kills them. They get more than a sporting chance. This one, though, I've had second thoughts, you know? I think I'm in love."

Stearman stands well back as Rosalind opens up the traveling cage. Just like her to let the 180-pound jaguar spring out of there, confident of her ability to control any creature in any situation. Let it loose to see him flinch, gain a minor edge in the relationship. He watches her in exasperation and, perversely, admiration.

(When Ros was sane, she was a charmer. In any of her other, morbidly errant states, she appealed to the recklessness that lies deep and fatally in the hearts of most men. Obviously Ros had not been a labor of love; she believed her underage mother had secretly cursed her before she was born—born in the image of her polygamous old man, with the doomsday belligerance, the sharp, cunning intellect of the congenitally depraved. Her life was informed by jumping-bean realities on a hotbed of psychopathology, fueled by a schemer's input of intrigue, lust, and duplicity. She was whimsically ruthless and morally brutal. Stearman's own ethics were priestly by comparison. He'd always been hot for Ros,

which she accepted as her due. Twice during fits of self-loathing he'd thought about having her killed, in spite of her usefulness professionally. Ros knew and doted on his quandary.)

With the back doors of the truck open, there is a gust from inside the cage, pure feral animal. His pulse rate elevates. He barely notices Rosalind peeling her tank top off over her head. The jaguar inside is lying down. It reacts slightly to the sound of Rosalind purring. No flicker in the almond-shaped yellow eyes. But Stearman has a vivid sense of the animal's savage heart, beating within the most frightening darkness imaginable. The jaguar is simply waiting, alert but unalarmed, perhaps waiting for Ros as she finishes undressing.

"Ros, what the hell are you *doing?*"

"Going inside for a little while. I'm going to lie down with Marco Polo. Maybe have a little nap. I told you, Jimmy's been wearing me out on the phone. I'm his only confidant. They have this gizmo called a gamma knife, which turns brain tumors into scrambled eggs. No invasive surgery. There's a gamma knife at the Med Center. I've been trying to talk Jimmy up here to give it a shot, but he thinks doctors exist just to punch his ticket to the tomb."

Stearman has seen Ros naked once before, the only time, the time he failed her. The scar like a pink serpent on one flank, motorcycle accident. Claw marks on one shoulder and her ribcage. Old scars. Her prehensile feet, racy long legs and elevated nipples. A long look over one shoulder at him, *remember?*

"Do you have your gun?" Rosalind says.

"Yes. Now listen, Ros, don't—"

Ros smiles.

"It's not for *my* sake. It's for yours, Dale. Marco Polo might be a teensy jealous. Another male around, you know. So take some advice. I saw a lion maul a man once. A jaguar's bite is worse. They have the largest canines of all the big cats. The advice is, put a bullet in your head before he gets to you. I mean, you know. Should it come to that."

"You crazy bitch."

"Love you too, sweetie. If we're both around later, how about dinner? I know a fabulous place."

"Where are Gabriel's tapes, Rosalind?"

Her shoulders sag for a few moments; she winces in annoyance.

"I don't have them. What difference does it make? EndTimes is a load of horseshit. Pappy's been conned out of millions, and that

Eurotrash arms dealer will keep on conning him, even though Suchary is dead."

"The Aum Shinrikyo are different. Worse than Hamas. They've probably already detonated a crude nuclear device underground in Australia. If they've been led to believe Rhondo has something even better, they'll kill to get their hands on it."

"It's a myth, Stearman. There's no device. The Dove don't fly. Suchary couldn't make it work. And if he couldn't, nobody can."

Stearman straightens and steps back, looking slightly glazed, as if accepting a mandatory eight-count. He breathes deeply, staring at her.

Rosalind grins, conciliatory.

"Maybe," she says, "I'll give you enough to put some people away for a while, if that'll take the heat off Pappy. We'll talk about it later." She strolls confidently toward the back of the truck, with that erotic sass and flagrant hip flaunt, so enticingly obscene. "That is, if I'm in a nice-enough mood."

●

Silverwhip Jack Waco comes slowly down the stairs inside the Crystal Chandelier, holding onto the railing. He wears his hat and carries his boots and there is a towel around his waist. Three steps from the bottom he notices Katharine Harsha. Stops.

"Hello."

"Hello."

"I was—you don't know where the sauna is, do you?"

"Sorry."

"Ros said there was one."

"Maybe back there," Katharine says, with a gesture.

"Okay." He limps down the remaining steps, stumbles, drops a boot, picks it up, grabs his towel as it is slipping.

"Sorry."

"Don't mind me."

"Friend of Ros's?"

"No."

"I'm Jack. Jack Waco. I used to be in movies."

Katharine nods, thoughtfully.

"But you'd be too young to remember me," Jack says, with a

slight injured knitting together of his still-dark eyebrows, too aware of his flimsy status in the gale of Time that howls around his ears.

"I'm sorry, I don't."

"Well, I'll just see if I can locate that sauna."

"Have a good one."

"Thanks."

Katharine watches the white-haired old man walk, painfully, through a doorway and down a hall at the rear of the Crystal Chandelier. She looks up as a fly circles annoyingly close to her head, then back into the wide shaft of sun, lighting up suddenly like a blip on a pinball machine. She turns and walks slowly out of the saloon and puts her shades on and after looking around for some sign of Dale Stearman stands with her arms folded, eyes hurting even behind the sunglasses, bridge of her nose simmering beneath its coat of zinc oxide. Every inch of exposed skin feels hot, her armpits are damp, she has a rash on her belly and pelvic area.

She is waiting for Stearman, but she is thinking about Rosalind Dubray. Katharine can't stop thinking about her. The back of her throat is dry. She has a doctorate in International Studies from Harvard. She was all-American in field hockey at Swarthmore. She is good at her work, commended by her superiors. Her parents adore Katharine. Her ex-lovers, both of them, speak well of her. Nobody, *nobody* has ever made her feel inadequate.

The sun. How she hates the goddamn sun.

14

IT WAS PEPPER WHO finally persuaded Shay to accept Tobin Bonner's invitation to dinner.

"I'll be okay," she insisted. The nausea had passed and she had eaten her own dinner, cleaned her plate in fact, and also the small dish of orangey pudding that came with a peanut-butter cookie, candy icing and M&M's making a face of it. Pepper saved the cookie for later. They had removed the IV and brought in a wheelchair in case she felt like going down the hall to the rec room to socialize with other ambulatory patients on the Pediatrics floor. The swelling of her knee had been reduced with ice packs. Pepper was getting used to the throbbing pain. And, truthfully, she was a little tired of her mother's company. She wanted to listen to music on her new headphones and watch game shows on TV. She had chatted with her maternal grandmother, who lived in Sausalito and operated an antiques shop with two other women. Shay nixed a call to Liam, who was just about inaccessible on the other side of the world, but promised Pepper a chance to phone her best friend, Angela, in North Hollywood, brag about her surgery and catch up on the gossip.

Shay went back to the Comfort Inn at seven to freshen up and change clothes. Pepper watched *The Simpsons.* At seven-forty the phone rang.

"Hello?"

"Hello." A voice she didn't recognize. He cleared his throat a couple of times. "Who's this?"

"Pepper."

"Oh, Pepper. This's your grandpa."

"It *is*? Where are you?"

"Well, I'm out of town right now. But I'm coming home soon. Maybe tonight. I heard about what happened. You doing okay?"

"Yeah. I had knee surgery this morning."

Hectic coughing and a winded sigh. "Knee surgery, how about that. Can you walk?"

"On crutches. I get them tomorrow."

"Listen, I sure am sorry, sweetheart. About not being there."

"That's okay."

"Is your mom handy? I reckon I ought to—"

"No, Mom went out. She went to dinner."

"She did. Uh-huh. You know what? I'm gonna buy you a horse. That's a promise. This yearling filly I've had my eye on for a while. Would you like that, your own horse?"

"Sure!"

"Well, you take it easy, darlin'. Real good to hear your voice. I'll see you soon."

"Where—?" Pepper alertly wanted a phone number, knowing it would be the first thing her mother would ask—it was the drill around their house, phone calls often meant money in the bank. *Always get the number*. But Silverwhip Jack had hung up with a signature fit of coughing. Wasn't her fault. Anyway, he'd said he was coming home right away.

Pepper had cut the sound on *Married—with Children* and didn't put it back on, an episode she'd seen already. She thought about having her own horse, a happy surge of anticipation after a lethargic day. There was only a slight tingle of doubt to spoil the rosy picture. Where would she keep it—they lived in a two-bedroom bungalow on a quarter-acre lot. But what Granpa probably meant was the horse would be *hers*, only he would take care of it. Then she could come up on vacations from school or spend summers here.

Pepper had a choice of bedpan or jump on one foot as far as the bathroom. She chose bathroom and made it inside, but the exertion left her feeling swarmy-cold and light-headed. She rested awhile on the john before returning three awkward jumps back to the bed. She lay down with her heart pounding and soon fell asleep.

At nine o'clock a nurse came in for blood pressure and pulse check, and asked if she wanted anything. Fruit juice. Pepper drank the tepid apple juice and dozed, intermittently waking up to the low sounds of TV laughter, the abrupt voice of someone walking by in the hall outside.

The next time she woke up, there was a Rockies baseball game on the wall-mounted TV, and someone was climbing into bed with her.

Pepper jerked violently, then relaxed when she heard a gleeful hiccuppy laugh. She had been lying almost flat with her bandaged knee elevated; she raised her head from the pillows. Gleam of spaced baby teeth and spit bubbles; borealis of TV light around the infant's curly head.

"Cym! What are you doing here?"

Cymbeline was a tireless climber, and even more peripatetic than the average 20-month-old. She had escaped the confines of the nursery on several occasions, but had never made it as far as Pepper's room, which was nearly at the other end of the hall from the nursery. She'd had to pass the nurses' station in order to get there.

Somebody, Pepper thought, *isn't paying much attention tonight.*

"Cym, I can't play right now—no, stay on this side; you'll hurt my knee. You'll make Pepper cry." Pepper's mouth folded down and she blotted pretend tears from one eye.

Cymbeline reached over and wiped the other eye solicitously. "*No llora,*" she said, then pointed at the tray beside the bed. "Papuh cookie?" eyeing the cellophane-wrapped treat. She started to crawl along the edge of the bed. Pepper put an arm around her so she wouldn't fall off. Cym looked at her.

"Yeah, okay. Party time. I'll split the cookie with you. But I better let them know where you are."

The call button alerted the nurses' station in the center of the Pediatrics floor and also turned on a pulsing light above the door outside. Having summoned someone to put Cymbeline back to bed in the nursery, Pepper unwrapped the cookie the little girl had her eyes on and broke it in half.

"Peanut butter," she said.

"Peen buh," Cym repeated, taking a bite.

Pepper wiped her slobbery chin with a tissue when Cymbeline was finished, brushed cookie crumbs onto the floor, and wondered where everybody was. She pushed the call button again. Maybe it wasn't working. The sound on the TV was off. The door to her room stood open a few inches. Usually there was some traffic in the hall, even after ten o'clock, or voices. Tonight it was utterly still out there.

Pepper looked at the wheelchair at the foot of the bed.

"Cym? Want to go for a ride?"

She wasn't understood. Too many English words at one time.

"Rye?"

"In the wheelchair. If I can get myself into it. Here, why don't you get down for a minute, okay? I'll try to work this out."

When Pepper put her hands in the child's armpits to lift her to the floor, Cymbeline's face bunched.

"It's all right. *No problemo*. We're going for a ride. Good girl. *Good* girl. I'm coming. See? Pepper's trying to get out of bed, but her knee hurts."

"Hurds."

"Yeah," Pepper said, gritting her teeth as she put one foot on the floor. "But I'll make it. You just stay put, Cym."

"Cym!" the little girl said ecstatically.

"That's you, punkin."

Pepper made her way to the foot of the bed and got a hand on the back of the wheelchair, pulled it toward her. That much exertion had her out of breath. She bumped the bandaged knee slightly on the bed frame and knew exactly what was meant by seeing stars. For a few moments she couldn't move at all, tears trickling down her cheeks.

When she could move again, she manuevered the wheelchair closer and sat down suddenly, bandaged leg outstretched.

"Made it. Come here, Cym. Climb up in my lap."

The little girl didn't budge. Pepper sighed and held out her arms, wondering when her mother was going to be back from dinner. If she'd stayed away this long, did that mean she was having a good time?

Cymbeline got Pepper's message and toddled closer. Pepper hoisted the girl into her lap, weight on her left thigh.

"That wasn't so tough. Let's get us turned around. Hold on to me. How do you say it in Spanish? I don't know. Ready?"

Using the wheelchair was easier than she'd anticipated. Chrome handgrips outside the wheels. Steering wasn't hard, pull on one wheel or the other to turn. Roll backward, turn, roll forward. Cymbeline liked it, settling back against Pepper.

Open the door wider, out into the silent hall. Turn.

No one in sight, at the nurses' station or farther down the hall.

Pepper heard a couple of TVs behind nearly closed doors. Mop and bucket against the wall past the nurses' station, a swirling gleam of still-wet floor. Someone moaning fitfully behind another door as Pepper rolled slowly down the hall. The girl had come in the day before, pelvic surgery, her quarterhorse had stumbled and fallen on her. Pepper knew that two-thirds of the rooms on the floor were occupied, and no matter how late it was, there should have been parents around. In the rooms with their kids, or taking a break in the lounge, chatting with each other about their children or their medical coverage. And at least three nurses on duty, always.

The elevator door was open, but there was no one inside.

So where had everybody gone?

She was still wondering about that when a man walked out of the nursery into the hall, turned toward them, and stopped.

Pepper, tiring again, braked the wheelchair.

He was ordinary looking, even though he wore earrings. Dark Hispanic, a little plump, brush-cut hair. The shirt was flashy, a scratch print in gold and black, unbuttoned past his breastbone. He wore a navy blue blazer with a crest on the breast pocket. He rubbed one deeply sagging eyelid with a knuckle and looked morosely at Pepper and Cymbeline. He sighed and nodded, raised a hand and beckoned. It signaled a change in his manner, to the sort of arrogant authority some adults conveyed when in the presence of kids.

"*Traeme la muchacha,*" he said to Pepper.

Pepper didn't understand the language, but his gesture was plain enough.

She looked around quickly; still no one was there. No one except the Hispanic man, who didn't appear to be a doctor. Although he was more than fifty feet away she could smell his potent aftershave, as if it had saturated the air like fresh oil paint while he was on the floor. A fluorescent bulb flickered like a flawed nerve overhead. Cym pointed at the man and said something unintelligible in her own nascent Spanish.

The man grimaced impatiently and gestured again. "*Ven acá.*"

A woman walked briskly out of a room behind him. She was tall, with skimmed-back, moussed black hair and elliptical eyes. She was sliding something that looked to Pepper like a gun into a citrus-colored leather shoulder bag.

"Esta ella?" she said to the man as she walked past him. He nodded.

She kept going, long strides, past the nurses' station, intent on Pepper and little Cym. The soles of her running shoes made rapid-fire sticking sounds on the asphalt tile squares of the floor.

Something came unstuck in Pepper's breast; fear beat against her rib cage like a trapped bat. She turned the wheelchair sharply left and rolled it onto the large elevator. The door was wedged open, she'd seen that, but there was no chance of escape anyway. The only thing she had time to do was reach out and hit the red alarm button.

Shay hadn't wanted to go, nothing to wear, etc.; then she didn't expect to have a good time, just be polite, eat, and run. But the Italian restaurant, in a converted home at the upper end of West Valley Boulevard, was intimate and not too effusively charming, a one-violin establishment with a good wine list. She had grown up knowledgeable about wine; one of her relatives was a Sonoma County vintner.

A glass of Castello di Fonterutoli smoothed the jagged edges of a trying day; she was able, after a half hour or so, and a second glass of the deep purple wine, to focus on Tobin Bonner. Gradually, while they worked their way through the expectable small talk, she altered perceptions based on what she'd seen of him while he was on the job. The cop eyes, a gray that could chill, softened with drink and let her in, to the threshold of the place in every worthwhile man that was secluded in personal mystery.

"How did you get into stunt work?"

"My background. Loved movies. When I got bored with high-school gymnastics and was looking for a way to earn some money, it was a natural transition."

"Lot of risk involved."

"A psychologist I dated told me there's a hierarchy of risk in nearly everyone's life. Risks beyond our control are scarier than those we take charge of. I take charge. Framing the risk in terms of injury or even death instead of achievement affects the judgment. Isn't that true in police work?"

"Now that you mention it. What's the best stunt you've ever done?"

"One I've never done for the cameras. But I win a lot of bets on locations. Okay, I stand barefoot on a four-by-four fence post pointed at one end and driven into the ground until it's rock-solid and perfectly vertical. I have someone blindfold me. Then I lift my left knee until my thigh is parallel to the ground. I move very slowly. When I'm ready, my arms rise into the air until they're fully extended at shoulder level. Then I jump straight up, turn a hundred and eighty degrees, and come back down on the fence post on my right foot, facing the other way."

He visualized her doing this, frowning slightly.

"Sounds impossible."

"Some of the best stunt guys in the business have told me they look somewhere else while I'm doing it."

Shay serenely sipped her wine.

"It's a trick? you can see what you're doing?"

"No. If I could see, I'd mess up, impale myself. I have to orient myself in perfect darkness. By the way, I've been doing it since I was twelve. Probably I should quit, I don't have the strength in my right leg any more. It's balance, see. I have perfect balance the way a few singers have perfect pitch. Balance, breathing, touch. My foot finds the post again because it *belongs* there. All of this can be a little hard to explain, except to a Zen archer or a Shaolin kung fu master. They know. They can do even more amazing things, and they probably would think my fence-post gag was childish."

"So you've been a professional stuntwoman for—"

"Oh, more than a dozen years now. When I was nineteen I earned enough to buy a car, and I had some college money left over."

"Where did you go to school?"

"Name it. If the college is in the L.A. area, I've taken courses there. I never cared much about getting a degree. I study this and that. I wander through curriculums. History, psych, finance—I needed to find out why I've never been able to save a dime. Money still melts out of my hands; the mystery is unsolved. Creative writing. Everybody in the movie business has written or is writing a screenplay. But I wrote a novel."

"Is it any good?"

She shrugged. "I may be short on talent, but I'm long on try.

Anyway, a couple of editors in New York said nice things about the book. They said I must have had an interesting childhood."

"With Silverwhip Jack, that was a guarantee."

"You could read my book," Shay said, with a look that implied it had just occurred to her she might want him to. "What did you do when you were a kid?"

"Got into trouble. I was the reason they needed a sheriff in Solar County in the first place. What's the movie business like? I've been to some locations in the county, but I could never figure out what all the fuss was about. Mostly it was people standing around or truck drivers playing cards."

"The movie business is pure addiction. They say not enough to want it; you've got to need it. Do you like Edward Hopper?"

"The painter? Sure. My old man's a nut for Hopper."

"Portrait of Hollywood. Sunday mornings in bright lonely places. People who look as if they've temporarily lost their memories. The vacant, glazed expressions of asylums. Marlon Brando shops for groceries in his bathrobe at three A.M."

"Who's your favorite actor?" He didn't really care, he just liked listening to her.

"Elisha Cook Jr."

"Don't know him."

"Played Wilmer in *The Maltese Falcon*. *Phantom Lady*, *The Big Sleep*? He had a petty-larceny face, like a choirboy with a bad haircut who steals from the poor box. He was always involved in intrigues that were over his head, and the suspicion that he was in over his head made him jumpy. Just before somebody killed him—and he got killed a lot, it was almost mandatory in *film noir*, Elisha Cook Jr. doesn't make it past the third reel—his eyes would get big with the knowledge that the world wasn't going to miss him one damn bit. I guess you know who I'm talking about now."

"Yeah. I've got a jail full of them, almost every day of the year."

⬤

The alarm was ringing, Cymbeline was howling, the tall woman with moussed hair was yelling at Pepper in Spanish as she tried to pry the child out of Pepper's tightly encompassing arms, but Pepper wouldn't let go.

She had wedged the wheelchair under the handrail on one side of the long elevator, which had doors at either end, and she held Cym like a football she was determined not to fumble, her chin pressing down on the top of the girl's curly head.

The would-be child snatcher shut up and stepped back for a couple of moments to assess the situation. Pepper heard the man in the gold-and-black shirt say something, then there was a third voice, also a man. That made three of them, at least. Pepper didn't look around. She was dizzy with fear and trying to swallow her heart, but she wasn't giving up Cymbeline.

They resolved the impasse Pepper had caused by pulling the chair roughly backward and turning it over, dumping both girls onto the elevator floor.

Pepper's bandaged knee hit first; she screamed in pain but held on to Cymbeline.

The woman leaned over and looked into her eyes and then looked, meaningfully, at Pepper's outstretched right leg.

"You doan let go the *nena,* you onnerstan, I'm hurting you worse, sweetheart."

Pepper put all the breath she had into a drawn-out wail for help.

The woman shook her head in annoyance, reached down and gave Pepper's knee and newly repaired patellar tendon a cruel twist. Pepper's mouth flew open, but she could barely squeal.

Cymbeline was shrieking in terror.

"*Rapido,*" one of the men said angrily. The other one said, laughing, "*Brujalita, no?*"

Pepper's fingers were locked on Cymbeline's taut belly. The woman pried loose a little finger and looked Pepper in the eyes once more, holding the finger at a taut angle in her ring-studded brown fist. She nodded and smiled. *Yes I will.*

Pepper moaned, closing her eyes tightly, and waited in a kind of trance to be cruelly hurt again.

●

Tobin Bonner's pager vibrated and he pulled it from his belt read the message. Del Cothern wanted him. Bonner grimaced in apology at Shay, but they had nearly finished eating.

His cell phone was in the car. He used the phone in Dominic's office. He was still suffused with Shay Waco, everything he'd absorbed of her while sitting there like a dry sponge, slowly finding his shape after a long spell of loneliness. He realized how like Luz she was: both seasoned, a little scarred; already, in their early thirties, beginning to show the hard-bitten spirituality of a ghetto grandmother. His bad luck to be attracted to both of them.

"Bonner."

"I'm out here in Starrettville, Tobe. You know those two drifters in the lockup, Hanratty and Mizell—"

"This had better be good."

"They might've been telling the truth about what they saw. They described Starrettville accurately, said they spent a couple nights out here, sleeping in the house where they shot some of *Butch Cassidy and the Sundance Kid*—you know, where Paul Newman is riding around on that bicycle wearing a derby hat and you hear "Raindrops Keep Fallin' on My Head" on the soundtrack? Hanratty says that's his all-time favorite movie, which is why they headed over this way in the first place—"

"Did you find a body in Starrettville, Del?"

"Tobe, I think I know where there *might* be a body, that's why I'm—"

"Where?"

"In the cemetery."

Bonner whistled a couple of bars of "Raindrops Keep Fallin' on My Head."

"Okay, Del. If I thought you had a sense of humor, but you don't, so who put you up to this, Mary Lynn?"

"Tobe, honest to God, I am standing right here next to my unit, which is parked in front of the old Mormon cemetery, and there's a grave that looks like it could've been dug up before the rain we had the other night. The grave is depressed because the dirt wasn't packed in firm enough."

Bonner put a fingertip to the circular dent on his right cheekbone, which was part bone and part titanium microcompression plate. There were those times, deep in the night, when he woke up in a panic after dreams of bullets flying at him, thinking *What am I doing here; I'm supposed to be dead.*

"Get a shovel, Del. Some help if you need it."

"What I'll need is a court order, probably. The whole town is under the protection, or whatever, of the State Historical Preservation people. Can't go digging in that graveyard without a show cause. You want it to keep until morning?"

Bonner thought about it. "No. Do what you need to do. I'll take Shay back to the hospital; be out there in a little while."

The elevator doors opened at lobby level. Pepper Waco lay in a heap on the floor inside, no longer holding Cymbeline. The security guard who had been alerted by beeper stepped in with wheezing breath and wordless expressions of concern to help her to sit up. She babbled vacantly at him.

"They took Cym. I'm sorry! I couldn't stop them. She was going to rip my finger off."

"Took who?" The guard was an overweight middle-aged man who had already put in ten hours at his day job in pest control. "Where did you come from?"

"Upstairs!" Pepper screamed, now focusing, frustrated by the confusion she saw in his face. "The nursery! They're kidnapping her!"

"I'm calling the police," the receptionist said. She was on the way back to her telephone console when the tinted glass front doors slid apart and Lucy Ruiz, off duty, walked in with her mother and two of her half-sisters.

Lucy took a second to recognize Pepper and sense trouble, turned to one of the girls, who was part-time with the Spanish Wells Police Department, and said, "Trudy—backup." She sprinted across the lobby to the elevator.

"Pepper, it's Lucy, remember me? What happened?"

"They came to get Cym!"

"When?"

"A couple—minutes ago."

"How many?"

"I don't know. Maybe three of them. They all spoke Spanish. One woman. She had a gun, I think."

Two minutes, with luck. Lucy lifted her head and yelled, "Trudy, armed abduction in progress! Nobody gets on the interstate! We need Hamblin blocked southbound and Division both ways off Hamblin! Possible three Hispanic, possible two males, one woman, an infant with them." To the security guard she said, "Everybody else who is on tonight, *outside,* now; cover all exits."

She took her off-duty pistol, a .38 Smith with a shrouded hammer, from her purse along with her ID, shoved her purse under her sister Magdalena's arm, said, "Don't let Mom wander off," and went running for the stairs.

Neal Bonner was sitting behind the wheel of his pampered '74 XKE on the ground floor of the three-story parking structure next to the Med Center buildings when two men and a woman with heavily moussed hair came in and walked up the ramp toward him. They were in a hurry, like people who are accustomed to being in a hurry, moving purposefully together, not talking. One of them, bringing up the rear, carried a large nylon duffel on a shoulder strap. The scarlet duffel was shaped to whatever filled it, different-sized bulges in the material.

Neal's low-slung Jaguar was backed between a 4-Runner and a Cadillac Seville in one of the blue spaces reserved for doctors and nurses. Neal was a man whose complex business arrangements and lifestyle kept him mindful of the need for fast exits, although he'd been sitting there for nearly twenty minutes. The engine was off. They were coming right at him, but the lighting was subdued, the kind of twilight atmosphere that makes tinted windshields even more opaque. Neal knew he hadn't been seen, if that was important. But something about the trio had set off a low-level alert in his primordial brain.

Halfway up the ramp they all paused, as if on a signal Neal couldn't hear. Then he did hear it: the siren of a city police car, distant but still of interest to the others.

After a couple of seconds they split up briskly. One of the men had an eye out of kilter, the lid half-down; it looked like a badly hung picture on a wall. He got in behind the wheel of a black Taurus sedan and pulled out of the space immediately. The woman unlocked the trunk of a Volvo two spaces away and raised the lid. The other man took the duffel and pushed it well back into the trunk. He stayed in there for another few seconds, retrieving something. When he backed away from the Volvo, he was holding a tactical shotgun with an 18-inch barrel. He racked the pump. The sound was jarringly loud inside the parking structure.

The man driving the Taurus had passed through the open gate at the entrance below—they didn't charge for parking at the Med after visiting hours, so no one was in the booth—and he had stopped there.

The woman with moussed hair climbed into the trunk and scrunched down on her back. The man passed her the shotgun, which she held at port arms. He closed the trunk lid and got into the front seat. Below them the driver of the Taurus beeped his horn once, warningly.

There were two sirens now, one sounding as if it were within three or four blocks of the hospital.

The driver of the Volvo laid down some rubber backing out. It must have been bumpy, Neal thought, for the woman cradling the shotgun in the trunk. Hiding, guarding whatever it was they had taken from the hospital.

Then, as if he were seeing it fresh in his mind, the duffel swung from the man's shoulder, the outline of the small, chubby body—head, shoulders, limbs—momentarily recognizable against the nylon as the duffel went into the trunk, Neal realized with a throb of apprehension in his throat what it all meant.

He started the engine of the Jaguar, but didn't make a move just yet.

Lucy found five people unconscious on the floor of the visitor's lounge, all of them shot, little tasseled darts stuck into various parts of their anatomies, as if they had been tagged for a future exhibition. Kapchur gun, used by vets, tranquilizers or sedative. If the kidnappers had used tranquilizers intended for animals, these people could be in real trouble.

She was relieved to see a nurse and a doctor get off the elevator when she left the lounge. "Medical emergency!" she yelled, and took to the stairs again, heading for the parking structure at the other end of the hospital grounds from the wing where Pediatrics was located.

Neal saw the hospital security man enter the parking garage and hold up a hand to the driver of the Volvo, who was speeding down the ramp.

Uh-oh.

He carried two guns with him in his car, a custom Kimber .45 with a match-grade barrel, and a Colt Defender in a nylon holster. The Colt was handier. Neal took it out of the console and put it on the seat between his long legs, eased the Jag out of the parking space and started down toward the Volvo, which had slowed at the appearance of the security guard. Then it speeded up again, and the guard was late getting out of the way. The right front fender threw him up against a cement column. Neal winced. The guard dropped and didn't move.

The driver of the Taurus, who had been waiting, stepped on the gas and made a fast left turn out of the structure, heading east. The Volvo went west, at moderate speed, toward the Mormon temple across from the Med Center.

Neal followed the Volvo, not sure what he was going to do. Then he saw his brother's Crown Vic police interceptor, two blocks south on Hamblin and coming toward the hospital. Tobin not using his lights or siren, maybe not knowing what was up.

The Volvo paused at the four-way stop, Neal coming up behind it but staying fifty feet back, thinking of the woman in the trunk with the shotgun.

In his right-side mirror Neal glimpsed Lucy Ruiz running out of the parking structure, wink of light on the nickel-plated revolver in her hand.

Two police cars were coming down Hamblin, lights flashing. They turned into the driveway at the front of the Med.

The Volvo started across the intersection.

Oh, hell! Neal thought. He turned the steering wheel hard left, hit the accelerator and pulled around the slower-moving Volvo, then cut across its path in the middle of the wide street. He gave the driver no time to react. The Volvo crunched into the right side of the XKE, jarring Neal.

He jumped out, Colt in hand, aware of his brother's car, headlights full on him. Tobin had to recognize him. Neal also was aware of Lucy, who didn't know him so well, and who might shoot him if she saw the gun in his hand. More sirens, cops; it was already mass confusion as he ran toward the Volvo, pointing his Colt and shouting, "Out of the car, get out, get out!"

The driver went into reverse instead, heading back toward Lucy Ruiz, who stopped, crouched, took aim—at the Volvo, at Neal, he didn't know which, she was shouting, too.

Neal shouted louder. "*Don't don't shoot kid in the car kid in the fucking car!* even as the driver, clear of the Jag, spun his wheel and peeled out through the intersection.

Another police car, eastbound, appeared at the southwest corner of the block-square temple grounds.

Neal turned around in the street, holding both hands high in the air, the colt by the barrel, trigger guard and butt visible.

"Tobin, it's me!"

Bonner jogged toward him as Lucy flashed by, intent on the Volvo.

"They've got guns!"

"Okay, okay, give me yours, Neal. Take it easy, what're you tonight, some kind of vigilante; just hand it to me slow."

The eastbound police car went into a squealing, sliding stop in the middle of the street in a futile attempt to head off the Volvo. All of the grid streets in Spanish Wells were 132 feet wide. But the Volvo had to swerve; it hit a speed bump doing 60 and was briefly airborne.

When the Volvo smashed down, an axle snapped. The Volvo careened out of control over the curb, missed a tree, sideswiped a gate post of the side entrance to the temple grounds, kept going, and piled into the rear of a florist's truck parked in the curved driveway.

Lucy Ruiz, running hard, was only fifty yards behind the Volvo when it hit the truck.

The driver tried to go into reverse, but all he got was smoke and spinning tires. He was out of there quickly, air-bag dust all over his hands. But he seemed a little dazed, disconnected from events. He wasn't looking to shoot. Instead he ran through trees and flowerbeds toward the back of the looming, floodlit temple.

Neal yelled, "Tobe! Woman in the trunk with a shotgun!"

"*Shit!* Luz! Luz, no, *shotgun* get away from there, back off, Luz!"

Lucy was running through the gateposts, two cops just behind her, when the trunk of the Volvo opened.

"Shotgun!"

The woman with moussed hair sat up in the trunk, racking and shooting, racking and shooting again. Deafening. Lucy Ruiz went flying away from the heat and the brightness, blood from her dark head dispersing like red dew as she fell, tumbled, lay dreadfully still. The woman racked the shotgun a third time, holding it in one hand as she climbed out of the trunk, dragging the duffel, which she held aloft by the strap crying, *Nena, nena!* She ducked her head through the strap and carried the duffel slung across her chest, both hands on the leveled shotgun now as she advanced down the drive toward the street. *Nena!* she warned again, and the policemen at the gate fell back with their weapons, letting her pass, the cry going up and down the street as more cops arrived. *No shooting/She's got a kid/Hold your fire.*

Tobin Bonner stood in the intersection with his own gun drawn, Neal's Colt Defender in his other hand, standing in front of his brother as the woman with the big-medicine shotgun came at them. Her teeth were clenched. Her eyes were out of this world, as if she'd been stoking on rock. Bonner could smell the murder on her skin from ten feet away. Nothing reachable left in her head, there wouldn't be any talk. She knew she was going down; she would go down killing.

"Okay, okay," Bonner said, both hands out from his sides, the guns turned harmlessly backward. "Whatever you want, don't hurt the kid. I know you didn't come here to hurt the kid."

She sidled around him, keeping her distance. A stoned, crafty smile came and went. She was grinding her teeth and maybe biting her tongue; bloody foam and spit leaked from one corner of her mouth. Low sounds in her throat. Eyes darting and blinking. No coherence. She was surviving on burnt nerve. It was unnaturally quiet now. Anything at all, the scrape of a shoe on pavement, a rumble of gas in Bonner's stomach, might goad her into that showdown frenzy they all seemed to be anticipating.

Bonner couldn't look at Luz lying inside the temple grounds, dead, or bleeding to death. He would go nuts, compound folly with madness. Had to keep working, find a way.

"Take my car," he said to the woman, eager to dilute the doom of her mood. "I'll drive. Anywhere you want to go."

Just a little late, he remembered that Shay was still sitting in the front seat of his Crown Vic.

●

Shay watched the woman with moussed hair backing away from Bonner and his brother Neal and cops crouched watchfully everywhere. The duffel hung across her back now, heavy with child, who seemed not to be moving. Shay thought she had better not move either, although it seemed obvious that the woman, glancing quickly around to get her bearings, intended to take Bonner's car.

She was going to need a driver, of course. Maybe she was thinking about that already. She came to the door on Shay's side, moving her left hand from support of the shotgun to open the door a couple of inches. She glanced down at Shay, who looked at her for instructions, realizing at the moment of eye contact *If she gets in the car, then we're all going to die.*

"*Tu quias,*" the woman said.

Shay's lips parted; she looked puzzled.

The woman yanked the door open, swung backhanded and hit Shay in the ear with her knuckles, knocking her sideways in the seat. Shay grabbed her head with the splinted fingers of her right hand and crawled over into the driver's seat, straightening her glasses and blinking away tears of pain.

Okay, so there wouldn't be any stalling. Shay sat up and fastened her seat belt, glancing at the woman as she backed into the car and dropped the duffel on the console between the seats.

Before the woman could bring her right leg and the shotgun into the car and pull the door shut, Shay pushed the duffel off the console with a sweeping motion of her right arm. It tumbled to the floor behind her. Shay put the Crown Vic into reverse, accelerating. The backward takeoff unbalanced the woman, pressing her momentarily into the curve of the seat. She had just changed hands with the shotgun, right to left. The door swung shut against her lagging foot. Shay grabbed the barrel of the shotgun and braked hard with the side of her right foot while keeping pressure on the accelerator, speed close to sixty. At the same time she made a full turn of the wheel with her free hand. The Crown Vic did a squealing 180, and for an instant Shay was afraid she had miscalculated and they were going to roll.

But squealing tires meant good traction, and the Interceptors were built to take this kind of abuse. The door on the woman's side flew open again. Her shotgun went off, blowing out half of the windshield, as the woman tipped toward the door space. Shay got off the brake, still accelerating. The woman rocked back toward her. Shay let go of the shotgun, spun the wheel with her left hand and shoved with her right. The woman and the shotgun tumbled into the street.

The back end of the Crown Vic bounced over a curb and Shay's head banged on the underside of the roof: she bit her tongue but barely noticed. She was busy, shifting into drive, the lightning of adrenaline ablaze in her breast. The woman, scrambling on her knees, was going for the shotgun, which she had dropped.

Shay went after her.

The car slewed sideways just as the woman picked up the gun and started to turn. The left rear fender came around and slammed her twenty feet away.

Shay kept going and stopped diagonally in the intersection, seeing the woman in the side view through a haze of burnt rubber and brake pads.

The woman got up slowly. She put one foot in front of another, balancing, like a high-wire walker, and remained that way, swaying a little. Blood dripped down her face from her hairline. Fractured skull, at least, heavy concussion. One shoulder down, as if broken. She had the shotgun in that hand and transferred it awkwardly, impulse of violence still glowing like a meteor in her dark, fixed gaze, while gun-toting cops closed in a semicircle, shouting at her.

Tobin Bonner was running toward the temple.

Shay didn't watch the rest of it. Her heartbeat was enormous, and her dinner was trying to come up.

She heard a cry behind her, the wail of a child lost in darkness.

II.

...RIDE
THE CEREMONIES
UNTIL THEY GROW DARK.

—MICHAEL ONDAATJE

15 **WHEN HER PAPPY CAME** around, with his quaking left hand and shuffle step and stuffy moon of beard, Rosalind kept the Aryan Brotherhood and most of the girls out of sight—not that Rhondo didn't know they were there, but he didn't like them and preferred not to see them, although he wasn't hypocritical about Ros's companions to her face. This evidence of tact was part of the new order of their relationship. Thus during the early hours of his increasingly frequent visits, it was just the two of them, downstairs in the Crystal Chandelier. Ros always had a gift for Rhondo, made étouffée, boudin and dirty rice for his supper, and after he'd eaten she washed his feet and trimmed his toenails and beard.

Like his daughter, the ninth of seventeen daughters he had fathered, Rhondo had unusually long feet, three knuckles on each toe. As a boy, he'd been embarrassed by this genetic quirk. He never let any of his wives see or touch his naked feet. He fucked, Ros had heard, with the Garment on. Long excommunicated from the Orthodox church, Rhondo still wore the sacred, apronlike undergarment designed by the Prophet, who personally communicated with Rhondo through revelations, gave freely of advice whenever Rhondo was stuck for a course of action, and generally treated Rhondo as a prince equal in stature to Smith himself. So it was in the revelations of Rhondo Dubray, a banquet of the imagination in a long fast of gratification.

Ros had learned to shuffle a deck of cards with her prehensile toes when she was still a kid, a knack that had made her an almost instant celebrity in Las Vegas, following her exile from Solar County at the whim of the sheriff. Her other talent, with either foot, was erotic in nature. Within a few weeks after her arrival, she was earning fifteen hundred a night, fulfilling the dreams of rabid foot fetishers. By day she worked behind the scenes for Siegfried & Roy, the show-biz illusionists with a menagerie of snow white, blue-eyed tigers and other jungle cats. Not because she needed a job but to satisfy her fascination, acquire an understanding of what she had begun to perceive as a potentially fatal flaw in her nature. At the age of five she'd wandered away from a family group and come face-to-face with a cougar in a wilderness area. The cougar had shown its teeth but had not attacked; it leapt away after only a few moments, but little Rosalind was hysterically mute for months afterward. Convinced the cougar would return. Hearing and smelling it in her sleep. Waking one morning to know that it *had* returned and become a part of her. She growled at and clawed other children, was delighted with their fear. It was not tolerable behavior, and she was beaten for it, made to sit for hours in a hot, dark closet, hands tied together, a soup can to piss in. The cougar retreated deep into her psyche and crouched there, waiting for her unpredictable spells of rage and malice. Her violence was always preceded by an overpowering whiff of carnivore, then a muscular, untameable explosion in the brain.

Her worst times had been childhood and early puberty. As an adult she still stalked with feline arrogance through the dreams of others, but Rosalind had better control of her appetites now, no longer just living for the moment. Her impulses had become less destructive. Before snuggling down with Marco Polo in his cage, she had made sure he'd eaten his chicks loaded with animal tranquilizer. (Still a kick, seeing Stearman oozing fear thick as suet from his pores.) Those weeks with Siggy and Roy before she was found out and fired, she'd confronted big cats, four hundred pounds or more, in their cages, with no protection but sheer nerve. Having educated herself through sin and hard knocks and belatedly discovering an intellectual bent, Ros turned to the great philosophers and psychologists for meanings. A new fascination, while the old cougar yawned and rested. She had made up with her father after working out his release from the Mexican hoosegow. Not at all sure why she had returned to him, and he to her, at this stage of their lives; something in the blood, in their cold, criminal genes, a marvel of destiny, perhaps.

Washing his feet, listening to him sorrow and rage, she was not deluded: he was a sick old fucker who had done many bad things, possibly even worse things than she had done. Yet she felt tender and protective. As she felt toward Jimmy Loza, one of the worst badasses who had come along in this century. Probably, Ros thought, when she attempted analysis of her relationships with these men, she loved them—if love was the word—because they were both powerful and stricken. They needed her because there was no one else in their lives who understood them half so well.

EndTimes, as once defined by the Prophet, was near, although these days the Mormon Orthodoxy was downplaying it, concentrating on positives such as the rapid growth and financial health of their church. But Rhondo clung to the apocalyptic promise of EndTimes. The death of his friend and fellow visionary, the Georgian nuclear physicist Suchary Siamashvili, he had taken as an omen. Lament followed lament like dry leaves falling in autumn. Rosalind, curled up at his bare, washed feet, head against his knee, listened patiently. In the kitchen one of the girls was cleaning up. Ros always left a mess when she cooked, but she cooked damned well.

The music of Rhondo's youth was on the stereo: "J'ai Été au Bal," "Jolie Blonde," "Les Valse des Grands Chemins." The great Cajun accordianists Nathan Abshire and Iry Lejeune, a Dubray cousin who carried his instrument around in a flour sack, hitching rides in the backs of pickup trucks. Nearly blind and barely earning a living, like most of Rhondo's family. But all Cajuns knew how to make music; Rhondo was precocious on the fiddle at the age of seven.

The family migrated after World War Two from the steeping backwater of Grosse Tete to "Big Texas." Rhondo was ten years old when Mormon missionaries stopped at their scratch farm. He hid from his Catholic parents the copies of the *Book of Mormon* and *Doctrine and Covenants* the missionaries left behind, studied them, absorbed the life of the Prophet Smith. He experienced a strange chill of recognition when dwelling on the portrait of the Prophet as a fanciful and penniless young man: the vulpine features, a hint of blandness belied by withheld mirth in the set of his mouth. Rhondo had his first revelation when he was thirteen, shortly after he experienced orgasm by his own hand. In his revelation, the Prophet advised Rhondo that his seed was strong and ready. The time was near for him to marry in preparation for his life-long task of establishing a New Zion in distant, desolate canyonlands.

Not long afterward Rhondo left for Utah, and within a week he was baptised in his new faith. He was fourteen and looked eighteen—six feet four already, and husky. He lied about his age and married the daughter of his first employer, who owned a lumberyard in Solar County. She was a plain, twenty-year-old woman who, he knew, through subsequent revelations, would not oppose him when it was time to take more wives.

Cunning and a quick learner, Rhondo already understood that most people simply waited on this earth for someone to tell them what to do. He had a good business head and no scruples when it came to exploiting the unwary. His visions of the New Zion were both a goad and an impediment. By the time he was twenty-five he had taken two more wives, while contemptuously failing to conceal his adherence to the principle of plural marriages from the Orthodox church. This earned him excommunication, but he was too busy making money to care. He had discovered how quickly paper trails disappeared in mazes of corporate activity as they wound through the bankruptcy courts, the vulnerability of insurance companies in liability cases, and the many loopholes in the public welfare system. He bought into businesses, siphoned off cash, bankrupted them, repurchased the remaining assets at twenty cents on the dollar through more dummy corporations. The penny stock market, when he got around to it, became a cash machine for Rhondo Dubray. He gave new life to obsolete and played-out mines throughout the West and in Canada. He had boiler-room operations in four states, selling stock to retirees over the phone, bidding up share prices on thinly traded issues at that swindler's paradise, the Vancouver Stock Exchange, selling out for big profits and letting the overvalued stocks collapse.

Early in his career, when he was keeping records in his head, he slipped up by signing the wrong name to a welfare check and drew probation. That was the most trouble Rhondo's business dealings ever got him into, until his zeal for greater riches affected his judgment, leading to a brief fling in the drug business. He was not up to the level of the competition in paranoia, treachery, and sheer terror, and soon gave it up.

His worst problems had always come from within the Brightly Shining: challenges to his authority, which was no less than the will of the Prophet. In the past, some challenges had been settled through blood atonements. Twice Rhondo had been arrested for murder, released both times for lack of evidence. But anyone could play the

Revelation game; and younger men, seeing what was left of Rhondo after his lengthy stay in prison, aware of millions of dollars in yearly revenue and nubile young women for their choosing, were eager for an opportunity to cast him out. The oldest principle of human history, reenacted at every level of power.

Rosalind knew that the unrest he was enduring now, with defections almost every day and fear in the hearts of many who remained in the Brightly Shining, was entirely due to Rhondo's pathological need to fulfill the most critical phase of his revelations by setting off a nuclear device at One Temple Square, thus eliminating much of his opposition in a stupendous blast. Then (as he constantly preached), through "heaven's awful rainbow" the returning Saints, those who were true to the Principle, would come marching in *zeitgeist* glory straight to New Zion, the Eden Rhondo had been preparing for them at unconscionable cost to himself.

As Ros had tried to make plain to that dickhead Stearman, it wasn't going to happen. Rhondo had never been able to accumulate—at a cost of more than a million dollars a kilo—enough black market, bomb-grade uranium (HEU) for Suchary Siamashvili to put together a briefcase nuke. And Suchary's other brainchild, a property-friendly "Dove," which was a deuterium-tritium device the size of a softball, wouldn't work either, without the red mercury rumored to be needed for a trigger.

Currently Rhondo was trying to work out trade agreements with a couple of peerlessly nasty anarchist organizations that might have former Russian physicists on their payrolls, and whose leaders didn't care how much of Utah he blew up. *Their pleasure the terrors of the earth*, Rosalind thought, watching her father and thinking of mad old Lear.

Ros was mildly concerned by this development. Not that she thought her Pappy could hope to realize his ambitions; but there were investigators, like Stearman, unwilling to take the chance. Rhondo, since getting out of prison, had attracted far too much hostile attention to himself, particularly in his dealings with Wolfgang Gehrin—who, Ros had heard, was high on lists of undesirables in several countries.

There was something she could do to divert Rhondo, while settling an old score of her own and having some mean, dirty fun in the process. Rhondo Dubray's revelations were dense with omens and rife with prophecies. Rosalind thought he was agreeable to be shown a way out of his present dilemma, while regaining a firm hold on the Brightly Shining. Ros wasn't the spellbinding equal of the Prophet but she knew how to capture Pappy's attention and influence the sometimes muddled processes of his mind.

When Rhondo's ramblings had slowed until he was talking in circles and he had wearied of his own anger, she poured him another glass of the hard cider he enjoyed on these occasions, cider she mildly spiked with a hallucinogenic. Then she turned on the TV and the VCR and started the tape she'd waited all evening to show him.

As soon as Vida's image appeared, Rosalind got that pleasurable singed feeling along her spine, and the taint of carnivore thickened in her nostrils.

Rhondo leaned forward in his chair, hands gripping his knees. His expression was horrified.

"Big, isn't he?" Rosalind said, with a faint smile.

A glistening fly slowly orbited his head, settled on a crumb of cooked rice that had stuck to his beard. Rhondo seemed not to notice.

"It's him, all right," Ros assured her pappy. "He's the sheriff's son, but not his natural child. Adopted. Bonner's been raising him in our midst all these years."

"We knew he had a black child."

"But you didn't know *whose* child." Ros stopped the tape on a looming closeup of Vida. "See there, at his temples?"

"Oh, my Lord."

"They're about to erupt. He doesn't come out in the daytime, by the way. Only at twilight. It must be something about the sun. As if you needed any more proof."

"In our midst. All these years. Growing up."

"But the Revelations told you he was coming."

Rhondo turned his face aside. His eyes were open, his senses in withdrawal. He screamed, violently. In response, the kitchen girl dropped something that shattered on the floor. Ros winced and turned off the VCR. She put a hand on Pappy's shoulder, digging in with her fingers, bringing her power to bear on him as a few more flies swaggered around, large enough to shoot down with a pellet gun. He observed them now and understood why they were there.

Roused by his manifest dooms, Rhondo looked at his daughter.

She relaxed her grip, grinning brutally.

"You can do it, Pappy."

"I don't—"

"The Prophet foretold this. Didn't he?"

"But I—"

Rosalind bent close to his ear.

"He's young, and strong. Getting stronger every day, from the looks of him. But not so strong yet you can't defeat him. Only it has to happen soon. Listen to the Prophet. He will tell you the time and place. Won't he?"

Rhondo's mouth was still, but his small eyes raved.

"This nigger will turn them all against you. All of the Brightly Shining. Turn them to *his* purposes. It's already begun. Remember?"

"Who?"

"Sarah. Why didn't she want to marry Frenchie? Ha. You know the answer. *He* has Sarah." Rosalind was beginning to get the feel of this, rhythm and nuance. "Do you want to see him again? The Antichrist? Destroyer of Eden? Who else knows? Who can stand in his way? Who can defeat him? *Who* will go straight to the throne of God when the Antichrist is dead? Rhondo Dubray. Rhondo. Rhon-do! Only Rhondo." She was nearly aglow with her heat, the righteousness of the preacher, arouser, avenger. At the same time she was sardonically amused. "Go and pray now. Forget about everything else. The Prophet has a new plan for you."

Outside she had to help her mumbling pappy down the steps to the car. Frenchie and one of Rosalind's brothers had been waiting out there for half an hour. Jake had his powerlifter's arms folded as he looked away from the night sky.

" ' . . . The stars, which are the brains of heaven,' " Rosalind said.

"What's that?"

"George Meredith. Read any poetry, Jake?"

"Shit no. What's wrong with Pappy?"

"A little indigestion. Put him to bed. How're you, Jake? Got any new wives since I saw you last?"

"Same precious three. Looks like you did some fixing up around here."

Frenchie got out of the backseat of his Cadillac and said excitedly, "Ros, you been watching the TV? Sheriff's deputy got killed at the hospital tonight. Some Messicans was trying to make off with that little girl, you know, the one that was left after all her family was shot over there by Desert Rose?"

"Fuck," Rosalind said, under her breath. Rhondo staggered and almost fell down.

"Help me get him comfortable in the backseat," Frenchie said. "What did you do, Rosalind, poison him with your loozy-anner cuisine?"

"It's not his stomach; it was food for thought," Rosalind said.

Her heart was hopping from displeasure, her mind on Steel Arm Jimmy, who obviously needed someone to do all of his thinking for him these days. Rhondo was breathing heavily, eyes unfocused. Ros turned him over to Jake, only a little shorter than Rhondo was, and just as wide. Rosalind leaned toward Pappy to give him a good-night kiss when the bullet went past her ear and took a piece out of his right cheekbone. The bullet made a sound like a sharp intake of breath. A little blood spritzed Rosalind in the face.

Ros recoiled, then, hearing the echo of the powerful shot, she jumped on both Rhondo and brother Jake, hitting them hard and knocking them down out of the throw of the Cadillac's headlights. She covered Rhondo with her body while he squirmed, astonishment appearing in his drug-sluggish eyes.

"Ros!" Frenchie squawked, "what do you think you're—"

Rosalind was the only one who seemed to realize what was happening.

"Sniper in the hills, Frenchie! The shot came over my shoulder!"

Her eyes were on her father. He stared back at her, his own eyes lustrous but without pain. There wasn't much blood. The bullet that had scored his cheek had apparently passed on through his beard without doing further damage.

Jake was trying to struggle out from beneath the press of their bodies and get at his pistol.

"Forget it!" Ros said. "Pappy, close your eyes and lie still like you've been killed. Let's get him up on the porch. *Now.*"

"Who the hell—"

"Frenchie, shut up and help us!"

They managed, with difficulty, to carry the 350-pound Rhondo back up the steps to the covered porch and lay him down.

Rhondo was agitated now. Ros blotted his cheek with a sleeve of her peasant blouse and put a hand over his mouth to keep him quiet. Jake, carrying his .40-caliber Smith shorty, went down to the end of the porch to have a peek back up into the hills behind Silverwhip Jack's town. Not that he was going to see anything, even with a three-quarter moon in the west.

Frenchie had his own gun out, a pearl-handled Air Lite that

wouldn't stop a cockroach at more than ten feet, his hand trembling. Looking around with his eyes bugged more than normal.

Ros snapped at him to put it away.

"He's gone by now."

"Who?"

"Crissake, Frenchie, the shooter! The technician. Five or six hundred yards. Five-percent error at that distance with night optics and a laser range finder." She put her face close to her father's, smelling blood and the odor of bullet-singed beard. "Pappy, one of us got lucky just now. And I'm pretty damned sure he wasn't aiming at me."

"Somebody sent a pro after Daddy?" Jake asked, coming back to them.

"I want to go home," Rhondo moaned. Bogged down by his own great weight, by shock and pain, his new identity as a marked man. He tried to touch the wound on his face. Ros held his hand back.

"Shhh, you can go in a minute."

"They might try to follow us," Jake said worriedly. "Maybe we'd better call—"

"Call nobody. The shooter was alone, or with a spotter. One shot. Every reason to believe Pappy's dead. He packed up and cleared out five minutes ago."

"You act like you know a lot about this," Jake said, with a hint of hostility.

"I don't know shit, Jake."

That wasn't true. Rosalind had a strong hunch; her hunches were based on her experiences in volatile societies of impulsive, ruthless, and chaotically brutal men. And she was made in her father's image, her father before his decline. She felt sore and provoked and welcomed the challenge that had been issued by the nighthawk shooter. Obviously the contractor not only wanted Rhondo Dubray dead but had contempt for *her*, staging the hit in her front yard. Nobody could get away with that.

She rose to her feet and gave Jake a light admonitory slap on the side of his head. Jake nodded and smiled apologetically.

"Now get your butt out of here. I'm going to find out whose D and B this was. Meantime, keep Pappy down home and under guard, you hearing me?"

"Will you need help, Ros?"

"I'll call you if I do, Jacob. Thanks."

16

FIRST THE DOGS, and obviously they hadn't been aroused by some nocturnal creature getting too close to their kennel runs. After thirty seconds of savage barking, as Hoyt Bonner was sitting up in bed shaken from sleep and out of sorts, the door chimes rang. Willa was awake too, next to him, motionless on her back, apprehension in her nearly sightless eyes.

"Who could that be? What time is it?"

Hoyt cleared his throat, a sound of annoyance, and pulled off the covers. He was a burly man who slept naked during the summer months. There was no clock in the bedroom. Hoyt's internal clock woke him promptly at five-thirty every morning. Five hours of decent sleep, now that his thyroid problems were controlled with medication. The cancer only a memory. Seventy-five years old, good muscle tone, he could hike for several hours over rugged terrain and not get winded.

He reached for a pair of faded, beltless Wranglers, a little frayed at the cuffs, pulled them on, wondered if he should choose a shotgun from the cabinet in his study on the way to answer the echoing chimes. But then he saw, past the foyer, a familiar shape behind the rectangle of etched and beveled glass in the custom-made front door, and, in the driveway, red flasher lights alternating behind the grill of Tobin's car.

Willa said from the doorway of their bedroom suite, "Do you know who it is?"

"The sheriff," Hoyt said, with a slight scornful edge to his voice.

There were others on the porch besides his oldest son. He felt a momentary tightness in his chest, knowing something had happened, and his immediate response was to think of Neal. But, no, Neal was there too; Hoyt heard his other son call out reassuringly to him as soon as he switched on the foyer and porch lights.

Hoyt unlocked the door. He knew when he saw Tobin's face that whatever it was, it was very bad.

"Sorry. I've got a problem. I need some help."

His tone said he was unwilling to hear an argument. His expression was that of a man whose life has advanced ordeal by ordeal. A jolt beneath the heart released the tightness and Hoyt felt a wary sympathy, realizing that it had been months since they had seen each other. And they had had nothing much to say on that occasion.

"Tobin?" Willa said, coming to the foyer, where she distinguished only shadows and phantom swarms of color but felt the tension of his presence like a storm front at their door.

Tobin Bonner came in, followed by Neal.

Their father looked at the woman on the broad flagstone porch; he had thought it might be Lucy Ruiz, but she was a stranger: good-looking, thick head of dark curly hair, wore rimless glasses. She was carrying a sleeping Hispanic child, wrapped in a blanket but with bare feet dangling.

There was, distantly, an eggshell paleness above the dark hills; the waxing moon was down. Neal's Jaguar was parked behind Tobin's Crown Vic, headlights still on. The right rear door and a fender were smashed in, bare metal showing.

"What's going on?" Hoyt asked, looking again at the woman and the child.

Tobin said, in a voice weakened and raw, "Come on in, Shay. This is my father. And my mother. Sorry to wake everybody. The baby's name is Cymbeline. I have her in protective custody. I need for you to look after her for a while. Except for the five of us, and Maria Elena, nobody will know she's here."

"Why?"

Tobin put a hand to his forehead, fingers and thumb squeezing at the temples. He looked into his father's eyes.

"She was almost kidnapped tonight. She might have been killed. I don't know why, yet. I'll find out. Meantime I don't know who else I can trust."

Neal said to his father, "I told him Poppy would be glad to—"

"Three kids in your house already. Kids in and out all the time. Word would get around. This is better."

Tobin felt his mother's hand on his sleeve, turned.

"Of course we'll take her," Willa said. "Where is she? Show her to me."

Hoyt cleared his throat again, exasperated.

Willa said, with schoolmarmish authority, "in this house we always do what needs doing, no matter what."

⬤

They sat in the great room drinking warmed sweet milk and nibbling on breakfast cake provided by Maria Elena, the portly housekeeper, who lived in a guest cottage nearby. In-slanting glass windows twenty feet high framed a good portion of Hoyt Bonner's two thousand acres of alpine meadow and canyon, and a nugget of sunrise gold in a notch of forested mountains. There was a stained-glass panel in the skylight above them, Mormon theme—covered wagons, the hegira led by Brigham Young. Sectional sofas in a deep wine shade surrounded square sand-painting tables. Green plants everywhere, vines scrolling along a staircase made from hand-hewn slabs of cedar, and, from what Shay could see, an impressive art collection on the sandstone walls of the gallery above them. Homer, Hopper, contemporary artists like Fritz Scholder, Native-American themes.

Shay was close enough to Tobin Bonner to make out, as the light slowly improved inside the house, traces of dried blood rimming his fingernails, in the creases of his palms.

Neal Bonner sat on the edge of one of the sofas, nearest his father, red-eyed and massaging his knuckles. They looked often at each other, motes of appreciation and fondness swarming in those moments of contact. Hoyt seldom spoke to his oldest son. The looks he gave Tobin were distrustful. Usually, Shay thought, the father favored the first-born. But Hoyt Bonner, obviously, was a man of means who also had reached a level of great prestige in the LDS lay clergy, a representative, perhaps, to one of the quorum of Seventies. She couldn't recall everything about the extensive networking of church leadership. At dinner—a few hours ago, but it now seemed like another lifetime—Tobin had made oblique references to a serious conflict with his father, a conflict that might have been the result of Tobin's indifference to the family's religion. Hoyt, Shay presumed, was a man who played hardball with his piety. When Shay looked at Neal she thought about his tomcatting—but he was the kind to maintain appearances for the sake of his father's approval. And the best shot at his money, in the not-so-distant future. Shay pegged Hoyt Bonner at better than seventy years of age.

She was tired, too, the fatigue of ongoing crisis, worried about Pepper, divided in her desire to be with her daughter and with Tobin, who had pulled too much weight for too long and was almost, but not quite, down in the traces.

"Who would go to such lengths?" Willa asked. "Who are these people, to steal a child from the hospital?"

"The woman's in surgery right now. The other one we have won't talk, not even a name. There was one more, but he got away."

His father said, "I don't think you've given enough thought to the situation you've put us in. We're by ourselves. How can you expect your mother—"

"A few days, while I'm make other arrangements. Meantime I'll pull a couple of deputies off their shifts and post them out here at night."

"I could sleep over with Patrick," Neal offered. Patrick was his oldest boy and, like his father, a competition shooter.

"I still don't appreciate it. You've involved your *family* in police business, Tobin."

"It's done," Willa said. "And we'll be fine. I'll enjoy having a child around again, even if it's only for a little while. Why were you at the hospital tonight, Neal?"

Her sudden shift of thought seemed to catch Neal by surprise. He smiled and shrugged, although she couldn't see.

"Oh, I was—visiting someone, that's all."

"Then you're feeling all right."

"No problems, Ma. Healthy as a horse."

"That's good. When I talked to Poppy last, it was the day before yesterday, wasn't it? We had a nice long chat. She sounded concerned that you're working too hard. All the traveling you've had to do. She heard you throwing up in the bathroom and thought you might have picked up a bug. It rains so much in those places. Panama? Nicaragua? And they keep the air-conditioning turned up too high in the hotels. Your father was sick for weeks at a time when he was president of our mission in El Salvador. He lost twenty-five pounds, and his color—"

"I might have had a touch of something; I don't remember throwing up. Poppy's a worrywart, you know that."

The sheriff gave his brother a glance as he stood.

"I have to be going. I'll be back. Neal, you'd better get hold of the insurance company about your Jag."

"Yeah, I should be going too."

Neal gripped his father's shoulder, kissed his mother.

After him, Tobin took the browned parchment of her small hand, his head bowed over it. Her smile, Shay thought, was somewhat warmer for Tobin.

"How is your son?" Willa asked.

"Good. He's good."

"I'm glad. Tobin? I know how very difficult it's been for you. And now Lucy. Tobin, I'm heartsick. I thought she was wonderful, and I hoped—"

"Yeah. Luz was—"

He shook his head sharply, as if he were banging it against an invisible wall, as if he could throw off a fiery clinging rage.

"I want to be at the funeral," his mother said. "*We* will be there."

She turned her face slightly toward her husband, whose expression was stiff with displeasure.

Tobin said, "I'll let you know. About the arrangements. It'll be— I know we'll have delegations from all the departments in the state. Some deputies from Nevada, Arizona, too. Luz—deserves that. Shay, I'll leave you where you want to go."

"Thank you."

"Miss Waco?"

Shay lingered as Hoyt Bonner said, "I haven't seen your daddy for some years. How is he?"

"Okay. I haven't seen him either."

"I never liked him. But I have to give him credit for—persevering. He turned out to be quite a businessman." His seamed lips turned up in a spare smile of approval.

"I believe so."

"I used to buy him lunch when he had no money at all."

"But you never liked him."

"It was my hope that he would one day embrace Jesus Christ."

From the strictness of his gaze, his uncompromising rectitude,

Shay drew hints of ancestry, cruel lives repeating like gunshots in dark family histories.

She drew a breath and said, "I'll tell Jack you said hello. Thank you for what you're doing now; that little girl doesn't deserve to suffer anymore."

He nodded, slightly, acknowledging that although they didn't share this concern, still he was pleased with her. Shay offered her hand. He took it, drew her toward him slowly, and down, and placed her hand on top of his penis, most of which was molded tightly to the denim of his washed-out Wranglers. He looked directly into her eyes while he did it. Willa sat a foot away seeing none of this, but perhaps not needing to see.

Shay swallowed and trembled; he released his strong grip.

"Come again," he said pleasantly. "I would enjoy your company."

She was closing the door behind her when she heard Hoyt Bonner speak to his wife.

"I have no intention of going to that funeral."

And Willa said, "Shut up, Hoyt."

"Willa!"

"Respect his grief. Respect your son, for once."

Neal Bonner had gone. The sun was rising. Tobin sat inside his Crown Vic, staring through what was left of the dust-dingy windshield, hands on the wheel.

Shay got in, still feeling a little stunned.

He didn't move for almost a minute. She watched him. His hands dropped into his lap.

Shay put her arms around him, tentatively. The poisons of the night had worked their way through his skin; he was rank as a dead snake.

"Sorry," he said.

"It's okay."

"I'm done."

"I know. I'll drive."

"Thank you."

His eyes had dimmed with the sleeps of hell.

Shay said, "Maybe you ought to go back inside, lie down."

"No. Take me home. I don't belong here."

Shay went around to his side of the car. He got out slowly. She held him again, grateful that he didn't shrug her off. As if *she* belonged. He seemed to have no bones; his body was a burden. He breathed against her neck. Over his shoulder she saw, through the decorative glass of the front door, Hoyt Bonner in his foyer, fractionated by the prisms. Motionless, head bowed a little, something sacrificial in his stance.

After a solitary daybreak plunge in a mountain pool, yelping from the violent, soaking cold, Rosalind dries off and puts her jogging duds back on, goes down a steep trail at a half-run to the river bottom. She makes herself comfortable on the pale trunk of a windfall, its branches now stubs, arced like a a flayed creature seven feet above the jogging path and the shallow, stony river. Waits, dark in her clothes, wet hair dark around her face, secure, as always, above pitfalls. On the park road, not visible from the place she has chosen, summer nomads are already on the move to the next American natural wonder. Ros can make out the tops of motor homes and vans, roof racks bulky with tied-down camp gear. She hears a snatch of a country anthem: Roy Acuff's "Great Speckled Bird." She is strangely charmed.

She studies the path along the river through a pair of Steiner binoculars. So she has time to look Vida over long before he can be aware of her.

He is only a few yards from the windfall when he glances up from the uneven path he is following, not running hard any more. She hears him breathing. How far from his house, six miles, seven? Ros hangs the binoculars from a stub and signals Vida with a wave of her hand.

"Hi, Vida!"

The sound of his name stops him. Watching Ros on the tree, one leg drawn up, the other down, foot swinging nonchalantly. He's curious, but he has nothing to say. The light in the canyon is still toneless, the sun shut out by the high walls. His features have a slight sheen but no modeling. When he cocks his head right a couple of inches, like a bird, she can tell there is something wrong with the right eye. A splatter of mercury on the dark pupil. It didn't show up on the tapes she's seen.

"I'm Rosalind."

That doesn't fetch a response either. After a few moments Ros pushes off from her perch on the windfall and lands lightly a few feet in front of Vida. Except for the movement of his chest as he breathes, he is still. Not afraid: there is an aura of youthful invulnerability around him, the toned, electric body. She is reminded of the jaguar, large for his species, her captive and nemesis. Now she can see the scars on Vida's broad head, raking back from the prominent temple bones and over his small, flat ears. Scars. Not from the shooting she has heard about, the ambush in El Paso fifteen years ago. They are, she thinks, surgical scars. And she understands a little more. He's a dummy. That beautiful body, the cruelty of his wounds going on and on. So what can she say to him now? Ros feels, not awkward, but oddly defensive. Out of place.

"I know your daddy," she says impulsively.

There is a crease of smile: such good teeth, an eagerness to share him with her. Ros feels better, having found a way in, past the word-lessness, the mild bloom of vacancy in his right eye.

"When I was fourteen, I got into trouble. I mean, real trouble. I was living with a man named Chamas Calder. A retired college professor. He was an anthropologist, and he'd been everywhere in the world. Did you know that four hundred thousand years ago hunters made spears that were as well-balanced and aerodynamically perfect as the javelins we use today? This is a long time before the so-called Advance Hunting Period of the Late Paleolithic Age. Calder always had something interesting to tell me. I got bored easily then, and I still do. I love the sound of Old English better than any music I've ever heard. Calder read Chaucer to me when he was mildly drunk. When he was drunker than that, he could be a real aggravation."

Rosalind pauses. Vida's expression is alert: he hasn't looked away from her. But she doesn't know if he is really listening, if he wants to understand.

"What really happened was, Calder and a friend of his, another boozer, got into a wrangle and the other guy, who had a temper, bopped Chamas on the back of the head with a shovel from the fireplace. You don't have to hit them hard, old people. His skull just collapsed, like a cement wall with too much sand in it. I came in right after it happened, and the other guy was such a mess, crying hysterical, I felt sorry for him. He'd always treated me nicely without once coming on to me. Who was going to feel better if he spent twenty years in prison? Not Calder. Not me. So I got him out of there without anybody seeing him and I made myself scarce, but they picked me up three days later. Some of my clothes were in Calder's house; it was no secret I'd been living there.

"They spent three days trying to break me down; no way, and I walked. You're not following this very well, are you, Vida?"

Vida shifts his feet a little restlessly and looks at the brightening sky as if he is beginning to fret about this delay in his morning routine.

"Wait. What I really wanted to tell you about was your daddy, the sheriff, what he did to me when they dropped charges."

Rosalind hears, above the sound of an ATV's engine, whoopings and loud laughter. The noise is somewhere behind them, the all-terrain vehicle perhaps coming from a KOA campground about half a mile farther up the Virgin River, just outside the park boundary. She turns her close-cropped head momentarily, doesn't see anything, then looks back at Vida. He is definitely showing signs of nervousness.

"He picked me up on the street one night and handcuffed me, put me in the back of his car. I said what for. He said I wasn't exactly an asset to the community and it was time I moved on. I didn't believe that. I thought it was going to be a sex thing. But I guess he had his standards then. He drove us down through the gorge and past Arizona and across the Nevada line. Turned off the highway there. Clear night, the moon full. Then out over the desert, I don't know, three or four miles. He parked in an arroyo, got me out of the car, and laid me across the hood, handcuffed like I said, wrists and then ankles. He slit my jean pants right down the back seam with a Bowie knife. Then he took off his belt and whipped me. He used the full strength of his arm. I said, 'If my daddy couldn't make me cry, you never will.' He never said anything, just rawed my bare ass. I thought I could take it, but I couldn't. I passed out holding my breath."

The ATV is closer, snarling around a bend of the river. Yelps and war whoops. Ros takes in a deep, shuddering breath as if she is only now coming out of that long-ago swoon and says hurriedly, "He gave me a skirt to wear instead of pants, because I couldn't have pulled on a pair of jeans after that whipping. Both cheeks of my ass felt bigger than the moon. He counted out eighty-two dollars from his wallet, all he had. Put the money in my hand. I don't want to see you again. *Okay.* You can get a lift on the highway. *I can't sit down.* Then walk. *Okay.* Am I ever going to see you again, Rosalind? Staring at me, our faces so close. I said, *Man, what you won't see is, you won't see it coming."*

The all-terrain vehicle, two youthful riders behaving like rodeo cowboys, careens on fat tires up from the riverbed and bounces toward them with lights still on and blazing in the calm twilight; Vida jerks his face aside as if he has taken an arrow between the eyes.

"Hey, there he is!"

Vida drops the hand that instinctively shields his face and runs, back the way he came, as the ATV pursues, passing recklessly beneath the windfall a few feet from Rosalind. A small stone kicked up by one of the tires chunks her on the breastbone, and it hurts. There is a lot of dust in the air. Her view turns red. Vida is fast, but they catch up to him, ride his heels in and out of the river until they all disappear from sight. But Ros can still hear them. Hoorawing, having a terrific time.

Ros retrieves her binoculars, takes a *Romeo y Julieta* from her fanny pack, and leans against a root of the windfall, smoking, rubbing the sore spot between her breasts.

Eventually the teenage boys return, laughing. They stop near Rosalind. They both have number-two buzz cuts. The driver, the older of the two, wears a muscle shirt and a red shooting vest with NRA patches, biker boots. He gets off the ATV.

"Hey, you okay?"

"Sure," Ros says, smoking. "Where're you guys from?"

"Wenatchee. You sure he didn't touch you or nothing?"

Ros shrugs, looking coolly at him.

"That coon," the other boy says scornfully. "We been watching out for him. What's he doing around here anyway?"

"We taught him a lesson. He won't come back."

Ros gets up and saunters over to them.

"I'll bet you scared him good."

"Man, he was flying like his tail was on fire."

"Hooboy," Ros says appreciatively. "Guess I owe you one. C'mere, guys."

One of them has front teeth that overlap a little; the other, a noseful of acne. Cute, though, both of them. Wholesome blue eyes. Ros gestures until they are standing side by side a couple of feet in front of her, grinning, one a little bashfully, the older boy thinking he is going to be kissed, finding her interesting.

Ros clamps down on the cigar and puts her hands on the sides of their heads, pats them disarmingly a couple of times, then smacks their heads together so hard the younger boy blacks out and drops where he stood. The other one staggers away, bleeding from a tear in his scalp, superficial but still a lot of blood. He falls into the tangle of roots, eyes dimmed, mouth open.

"His name is Vida, you little shit. He belongs to me. Don't go near him again. Got it?"

●

After a mile or so Ros is up to speed and running easily when she comes across Vida again. He is sitting on the bank of the river with his left leg outstretched, grimacing.

"You hurt?"

Ros kneels and gently pries his fingers from the inside of the thigh, where the muscle has cramped, a knot like a golf ball.

"Yeah, I'll bet that hurts. But rubbing won't do much good. Just sit still."

Ros goes into the river and finds a flat, submerged rock, takes it to Vida, and presses the cold rock gently against the cramp. She has him hold it there and goes to find more rocks, then handsful of wet sand.

After fifteen minutes of this treatment he can stand and put some weight on the leg. He walks around gingerly. But even a sedate jog is out of the question.

"I'll go home with you." When he looks questioningly at her, Ros smiles and says, "Hey, I don't have anything better to do this morning."

17

ALMA DARKE WAS GETTING into her car when she saw Rosalind and a limping Vida come up from the river and cross the yard to the house.

"Vida, I was beginning to worry about you! What happened?" But she looked to Rosalind for an explanation.

"He's okay. Cramp. I found him on the trail up by the park."

"Oh, my."

"My name's Ros."

"Thank you so much for seeing him home. My name is Alma. I've worked for Sheriff Bonner, oh, it's nearly ten years now. I was about to do the marketing."

Ros looked at the Crown Vic Interceptor in the driveway. "Sheriff home?"

"Yes. But he's sleeping. He's just exhausted. There was a terrible tragedy last night, a shooting. Lucy Ruiz was killed. He was exceptionally fond of Lucy, and he's taking it very hard."

"I heard about it."

The sun, at a few minutes past eight, was beginning to glare, and although Vida kept the sun to his back, still he was shielding his eyes. Rosalind wondered about that.

"Go on in now, Vida," Alma told him. "I've kept your supper warm."

Vida smiled slightly at Ros, *thanks,* and went to the house, hurrying, hand to his forehead. "Be seeing you, Vida," she called. "Remember to ice that leg, and stretch it slowly." She looked at Alma. "Supper?"

"Yes," Alma said. "Because he lives, oh, topsy-turvy, we call it that. It's Vida's main meal of the day. He'll have his shower first, then eat, and in an hour or so he'll go to bed. He sleeps until late afternoon."

"Then he's awake all night?"

"The problem is a brain injury, you see. Vida is unable to tolerate bright light. Should he look directly at the sun, although we're still quite early, he could have a potentially disastrous seizure, in spite of his medication."

"That's rough."

"Well, thank you again for your consideration."

"No problem, Alma. Do you suppose I could have a drink of water?"

"That is so thoughtless of me! Of course, Ros. Come right in, dear."

Alma, apparently, didn't lock up when she went shopping, but after all it was the sheriff's house. In the kitchen Rosalind had her drink while looking around. A cheery kitchen, good light, solid cabinetry. Pancakes and scrambled eggs for Vida's supper, keeping warm in a chafing dish beside the island range. Ros heard a shower running in another part of the house.

"I'll just go out the back way," Ros said to Alma.

She crossed the wide flagstone veranda and walked slowly down toward the river, listening for the sound of Alma's car. When she heard it, she turned around and went back to the house, let herself into the kitchen again. The shower was still running. She walked through the breakfast room and turned down a hall in what she thought should be the bedroom wing, the sound of the shower louder. She didn't know where she was going, but she made no attempt to be surreptitious. She whistled tunelessly to herself, barely audible, and looked through an open doorway. Tanks of tropical fish, which she remembered from the tapes. So this had to be Vida's room. She heard him getting out of the shower. The bathroom door was half open. She saw a bare-assed reflection in a partial misted mirror. And what an ass it was.

Across the wide hall another door was closed. Ros tried the knob, which turned easily. She listened for a few moments with the door open a crack. Muffled snores. She went in, closed the door behind her.

The blinds were half closed. The sun had risen at the front of the house, so the sheriff's bedroom was still in twilight. He was there on the bed wearing only boxer shorts. *Like a beached whale,* she thought. But actually he wasn't all that bad; she didn't mind beefy men. It would depend on how he smelled. Years ago he had favored a spicy aftershave that didn't work against his natural scent. He'd had more hair then, but he still cut it short. In this light it was a mushroom shade, between pearl and gray. Asleep on his side, breathing hard, sheen of perspiration on his bare, freckled shoulders, hair wet around the ears. Boxer shorts gaping a little, puff of dark pubic hair, a liverish length of penis.

Rosalind licked her lower lip with her tongue, as if she were salving a sore spot. She was surprised by the scars, how many rounds he had taken, and survived. Eight healed bullet wounds, entrance and exit, that she could see, a few the size of his thumbnails, others that had been pulled tight by stitches, now resembling wizened eyelids drawn into empty sockets. Scars like a worm hatchery. Shoulders, arms, ribcage on his left side. One shot had just missed the spinal cord in his lower back.

His messy suit and shirt were thrown across the arm of a rocker. The holstered pistol was on the seat cushion. Ros picked it up. Revolver, commonplace Chiefs Special model but with a bulkier grip molded for his hand. She took the revolver from the belt holster and carried it with her while she explored Bonner's bedroom.

Full-length portrait of his Peruvian-born wife on his dresser. Wedding dress and veil, bouquet of tiny flowers. The bride stood pigeon-toed, with a pleased shy smile. Some family pictures on the paneled walls. Little Vida. A much younger Tobin Bonner, an arm around his brother, Neal. Big grins in western daylight. Fishing trips, family affairs.

Ros heard Bonner moving on the bed and, reflected in the glass of one of the framed photos, saw him sit up part way, catching his breath, scowling at the sight of her.

"Who are you?"

"Rosalind Dubray. You remember me."

"Yeah. What the f——. You had better be on the gone side of leaving."

"Just stay put, Sheriff. Relax. I brought Vida home. He had a cramp, but he'll be okay."

Rosalind turned from the wall of photos to face him, holding his gun in the palm of her hand at about the level of her waist, but not pointing it at him.

Bonner said carefully, "Better put that down, Ros."

"Just hold on. I told you to relax. I found this on the chair. The trouble is, you know, I'm a terrible klutz with guns. No idea of what I'm doing. But that's bad. I might accidentally do the wrong thing."

Bonner knuckled his stubbly jaw and sank back against the pillows.

"I'm telling you one time. Get out of here, now. Trespass is the least of your problems."

"Vida was having some trouble with a couple of kids who thought it was fun to dog his heels on an ATV. They won't try it again. Alma invited me in after I walked him home. She's out shopping. I was looking for a bathroom. Getting some girlish pains, you know how it is."

"Put down my goddamn gun, Ros!"

"Oh, I don't think I will, Sheriff. You're making me nervous. I might drop it, and it could go off. I'd better just hold on to it. For now." Her tone was earnest, not playful. "What do you say?"

"I'd say you haven't changed much since I last knew you."

"Oh. Painful recollection. Sure I've changed. I'm older. I've seen the world. Those parts of it that interested me. I've met interesting men. Assuming I intended to shoot you, well, you'd already be sprouting lilies, wouldn't you?"

"Does that mean you want something?"

Ros glanced at the bridal portrait on his dresser.

"What did they hit you with, that time in El Paso? Assault rifles?"

Bonner rubbed his jaw again, still angry but curious now, reading her a little differently.

"What do you know about it?"

"I know you've wasted a lot of time trying to pin the whole thing on Jimmy. Fact is, he only heard about it after it went down. Annoying him one hell of a lot. A matter of professional courtesy, right?"

"I said, *what do you know about it?*"

"The technicians came from way down yonder in Morelos state, another outfit altogether from those the CIA has done heavy business with."

"How do you know Jaime Loza?"

"Two lonely souls meeting in the night."

Bonner sat up suddenly. Ros gestured pacifically.

"Don't go hot-headed on me. I know Jimmy; he knows me. He's dying, by the way. Or thinks he is. We talked about you a lot, because you were causing him problems in the organization. Two years ago, when you sliced a thumb off Pepito, Jimmy was ready to have you done then and there. I talked him out of it. So *tranquilo,* hear what I have to say. You were assigned to an intelligence unit, El Paso Center. Tracing the money, right? Accountant's work."

"Basically. And?"

"There are good banks and bad banks along the border, on both sides. Remember BCCI?"

Bonner was over his first wave of blind anger at her intrusion—his own gun in her hand, although not held threateningly. Maybe the best thing to do was pay attention while trying to take her advice and chill. There would come a time. He yawned.

"BCCI? The death-squad bankers? Who could forget them?"

"They got into a good bank in Arizona, through one of their holding companies. What the bank turned into, it wasn't a laundry, it was a fuckin' car wash. Carloads of cash, every week. How do they do it? Well, they need legitimate accounts, big ones, to hide all the activity, and they need powerful friends, from U.S. district courts all the way up to the House Banking Committee and the Federal Reserve. Not to mention the PRI in Narcomex. Better friends and allies than you had, when you got lucky—or unlucky I guess—and found out how some of the protection money was being distributed."

"And who was getting it. All of them above suspicion. Respectable married women, down in Mexico to shed a few pounds and tone up at Las Damas. Going home with half a million or so in uncut diamonds in their luggage, getting waved through customs. Exchanging the stones for cash at jewelry stores owned by Arabs in Washington and New York. Then the cash went by diplomatic couriers to the banks of their choice in Luxembourg, Malta, or the Jebel Ali Free Zone."

"Who was the one you set up? I forget the name."

"Trish Hagood. Second, and very young, wife of a Federal Reserve Board member who had a serious gambling problem. Trish's problem was a Latina masseuse she couldn't get enough of during her visits to Las Damas. The masseuse was tied in with some local traffickers, and they had a brisk business going at the health spa. Trish liked to do a few lines to loosen what inhibitions she may have had when she was with Claudia, who was nicknamed *la araña terciopela* for her seductive ways. My team got videos of Trish and 'the Velvet Spider' diddling each other.

"I thought it could be useful. We picked Trish up, very quietly, before her plane left the Las Damas air strip. My paperwork was a little incomplete. Those things happen in Mexico. I never bothered to notify the *judiciales*. I only wanted to ask some questions about Claudia. I didn't know we'd find diamonds. Trish had been muleing them northbound for over a year. Doing all the legwork for her husband. Diamonds into cash, cash to the Bahrainian embassy in Washington. Trish opened up about that, and a good deal else involving her husband, when we played the tape for her."

"Some unexploded bombs you just don't want to tamper with. Too many alarms go off in high places."

Bonner nodded. "I made myself immediately expendable. I just didn't think—" He paused, biting back pain. "If not Jimmy, who was it?"

"Whoever you trusted most at EPIC. But you've always known that. I guess you got a little crazy, grabbing Jimmy's people like you did. But it's a big maze. No trail to follow. He's great at the game."

Bonner nodded again, acknowledging what they both knew.

Ros began to prowl around the bedroom.

"Stearman's in town. Have you heard?"

His eyes were very tired. Sometimes he lost focus, as he did now when she moved. There was an afterimage of the other Rosalind where she'd been: ghostly, threatening in its stillness and silence.

"Sure. Did me the courtesy of checking in with my office before taking over the Santero murder case. Anyway, Santero's the name Gabriel was given by the WPP. But I'm not telling you anything."

"No."

"Where do you know Dale Stearman from?"

"Vegas, of course. The crossroads of the civilized universe. I helped Dale out with a little matter involving a U.S. senator he, ah, needed to get a yoke on. We've been pallys ever since."

"I don't suppose you could tell me who did Gabriel?"

She shrugged. "Pretty obvious. Gabriel's brothers found him and sent pros to kill them all. Now that's sick. But it's the way those crazy assholes are."

"Contracted to the same people who went after the little girl at the hospital last night?"

Ros was quiet for a few moments, thoughtful.

"I seriously doubt it."

She was good at her own game, but Bonner knew she was holding out. He was getting angry again. And he wanted his gun back.

"If you didn't come here to plug me for flogging the skin off your teenage butt, then lay my piece down on the dresser. Nicely. And we'll do some real talking. Otherwise I'll execute the warrants and have you picked up and held in my jail for as long as I can think of a lawful reason. We'll continue this conversation on *my* terms from now on."

"Okay." Ros slid the gun onto the dresser top. "I meant it, these things make me squirm." She turned to face him. "Real talk, no fluff."

"What do you want?"

"Stearman has an assassin traveling with the team. I have a hunch who it is; I usually know them when I see them. But I want to be sure. I'll give you a name; you can check it out for me."

"I'm a county sheriff, not the FBI."

"You're a county sheriff *now*. But you know some useful people. Just do it."

"Why should I?"

"Stearman's sniper took a pop at Rhondo a few hours ago in front of my place. From up in the hills somewhere. Very long range, probably a .50-caliber rifle, judging from the chunk the slug took out of his cheekbone. Missed killing him by a quarter of an inch. I don't want it to happen again."

"Why would Stearman want to take out your old man?"

"Shit, Bonner. His reputation. Stearman thinks Pappy has a lunchbox nuke."

Bonner almost laughed.

"Right. It *is* ridiculous. I didn't say Pappy hasn't tried. He's spent millions. But the thing doesn't exist. In a usable condition."

"Christ, you're *serious*. Rhondo Dubray's been working on a— Christ. This used to be a nice little place to settle down, not the anarchists' Los Alamos."

Ros said, with her jutting grin, "I can handle Pappy. We both know he's delusional. Anyway, get me the information I want, and you'll find out how grateful I can be."

"Yeah, right. I'm not working with you, Ros."

Ros whistled a breathy little tune, considering his denial, rejecting it.

"Oh, I think you will."

"Then you're as delusional as your old man."

"Am I? Here's what *you* get. I hand you Stearman. Not for the murder of your wife; there's no way I can help there. But I'll give you enough about his connections with certain people to put Stearman and a gang of them away. I'm not talking about a couple years in Club Fed. I can deliver by-the-book shit that will stand up in any court. Photographs, tape recordings, copies of incriminating transactions."

"You have them?"

"No, my main man Jimmy does."

"And he's so nuts about you, he'll gladly hand them over."

"I can say he wouldn't be sad to see Stearman go down. Stearman's too powerful these days to suit Jimmy. To put it in Jimmy's language, *Ya no puedes fejarte en el.* 'You can't see his shape anymore.' "

Bonner said, passing a hand over his eyes, "I can't make out yours all that well."

" *Mano,* what do you have to lose? Your integrity? You took a fourteen-year-old across two state lines and whipped her naked ass with your belt. It amounted to rape. What I could have done with that."

"Your word against mine. You killed an old man with a shovel and walked. I didn't lose my integrity with you, Rosalind. I was trifling with some of the rules long before I came home to Solar County. Occasionally I still get fed up with the bad laws, those that offend common sense and create an inordinate amount of work for an understaffed enforcement agency. I slide by here and there. I don't apologize. I've done a good job and I've kept my sanity. Until now."

Rosalind said, looking steadily at him, "Lucy Ruiz."

Bonner's face had thickened from the torment in his blood.

"She's still alive to me. But memory never holds; it's like water in my hands. I've been through it before. I hope there are candles and saints where Luz and Connie have gone. I don't know. Where I am it's dark, freezing night."

After a few moments, seeming to remember that Rosalind was still in the room, he looked up curtly.

"What I *do* know, I'm not fucking with you just to get at Dale Stearman."

"Interesting choice of words," Rosalind said, not following through on the beginning of a smile.

Bonner said, edgy and smarting, "You always had a line of talk, and a quick comeback. You were a cheap little charmer with the ego of a mercenary. Maybe you're telling the truth, but even so you don't add up. Somebody shot at Rhondo? Have him file a complaint and I'll go to work on it."

She gave him a look, a momentary pulse of havoc in her eyes until the congenial grin returned.

"You've got a lot on your mind. We'll talk again. You haven't used up all of your credit with me. Yet. The first law of nature is to pardon each other for our follies. Some Frenchman said that. It might even be true. What do you think?"

The door opened and Vida looked in, astonished to see Rosalind.

Bonner said, "It's all right, Vida."

Rosalind said, "So I'll be on my way."

She walked toward Vida, who was wearing only a pair of blue running shorts. She paused, smiling, put a hand on Vida's shoulder and kissed him on the lips, shot a bold, mocking look past Vida at Bonner, which froze him.

"By the way," she said, "it wasn't me who killed Calder. The whole thing was pointless anyway, a couple of drunks scuffling. You could probably figure out the rest. If you think it's still worth your time. 'Mordre wol out, that se we day by day:' The Pardoner's Prologue."

She left the bedroom, whistling on her way down the hall.

Shay Waco had been driven from Bonner's house to the Medical Center by a deputy. At seven-thirty in the morning the Pediatrics Department was already a busy place: breakfast trays were being distributed and a couple of doctors were on the floor, including the orthopedic surgeon who had repaired Pepper's knee the day before. Shay intercepted Verger on his rounds.

"I don't know if she'll need surgery again. There's a lot of swelling. I've scheduled another MRI for later this morning. You look like you could use some sleep."

"Right now I could use a new life."

"There was a TV news crew up here earlier. Somehow found a way in past all the cops. They were looking for Pepper. Your father kicked them off the floor. Real rugged for his age. Understand he used to be a cowboy actor."

Shay said wearily, "Jack's here?"

"He's with Pepper now. She's finally dozed off, I think."

"If the MRI is negative, I'm taking her home. Soon. I've had enough of Solar County."

"Couldn't blame you. We're not like this, really. It's a quiet place. I don't know what's going on lately."

Shay walked on down the hall and pushed open the door to Pepper's room.

Silverwhip Jack Waco was sitting in a chair beside Pepper's bed, long legs outthrust and crossed at the ankles. He wore a fancy pair of black boots. Hand-stitched red-and-silver eagles on the boots and on his leather vest. The familiar black Stetson was in his lap. Pepper had fallen asleep on her side, holding his hand. Jack's eyes were also closed and he breathed through his mouth. Shay stood in the doorway watching him. Twenty years later. His face now like a dry riverbed, but he still had the square chin and imperial cheekbones.

Shay whistled softly, twice, a three-note summons. His eyes tweaked open and he stared at her with a slowly broadening grin.

"While I was settin' here with Pepper I came up with a hell of a notion for a TV show," he said. "I could probably finance the pilot myself. We'd play undercover investigators, father-and-daughter team, only your day job is stunt woman? Get some good-looking guy in it who's a whiz at computers or something. I think we could sell it pretty quick after what happened last night. You're all over the news this morning, honey, did you know that? Jesus, if I ain't proud of both my little gals.''

Shay's eyes felt gritty. She took off her glasses and rubbed the closed lids gently and wasn't all that surprised when the tears started coming.

18

THE SHORT WOLF CAFÉ, on Division Boulevard six blocks west of the interstate and the Ramada Inn, had been Dale Stearman's choice for breakfast since his arrival in Spanish Wells. The Short Wolf had been in business since before World War Two. It was popular with local politicians, attorneys, and courthouse personnel; and it could be tough to get a seat before the courts convened in the morning. About nine-thirty the low, pungent haze of smoke that was partly kitchen fry grease and partly tobacco thinned out along with the crowd, most of them men: longtime residents, ranchers and retirees with time on their hands clustered at the counter, nursing their coffees until it was time to go to the doctor's or to the post office to pick up their mail.

Stearman had been at the café for about an hour with two of his handlers when Katharine Harsha came in, having risen a little later than usual. There were laptops with modems and printers on the table. Stearman had his handlers remove the gear, and themselves, to another booth.

Katharine sat opposite him with a spare smile, lifted the coffeepot. It was empty. Stearman signaled the waitress.

"Want anything to eat?" he asked Katharine.

She glanced at the menu, then at the waitress, a thin kid with tar black, spikey hair and starkly made-up eyes, who reminded her of someone. Katharine met the girl's eyes for a few moments. Not bad-looking, in spite of the standard rebel facial piercings and adornments, small diamonds in each wing of her snub nose. There was a spice of sulfur in her deep brown eyes. Katharine was sure she'd seen her somewhere, in passing, but couldn't remember. The girl had a one-side-of-the-mouth smile. Depending on her mood, it might be disarming or a vulgar smirk.

Katharine lowered her eyes to the nameplate on the waitress's checkerboard tunic.

"Could I have a slice of honeydew and, oh, buttered whole-grain toast?"

"We're out of honeydew, but there's some nice Crenshaw melon left."

"Good. And decaf, please, Charmaine."

"Yes, ma'am."

Katharine put the menu back and looked at Stearman with a more confident smile. His expression was neutral.

"I'm not apologizing."

"Did I say anything?"

"Six hundred twenty-five yards. I won't miss that take, even at night, twice in a hundred tries."

"Look, it happens. You don't have to tell me. I know you're the best."

Katharine responded with a small nod, then bit her lip in exasperation. The surface of the heavily laminated table contained a display of old cattle auction and rodeo handbills from the forties. Casey Tibbs. Jim Shoulders. She looked at Stearman again. He was chewing gum. His reddish orange hands were loosely clasped on the table, as if he might be concealing something precious from her.

"What do you want to do now?"

"Well, another take on Rhondo would be hard to arrange. They'll keep him under wraps until the meet comes off."

"And we still have no idea when that is."

"There's no movement yet in Australia. Hayakawa is still holed up, if you want to call half a million acres of sheep country a hole, near Banjawam. But he won't be publishing his travel plans."

"It has to be soon. We can be reasonably sure of that, from what Gabriel passed on before they killed him. Gehrin is home, after his visit to the Outback. So—"

"It'll happen. The anarchists' summit. Aum Shinrikyo and the Brightly Shining."

"God, I get cold chills."

Stearman yawned. Katharine's sensitive high-bridged nose was smarting. She resisted touching it. She was a little stiff this morning, from the hours she'd spent in concealment high above Rosalind Dubray's place, waiting in desert camo with her full sniper's kit—.50-BMG-caliber semiauto rifle crafted to her specifications by Harris Gunworks, ear protectors, 20X Leupold scope, laser range finder, flash/blast suppressor—long hours devoted to the quality take. Additional sleepless hours after she'd missed, analyzing it. Rhondo's slight turn of the head to accept Ros's kiss just as she squeezed off the round. Otherwise, right through the rosy sunset of his laser-measured eye.

The waitress returned with Katharine's order. Katharine couldn't find any Sweet'n Low for her coffee, decided to drink it black.

"Maybe we should focus now on Gehrin," she suggested.

Stearman locked his hands behind his head and stared up at the stamped-tin squares of the ceiling, which had been painted white once but now were gummy and yellow from nicotine.

"Paraguayan national with a diplomatic passport, cabinet level, international trade specialist. I can't put any heat on him. What did he do anyway? Even if we had specific conversations on tape, Gehrin's simply acted as an intermediary, for a fee. Arms dealing, uranium smuggling, forget it. Interpol's been trying to make that connection for the last four years. The trail dead-ends in Paraguay, with its long history of accommodation to the high-tech black market. No, we need the device, even though Rosalind assured me Suchary's Dove can't fly."

"Rosalind," Katharine said thoughtfully, and bit into a triangle of buttered toast, "do you believe her?"

"She said Suchary couldn't come up with a reliable trigger. But he was a sick man for almost a year before he died. Maybe he was very close to making the Dove work, and the Aum Shinrikyo have just the man to finish the job Suchary started."

"How did Rhondo and Suchary get together in the first place?"

"When the Cold War ended, a lot of Russians were left without much of anything to believe in. Some of Rhondo's own missionaries went looking for apostatized Russian nuclear whizzes. Their interpretation of the faith was just what a hard-line old Stalinist like Suchary Siamashvili required to fill his spiritual void. From Uncle Joe to Prophet Joe."

Katharine was silent for a while, looking speculatively at Charmaine, the waitress, who was talking to another waitress near the kitchen. Business in the Short Wolf had slowed considerably.

"Some tapes of Gabriel's are missing from his inventory," she mused. "Probably the technician took time after he shot them all to remove as many tapes as he could carry, in a garbage sack, let's say. It looked hasty to me, as if he couldn't be sure of what he was after. We've listened to enough tapes to know Gabriel recorded everything, even his own telephone conversations. And his daughter's. We know she had an Anglo boyfriend. Because Graciela had very little English, he spoke Spanish to her, badly enough to make her laugh a couple of times."

"What are you thinking?"

"Whoever came into the house that night may have been expected. The boyfriend? Or someone else who didn't arouse suspicion."

"Friend of Gabriel's."

"Um-hmm."

"You mean Rosalind Dubray." Stearman thought about it. "Ros doesn't like guns. I know that for a fact. She's used a single-edge razor blade and the sharpened end of a rattail comb on a couple of occasions, but unless she'd had a change of heart and really worked on her marksmanship—that was pro-style shooting."

"Yes, it was. Which made me think—"

Katharine opened her cream-colored leather shoulder bag and took out a folded report.

"I had Sweets work this up yesterday. Just acting on a hunch."

Stearman picked up his Ben Franklin glasses and put them on, massaging his forehead with his fingertips while he read. When he was finished he refolded the pages and passed them back to Katharine.

"Quite a debt load he's accumulated."

"Most of it due to the expense of taking care of his adopted son. I couldn't believe those pharmacy bills; the co-pay has been killing him for years."

"How close are they to taking his house away from him?"

"He has a little time to cure the arrears; another ten days and foreclosure automatically kicks in."

"He'll have to file for bankruptcy."

"And forget about reelection, although that doesn't look good right now."

"Damn shame. I'm sorry for him. What does it prove?"

"What does desperation do to a man? My half brother was as brave as they come. Platoon leader, Vietnam, two tours, highly decorated. Rotated home, floundered, got married, couldn't hold a steady job. Couldn't support her or the kids. She threw him out. He took his last five hundred dollars to Vegas. Lost at blackjack. Cut an artery that night. Lengthwise, from the hell of his palm to his elbow. Methodical, meticulous."

"I don't know. Tobin Bonner? It's a reach."

"He was off work for three days. Gave a deposition in Vegas, then went fishing, alone, up in the Cedar Breaks, which is a wilderness area about eighty miles from here. Driving time, each way, about an hour and a half. In the rain, longer."

"Stolen vehicle involved, which he's been careful not to let us in on."

"Motive, alibi, access to privileged information as the sheriff of this county, knowledge of firearms, qualified expert marksman on a yearly basis, control of the subsequent investigation. Because of his time with the DEA, it's a cinch he would have known how to make contact with the other Sinaloas. How much do you suppose they were willing to pay?"

"To do the whole family? Half a million or more."

"He needed the money, Dale."

"Tobin cut some corners while he was operating out of the El Paso Intelligence Center. We all did. They say in Mexico, 'You wash dirty clothes with dirty water.' I know he went off the trolley tracks temporarily after his wife was killed. He was on the psychiatric tit for a while. I haven't picked up anything in my conversations with him that bothers me, and I've got an ear for that kind of subliminal noise."

"But you'll think about it."

Stearman grinned and reached across the table to touch her sore nose with a fingertip; Katharine recoiled as if violated, with a sickly grin of her own.

"I think about everything."

●

Sarah Dubray had been too anxious to sleep much, particularly after being awakened in the middle of the night by Shay's daddy, who was surprised but affable upon discovering her in the guest bedroom of

his house. Silverwhip Jack had hung around for a while in the doorway, while she sat there with the bedclothes clutched to her throat.
He told Sarah what he knew of the shooting at the hospital, everything he'd heard about the gutsy part Shay had played in preventing
more bloodshed. Sarah was already in love with Shay; she listened
with a teeming, proud heart, heat rising to her pallid cheeks. Jack
asked Sarah if she'd like to have a drink with him. Of course not. He
allowed he'd just have one himself, get duded up, and return to the
hospital to be with his l'il granddaughter. "Make yourself right to
home, honey. You're welcome to stay long as you please."

By eight o'clock Shay hadn't appeared. Sarah had a glass of apple
juice and a buttered biscuit for breakfast. Her own things were still
in the room she shared with two other girls at the house in town,
but most of Shay's clothing fit her well. She thought she looked really
nice in the yellow-and-midnight blue Lycra biking shorts. One of the
mountain bikes that Shay and Pepper had brought with them from
California, a Kelly Hard Tail with a nineteen-inch frame, had become
detached from the rack and thrown clear of the tumbling Tahoe.
With some cleaning up it was okay to ride. Except for two Hispanic
female servants, there seemed to be only men around the ranch. At
least one of them got on Sarah's nerves just by looking her way—it
was the duration of the looks Tom Leucadio gave her, sometimes
touching his lower lip with a tongue of avarice. Except for those
evenings she'd spent with poor, doomed Suchary Siamashvili, she'd
never felt comfortable around men. She wanted to be off on her own
for a while, pedal hard, get up near the clouds, think blissfully of
Shay, only Shay, enjoy the revel in her heart.

Starrettville had never been much of a town, though it occupied one
of the most attractive little valleys west of Spanish Wells, with good
water and shade trees. In 1874 six polyg families had lived there, a
population of 57. The founder was one of Brigham Young's Danites,
or Secret Police, and a member of Melchizedek, the highest Mormon
priesthood; Boyd Starrett had his choice of land on which to settle
during the southward migrations from Salt Lake. A few skirmishes
resolved matters with the local Indians, but hoof-and-mouth disease

eventually decimated their cattle, the principal spring was poisoned by an earthquake, and the seven-year winter, lasting into late April of '77, brought sickness and death. The survivors moved into the larger towns of Windbow or the Wells, leaving a few dwellings and barns behind, and a hillside cemetery with a picket fence around it. What was left of Starrettville became a minor state historical site, three miles from the nearest paved road.

Bikers from the fitness center in Windbow liked the switchback trails and runouts in the hills surrounding Old Starrettville. So did Sarah.

After a nonstop fourteen miles from Silverwhip Jack's place, Sarah got off her borrowed bike in a breezy copse halfway up a hill. Cow patties and glistening flies on one side of a trickling creek, sunlight blaze on the open meadow above Starrettville. Sarah drank from the water bottle clipped to the bike frame and walked slowly around so that her muscles wouldn't tighten, feeling pleasantly winded, her quadriceps fiery, ears tingling, heart warmed like an egg in a nest. After a while she sat down and took off the vented helmet, feeling tired. Fifty yards away there were other bicyclists, a group from the fitness center taking photos of the old Starrettville cemetery. Sarah suddenly was tearful and wished that she had a camera with her. But all of her photography gear was safely stored, along with Suchary's remembrance, in a locker at the airport.

Sarah had not been invited to the midnight burial, nor had she had the chance to say good-bye to Suchary Siamashvili. During the ten days before he finally passed on, he'd been heavily sedated—unaware, Sarah was told, of who was in the room with him. But she'd had a great deal of time to talk to Suchary in the months before his death, during off-hours at the Captain's Table. Usually he wanted only coffee and something sweet. Sometimes she was able to coax him into eating more than dessert: a cup of chowder, a salad. But food frequently gave him distress, as if his digestive system was in runaway decline.

Suchary was a convert to Rhondo Dubray's brand of Mormonism, but unmarried. It was not in him to have children, he explained. There was a rumor in New Hebron that he was a eunuch. His health had been dicey for many years. He was a tall, shapeless man, with the neon blue eyes of some Svanetian Georgians and a brain filled with the dark esoterica of doomsday mathematics. He chain-smoked, gasping, scratching, made miserable by a blood disease, by his half-combusted lungs. His large, gray-whiskered head hung forward on a thin, frail neck, like an isthmus to the ungainly continent of his body. The lowered head gave him a look of abashment that always aroused Sarah's sympathy.

They never talked directly about what he was doing, his part in the fulfillment of Rhondo's elaborate vision of EndTimes. Knowing that his own days were numbered, Suchary seemed to have reached a deep spiritual gulf he hadn't the strength to navigate. Sarah's own tribulation was modest in comparison.

He liked to reminisce about his boyhood. He was the only child of a family prominent in the arts: his father had been the director of the Tiflis Opera Company, his mother a tall red-haired Russian actress. Both were devout Stalinists, and her father was a senior party official. The first goal of a revolution in any society is to intimidate or destroy the best and most skilled people in that society, but Stalin had been a mediocre poet in his youth, enjoyed good theater all of his life—aside from the political *Grand Guignol* of his regime—and tended to leave alone those artists and writers who were faithful to the party. Thus Suchary's family retained its privileges through those years of famine, widespread terror and in-house purges, orchestrated according to Peter Tkachev's inspirational maxim for the formation of a successful socialist state: "We must ask ourselves how many people we need to keep."

The Siamashvilis had the use of a large government dacha in the northern Caucasus Mountains, and they often summered in Sochi, on the Black Sea, where little Suchary kept a pet fox in the walled garden. As a child he loved the pyrotechnic displays on holidays by the sea; by the time he was ten he loved bombs even more than fireworks. He was fascinated by the physics of extreme destruction: high pressures, cosmic velocities, the structure of detonation waves. He had the touch of a gifted engineer, the theoretical brilliance of great Russian physicists such as Igor Kurchatov and Yuli Khariton, who discovered Suchary's prowess while Suchary was a student at the Chemical Physics Institute. Khariton's interest in Suchary resulted in an assignment for the young physicist that was to last for forty years: Arzamas-16, the atomic city founded in the cells of monks expelled from the Sarov monastery that lay some four hundred miles to the southeast of Moscow.

Arzamas-16, even in its crude formative years, was a paradise for scientists accustomed to the deprivations of postwar Russia. Paradise with barbed wire, of course, on the perimeter of the restricted zone and wound laurel-like around the minds of those who worked there. Punishment was the mirror image of reward at their elite level. Spies were everywhere inside Arzamas-16. The scientists were never free of suspicion and restriction while they pursued the work that led to the USSR's first thermonuclear bomb—which nearly everyone assigned to the project believed was vital to the survival of the Soviet Union. Moral issues—a demonization of scientific values—were never discussed. Project secrecy was so intense that many were clinically depressed, and a few vulnerable souls committed suicide from fear of making a treasonable error.

Suchary, twenty-two years old and enthralled by his research into critical mass, was not intimidated. The advent of the bomb was the realization of a romantic dream that had first occurred in Suchary's boyhood: the slow melding in his mind of mass murder and utopianism—the ideal that was unobtainable without necessary bloodshed, a drastic reduction in human numbers. Visionary fervor like Tkachev's fused with the social idealism of the Russian professional intelligentsia had created in many of Suchary's fellows a yearning for Utopia; it was one topic they could discuss in their social hours without fear of reprisal, since the official view of Soviet Russia was that the evolution into a perfect society—"scientific free thought and popular labor"— had all but been completed.

Sometimes in sorrow, his vivid eyes tearless but half-blinded by memory, Suchary would reach for Sarah's fine, pale hand across the table. His speech would turn from English to Georgian or Russian; he would lose her comprehension. She listened with small shifts of expression, silent but sympathetic notations, until he began speaking English again. His descriptions of Arzamas-16 reminded her of New Hebron, Rhondo Dubray's version of Utopia, isolated amid sun-blasted cliffs on the Arizona border.

The last time they had been together Suchary had said very little. It hurt him to breathe, to live. He no longer could see himself among the angels. She comforted him. They were in an isolated booth of the restaurant, the chatter of early diners in their ears. Lobsters with bound claws crawled over one another in a saltwater tank nearby, antennae wavering in the streams of bubbles from the aerator. In another five minutes she would have to go to work. One of her broth-

ers, David, was waiting outside to drive Suchary back to New Hebron. Three of David's children were in the car with him, eating ice
cream. The sky outside, its blue reduced to a wan luminosity, was
streaked with sunset orange. Suchary was dying.

"What did Jesus say?"

Sarah could barely hear; she leaned toward him.

"About what?"

"About the Kingdom. When he was asked by the Pharisee when
the kingdom of God would come."

"Oh." Sarah did a quick mental review of the New Testament.
"Jesus answered, 'the kingdom of God is within you,' Luke seventeen, and—ah, I'm not sure which lines."

Suchary nodded as if he were having trouble keeping his head
from falling to the table. A last cigarette burned between the mustard-
colored fingers of his right hand.

"It's so beautiful, isn't it? Beautiful, simple, and the truth. The
truth I have neglected, or been opposed to, nearly all of my life. Do
you love Jesus, Sarah?"

"Oh, yes. I love Him."

"But Rhondo has forsaken Jesus. He thinks only about destroying his enemies on *this* earth. What can that matter now?"

Sarah said with lowered eyes, feeling a chill at the heart, "I'd
rather not talk about—"

"I don't say he's an evil man. I believed, too. First the great fire,
the cleansing . . . then the Perfection. That perfect order men have
always dreamed of. So foolish. I have been near the Kingdom all
along, without realizing. We all are. But we forget . . . the words of
our great Teacher. Sarah?"

"I'm sorry." She wept, overcome by his pathos and longing.

"No, no, don't feel sorry for me. Look, let me show you something."

He needed a couple of minutes to untie the ribbon from the box
he took from his knapsack. Leftover Christmas ribbon, wrinkled paper
with multiple Santa Clauses on it. His fingers shook. Sarah knew she
ought to be at her station; cars were pulling up in the parking lot.
She felt anxious, but her curiosity was great.

The box Suchary unwrapped had contained a set of a child's interlocking building blocks, plastic pieces in primary colors. He used
a knife to sever a strip of transparent tape, opened the lid, lifted out
a polished nickel sphere easily contained in his cupped hands. It was

about four inches in diameter. He placed his shaking hands quickly on the table. Sarah had an inkling that the sphere, for its small size, was quite heavy.

"What is that?"

"A Dove. The only one of its kind. There are others, failures. But this one—it is the culmination of a lifetime of experimentation. I think—I *know* it will work."

Suchary's breath made a sound like a bad wind. For a while he had no speech, only the genius of his look, head bent over his cradled creation.

"Dove?"

"It was first conceived in this country, in the Livermore Nuclear Weapons Laboratory in 1958. A physicist who took part in the Manhattan Project came up with the idea while working on the laboratory's peaceful explosives program. The code name was 'Dove.' The bomb contains no fissionable material, only the deuterium-derived isotope tritium, plus a trigger of mercury oxide. There is almost no detectable radiation when it explodes. The force of the explosion itself has little destructive power, scarcely enough to shatter glass in the immediate vicinity. The neutrons that are disseminated by the detonation kill every living thing within a radius of several hundred yards; the practical range may be much greater than that, the effects long-lasting. The electromagnetic pulsation waves instantly knock out all electronics transmissions."

Sarah's mouth formed a perfect O. The aftermath of his description pressed against her consciousness like fog at a cold window.

Suchary replaced the neutron device inside the Lego box.

"I want you to have this, Sarah."

"Me!"

"There's no danger. The firing circuit is not connected to the detonator. You could drop my Dove, throw it against a wall—remarkably stable. I don't want it in anyone else's hands after I'm gone. I've heard rumors. The Iraquis, the Libyans, the North Koreans, all are working on their own versions of the Dove. Many of the physicists they now employ once worked under me. Capable men. But the technology of the detonator, so very difficult. I'm content to know that I alone have solved the puzzle."

"What am I going to do with—"

"I have thought about turning it over to your government, but that may not be a wise decision." Suchary belched consciously and violently, making of it a curse. "I think it is important to remove the Dove from my workplace. I have several prototypes, without triggers. They all look the same. Tonight I'll alter all of my research in my files. I've told no one else that I have succeeded. Take the Dove, Sarah. Say nothing to anyone. Keep it in a secure place until we speak again. Then I'll let you know how I want you to dispose of it."

At some point during the night Suchary suffered a stroke. His kidneys, already failing, shut down a few days later. He lapsed into a coma. His lungs filled with liquid; his heart faltered. Sarah never knew if he'd been able to delete all of a lifetime's work from his computer files.

She must have slept for a little while, on the hillside overlooking the Starrettville cemetery. She dreamed about the henhouse. One of her jobs, when she was small, was to collect eggs in the morning. She wore an apron over her ankle-length dress. She carried the gathered eggs carefully in the hammock of her apron, the corners of which she held in one fist at her waist. Usually she could manage to carry two dozen eggs at a time, but in her dream she was laboring under the weight of only a few.

Something was odd about the eggs today. They were spherical, shiny as polished metal and as large as croquet balls. The hens squawked loudly when she reached into the nests. They were all out of sorts. It was very hot in the henhouse. She was perspiring and her palms were wet. *Better not drop one.* She could barely breathe from fear. She had enough now, all she could carry. The dusty light of the sun coming into the henhouse at stiletto angles blinded her wherever she turned. The floorboards were rough and sprung in places. She tripped and lost her hold on her bunched apron. The glistening metal spheres rolled free, making a noise that hurt her eardrums. They fell through wide cracks in the floorboards. *Hopeless.* She could never find the right one now. She would have to endure another lecture.

Sarah woke up drenched in daylight and perspiration, needing to relieve herself. She searched for a sufficiently private place, in deep shade. While she was moving her bowels, eyes adjusting to the change in light, she saw the rattlesnake.

Not far away on the ground and motionless: if she had taken a few steps in that direction she might have stepped on it. She watched the Great Basin rattler without fear. Snakes had never bothered her; she knew how to handle them. And this one had fed recently. It was too sluggish to reach its den while digesting the vole or pica it had swallowed.

When she had finished her toilet with a wad of tissue, Sarah walked out into the noonday sun again, looking past the black Angus cattle that had gravitated uphill to the perimeter of shade, their heavy bodies reeking of dust and dry vegetation, somnolence in their gazing. She looked down at the cemetery and trembled slightly from shock.

Two Explorers from the sheriff's department and a midnight blue hearse were parked outside the cemetery gate. She saw three men wearing orange jail jumpers working with shovels, digging up a grave. Deputies stood around with folded arms. Another deputy was eating a sandwich, the foil it was wrapped in reflecting sunlight.

She knew whose grave it had to be. Indignation followed shock, then outrage: *Why were they doing this? Why couldn't they leave him in peace?*

Another car came down the uneven wagon road to the ghost town. No markings, but the windshield glittered icily around a big hole on the right side, as if someone had heaved a bowling ball through the glass. Cracks radiated across the driver's field of vision. Sarah recognized Tobin Bonner even before he stopped his car behind the hearse and got out.

A shovel blade struck the top of the coffin the work crew from the jail was digging up. Bonner walked over to the grave and had a look. He'd been expecting a cheap coffin, maybe just a homemade box, but the coffin had a rosy glow of lacquered mahogany and expensive trimmings.

"We'll want to know where that box came from," he said to Del Cothren.

"Yes, sir."

"Let me see the paperwork before we pull it out of the ground."

Del handed him the original court order. Bonner read it carefully, handed it back.

"Okay, get it done." He started back toward his car.

"Where're you going to be this afternoon, Sheriff?"

"Luz's family: then I'll drop by the funeral home later this afternoon."

He looked up then and saw the girl in the bicycle helmet standing rigidly near the top of the hill a hundred yards away. Even at that distance he was sure it was Sarah Dubray. Hard to read her expression but not her body language as she turned quickly away and picked up the mountain bike lying in the pasture. She was angry, and he wondered why.

Dubrays were turning up in a lot of unlikely places today.

Sarah was quickly on her bike and peddling down the other side of the hill. Bonner didn't think he could head her off. But he thought it might be worthwhile to track her down and see if she knew anything about the illegal burial in the Starrettville cemetery.

Sarah's anger had acquired a hard focus upon seeing Bonner at the cemetery.

So this was *his* doing.

Tears welled up as she bicycled restlessly down the path. A vision of the rattlesnake crossed her mind. She imagined its fangs sinking into Bonner's flesh. Next time she wouldn't kill the rattlesnake with the .25 automatic Dally had given her. She'd put a live one in his mailbox. He had it coming.

Sarah was on the road back to Desert Rose and Silverwhip Jack Waco's place, peddling like a whirlwind, when she heard the motorcycle come up behind her. She glanced in the small dentist's mirror mounted on her helmet and saw her sister on a big heavily chromed Harley. Instead of whipping on by, Rosalind slowed to Sarah's pace, staying almost on top of her. Sarah didn't look back, didn't want Ros to recognize her.

But Ros must have had one of her infernal hunches or had noticed Sarah as she was cycling past a Chevron Mart a mile back along the road. After a short interval of tailing Sarah, waiting on an approaching pickup truck, Ros pulled even with her and gestured.

Sarah turned down a dirt farm road, stopped in the shade of some cottonwoods on the bank of a barely trickling creek. She took off her helmet, mopped perspiration at her hairline, and faced Rosalind hostilely, hands on hips.

Ros remained astride her Harley, the wind-ruffled crown of her head like a rooster atop the dawn. She lighted one of her *Romeo y Julietas*. The smoke that drifted her way was almost enough to turn Sarah's delicate stomach. She looked away when Ros smiled.

"Hey now, li'l sis. What have you got to be sore about?"

"I'm not taking any more pictures for you, if that's why you stopped me!"

"Thanks, I've already got enough. Just wanted to pass the time of day, that's all."

"Oh, *sure.*"

"Never understood what you hold against me, Sugarpea. I've always had a weak spot in my heart for you."

"For one thing, the way you treated Dally."

"That butch roommate of yours?"

"My best, my *dearest* friend."

Rosalind sighed, then smiled her brutal smile.

"Those martial arts types rub me the wrong way. I told Diesel Dally when it came to my favorite sister it'd better be love, or I'd use her ass for a trampoline. So I tend to be protective. It's the curse of my character sometimes. You want her, your business, but make sure you see a blood test."

A puff of breeze brought more smoke to Sarah's eyes, stinging them. Her brow wrinkled and her mouth flexed.

"They're d-digging up Suchary," she said forlornly.

Ros got off the Harley and stretched her long body, cocked her head alertly.

"Who is?"

"The sheriff. I saw them, back at the S-Starrettville cemetery."

"I wonder how they knew? Well, a fresh grave in that cemetery; dead giveaway if you'll pardon the expression. Kind of dumb of Pappy, but his mental processes are hand-cranked these days. So what is it to you?"

"Suchary was my friend, too. He's dead, and Dally wuh-won't talk to me. I've called and *called* her. Damn you, Ros!"

"You're well rid of Miss Pose-Off, believe it. I've seen more of her underworld than you ever will, Sugarpea."

Sarah, struggling amid the maze of her thwarted affections, broke down. Ros smoked calmly and watched her get through it.

"Let's go have lunch," she suggested.

"I don't want to. Just luh-leave me alone."

"Can't do that, Sugarpea. I need you to help me with something, a little *affaire de coeur* of my own. That's French for I crave some carnal satisfaction."

"Oh, you've got . . . suh-some nerve, Rosalind!"

"Her name's Katharine Harsha. She's a fed, and I have to be careful who I'm seen talking to these days. So you'll set it up for me. Kate'll like you. She'll probably trust you. Just enough. Tell her . . . you have to talk to her about Suchary. Oh, yes. That'll get her juices to stewing. The chance to go one up on Stearman. Those two, the competition's there; I could see that. So we'll exploit it."

In the hot haze beneath the swaying cottonwood boughs Sarah's small, demure face seemed barely three-dimensional, as if the armature beneath her flesh were as fragile as church wafers. But Rosalind knew better. Of all her sisters, Sarah was most like her.

Sarah's eyes had cleared. Her gaze had a certain pitiless vacancy.

"It's not just the sheriff," Ros explained. "The feds are in on it too, or soon will be. They'll learn who Suchary was. They'll do an autopsy to find out how he died. Those are pretty damned ugly, Sugarpea. Like a butcher taking a meat ax to his bones. Suchary doesn't deserve to get chopped up before they put him back in the ground again."

Sarah shook her head slowly. A flush had crept into her cheeks; it seemed amatory. Her body trembled again, as if the effort of speech was an act of war. A shaft of sun caught the small, round mirror on the biking helmet she held in her hands; it reflected a smaller, trembling sun to the middle of Rosalind's forehead.

"What are you going to do to her?" Sarah asked.

19

T. FRENCHMAN DOBIE PARKED his dusty Cadillac in the driveway of Wolfgang Gehrin's pyramidal mansion, its inward-slanting adobe walls a rusty ocher color against the green surround of lawn and tall Italian cypress, the showy pink and purple of tree-size crape myrtles. He got out, adjusted the tilt of his wide-brimmed Stetson against the angle of the afternoon sun, which had the sting of jellied gasoline on his skin. He rolled his shoulders uneasily, hearing activity in the pool fifty yards beyond the house, practiced a smile that would belie an uneasy mind, and went along the terra-cotta path toward the pool and the gazebo built over a waterfall at one end.

Wolfgang Gehrin was doing laps. A hippy Latin housegirl with high-rise breasts and flagrant nipples in a peasant blouse was setting the table in the gazebo. Gehrin wore swim goggles and a French bathing strap. He had heavy, hairy arms and shoulders and a ponderous stroke.

Frenchie stood near the waterfall end of the pool flicking a fingernail against his pale mustache as if dislodging mites and waited for Wolfgang to finish his constitutional.

"Where's the little woman?" Frenchie asked, just to get the conversation going after Wolfgang paused and clung to the edge of the pool.

"Shopping, I suppose. She's in Los Angeles."

When he had his breath back Wolfgang pulled himself slowly out of the water, took off his swim goggles, and reached for a blue-and-yellow-striped terry robe.

"So how're you this fine afternoon?" Frenchie asked, his other conversational opener.

"Wet."

The nonskid pavement around the pool was hot; Wolfgang stepped into a pair of leather thongs and walked up to the gazebo without looking at Frenchie. After a few indecisive moments, Frenchie decided he wasn't going to be formally invited but was meant to follow. Wolfgang sat down at the glass-topped table, smiled at the housegirl, then glanced at Frenchie and inclined his head slightly toward a vacant chair. The blue-eyed family cat was dozing, cloudlike, on a third chair.

"Would you care for sangria? I assume you've had your lunch."

"A couple of hours ago. You eat late."

"After crossing several time zones, I allow my body to adjust at whatever pace is necessary."

"You sure get around. I'm not a traveling man myself. Vegas and Mexico about the only places I ever go. You like to gamble?"

"Games of chance bore me."

The housegirl leaned over the table slightly to pour sangria for them. She wore a large gold cross between her breasts, but Frenchie wasn't interested in the cross. Frenchie had four wives and one pending, at least he liked to think so; no time lately to concentrate on Sarah Dubray. Looking at the housegirl's marvelous tits had him randy and resentful too. He reminded himself that he needed to attend to Sarah, and—Frenchie touched his split sore lip—her friend, whose swift foot and sneak attack had cost him three hours in the dentist's chair, $650 dollars' worth of repair work.

"What's your name, honey?" Frenchie asked the housegirl. Her ripeness and delicious sun-warmed scent were making him dizzy. She would have been beautiful, but her left eye wandered and her nose had been broken once, then badly reset.

"Conchita," the girl said, with a perfectly blank expression.

"Spick English, Conchita?"

"A little."

"Think you and me could have us a real good time together, *muchacha?*"

Conchita studied him opaquely, then lifted her shoulders as if puzzled and glanced at Gehrin.

"You handle it," Wolfgang said to her.

Conchita nodded. She turned and emptied the pitcher of sangria in Frenchie's lap.

"Goddamn it! Goddamn you, you cockeyed greaser bitch!"

"Oops," Conchita said. "Sorry." She looked at Gehrin again. "What is meaning, 'greaser bitch?' "

"It's an ethnic slur, darling."

"Oh." Conchita's English improved suddenly. "Then it would be all right if I cut the *huevos* off this *pinche qusanito* the next time I see him on the premises?"

"I don't believe there'll be a next time, Connie—but, yes, you have my blessing."

Frenchie, his hyperthyroid eyes bulging, used a napkin to brush wine and pieces of marinated fruit from his stained crotch. His curses stayed low in his throat, more or less strangling him.

"Would you like your lunch now?" Conchita asked Wolfgang.

"What are we having?"

"Salmon mousse with ginger-flavored mustard, steak tartare seasoned with hazelnut oil and white pepper, a brioche filled with black fig jam for dessert." She glanced at Frenchie. "And I'll make another pitcher of sangria. I apologize for being wasteful."

"No problem. Thank you, Conchita."

"I wonder if you'd mind if I took a couple of hours later this afternoon to work on my master's thesis? I've recently come across some interesting monographs on the Internet relative to Gustav Klimt's visits to Italy in 1903. The influence on Klimt of the San Vitale mosaics is quite evident in his subsequent work, the *Stoclet Frieze,* for instance."

"A very beautiful mosaic in its own right. The only one Klimt produced, I believe. Sit down, Frenchie, where the devil do you think you're going? We have business to discuss."

"I'm not used to being treated this way!"

"By women? Of course you are. We'll exclude the devout youngsters required by the tenets of your religion to bed down with you. A certain cultish sanctity being your only advantage; I wouldn't call it cachet. In the workaday world you have the sensual appeal of a dog with a shaved ass."

As Conchita walked away with a trace of a smile on her full lips, Frenchie slumped lower in his seat, too craven to be insulted by a man who could make him extremely rich.

"Rhondo was shot at last night."

Wolfgang said with a flicker of surprise, "Missed him?"

"Just barely." Frenchie tapped his forehead with a finger. "Gave him a setback, though."

"Not surprising. Who do you suspect?"

"Well, we know there're feds in town. Maybe no reason to look further than that."

"Umm-hmm. At any rate, it's not good news. We should be done with our business all the more quickly." Frenchie's eyeballs were tense and glistening. Wolfgang said sourly, "I hope you haven't come to tell me that you can't locate the Dove?"

Frenchie raised both hands defensively, as if Wolfgang were about to chuck a medicine ball at him.

"No, no, there's no problem; matter of fact, we've found half a dozen of them. All alike."

"I see." Wolfgang studied him for a few moments, then shifted his gaze to Conchita. Her back was to them as she prepared the steak tartare on the elaborate brass and stainless steel chef's cart a dozen feet away. "So there are several Doves, which may not be of any value without Suchary's research, diagrams, and test data. He did conduct tests?"

"Sure, he must have. I mean, that's why he had Rhondo put in that one deep tunnel. Two hundred yards bored through solid rock. You talk about gonzo expensive—"

Wolfgang cut him off with a flick of one hand.

"The data, Frenchie. Suchary's computer files. *Those* are what matter, with company coming."

Frenchie was sitting half in sunlight; there were dribbles of perspiration on his forehead as he looked down at the wine stain on his whipcord trousers. He fumbled for his sunglasses hanging by a temple bar from the breast pocket of his rancher-style suit coat and raised his head to put them on. Wolfgang leaned toward Frenchie and took the shades, not wanting Frenchie's eyes to go into hiding.

Frenchie squirmed a little, surprised by the strength of Gehrin's grip.

"The files I've seen are in that Russian writing, you know, acryllic—"

"Cyrillic. But mathematical formulae are a universal language. What do you mean, the files you've seen?"

"I don't know almighty much about computers. Now Tyrell— that would be Rhondo's fifth son by Carlene, who is Rhondo's—"

"Let us not get into the convoluted genealogy of clan Dubray. Just who is Tyrell, and why does he matter?"

"He worked the closest with Suchary, and he had the education, you know, to understand most of that physics stuff. Also computers. Tyrell is real gonzo with computers. Anyway, Tyrell had the access codes, but when he got down to work he had to back off in a hurry—"

"What?"

"Tyrell says he's pretty sure the encryption software he was using turned loose some kind of germ in the, what do you call it, the hard drive—"

"Germ? You mean a virus."

"Yeah, that's the word, virus. Which I guess means—"

Wolfgang let go of Frenchie's wrist and sat back, a lot of air leaving his chest even as he smiled tautly.

"What it means is, Suchary tried to fuck us. May have done. One small change in the code, and Suchary's files turn to gibberish. Calculations become nonsense, or—better still—lead to erroneous conclusions that might take months to rectify. So the hard drive was infected. What about the ZIPs?"

"The what?" Frenchie said, blotting his face with a linen napkin.

"Backup disks. Copies of all the files that were in the hard drive before Suchary poisoned the well."

"Yeah. Copies. Tyrell tried one on a different mainframe. They look okay; then, before you can blink, everything turns to—garbage, Tyrell said. He was pretty put out about it."

Frenchie shied away from the expression on Wolfgang's face, staring at the ribs of blue water on the surface of the breezy pool.

Wolfgang said, "Handwritten notes? Scratch work Suchary overlooked? *Anything?*"

Frenchie shook his head. "We've still got the Doves. Six of them, like I said. That ought to be enough."

"All that we have, I'm sure, is a set of dummy N-bombs, each containing—it's no secret what they contain. The Aum Shinrikyo are not about to pay twenty million U.S. for tritium they can buy in the open market at half the price. So why—"

"Why what?" Frenchie asked cautiously after a few moments.

"Why would Suchary Siamashvili decide to destroy the most brilliant achievement of his life? Why the change of heart? What—or who—influenced his decision? We need some answers, Frenchie. Fast.

Because company is coming. Certain guarantees have been made. Our asses are on the line, Mr. T. Frenchman Dobie."

One corner of Frenchie's mouth twitched. "We can explain to them that—"

"No, no. You don't get it. No explanation will be accepted. Not by the Aum Shinrikyo."

"But—" Frenchie protested, his hope falling like a bucket into a dry well.

"The Aum Shinrikyo, if you may have forgotten, redefine the term 'homicidal paranoiacs.' "

Frenchie moved his chair, taking his face out of the sun. Conchita approached the table and placed Wolfgang's lunch in front of him. She gave him a sympathetic glance, as if she knew he had lost his appetite. Wolfgang thanked her anyway. Conchita returned to her cart and began slicing oranges for another pitcher of sangria.

"We can't call it off?" Frenchie asked.

"Let's not be hasty," Wolfgang replied, deep in thought. "Lord knows I need my end of the twenty million, but it's not worth— Tyrell isn't going to be of any help to us?"

" 'Fraid not," Frenchie said.

"Did Suchary correspond with other physicists, attend conferences?"

"No. He was a real loner."

"He had no confidants in New Hebron?"

"Last couple of years, knowing his health wasn't going to improve, all Suchary did was work and watch western movies when his brain went numb on him. He must've seen *Red River,* that was his favorite, twenty times. He almost never left his compound. Tyrell says there probably wasn't five men in the rest of the world who could hang with Suchary in his area of expertise."

Wolfgang picked at his salmon mousse. "I know he wasn't married. But who was he fucking?"

"Suchary?" Frenchie laughed. "Couldn't. Something to do with radiation when he was a lot younger, working at that nuclear lab in Russia. An accident that permanently wilted his pecker. And I believe he mentioned once he had to have his thyroid gland removed."

Wolfgang was thoughtful again.

"No," Frenchie continued, ruminating, "there wasn't any little gal Suchary could get it on with, but if he could have, reckon I know the one."

Wolfgang looked alertly at him. Frenchie was making a wry face.
"Yes?"

Frenchie shrugged. "Suchary might have had a little crush on *my*
intended. Can't say I blame him; Sarah stole my heart away when she
was only eight years old."

"Who?"

"Sarah. Sarah Dubray. Rhondo's first and only daughter by his
wife Leona, who died when Sarah was just three years old."

"Did they have a relationship of sorts? Sarah and Suchary?"

"It didn't amount to anything; I know that. Sarah worked at one
of Rhondo's restaurants in town, and maybe once a week Suchary
liked to have a meal there. I heard they'd sit and talk. That was all."

"Was it?"

"Hell, I told you! She's been my intended for the last eight years.
I was set to marry her when she turned thirteen, but—"

"Thirteen?"

Frenchie hunched his shoulders slightly, began flicking at his
mustache again with a fingernail.

"Morbid curiosity on my part, but why didn't the marriage take
place?"

"Oh, she, uh, swallowed some stuff that just about killed her,
and she was in kind of a bad motional state for a while. Rhondo had
to send her away to a clinic up in Oregon. So I figured, well, I would
just bide my time."

"Very decent of you, Frenchie, I'm sure. I would like to have a
talk with Sarah."

Frenchie froze, a fingertip poised against his upper lip.

"What for?"

"Because she's the one, Suchary's confessor. The dying need
someone to whom they can open their corroded and insulted hearts,
absolve themselves of their wretched sins. One needn't be religious.
It's human nature."

Frenchie moved his chair a little more to the side as the sun
reached his eyes again.

"I don't know what you—"

"Suchary sacrificed his potency and his thyroid to science; who
knows what else decayed inside due to his lifetime of exposure to
lethal isotopes? But the last thing to die in a man like Suchary is the
ego. It lives on well beyond the last beat of his heart. All brilliant but
antisocial loners with a sense of destiny want vindication for their

trials and suffering. *Red River?* Suchary may have loved that movie because he felt a kinship with the lonely, driven man whom John Wayne played so effectively. Suchary mangled his research during his last days, possibly to keep lesser men from exploiting his work—for other, ethical reasons. Who knows? Sarah may have had a part in his decision. Whatever, I understand quite enough about Suchary Siamashvili to make an assumption. Suchary's ego would *not* let him totally destroy the Dove, the hard-won knowledge for which he gave his life. The trigger for the Dove exists. And Sarah may know where it is."

Frenchie felt his heartbeat accelerate. Adrenaline shook him like a depth charge.

"I don't think—"

"No need for you to think about it at all," Wolfgang said smoothly. "Just produce Sarah for me, and quickly."

20

NEAL BONNER FOUND HIS mother on the terrace with Maria Elena. Near them the infant Cymbeline splashed naked in an inflatable pool. She had a couple of bruises from being slung around in the duffel bag the night before, but she had slept off the dose of chloroform given to her by her would-be abductors and showed no other signs of trauma. She was having a good time with toy boats and wind-up dolphins.

Neal sat down beneath the mesh sun shade that extended the length of the terrace and took off his cocoa-colored Panama hat. There was a sting of sweat at the corners of his eyes, in the creases at the back of his neck. He loosened his tie.

His mother smiled when he took her hand. She turned her head to look at him with eyes like canceled stars.

"This is a delightful surprise."

"Just wanted to stop by for a few minutes. I'm on the five o'clocker to LA."

"Always on the go," she chided. "Have some lemonade."

"Thanks." He poured a glassful on top of three ounces of vodka from the pint in his coat pocket. "Where's Dad?"

"He's off somewhere with Charlie Barnhofer. Drinking again?" She couldn't smell it, but she had caught the sound of him screwing the cap back on the bottle.

"Aw, Mom. It relaxes me. I haven't had any sleep for twenty-four hours. My head's going at warp speed."

"You might have been killed, from what I've heard."

Neal looked at Cymbeline, who was babbling in Spanish to the watchful Maria Elena. There were butterflies on the terrace, the sweetness of roses. A stiff-legged old border collie named Groucho came up to Neal for a head scratch, then stretched out slowly and painfully on the flagstones. Neal swallowed half of his liquored-up lemonade. He put the glass down and cracked the knuckles of his left hand.

Willa asked, "You're in trouble, Neal?"

"What makes you ask that?"

"I always know. What is it this time?"

"Nothing my lawyers can't handle. I'm meeting with them in the morning."

"I don't think you're as sure as all that."

"Mom, some allegations have been made. I'm used to it."

The vodka was having an unusual effect on him. His body was okay, but his heart felt as if it were about to go mad. Splashings from the small wading pool sparkled in the sun. He stared at the child and imagined how it might have turned out, gunfire erupting, mulberry blotches around the bullet holes in the red duffel bag. His mouth went dry; a muscle in his cheek trembled. But here she was, just ten feet away, unharmed, unaware. He wondered if Tobin knew what it was about yet, the kidnapping attempt. Neal hadn't been able to contact his brother. Mary Lynn, who was handling funeral arrangements for Lucy Ruiz, had told him the sheriff had already received two hundred calls today. Calls he had no time to return.

"Your father can't help this time," Willa said.

"I don't need his help. It'll get straightened out."

"I would hate it if you've jeopardized Poppy or the children in any way."

"What are you saying? I would *never*—my wife and children are my most precious—"

"It would put my mind at ease to know more about your problem."

"Computer glitches. Clerical errors. Some clients were overbilled. A few of them just haven't been willing to cooperate, give me the time I need. They'll get their money. Business has been slow, you know how it is; there are more lawyers in this country than there are pigs in shit." Neal laughed derisively and reached for his spiked lemonade. "Nobody takes into account the work I've done on the cuff. Pro bono, fund-raising. You name the cause, I've always been available. I'll pay Dad back too, those other loans. One hundred ten percent. You don't have to worry."

Willa looked at him, reading his face from memory.

"I'm only concerned about you and your family."

Neal stared again at Cymbeline; he couldn't help himself.

Willa said, "You know I have the money my father left me. If that would—"

Neal laughed again.

"Mom, absolutely not. I wouldn't touch it." He leaned over to kiss her. "Put that thought out of your mind."

"I'm not even sure how much it is now."

"I invested the money well, rock-solid securities. Nothing speculative. You're comfortable. Very comfortable."

"Couldn't I borrow against—"

"As trustee I absolutely forbid it. I don't want your money. The subject's closed."

"All right."

"Mom, I love you. I have to run."

"How long will you be in Los Angeles?"

"Two or three days."

Maria Elena had taken Cymbeline out of the pool and wrapped her in a beach towel. Cymbeline ran across the terrace toward Willa as Neal got up from the patio chair.

On his feet he felt dangerously tipsy, not as if he had drunk too much—although the pint in his coat pocket, nearly empty, was his second of the day—but as if his insides had been sucked away, nothing left but the fruitless seed of his heart. His mother offering him money that hadn't been there for years. It was like a faint, final blow to his nearly demolished pride.

The little girl stopped and looked up at him, beads of water on her face, dark as a sunspot in the explosive glare. So many strangers coming and going in her life. Neal smiled reassuringly at her, wondering what it was like to see with her eyes, breathe with her lungs. Childhood. He'd been safe then, way back there before the world ganged up on him. Cym's nose was running. Neal reached for his pocket handkerchief and gently cleaned her up. Cymbeline didn't flinch or take her eyes off him. Amazing, he thought, how full of trust she was. He felt unexpectedly calm now, almost peaceful, dabbing gently at her button nose. Just as he had done for each of his own babies.

Tobin Bonner paid his respects to Luz's extended family, gathered at the home of her oldest brother. So many relatives that they overflowed the house into the shady, red dirt front yard on a side street in the community of Rocky Mount. He didn't know most of them. Men in their church suits, boys in short-sleeved white shirts and dark trousers, girls who wore new dresses as crinkly as paper hollyhocks. In the lifeless heat the men came to Bonner to shake his hand or wordlessly embrace him. Mary Lynn had made sure that there were flowers and food. Luz's old mother was chatty and convivial, thinking it must be a party—first communion *quinceañeras*. They tried to hide their tears from *mamacita* until it was time for her nap.

A TV crew found Bonner there; he wouldn't talk to them. New arrivals, from more distant places, prompted fresh outcries of grief inside the cement-block house. He left as soon as he decently could. He wanted to see Luz, if she was ready to be seen. But he wasn't far from Desert Rose and Jack Waco's place.

In spite of the tragedy, he still had work to do.

Silverwhip Jack took a long pull at his bottle of Dos Equis and said, "I was there at the Mesquiteer from about three in the afternoon until I don't know when. Early hours of the morning, but I was out of it long before then, I expect."

"So while you were boozing at the Mesquiteer, your Silverado was taken. Keys were in the ignition when we found what was left of it."

Jack shrugged. "I always leave the keys under the floor mat."

"Jack, there was blood found on the front seat."

"I'll give you some of mine; odds are it's a match." Jack held up his right hand and pointed to a minor scar where his palm met the wrist. "Hooked it on some barb wire I didn't see when I was out hunting woodcock last fall."

Bonner nodded. "Where'd you go after McMurtry's place?"

"Friend of mine came and collected me."

"Who would that be?"

Jack looked away, at the lowering sun across the pond next to his log ranch house, and adjusted the brim of his black Stetson. After a few moments, he winced and said, "There's bound to be plenty of regulars at that biker bar who'll swear I never left during the time those murders were committed."

"We'll verify it. What I asked was, who were you with for the next day and a half?"

"Can't see how it's a question of the law."

"Jack, look at me. You see what kind of mood I'm in?"

Jack's pale eyes touched on Bonner's face. He nodded, chastened. "Hell, Tobin, I'm not very proud of myself."

"Come on."

"It was Ros Dubray."

Bonner sat slackly in the cedarwood Adirondack chair stroking his lower lip with a thumbnail, looking at birds strung together like black static on a telephone line.

"Where do you know Ros from?"

"I gave her flying lessons once upon a time."

"How old was she?"

"Just a kid. I knew her because she was living at Chamas Calder's. You know all about their arrangement. Chamas and me were drinkin' buddies."

"Flying lessons?"

"She wasn't good at it. No depth perception. After a couple landings that like to bust the fillings out of my back teeth, I gave up on her."

"So you were sharing a fourteen-year-old kid with Chamas Calder before she whacked him with a shovel."

"Hell no! It wasn't never anything like that. I could tolerate what was going on with her and Chamas, but I never wanted no part of it."

"After all these years Rosalind remembered you and gave you a place to sleep off your drunk. Guess what, Jack? I hate this story."

"It's the plain truth. See, I ran into Ros at McMurtry's, I don't know, a couple of months back. Talk about coincidence, she's living at my old town, up by the park. Rhondo Dubray took it off the bank's hands years ago. Ros has the saloon fixed up real nice."

"You ran into her, and it was just like old times."

Jack shifted his weight uneasily. His tooled silver belt buckle flared in sunlight that came through a space in the bamboo shade that was rolled partway down at one end of the porch.

"That's about how it was."

"Are you fucking Rosalind now that she's all grown up?"

Jack flinched slightly, then shook his head in disgust.

"Then what's the attraction? Why does she want to do you any favors?"

"What does this have to do with—?"

"Maybe Ros borrowed your truck while you were there in the Mesquiteer getting slopped. She took a run down to Desert Rose in the rain, shot three adults and two kids to death, drove up to Caballo Rojo and rolled the Silverado into a canyon. Hopped on the motorcycle she had stashed there and picked you up a few hours later, around closing time."

Jack looked appalled. "Hell, I can't believe that!"

"It's a fact that they're dead. And it's a fact that Rosalind Dubray had better than a nodding acquaintance with Gabriel Sinaloa; they were seen around town together."

"Sinaloa?"

" 'Santero' was the name the federal marshals gave the family. They were stashed in the Witness Protection Program."

"Murder? Ros has always been rough as a cob, but I'm willing to bet the ranch she never killed nobody."

"With the likely exception of Chamas Calder."

"I-I never did believe she had anything to do with that, neither."

His breath hung in his throat; momentarily there was a tiny flicker in Jack's eyes, a forbidden thought slipping out, cryptic to Bonner but still worth remembering. Then Jack's expression changed; a smile of relief added creases to his weathered face. He tried to jump to his feet in a move that startled Bonner, but Jack's old bones wouldn't permit that. He wound up staggering, grasping a porch post for balance.

"Here they are!"

Bonner turned to see a van with Shay Waco at the wheel. Her daughter leaned out the window on the passenger side, ecstatic, waving; Shay honked.

"Granpa!"

"Ain't my granddaughter a little beauty?"

"Yeah," Bonner said, rising, realizing there wasn't much more he could do with Silverwhip Jack. But he was sure that Jack knew something he would let go of at another time, when Bonner could bear down and pry it loose. "Doesn't look anything like her mother."

"I'd say she got the best of what her Irisher daddy and his side of the family had to offer. Although I never have laid eyes on him."

Jack went down the steps, trying to appear spry, to help Pepper out of the van.

"Take it easy, now, don't you give that knee a whack. Where's your crutches, honey?"

"I don't need to have another operation! I don't have to go back to the hospital, Granpa!"

"*There's* some good news."

Shay, getting out on her side, took off her sunglasses and forced a smile for Bonner. She seemed looted of energy.

"Social call?" she asked warily.

"No. How are you?" He didn't need to ask; his wife had suffered from migraines, and he knew the look. A muscle crept below Shay's pained right eye, like a caterpillar beneath the skin.

"Just getting Pepper out of the hospital is a great relief." Shay put her sunglasses back on. "Maybe now we can—"

"Granpa, wait'll I tell you! There's this TV show, it's *syndicated.* They want to *pay* me to be on television!"

"Forget it," Shay said.

"Mom-mm, *Godddd!*"

Bonner wanted very badly to touch Shay; hell, put his arms around her and hold tight. There were twin images of himself in the oval metalized lenses of her glasses: a man who was tired of seeing and knowing, another man hanging on to the edge of the world, cauldron of sun behind him.

"You're going to be around for a while?"

Shay turned to watch Jack and Pepper, who was struggling with her crutches.

"She doesn't have the hang of those yet, Jack. Be careful."

"What do you say I just carry you up to the porch, Pepper?"

Shay lowered her voice, looking at Bonner again.

"I think we'll head home to California after the funeral. When will that be?"

"Three days. Second of July."

"I never thought I'd be camera shy, but Pepper and I have had enough attention. It still worries me that he's on the loose."

"I understand. I wish I could say I was getting somewhere."

Shay was sympathetic. "Do you have to rush off?"

"I'm going to see Luz now. And there's some other business. An unidentified body we took from the Starrettville cemetery today."

"Does it ever end?"

"Would you like to meet my son?" Bonner asked.

Shay looked momentarily confused. "Well—I—yes."

"Good. My place, about eight-thirty? I'll put some ribs on the grill."

"I don't remember how to—"

"I live in Trampas. Twelve miles the other side of Spanish Wells, on the road to the park. Take a right at the Shell Mart, two blocks, turn left. We're the second house; you'll know it when you see it."

"Okay."

"Pepper's invited, of course."

"I don't know." Shay looked at the porch. Silverwhip Jack had her daughter on his back, carrying her. They were both laughing, Jack so hard it triggered a coughing fit. Shay was about to warn him, decided against it. She shook her aching head gently. "I want her to settle down, and she still has spells of nausea from the anesthetic. Jack can look after her."

"I'd say they've really hit it off."

"They *adore* each other. Now I feel guilty that they didn't get acquainted sooner. What did Jack have to say about his truck?"

"Stolen."

"Then he—"

"No, I don't believe he had anything to do with those killings. He's accounted for his time."

Shay's mouth flexed, softened. "Where was he?"

"Bending his elbow."

"Oh, well, of course."

"Don't be too hard on him, Shay. Told me he had a case of nerves waiting for you guys."

"I guess I can understand that," Shay said doubtfully. "Sher— Tobin, I *really* need to soak in a tub and catch a nap if I'm going to—"

"Sure. And thanks for—"

Shay smiled, a little anxiously. A breeze off the shining pond combed through her hair.

"You don't want to be alone tonight. I don't either. I mean— I'm not ready for Jack, just yet."

"A lot to be settled, is that it?"

"Oh, God. I suppose. I *hope*. You can wear out your heart, can't you? And never get rid of the anger."

"Yes."

21

THERE WAS A PANEL truck with a stylized peacock on both sides parked across the street from the funeral home, white uplink dish on the roof. A good-looking VJ from the Spanish-language network Univision was touching up her makeup in the front seat of a van with California plates, while her crew prepared to tape a report. The police department had a car there. Nobody knew what the hell was going on in Spanish Wells, but the TV crews were all over town now, from the seats of city and county governments to the Medical Center, contributing to the doom, the tension that enclosed the town like an electrified fence. Everywhere they parked they collected small knots of townspeople with nothing else to do but gossip and speculate.

Bonner, driving a pickup truck from the county's motor pool while they put a new windshield in his car, drove around to the back of the frame building and parked behind a hearse that was getting a wash job. He went in through the basement entrance and was met by one of the Edoway Brothers, members of an extensive family that had been in the mortuary business locally for nearly a hundred years.

"I have something for Luz," Bonner said to Pike Edoway, a pleasant rube of a man with a shingle of wavy hair flopped across one side of his forehead and coppery tufts of sideburns. "If she's—"

Pike nodded. "Yes. She's upstairs now. Come this way, Sheriff."

"Did Rudy get to the body that was brought in today?"

"We're waiting on Cas; he should be here any moment."

They had placed Luz in a small parlor at the back of the first floor. The parlor wasn't intended for viewing. She would remain there until they took her to the Catholic church and then to the cemetery. A long cortege down Division Street, which would be lined with sheriff's deputies from every county in Utah, delegations of peace officers from surrounding states.

Luz was wearing a dark blue dress with a high neckline of lace. He didn't think he'd seen her in that dress before. He wasn't used to seeing her in a dress at all. Most of the damage had been to one side of her throat and head as she instinctively pulled back and looked away from the muzzle of the shotgun. Three hours in surgery before they lost her. All of the wounds had been repaired or camouflaged by the mortician's art; she didn't look injured at all.

Bonner felt grateful as he leaned over the casket, awkwardly pulling from his coat pocket the crucifix that had been on the wall of her bedroom. He placed it under her clasped gloved hands. She had no jewelry with her, never cared for it. Luz and Christ, they would endure together. The mortician had filled three of the gloved fingers with—something; Luz had one remaining finger on her left hand, the hand with which she had tried to fend off the velocity of pellets, the metal storm she had plunged into headlong.

He sat down beside Luz in a chair Pike Edoway brought to him. Saw her look of soft, eternal imperviousness. He didn't like the lip gloss they had used. Too light for her complexion. The shape of her mouth was all right. He reminded himself that she wasn't there, wasn't there, his heart beginning to buckle from strain. Pressure in the front of his head. The awfulness of Luz not being there. The bad luck and inevitable guilt.

I didn't take good care of you. I failed again, Luz. But we have two of them. I swear to you, others will pay. Please. Use what power you have, wherever you are, use it to keep me going. I don't want to end up the way I was those months after they took Connie away from me. It's too hard now. Too hard to make it back from that kind of grief.

"Sheriff Bonner?"

Bonner looked back at the doorway and wiped his sultry eyes.

"I'm sorry," Pike Edoway said. He looked uncharacteristically flustered. "But we have a problem downstairs. There are men here from a government agency. They say they're authorized to remove the body; the old man who was buried in the Starrettville cemetery. What should I do?"

Bonner followed him downstairs and into the embalming room where the body from the cemetery, in a black rubber bag, lay on a gleaming zinc table with gutters and drains. The air stenchy, carbolic. That cold, astringent air of death tidied up, finalized. On a shelf there was a foetus in a storm of fluid, more like a mushroom than an incipient child except for its bland, mad eyespot.

Three men in dark suits were waiting for Bonner.

"What's this about? Show me some ID, please."

"Sweets, Wyrick, and Peyton," one of the men said. Sweets had his folder in his hand, but Bonner had seen him before, at the Santero house.

"What do you want with that body?"

"That's privileged information, Sheriff."

"Do you know who he was?"

"Also privileged." Sweets handed him a faxed authorization for removal of the body, signed by a federal district court judge.

"If you find this in order, we'd like to proceed."

"Do you have a phone on you, Mr. Sweets?"

"Yes, I do."

"Get Stearman for me."

"I don't see the necessity for that. We're legally authorized—"

"Until I read over this Direct Action Order with the county attorney present, or talk directly to your boss, that body's going nowhere, gentlemen. We have evidence of an illegal burial, with a possibility that foul play was involved, and that places the matter squarely in *my* jurisdiction."

Sweets looked at Wyrick, who looked at Peyton, who pondered Bonner's ultimatum, and nodded.

"Would you excuse me for just a minute, Sheriff Bonner?"

Bonner felt his dangerous pulse like a tightly wound clock in his head.

"You can have a minute."

Peyton went out the door.

Bonner leaned against a wall with his arms folded, looking at the body bag. His mind was tired; his legs ached. They waited.

Scrape of shoes on the hard surface of the hall outside.

Dale Stearman came in, ducking his head slightly. He didn't quite fit through most doorways.

"Tobin."

"Dale."

"I'm extremely sorry about the loss of your deputy. A personal loss, I know."

"Yes, it is. What's going on here? Why do you want that body?"

"It's relevant to our investigations, which is about all I can—"

"Dale, don't give me hand jobs; that's proof to me of intoxication. I'll have to tank you for public drunkenness."

Stearman's jaws stopped working on his wad of gum. He pinched the bridge of his nose with thumb and forefinger, eyes growing a little weary. He looked at the body bag.

"Everybody outside," he said, "except the sheriff."

When the door had closed behind them, Stearman said, "You take a look yet?"

"I saw him this morning. Natural causes, but us old lawdogs like to be sure. The body was embalmed, but there's no relevant death certificate on file in Utah."

"There won't be a death certificate anywhere. I expect they had the job done out of state, maybe even shipped the body to Mexico and back."

"Who are we talking about?"

"The Brightly Shining."

"Figures."

"This is highly classified, Tobe. I'm only telling you because I know if I don't you'll work yourself into such a state you may have to take a medical leave of absence from your job."

"And enroll in the weight-loss program at the Cube?"

Stearman smiled. "There's all kinds of therapy available at the Cube for overstressed government employees."

"I don't work for the government anymore."

"Your time with DEA accords you all the benefits of the Cube: golf, tennis, swimming."

"Mind control."

"Relaxation therapy is the preferred terminology."

"Out of curiosity, having heard a few rumors; just where is the Cube, at Area Fifty-one?"

Stearman shook his head. "All I can tell you is, you wouldn't enjoy the winters there. Now do you want to hear about Suchary Siamashvili? I'm assuming that's who we have here, although it's not a hundred percent certain. Which is why we need the body."

"Russian?"

"Georgian."

"Go on."

"Suchary was a nuclear physicist. Employed for most of his career at Arzamas-Sixteen. For the last four years he was a member of the Brightly Shining, living and working in New Hebron."

Bonner leaned alertly against the wall, thumbs in his belt, his gaze sharpening, a lone wolf sort of look.

"Working on a lunchbox nuke?"

"Good guess."

"I'm not guessing. It's not the first time I've heard about it. How far did he get with his H-bomb project?"

"Suchary abandoned conventional means of mass distruction for something that intrigued him more. Neutrons. A fusion bomb. Neutrons are deadly at short range: we're assuming a kill zone of a thousand yards from ground zero for a bomb the size of a grapefruit, but who knows? There are no aboveground barriers to neutrons. It might take less than a crate of Doves to extinguish the human race. We could vanish like the dinosaur. The radiation kills in minutes. Electromagnetic pulsation blows out computers. As the planet rolled around hebbin all day with that lucky old sun, fish would still swim in the sea, flowers would bloom, simple mechanisms like parking meters and Coke machines would continue to function. But human history would be one big dead-letter office."

Bonner tried to feel this news in his soul, and failed.

"How much bullshit are you handing me here?"

"We were well along the road to building Doves forty years ago. A very influential man in our government at the time, you'd recognize his name, realized what the Dove would mean to his attempts to establish a nuclear-proliferation treaty. The Dove would make any such treaty unenforceable. So he killed the project. But the Russians, including Suchary Siamashvili, kept working on the concept. Doves are relatively cheap to manufactures because they contain no fissionable material. A million dollars a pop? Cheap and portable. Undetectable by nuclear energy search teams."

"The guy in the body bag came up with a workable neutron bomb in a garage workshop in New Hebron?"

"He had better tools than your average home shop mechanic. Probably about thirty million dollars' worth of equipment. And yes, Suchary solved the problems of a trigger for his device, or else he was so close others of his ability could take over now and finish the job."

"Call in the Working Group."

"The Working Group is interagency, with all the potential feuds and fuckups inherent in such groups. We found that out during a trial exercise in New Orleans a few years ago, involving a theoretical malevolent nuclear threat. So that's why there's FIAT. A no-notice, final-initiative force. No point in swarming over New Hebron with NESTs, the FBI, and assorted SWAT teams. Suchary may have booby-trapped the place with a Dove or two. There wouldn't be time to reach for the aspirin. For want of any concrete data, let's assume wide-scale lethality. Every man, woman, and child living within a fifty-mile radius."

It was surreal, too epic for Bonner to get a grip on. His reaction was a yawn.

"I thought I had problems."

Stearman removed his wad of gum and rolled it into the wrapper of a fresh stick, which he began to chew.

"How do you plan to work it?" Bonner asked.

"My priority is to make sure that if we *are* sitting on a cache of live Doves right here in Solar County, none of them get out into the wide world."

"For instance?"

"I can only say there are other interested parties. Real scary folks."

"You tried to assassinate Rhondo Dubray last night, didn't you?"

Stearman's jaw stopped working for a few moments; his eyes cooled.

"Now we're going beyond the bounds of this conversation."

"Ros is real hot about it."

"How would you know?"

"She told me. Stopped short of filing an official complaint. So I guess I don't have anything to investigate."

"That's logical."

"To put her in the best light possible, Rosalind is volatile and unpredictable."

Stearman smiled knowingly and shrugged.

"She's the least of my worries."

"Dale?"

"Yeah?"

"You pull anything like that again in my jurisdiction, I don't care about your priorities. I'll fix up you and your gang that can't shoot straight with my *own* version of the Cube. And I'll be doing you a big favor. Because it's my conviction that Ros Dubray is definitely not the least of your worries. See you around, hotshot."

Bonner went back to his office from the funeral home and began returning the calls that were urgent. One of them was from his sister-in-law, Poppy Bonner.

"Oh, Tobe, I'm so sorry. I haven't been able to stop crying."

"It's tough, Poppy."

"I didn't know Luz all that well, but I loved her. How can I help you?"

"It helps just to hear your voice. To know you care."

Poppy sniffed a couple of times. "Tobin, this is the—absolute *wrong* time, I know, but I—I really must talk to you."

"What's the matter, Poppy?"

"It isn't—something I can discuss over the phone. Honestly, I hate to—"

Bonner glanced at the office clock. "You at home?"

"Y-yes."

"I can be there around six."

"Oh, gosh, I feel so *bad* bringing you my little problems at a time like this."

"That's what I'm here for. Where's Neal?"

"On his way to Los Angeles. Meetings, he said." Bonner detected a tone in her voice that was unlike Poppy. Cynicism. Well, she was long overdue. "I'll make dinner for you, Tobe. It'll just be us; Walton and Kyle are away at soccer camp, and Biffer has Girl Scouts."

When Bonner pulled into the driveway of Neal and Poppy's bluff-side house on Rocky Lane, Poppy was in the small front yard watering the feather-duster palms in plots of red volcanic rock. All three of the family dogs, plucked from death row at the county humane shelter, were engaged in mock combat on the lawn. Big shaggy beloved pooches. Poppy seemed frail in their rollicking midst. She was forty-two. From a distance of thirty feet she looked to be about sixteen. Richly tanned, slight figure, gamin haircut.

She put down the hose and ran barefooted to Bonner as he got out of the pickup truck. He gathered her in, and she pressed her face against his chest. Neither of them said anything for almost a minute. Then he pried Poppy loose and smiled at her.

"You mentioned something about food?"

"Caca! I forgot to turn down the corn chowder!"

She ran into the low stone-faced California-style house. Bonner turned off the water and coiled the hose. The dogs followed him into the house and through it to the terrace with its terrific view of large portions of Solar County. Poppy had the Bose radio tuned to an Arizona station that played *ranchera*. He called to her in the kitchen.

"I'm having company later tonight and I planned to put on some ribs, but I could handle a plate now."

"Chicken and dumplings?"

"Fine."

"Do you want a drink? You know where Neal hides it."

"Just some iced tea, Poppy, thanks."

Bonner made himself comfortable on a wide lounger. There was a stiff one-note wind, almost a daily occurrence up here in the late afternoon, the wind nicely deflected by angled glass panels at either end of the terrace. The oldest of the dogs—scarred, wiry, and enduring—took her place at the foot of the chaise, still panting from her romp, an ear drooping like a jester's cap.

He looked at the familiar landscape, familiar but never boring: homeland. Lucky to have been born in a place like this. A vista of mesas, benchland, cliffs, invisible streams choked with green trees, their roots deep and claiming all the water that, except on the wettest days, sank swiftly beneath the strewn boulders. To the east, where Bonner lived, there were bare, rusty cliffs with striations made by the wave action of seas that had retreated millions of years ago. Due north, blue-toned mountains were thick with ponderosa pine, lustrous with deep snows in winter.

He liked this house, and everything in it, as well as he liked his own. He adored Poppy. He felt a mild sense of dread, half-knowing what he was in for. Anxiety was all over Poppy, glaring like a rash.

She brought him chicken and dumplings, corn chowder, and sourdough rolls on a tray. She had a plate for herself, which she balanced on one bare knee, sitting on a low ottoman opposite him.

They ate first, talking mostly about the kids, avoiding the painful things in his life. Poppy had developed a habit of abruptly cocking her head to one side, as if she had a flea in her ear. Her normally astute brown eyes looked vague, watered down. Bonner was disconcerted. Six kids, one adopted, and Poppy, through all the tribulations of marriage and motherhood, had been a miniature fortress, maintaining the complex flow of family life and good works with her healthy life-giving vibrations.

Bonner's appetite failed him.

"What's wrong, Poppy? Is it Neal?"

She trembled, but looked him in the eye.

"What's he done?" Bonner asked.

"I'm not sure. But I think it's something bad. He could—*we* could lose—everything." Her eyes swept around the house like trapped birds. *"Everything."*

"It's business then? His practice?"

"Uh-huh."

"Well. Maybe you're overreacting. Neal's been in tight corners before; he always comes through."

"I don't know. This time—I overheard him on the phone, and then I—oh, God, Tobin, I *snooped*. Found some papers. I'm not sure what it all means, but—excuse me."

She ran from the terrace, exciting the dogs, to the nearest bathroom. In too much of a hurry to close the door. He heard her retching.

Bonner shook his head, carried the plates to the kitchen, scraped and rinsed them, put them in the Rubbermaid dish rack. Then he prowled through the back of the large pantry and part of the stores of food they maintained according to one of the dictates of their faith, came up with an unopened bottle of expensive scotch.

Poppy returned from throwing up with her face clean and bloodless, skimmed-back copper hair, a high forehead, dark brows with a touch of fire in them.

"Have you talked to Neal?"

"How could I? I told you. I snooped. He would never forgive me for that."

"What do you mean, Poppy?"

"I opened his safe. When he was gone a couple of nights ago." Her face changed suddenly with another cock of her head, a look he'd never seen before, that gave him a chill. Her teeth were gritted.

"Seeing that *woman*, I'm sure. That damned *Valkyrie* he can't seem to get enough of. I ought to tie a knot in his faithless prick."

"Poppy."

"You know me. I have *never* allowed bitterness to come into my heart. But he just won't quit, ever. Will he? We've been married twenty-two years. Okay. Let's get straight about it. He's a liar and a philanderer. He has the morals of a mink. How much am I supposed to be able to stand? What are you drinking?"

"Scotch."

"Pour me some."

"Poppy!"

"Oh, don't you start. Poppy, how *could* you? Poppy, you're so *per*fect. Caca. I'm *not*. I'm sick of hurting. I want some whiskey."

Bonner poured her a small shot.

"If you're not used to that—"

"Well, maybe I am," Poppy said with a sly glance, and downed the scotch, two gulps. She wiped her mouth with the back of a slender wrist and endured the burning with satisfaction. "Okay."

"Okay."

"Let's sit down again, shall we? Maybe you can tell me what to do because I'm at my wit's end."

●

Bonner listened to Poppy, then went with her to open the safe in Neal's home office.

She was jumpy from her perceived misdeeds, but another whiskey swung Poppy around into a sheltered anchorage of the mind. She watched listlessly while Bonner read through the documents—articles of incorporation, bank statements, a stack of computer printouts—and finally put it all together: some evidence, the gaps filled with educated guesswork. Facing a few truths he'd only half-faced before, the fundamental venality of his brother, the tainted center of an ambitious, unprincipled man.

"How bad?" Poppy said, after her third scotch.

"Poppy, you know I can't lie to you."

"I don't want you to." She stared at wisps of dark cloud flowing across the sky like ghosts leaving an exorcised house. "What did he do?"

"Juked around with his law practice. Recruited star kids out of big-name schools with promises of high starting salaries. He sold a million and a half dollars of projected receivables to a shell company, and used those"—Bonner hesitated—"bogus receivables to borrow money to keep the firm solvent. Which it isn't, of course. The loans are past due. He's short, way short."

"That's what I thought. Neal needs money again. But he isn't able to raise it. Your father—he's gone to that well too often."

"Don't count Neal out yet. Maybe that's why he went to Los Angeles. He's made a lot of friends, a lot of contacts over the years."

Poppy took a deep hopeful breath.

"You mean there's a chance he can fix it?"

"I don't know."

She shied as if he'd slapped her.

"Oh, Tobin."

"No, I don't think he can fix it, honey. The least he's looking at is disbarment."

"Wonderful. What else? Go ahead. I can take it."

"Three to five, federal. Minimum security, country club time, that sort of—"

"DAMN him!"

Ripped loose from her emotional moorings, Poppy raged. Bonner didn't try to stop her. There was nothing he could do or wanted to say. His nerves shimmered at each high note of invective, but he maintained a woeful silence. The folly of his brother, however injurious it might be to the future of his large family, was only an unwelcome distraction. Every breath Bonner had taken that day was clotted with evil. Waking to the sight of Rosalind Dubray in his own bedroom. A man with a depraved talent in a body bag. Luz trying to rise in the dark beyond of his mind, catch flame, open her stricken eyes.

The ceremony of God's disapproval would be vast, silent, and final.

22

KATHARINE HARSHA, DRIVING a black rental Tempo, reached the community of Rocky Mount a few minutes before midnight.

Rocky Mount wasn't much to look at. It was named after a stand-alone monolith of red sandstone at the southern end of Shining Butte State Park. The streets were laid out in the familiar grid pattern. A lot of prefab shell homes with stunted, dusty trees in the yards, tumbleweeds piled against chain-link fences. Pickup trucks, motorcycles, horse trailers; a complacent rural ambience. The small business strip had the post office, a Laundromat, a hair-dresser who also sold insurance, an Allis Chalmers's dealer, a café with a beer license, a trash-food mart with off-brand gas pumps out front. Everything but the café, identified as SINGIN' SANDY'S on a badly lettered sign, was closed at this time of the night. And Singin' Sandy's parking lot was nearly deserted.

Katharine pulled up to the gas pumps as she'd been instructed, left the motor running, and looked around. She had on a faded jeans outfit with desert boots. Under her denim jacket she wore a Glock 19 in a belt scabbard with the FBI tilt.

The first-quarter moon, about two days from the full, was squarely over the monolith. A scrawny dog limped down the middle of the road that ran in a straight blacktop line toward the monolith, which was about two miles away. She saw the lights of a car in her rearview, but it turned right a block from the food mart. Katharine uncapped a bottle of spring water—she'd been trying to drink a lot more water since arriving in Utah, for the sake of her complexion, which was getting blotchy. Her poor nose, forget it.

Behind the business strip, with its ramshackle buildings, was a sweep of desert, no houses on it, nothing. The digital clock on the dashboard changed. Eleven fifty-eight. Katharine raised her elbows and pressed her palms together, doing an exercise that was great for the bustline. Her eyes were never still.

Across the wide road a screen door banged. A man who was bare to the waist came out, loitered on a small front porch with a metal sunshade for a few seconds, was yelled at by someone inside, yelled back, then braced himself and began to butt his head against the aluminum siding of the house. Gently at first, then with real force. Katharine could imagine the furniture dancing. After a while a woman with big hair opened the screen door, reached out with a yammer of annoyance, grabbed him by his belt and pulled him stumbling back into the house.

Twelve oh one A.M.

An SUV hauling a horse trailer with hay bales piled on top pulled up in front of Singin' Sandy's. The driver honked. The lights went out inside. A stringy man with braids down his back came out, locked the door behind him, and got into the SUV. It drove past Katharine's Tempo. She glimpsed curious male faces.

Katharine glanced to her left and saw, through the space between the food mart and the farm equipment building, a figure walking in the moonlight on the desert. Walking her way. Maintaining a brisk pace over the uneven, rocky ground, making small detours around spikey fists and bristling bayonets of desert growth.

Interesting.

Now Katharine devoted all of her attention to the walker on the desert. Measuring distance with her acute sniper's eye. At a hundred yards she made out a pale oval face beneath the bill of a baseball cap. A youthful face. Boy or girl, couldn't tell yet. Katharine relaxed her vigilance somewhat, her pulses slowed. When the figure reached a trash pit behind the food mart, now obviously coming toward the Tempo, Katharine knew it was a young woman.

Katharine opened the door of the sedan, and the interior lights flashed on. She stepped out.

"Hi, there. You Sarah?"

"Yes."

She was wearing a windbreaker, khaki slacks, and high-topped hiking shoes. She wasn't breathing hard. She stopped on the other side of the gas pumps, gave a quick flick of her fingertips to an insect attracted by the moisture on her brow.

"I'm Katharine. Where did you come from?"

Sarah turned, gesturing vaguely.

"Oh, back there. It's a couple of miles by road, but less than a mile cross-country. I walked it because I don't have a car."

"Why are we meeting here, Sarah?"

"Oh, because I—didn't want anybody to see me."

She looked cautiously up and down the street, having reminded herself of this concern.

"That answers only half of my question, Sarah. You said you had something important to tell me."

"Yes, I do. I mean, there's something I think I ought to show you."

"What would that be?"

"I can't describe it, exactly. But it's—something Suchary Sia-mashvili gave me."

"Yes?" Katherine said mildly, but her pulse rate had picked up again.

"Do you know who he is?"

"Yes, I do. But how do you happen to have known him?"

"We were friends. We talked a lot, at the Captain's Table. That's where I work most days. Before he died, he gave me something he wanted me to keep. But I don't know. I don't know if I want to keep it. I'm sort of scared of it."

"I understand. Suchary called this thing he gave you a 'Dove,' didn't he?"

Sarah nodded. "You know about it?"

"I know. You're smart to be concerned."

"He said I had to be really *really* careful with the Dove. That got me to thinking, what if—well, it could be dangerous, couldn't it?"

In spite of the dry air Katharine's mouth was watering so much she had to swallow twice before she could speak again.

"What did you do with the Dove?"

"I'll take you."

Katharine, hardly able to believe her luck, motioned to the car.

"Is it far?"

"No. Only a couple of miles, like I said. Just down the road, at the theater."

"Theater?"

"You'll see."

Sarah walked around to the passenger side of the Tempo, got in, sat with her hands loosely joined in her lap, staring through the windshield. She didn't look at Katharine again until they were a mile down the straight road to the monolith. The headlights picked up a signboard. It was an outdoor amphitheater they were going to, Katharine realized, in a canyon west of the monolith.

A musical pageant of the Mormon hegira, called *Brigham!* was the summer's attraction at the amphitheater, which was surrounded by impressively high walls and slopes littered with boulders, some larger than the car they were in.

The gate at the entrance to the empty parking lot was open. No one was in the gatehouse.

"Do you work here, too?" Katharine asked Sarah.

"Sometimes," Sarah said remotely. "I'm a stand-by usher."

"You must have been working tonight then."

"That's right; I was."

"Why so late? I could have met you right after the show."

"Well, like I said. I didn't want anybody to know. And I don't know you."

"Don't be nervous, Sarah."

"I can't help it."

"How did you know to get in touch with me, Sarah?"

"Oh—one of my Utah State friends, Mary, works the desk nights at the Ramada. She has bangs, kind of a wide mouth?"

"I may have seen her."

"Anyway, her father's a retired treasury agent. She knows, uh, people like you from Washington when she sees them. And it's no secret, I mean, about the FBI being in town." Katharine let that ride, with a slight smile. "Mary said you seemed real nice, and if I had a problem maybe I should try to contact you."

"You're doing the right thing."

Sarah hunched her narrow shoulders.

"Just park by the steps there; we'll go on in."

"Why don't you bring it out to me, Sarah?"

"I don't want to touch it. Anymore than I have to."

That seemed reasonable to Katharine. "Okay. You're right. I'll handle it from here on."

Sarah was out of the car even before Katharine had come to a complete stop behind a night watchman's golf cart. She all but sprinted up the wide steps, bordered on one side by a gradual seven-step waterfall, to the open-air court of the amphitheater. Still full of nervous energy, even after her cross-country hike.

"Wait for me, Sarah."

Katharine closed the car door that Sarah had left open, feeling the butt of her automatic inside her left elbow. The sound of the door chunking shut echoed from the canyon walls. Then it was quiet, except for the pouring of water down the seven steps, a wandering evanescent line pure as mercury in the moonlight.

Sarah hesitated beside a pedestal with a larger-than-life bronze figure on it; the whites of her eyes flashed as if she were searching for something in the deep shadows at each end of the stone-paved courtyard. She turned again, perhaps galvanized by the needling of adrenaline or a sound only she had heard, recognized. She bolted up a short ramp, disappearing into the darkness of the amphitheatre.

"This way!"

Katharine waited a few seconds, very alert, reaching without thought to undo the Velcro strap of the holster on her belt. She waited a little longer. She heard a horse somewhere, snuffling, the sound as clear as if the animal were standing a few feet away. Sound carried marvelously out here at this hour. Maybe they used horses in the pageant. Covered wagons and Indians on horseback were featured on the circular posters by the columns that flanked the entrance.

She started up the steps to the courtyard, jacket on her left side tucked behind the butt of the Glock.

Katharine had explored several religions until her junior year in high school before deciding that all belief systems were irrational. Clannish people, like the Mormons, didn't annoy her as long as they were civilized. It was also true that the devout, no matter how wishful and uninformed the content of their ethos, usually earned their way in life through hardship and oppression . . . Katharine's only faith was in the sanctity of the sure shot, the lonely theater of political assassination as a means to achieve a more easily unified, less troublesome society.

She heard the horse again, or it might have been two horses; the breeze that came down from the high dark cliff behind the amphitheater brought with it a tang of stables.

"Sarah?"

"I'm h-here."

She sounded upset, or unnerved.

"Where?"

"Inside. Are you c-coming?"

"Yes."

The post-midnight hour seemed a little chilly. Growing skepticism and caution inspired Kate to draw the pistol, which she carried, cocked and unlocked, against her thigh as she walked slowly up the ramp and into the open-air arc of seats facing an impressively large stage of polished cement. Artificial rocks and a cave stage right, a permanent set representing a pioneer fort at stage left, a façade of a simple homestead with a corral in the center.

Sarah had taken a second-row aisle seat. Her chin rested on her fist.

Katharine had another thoughtful look around. She was unable to tell if they were alone. A lot of hiding places, below and also behind her in the lighting booth. She now suspected that they were not alone. She went down a dozen rows and slipped into a chair behind Sarah, laid the barrel of the Glock against the girl's nape.

Sarah jumped and looked around, eyes glassy in the moonlight. She was frightened. Katharine felt solicitous. And rousingly salacious. Such a náive little cutie; she had appealed to Katharine at first sight. One of those magical things.

"Sarah. Have you been bullshitting me?"

"I—I didn't want to do this."

Katharine moved the muzzle of the Glock to Sarah's armpit and put her other arm around the girl's shoulders, holding her still.

"Don't!"

Kate sniffed Sarah's hair, the back of one waxen mildly scented ear, and gave her a fond rabbit-nibble. Sarah trembled. That excited Katharine, although not enough to dull her judgment.

"You're sweet. You really are. Now stop your fretting and tell me why you brought me here. Are we waiting for someone else? Is that it? Is it possible, little luv, that you've set me up? Whatever for?"

There was movement on the stage below, and Katharine tensed. She had an impression of oiled limbs in the moonlight, a nearly naked figure creeping on all fours to the brink of a ledge atop the rocks. Then came a long gymnastic leap to the stage floor. He crouched there, scouting around, knife in hand, an Indian on the warpath.

Katharine's impulse was to shoot Sarah through both lungs and make a quick retreat. No, better to make a retreat with Sarah as cover. On the other hand, she didn't feel all that threatened by a stage Indian, who was motionless now, as if waiting for the lights to come up.

While she thought about it, another Indian appeared, surreptitiously, from within the mock fort. He had no weapon. He posed with flair, making signs to the Indian who had preceded him onstage. Both of them were nicely muscled and wore only moccasins, breechclouts, and black wigs with beaded braids that bisected their gleaming pecs.

"Who are they, Sarah?" Katharine whispered.

"They're in the show."

"Am I going to a see a show?"

"Maybe," Sarah said, and she didn't seem as intimidated as she had been when Katharine laid the Glock against the back of her neck. A well-honed sense of jeopardy clashed with Katharine's curiosity, the sensation that she was, in a spooky way, enjoying all this.

Two more Indians were jogging down the long slope beneath the canyon cliff behind the stage, dodging agilely from boulder to boulder. Real boulders, a panorama that no painted backdrop could duplicate.

The stage began to glow as lights mounted on grids on either side warmed up.

Then music, full orchestra, a canned overture that reverberated stirringly through the canyon. All of the Indians went to full alert, facing stage left, two of them drawing arrows from the buckskin quivers hung across their backs.

A piebald stallion burst from the wings at almost a full gallop, circling the broad, deep, pageant stage. Katharine gaped at the sight of Rosalind Dubray crouched over the horse's thick black mane, reins between her startling, strong teeth, toy six-shooters in her hands, firing at the redskins, who clutched their anatomies and toppled one by one.

Rosalind straightened and took the reins in one hand, circled the stage again and jumped her horse over a line of hay bales into the orchestra pit thirty feet from where Kate had Sarah pinned to the back of her seat.

Firing more caps at the sky, Ros urged the stallion up the steps of the aisle past Katharine; they came to a stop just shy of the tunnel to the courtyard and Ros yanked off her Annie Oakley Stetson, flourishing the hat in Katharine's direction. Anticipating applause for her capering?

Katharine, totally absorbed in Rosalind's theatrics, wasn't aware of the night watchman who had come along the aisle behind her. Until she felt the muzzle of his shotgun pressing into her back between her shoulders blades.

"It's a twelve-gauge, darlin'. Why don't you just hand me the Glock, after you ease that old hammer down?"

Sarah, still being strong-armed by Katharine, managed to turn her head and smile wanly at the whiskery old gent, who had a breath like day-old roadkill.

"Hello, Uncle Job."

Ros was walking the piebald stallion down the steps. The horse wore hard rubber shoes and didn't make much noise.

"Give it up, Kate," Rosalind said cheerfully. "You're outflanked."

"What's the point?" Katharine said coolly. She withdrew her piece from Sarah's armpit, held it aloft while she lowered the hammer with her thumb, and allowed portly Uncle Job to remove the Glock from her hand. He kept the shotgun where it was, planted deep enough to be uncomfortable. "Either I walk out of here now, or your tit goes into the wringer."

Sarah said, "Can I leave, Rosalind?"

"In a minute, Sugarpea." Ros put her index fingers in the corners of her mouth and whistled piercingly. Then she said to Sarah, "You did good. What did you say to her?"

"I just told her a big story. I *lied.*" Sarah looked as if she could spit.

In the courtyard a motorcycle engine was kicked over and revved. The ironhead rider came up through the tunnel and screeched his hog to a stop above them. The piebald shied nervously.

"Here's your ride," said Rosalind. "—Hey, Kate?"

"What?"

"Step on up here behind me and let's mosey along while we have our chat."

"To where?"

"Up the canyon a ways. No particular place. No hurry. Sun won't be up for a few hours yet. We'll find a good spot for you to watch it rise."

Katharine looked away from the heat in Rosalind's eyes, giving herself a moment to deal with the terror this otherwise innocuous remark inspired.

"Oh, fuck you, Rosalind."

" 'Truly, Kate, I would the gods had made thee poetical.' What play is that from? Helpful hint: I'm the namesake of the lead."

Katharine looked at Sarah.

"Would you listen to reason? You're not in big trouble, *yet*. But don't let this continue."

Sarah rubbed the piebald's nose, glanced blankly at Katharine.

"He's my father, too," she said. She hurried up the steps to the motorcycle, put on the helmet the ironhead kid handed her, and climbed aboard.

Rosalind said, "You look unhappy, Kate. But our revels are ended. Time to be on your way."

Someone else had sauntered onto the stage, doing a few dance steps, waving to the audience of three as she joined the group of pretend-Indians. With their wigs off, they revealed uniformly buzzed heads. A few of their tattoos showed through the streaky redman body makeup. The girl cinched an arm around one of the boys and playfully grabbed his breechclout away.

Kate was a little slow remembering where she'd seen her before. But it hadn't been long ago. Just that morning, in fact, at the Short Wolf Café. The girl had waited on the table where Katharine had sat with Stearman talking shop. Saying far too much, Katharine realized now, remembering the conversation in excruciating detail.

The motorcycle went thundering through the tunnel and across the courtyard. Katharine glowered at Rosalind, and got a push from the muzzle of Uncle Job's shotgun.

Rosalind took a tape cassette from her vest pocket, letting Katharine have a good look.

"Can't help myself, Kate. I just have to know what's going on in the world."

Katharine nodded. Obviously she was going to hear herself again, bragging about her prowess with a sniper's rifle. Where had that bitch with the spikey hair planted the microphone? Under the table probably.

"I don't suppose there's anything I can say."

Rosalind put her cowgirl hat on and cinched it under her chin.

"Like, 'sorry?' 'Fraid not. Ready to ride?"

Katharine lowered her eyes and lifted her shoulders, thinking of the knife in her boot, wondering if Rosalind could possibly be that stupid. Then she realized she was the one who was being stupid, but only got half turned around as Uncle Job raised the shotgun butt first and snapped her lower jaw in three places with a solid uppercut to the chin, impaling her lower lip on her front teeth.

That blow only stunned Katharine; it was the hard fall down the concrete steps into the orchestra pit that knocked her cold.

Rosalind, gazing down at the body in the pit from horseback, said, "Little rough on her, Uncle Job."

"Reckon my timing's been off since I retired from my prison job. But it's a cinch she's got 'nother weepon on her somewhere. Just looking out for you, Ros."

"Oh, well. Heave Katharine up here, and we'll get on with it. For sure I need some sleep tonight. I'm expecting an old friend. And I guarantee it won't be restful, having Jimmy around the home place."

23

THE PHONE BESIDE Signe Gehrins's bed in her penthouse suite at the Century Plaza Towers in Los Angeles woke her from a sound sleep a little after midnight.

"Would you get that?" she muttered.

The phone kept ringing.

Awake enough now to be annoyed, Signe pushed her sleep shade up to her hairline and rolled over on her naked belly to reach for the offensive phone, discovering as she did so that she was alone in the king-sized bed.

"I need you at home," her husband said.

"Run out of cunty playthings, darling?"

"No."

"Do you miss me?"

"Always."

"That's lovely," Signe said, concluding with a purring sound deep in her throat.

"And I have a problem you can help me with."

"Oh? I'm intrigued. What could it be?"

"We won't discuss it over the phone. But you can be sure it will appeal to your special sense of fun."

"Wolfie. How thrilling. But not even a hint?"

"A limo's downstairs. There's a charter waiting for you at the Santa Monica airport. Don't dawdle."

"On my way. Ciao."

Signe stretched and yawned. The only light in the bedroom was from shaded twenty-five-watters in wall sconces. The door to the sitting room of the suite was partly open; so was a sliding balcony door. All of stale, stenchy Los Angeles was seeping in, giving her a chill. Goose bumps. She picked up a large pajama top from the foot of the bed and put it on, looking at the hunched figure on the twelfth-floor balcony.

She heard the tinkle of ice in his glass when he raised it to drink. He was facing the Mormon temple, a towering plinth on a hillside on Santa Monica Boulevard, a couple of miles west of Century City. The temple's outlines were vague, the skyward figure of the trumpeting angel dressed in twenty-four-carat gold, like a treasure long out of Neal Bonner's reach. The night was filled with mist from the ocean that was not far away.

Neal had wrapped a blanket around his own nakedness. His bare feet were propped on the balcony railing. His face was drawn, the face of a man mobbed by despair. He'd provided her with a less-than-able fuck, but Signe forgave him by putting her arms around him. Men had days like that.

"I'm broke," Neal said. He was also drunk, and acrid from dried flop-sweats, a leeched remorse. He needed a bath.

"You've been broke before. We all have been, we live like riverboat gamblers."

"Never broke like this. You've got to help me."

"But I've already done. Wolfie isn't pressing you for your end of the Oro Cruces funding."

"Christ, I hope not! I've already put so much money into that one, it's like a black hole." He shuddered. "No, I mean—I want him to float a loan."

Signe took each of his cold feet down from the wall, then nestled her ass in his blanketed lap. She sighed.

"I don't think so."

"I'm not talking about a *personal* loan. Wolfgang owns a bank in Sark. Another one in Vanuatu. I just want him to make it *happen* for me."

"How much money? I have a couple of accounts, if—"

"Two million U.S."

The sum took her breath away, momentarily.

"I had no idea. Well, it's far beyond my means. I *am* sorry."

"But if you talk to Wolfgang—. Listen, he said *six months* on

Oro Cruces, I'd quadruple my investment. It's been almost a year and a half and nothing, *nothing*. The assays are for shit."

"Are you really desperate?" she asked, with a hint of distaste.

"I don't have any more *time*." His voice had become a dirge. "Talk to Wolfgang. Please."

Signe was astonished to see tears sliding down his cheeks. She thoughtfully wiped them away with a fingertip.

"It's a closed door, Neal."

"No. Don't say that. You don't know what I've been *thinking*. Sitting here. I've got to have the money, or—"

Signe looked over her shoulder at the lights of West LA afloat in gray mist like dwarf abyssal suns. She didn't want to know what he'd been thinking. For the first time in their relationship, she was bored.

"Neal, I have to run home for a day or so. I'll keep the suite. You're free to use it. I'm sorry they canceled your platinum card."

"Signe," Neal moaned, "don't leave me. You just don't know. Poppy hung up on me—when I called her. *Poppy*. Oh, God. I can't be alone tonight."

"I have to go. Wolfgang's waiting. Now promise me, Neal, that you'll go back to bed and sleep it off. You won't do anything dreadful or messy. Tomorrow you'll be full of good ideas. It's only"—she lifted herself from his lap, gently pushed away the hand that tried to restrain her. She grinned—"two million dollars."

He looked at Signe with reddened, stifled eyes, possessed by a lifetime of betrayals, nearly all of them his.

"Talk to Wolfgang, Signe. I'm . . . begging . . . you."

At the balcony door she turned curtly to him, with a bitch of a pout.

"No, I won't. Because the truth is, Neal, Wolfgang thinks you're a schmuck."

●

In Shay's company and with the phone turned off, the daylong fury ebbed from Bonner's mind. He allowed Luz some peace, himself as well. He drank sparingly, because his stomach couldn't take it. But enough liquor to tone down the blitz of emotion that had accelerated at every insult to his reason, to his heart. The family welfare people, outraged that he had removed the infant Cymbeline from their jurisdiction, had finally given up threatening him and planned to pursue the matter in court. He knew he could stonewall for a few more days and keep the baby safe.

"Do you have any ideas?" Shay asked him.

They were on the terrace behind his house, listening to the river, the pulsations of desert night. Bonner didn't know what time it was. He had left his watch off after showering. Vida had taken his leave after eating a side of ribs and a baked potato; he was cleaning one of his tropical fish tanks.

Shay and Vida had hit it off effortlessly. She had brought with her a video of a recent movie in which she'd done some stunt work. Of course she wasn't recognizable, pretending to be the star; but the fight scenes and an unfaked close call on camera, as she rolled out of the way of two cars about to crash head-on, impressed Vida. He watched the gag three times. And Bonner, watching Shay, thought she was better looking than the star. Her body lean, elegant, warrior-useful.

"I haven't had much time to really think about her situation. Was Cymbeline overlooked by the gunman who killed the others in her family? That would mean he didn't know the family. But if he was calling on them for the first time, would he have walked in the front door? The patio would have been a better approach. In the rain none of the family would have seen him. Also, I think he would have used an automatic weapon or a shotgun. Why fuss with head shots from a nine-millimeter automatic? Because he had the gun concealed on him when he got there. And he was let in by one of the family members. Probably that was Graciela."

"Why Graciela?"

"She was the only one on her feet when the shootings began. As if she'd been bringing dishes to the table from the kitchen."

Shay said, "If he did know the family, then he knew Graciela had a child. So it was a deliberate choice, not to shoot Cymbeline." She grimaced, settled down to thinking of a reason. "But it didn't bother him, killing Graciela's brother and sister. How old were they? Ten, twelve at the most?"

"Something like that."

"Or else—you'll have to excuse me, I've done a lot of movies, read so many scripts—"

"Go on."

"He had to kill them. He was *paid* to kill them, even the kids.

But either he was told to leave Cymbeline alone, or he didn't think she mattered. Or—"

"After blowing away five human beings in quick succession, the rush died down, he lost his stomach for it. Or he had one more job to do, and he was in a hurry to get out of there."

"What job?"

"Gabriel was snooping on his neighbors, stockpiling taped conversations and possibly infrared videos. Apparently none of those tapes remained in the house. The gunman may have dumped them into a garbage bag and hauled them away. Why?"

Their eyes met; Bonner smiled slightly. So did Shay.

"You want me to answer that one."

"You're good at this."

"Okay. He couldn't be sure he wasn't on some of the tapes or videos."

"You're very good at this."

"Logical. If there can be any logic to a massacre. Now I have a question."

"About the attempted kidnapping? The two events are connected. But the gunman was not a part of the team that snatched Cymbeline from the hospital."

"How do you know?"

"If he wanted Cymbeline, for whatever reason, he would have grabbed her the night before."

"Oh. I suppose so. Then who were they?"

"Hired hands. They'll never talk. That's a certified death sentence, once they get to prison. That kind of fear, and compliance, can only be assured by a drug family like the Sinaloas."

"Gabriel's real name."

"Yes. Or the Loza family in Chihuahua. With whom I've had some dealings. The fortunes of both families are intermingled."

"So Cymbeline's mother and father are both dead. Who do you think her godfather is? Godparents are very important in Latin families, aren't they? Like the Irish. They take their responsibilities to the child very seriously."

"Yes, they do. And now that we've been talking about it, my hunch is that Steel Arm Jimmy Loza is Cymbeline's godfather."

"And he's the—"

"Head of the family. In Spanish, *el padron*."

"If he's at all interested in Cymbeline's welfare, why would he send those—murderers to steal her from the hospital? Legally he may have some claim to her."

"Two reasons why Jimmy wouldn't go through channels. One, he doesn't go through channels. Bribery, intimidation, and murder get things done faster, and there's no paper trail. Two, he might have acted out of a sense of urgency."

"Because he thinks Cymbeline could be in danger?"

"If we accept the hypothesis that Gabriel Sinaloa's brothers arranged to have Gabriel and his family killed for his transgressions, and the technician didn't complete the assignment, for whatever reason, then I'd have to say that Cymbeline is marked. Jimmy would be well aware of the consequences. Because in vendettas nothing short of complete annihilation of the offender and his blood is acceptable."

"Like in Part Two of *The Godfather* when Robert De Niro goes back to Sicily with his family, you know? And while he's there he sticks a knife into that blind, senile old man who had Don Corleone's family killed when he was a little boy. They never forget: they never give up."

"No," Bonner said, "they don't. How about another beer?"

"Good. My mouth is really dry. Could I tell you something?"

"Sure."

"I think I'm a little scared. No. I'm very scared, for Cymbeline."

"So am I."

"Have you called?"

"Twice. She's fine. I've got two deputies out there tonight, two of my best."

"How are your parents?"

"My mother's a rock, like always. My father—in spite of his age, and our differences, I don't know anyone I'd rather have backing me up in a fight."

"What are those differences?"

"Religion, for one thing. Believe me, when I was growing up, there was God in every frown. My blood has never jumped to that beat. I think I've always been in a state of rebellion against those people, like my old man, who are determined to legislate their personal views. Also, he's had a hard time accepting Vida. Not that he's made much of an effort."

Bonner went into the kitchen for the beers. He lingered there, observing her unawares through a window, reading, by moonlight, the romance of her still face as she gazed at the river.

Shay smiled at him when he handed her the beer.

"I ought to call too, see how Pepper is getting along. Although she really ought to be sound asleep by now."

Jack Waco said to Pepper, "I think I'd have been more successful if I'd had a good sidekick. Gabby or Smiley or even Fuzzy St. John. Smiley was the best. When Smiley was around, and Gene's writers gave ol' Frog some good business to do, you didn't notice so much that Gene couldn't act. About six words at a time was all he could manage. Of course he was great at singing and riding. Fearless, too. He did a good many of his own stunts. Roy could act some, but he was from Cincinnati, Ohio. To my mind Gene Autry was the true King of the Cowboys. He was also a fine gentleman and faithful to his word. I met him during War Two, where both of us were in the Transport Command flying C-109s from Karachi to Kunming, China across the Hump. That's the Himalaya Mountains, sweetheart, the highest mountain range in the world. You probably read about them already in geography class? What grade'll you be in next term, the seventh? Anyway, I'm getting away from my story. Gene and I hit it off, being native Texans and country boys that grew up on horseback. Gene was born in Tioga and I'm from Fort Stockton. I let him know I wouldn't mind giving the movies a whirl if I ever did make it back home, which was a big *if,* you know, 'cause those old 109s were the clumsiest aircraft you ever tried to fly, and all of 'em loaded with ten thousand gallons of fuel. You had to wrestle them up off the runway. But I had some luck, and I was decommissioned at March Field the fall of forty-six.

"Next day I was on the Republic lot in Gene's office, and the day after *that* there I was in Lone Pine doing my first movie. Played a bad guy, what we called a 'dog heavy.' Then Gene took me on the rodeo circuit with him because I was so good with a bullwhip. I could pop a playing card from between a cowgirl's teeth while riding at a full gallop. Let me tell you, the crowds ate it up. Sunset used a bull-whip in his pictures and then there was Lash LaRue; but what I had was a *trademark*: the silver whip, which had been in my family for three generations. Granddaddy Ezreel Lamar Waco won it from a Mexican *hidalgo* by filling an inside straight in a poker game, that was before the War Between the States.—You going to sleep on me, Pepper? How about if I bring you something to drink from the kitchen?"

Pepper stirred on the guest room bed and opened her eyes.

"No, thanks, Granpa."

"Guess all my talk about how I got into pictures is boring to a young lady."

"No, it's not."

"Let me fix that cushion, make you a little more comfy. Knee paining you? Are you needing another pill?"

"No, sir. I'll wait til Mom comes home. Granpa?"

"Yes, darlin'?"

"Why did Mom shoot you?"

Jack sat back on the edge of the bed, ran his fingers through his poet's shock of hair, pulled at his jaw, looked mournfully at Pepper.

"She told you that story?"

"No. It's just something I kind of put together from stuff I've heard. Like, Mom and Liam talking one night, and she said the first time she ever picked up a gun she took the seat out of your best pair of jeans with it. Was that an accident?"

"Wish I could say so. But she did it for a purpose, and I had it coming in spades."

"Why?"

Jack tugged at an ear, lowered his eyes, shuffled his handsomely booted feet.

"Well, Pepper. I used to get liquored up. Not just once in a blue moon, which a man is entitled to do, but pert near all the time. Didn't know what else to do with myself. I was a disappointed man. My movie days were over with. Couldn't scare up much of a living. I never blamed anybody but myself, you understand. But I'd been a high-flyer, and I didn't know how to handle it when I finally crashed and burned. So I took out my disappointments on people I loved. Like your dear grandmama Sophia."

Pepper bit her underlip and regarded him steadily.

Jack rubbed his shaggy head again.

"I didn't treat her the way she deserved to be treated. She got all the worst of my bad spleen. Because, I guess, she still couldn't speak English good enough to suit me. Or some other cockadoodle reason. Then when I'd work myself into a low mood, sometimes I'd just let fly with my fists."

"You *hit* her?"

"I'm not going to tell you any lies. I'm ashamed to say I did. On more than one occasion."

Pepper pulled a stuffed animal closer to her breast and didn't comment.

"I'm a do-right papa now. I've got more to live for. I bought a Bible. Those days, I was a stranger to my own heart. Sophia forgave me a long time ago. Shay, well, I can't say. Fact is she's here, at long last. She brought you, so that means something, don't you think?"

Pepper nodded, and found her voice.

"Did you ever hit Mom?"

"Never raised a hand to her."

"But you must have really got her mad."

"I don't remember how it started that particular night. I do recall Sophia lost a useful tooth. There was blood on her lip and chin. I cleaned her up with a cold cloth, and I did try to make amends, but she couldn't stop crying. It was just a torrent of heartbreak that poured out of her. I was sick to my stomach by then. Sick of being a rounder and a scoundrel. I needed to get out of the house—that little place we had then over at the western town and rodeo, it got buried in a rock slide some years ago.

"Anyway, I had just put my hand to the screen door when *powie!* that shotgun went off behind me and my rear end blew up. I looked back at Shay and then at the seat of my pants, and Lordy I was *smoking.* My butt was loaded with hot lead like a loaf stuffed with raisins. And my ten-year-old daughter stood there petrified, holding that long-barreled shotgun I kept in the closet and had all but forgot about. She was white-faced to the tips of her little ears, a startling sight. But you never can tell, in a situation of a critical nature. She might not have been so petrified she couldn't pull the trigger again and plunk me in the shortbreads. So I dabbed up some blood from my heinie and shook a drop off my thumb. You could bet I was dead sober by then. I just said, in the calmest voice I could find, 'Don't do it again, Shay. I'm sorry. I'll spend the night somewhere else.' So I did. And a few nights after that, and when I finally had the courage to show myself at home again, Sophia and Shay had left me. All because of John Barleycorn. I deserved what I got, but it was a hard lesson. I hope now we're going to put it all back of us and have a family again. I need that, Pepper. I know I ain't going to last forever."

Pepper looked at his downcast penitential face.

"It's okay, Granpa. Granpa?"

"Yes, Missy?"

"What are 'shortbreads?' "

"Well, I think it's referring to the liver and the kidneys."

Pepper's cell phone rang. She'd kept it close to her all evening with her mother away.

"Uh-huh. Hi. Not too bad. When are you coming back? Uh-huh. I'm all right. Grandpa's here. Oh. Okay. Do you want to talk—? Well, don't be *too* long. Love you, too."

Pepper looked at her grandfather. "I'm supposed to go to sleep now."

"Reckon it's that time for me, too. After I take my nightly stroll around the place. Kiss you good night?"

"Sure. Do you think we could go see that filly in the morning?"

"Nothing I'd like better." Jack bussed her on the forehead. "Should you need me, just give a holler. I'm a light sleeper."

"I will. Leave that little lamp on, please?"

Vida sat in the rocking chair in his room watching television with the sound off. He had a sketchpad in his lap, a box of colored pencils close to hand. In a freshwater breeding tank, a blue Siamese fighting fish bristled with danger. Three spiny puffers in the largest tropical tank hovered above the sandy bottom like mines in a harbor. Rippling patterns from all of the tanks were reflected on the ceiling. The motion of the waters never ceased. By day, as Vida slept, his fish swam in and out of his head.

He liked TV best with the sound off, whether he was watching a talk show, an MTV video, or a kung fu movie. Fact or fiction, it was all the same to Vida. What interested him was the play of light and shadow, kinetic energy. Tension, action, emotion. He watched lovers and murderers, dancers and athletes. He never tired of faces.

He often sketched personalities he saw on TV more often than he saw his own father.

CNN was devoting thirty seconds to the latest Mideast flare-up. Palestinian youths attacked Israeli soldiers with firebombs. Long scarves of flame trailed from the mouths of gas-filled bottles. The Palestinian kids wore T-shirts, jeans, and sneakers. The soldiers fired back with rubber bullets. Scuffling, running, writhings in the street. It was a cloudless day. Some of the youths had dark faces, but a different dark from his own. Brutality, hatred, fear. Vida had no sense of history or politics, no references to provoke feelings of outrage or dismay. He lived in a room with beautiful fish, slept days, worked nights at small, satisfying tasks. He changed channels.

A naked blonde woman with blue eyes was making love to a man in a hot tub. He'd seen this before. They would kiss, and then she would turn into an alien life-form. Such things no longer made him nervous. He knew it wasn't real. He'd watched, on another program, as hideous faces and bodies were made from materials not unlike the cement and plaster he and his father had used to build the patio and the new wing of their house. But he didn't change channels; he continued to watch the blonde woman press her lips against the lips of the man, who struggled as if she were trying to eat him.

He had seen her do this at least three times. For that matter, he'd seen kissing every night on the tube for years, men-women and sometimes women-women, but usually it was not like his father kissing him, on the cheek or forehead, good-natured affection. The kissing he saw was different, the expressions of the lovers not always friendly and smiling; they frequently seemed to be in torment.

Now Vida understood—and the revelation had been profound—that it wasn't painful. It was a desirable thing.

This morning he had met Rosalind Dubray. Tonight there was more than fish swimming in and out of his mind.

He was thinking ahead now, thinking of the first faint streak of dawn, his running time. It seemed reasonable to Vida, that, having appeared once, dropping from the arc of the tipped-over tree, Ros would be there again.

Because he wanted her to be there.

The thrashing of the doomed man in the hot tub ceased. There was blood in the water.

Vida changed the channel.

Riding on the back of the motorcycle behind a guy she didn't know, and whose leather vest had an odor she could only avoid by tilting her head into the airstream, Sarah passed the few miles from the amphitheater to Silverwhip Jack's place, mooning over Shay Waco. Sarah had put Katharine Harsha firmly out of her mind.

She hoped Shay would still be awake. They could have something to eat—a shared glass of wine also would be nice—and talk for a while. An hour to sit close to Shay and listen to her, while studying her beautiful face. The face that Sarah recalled in detail and read with care and longing, turning over one impression after another in her mind as if they were the pages of an exquisitely illuminated manuscript.

Dally, by comparison, had flaws. The pores in her nose were large, and there was an aggressive simmering tone to her eyes. How could she ever have cared that much about Dally? Sarah thought Shay's eyes were the loveliest shade of brown she'd seen; in a certain light they were like . . .

Sarah had only a glimpse of the big car that came barreling out of an orchard lane into their path, blocking the dirt-and-gravel road. The cyclist had less than thirty feet in which to stop, and he had been going very fast in spite of the ruts on Jack's road. When he panicbraked and veered left across the hump that went down the middle of the road, the back end bounced hard and Sarah lost her grip on the chrome handhold behind the saddle. She flew sideways as the bike began to flip over in the air, then skidded headfirst across the hood of the Cadillac. All of this in three blinks of an eye.

The motorcycle crashed down on the trunk of the Caddy, and the ironhead cyclist, bare-armed in his black leather vest, was flung into a ditch with a little muddy water in it.

"Christ's sake, Frenchie!"

In his Cadillac, T. Frenchman Dobie sat stunned behind the wheel, retaining an image of the body flying past the dirty windshield. He twisted around in the seat to look at the motorcycle that had caved in his trunk and shattered the back window. There was smoke and dust in the air.

"Cut it too close," Tom Leucadio said. *"Hijo de la Santisma Virgen!* You probably killed both of them."

Numbed at the heart and trembling, Frenchie opened his door and got out of the Caddy. He put his white Stetson on, then snatched it off again, threw it in the road, stomped on it, kicked it to a drooping limb of a fruit-filled tree.

"Son of a bitch! He was going too fast. Didn't he have sense enough to know he was going too fast on this road? *Son of a bitch,* the asshole deserved to get killed!"

Tom Leucadio got out on his side and said grimly, "Let's see how bad off they are. Maybe they got lucky."

"We're not reporting this. We can't. You know we can't report it."

"The insurance company may be a little curious how you came to have a Yamaha grafted onto the rear of your vehicle."

Leucadio went into the ditch and crouched with a flashlight by the face-down body of the ironhead kid. He turned the kid's head cautiously and saw a flicker of an eyelid. His helmet might have saved him from a fractured skull or broken neck, Tom thought, feeling marginally encouraged. The kid was breathing audibly, but not desperately. Tom couldn't tell if there were broken bones. Now the boy's eyes were partly open, but he was dazed and couldn't speak. He moved his legs a little, then grasped at Tom's sleeve. That much spontaneous movement probably meant the spinal cord hadn't been injured. Still, there could be soft tissue damage, a ruptured spleen.

Call an ambulance right away.

Tom put the boy on his back and crossed the road, taking a cell phone from the pocket of his denim jacket.

"Where's Sarah?"

"I can't look," Frenchie moaned. "I just can't do it. What if I killed her?"

Tom glanced at him, regretting, again, that he'd ever let Frenchie know Sarah Dubray was staying on the place, that an ironhead on a motorcycle had called for her around sundown. They'd been waiting in the orchard for almost two hours for Sarah to return. Frenchie nodding off, then waking up disoriented when Tom, hearing the motorcycle, nudged him. No call for him to pull out like that and block the road, no matter how impatient he was to get his hands on the girl. But some men had a genius for doing the wrong thing in a critical moment.

Frenchie proved that again by snatching the phone from Tom's hand as Tom turned his attention to the still form of Sarah Dubray by the side of the road.

"What are you doing? I told you, nobody finds out about this!"

"What are we supposed to do? Leave them lying here?"

"Sarah's coming with me. I don't care about the other one. Do what you want about him, after I'm gone. Now help me get Sarah into the car."

"Could be a bigger mistake than you've made already, moving her." Tom hesitated for a few moments, then said, "Okay. I'll clean up after you, Frenchie. But it had better be worth my while."

"I told you, a few more days, and I'm a rich 'un. You'll get twice what you've been draining from Jack's accounts."

"I don't know what you mean, Frenchie."

"The fuck you don't. I can examine any account, at any bank in Solar County, whenever I want to. You're real clever. But figures have always been my business, and I been at it a sight longer than you have, Mr. Stanford University MBA."

With the sensation that he had acquired an ice pick in the back of his neck, Tom passed through the headlights that were ghosting down a tight alley of trees and kneeled beside Sarah Dubray.

She was wearing a good helmet with a chin guard. But her body was slack, her nose trickled blood, and she was unconscious. He put two fingers on the pulse in her throat, found it steady. He looked up. Frenchie was hovering nearby.

"How is she?"

"What do you want from me, Frenchie? I'm not the fucking Mayo Clinic. She must've been thrown twenty feet. Came down hard on the hood. I don't *know!* Get the door open, I'll put her on the backseat. Then she's your responsibility."

"We have to get that bike off my car."

"That's next. Open the door, man."

Tom slipped an arm carefully under Sarah's shoulders, raising her slowly from the ground. Then, with a hand behind her knees, he picked her up and carried her to the Cadillac. For a tall girl she was surprisingly light boned. Sarah groaned softly as he arranged her on the seat, but her eyes remained closed. He backed out of the car and shut the door with the feeling in the pit of his stomach that no matter what he did next, sooner or later it was going to be bad news.

With Frenchie's help he was able to pull the rice rocket off the trunk. The Yamaha didn't appear to be severely damaged, but it probably wasn't driveable. At least the gas tank hadn't sprung a leak. Frenchie got into his Caddy immediately. The engine had continued to run. Backup lights flashed on. Tom hopped out of the way and looked around for the ironhead kid. He didn't see him.

Muy gachos indeed.

Tom jerked his face aside as Frenchie gunned the Cadillac and drove away, spraying dirt and gravel. He brushed himself off, staring for a few moments at the receding taillights, trying to think. Then he swept the beam of the flashlight through the settling dust. He looked along the road in both directions. Down several rows of squat small-leafed trees. *Nada.* So there *he* was, half a mile from where he'd left his customized pickup truck parked behind an unused storage building, standing beside a wrecked motorcycle. The kid having somehow dragged himself off, vanished in the dark. Why? Dazed and confused maybe. Or there could be a reason why he didn't want to be identified with this particular machine, wasn't disposed to talk to the law regardless. That might be a break. But if the kid had been conscious enough to leave the scene, there was a chance he'd heard Frenchie shoot his mouth off, to Tom's detriment.

No sense wallowing in regrets. Tom figured it would be prudent to get the motorcycle out of there and just go home. Fortunately his pickup was equipped with a power-lift tailgate. Loading up the Yamaha wouldn't pose a problem.

It took Tom ten minutes to hike back to where he'd parked the Dodge Ram truck. When he used the key chain remote to unlock it and turn on the cab lights and the engine, he saw someone leaning against the tailgate, arms folded. It startled him. He needed a few seconds to recognize Jack Waco.

"Hey, Jack. Up kind of late."

Jack turned his head to look at him.

"I went out walking, after I put my little granddaughter to bed."

"Yeah? Well, it is pretty late, and I—"

"You're getting off my property, Tom. And don't you ever come back."

"What are you talking about?"

"I heard the crash. Voices carry at night, Tom. Don't know what

Frenchie Dobie is up to, and I don't care. Just can't believe you'd get involved with him in any way. Which isn't all I find hard to believe. You steal from me, Tom?"

"Now look, I don't know what you think you heard, Jack, but—"

"Nothing wrong with my hearing. Good ears, good eyes, sound teeth in my head. I still wake up with a hard-on, almost every morning."

Tom grinned tautly. "Oh, swell, Jack."

"Got all my faculties. You know, it's too bad, Tom. Once you whiff a skunk, you never forget the smell. Get out of here and stay gone."

"Fuck that, old man. I'm the best thing ever happened to you! I made this place."

"Part of it was going to be yours, some day."

"Oh, yeah, *well*. Now that your daughter's back, I'll bet you can't wait to change your will. Why should I wait for 'some day'? It wasn't all that much money, Jack. I swear. Just something extra. A little sweetener. *Y qué?* Tell you what, we'll just forget about it. We didn't have this conversation. You can't get along without me, Jack, so don't even think about trying!"

Jack moved smartly from behind the truck. Tom saw his right arm cock, then the back swing of the great bullwhip, a gleam of woven silver in the moonlight. The shocking touch of the lash along one cheekbone. He reeled back, gasping. His fingers came away bloody from the laid-open flesh.

"Chinga!"

"Get moving, boy. Out of my sight."

"You're crazy, Jack! This is one mistake you can't afford to make. Put that whip away. Think about what you're doing."

Tom lunged for the door of his pickup, scrambled inside, blood dripping on his shirt collar. He shifted into reverse, put the tinted window down a couple of inches. Jack hadn't moved except to coil the blacksnake around his bent right arm. He stared, unnervingly, at Tom Leucadio. His eagle-eyed closeup look, from forty faded old movies. *Hell Town Outlaws, Ridin' the Renegade Trail.*

"You can't throw me away, Jack! I know where the money came from. I know how you bought each and every acre of Lucky Orchards, and I can prove it. So cool off."

Tom couldn't take his own advice. He felt as if all of his insides had liquified and were shooting up, volcanically, through his constricted throat. Spewing out, poisoning the air and the ground he cherished.

"This didn't happen. Nobody said anything tonight. Nothing's changed. We love, we forgive, we forget. Jack, I've *always* loved you! Why did you have to hurt me?"

Jack stood in judgment, still unyielding.

Tom put his truck into reverse, backed up a hundred feet, stopped, waited there. High beams on Jack, who didn't move though he had to sense what was coming. Tom shifted again, floored it. Headed straight for Silverwhip Jack. Cattle stampede, *Rustlers of the Rimrock*. There was a tightening in Jack's face, not from fear but disgust. His eyes sharply blue in the tremendous flux of light. He seemed to be seeing, instead of the shapely chromed front end of the onrushing Ram truck, a familiar nemesis that had no earthly name.

Tom stopped two feet short of drenching himself in murder and slumped at the wheel, his eyes closing from exhaustion.

When he opened them again, Jack was gone.

24

SHAY PICKED THE BOY up on the iron bridge that spanned the Aquiles River just before the turnoff to the road that went past Simba Spring Ranch and on to Jack's place. Not something she'd ordinarily consider. For one thing, it was one-twenty in the morning, not another soul around; she hadn't seen another moving vehicle for at least five miles. Also she didn't want to be getting to bed when the roosters were waking up.

But something about him signaled distress, even though he didn't make an effort to flag her down. He barely looked up at the approach of the Windstar she was driving. He had tattoos and a bad-boy buzz. Biker garb and boots, but no bike in sight. He was leaning against the wooden bridge railing, clinging to it with one hand. His left forearm was across his midsection, as if he were trying to hold something in.

Shay thought, *Drunk or stoned*. Stoned might be dangerous, if it was crank. Just move on. But he raised his head a little higher, mouth working as if he wanted to speak. Instead of producing words, he leaked a little fresh blood.

She stopped and put the window down a few inches.

"Hey, bud. What's going on?"

"Can't make it."

"You hurt?"

"Something inside."

"What happened?"

"Didn't see it coming. Right in front of me. Must have crashed."

"You were on your bike?"

"On my bike."

"Where is it?"

"I don't know. I can't breathe very good. Don't make me talk so much."

Shay got out of the van and helped him inside, a painstaking process. He blacked out on his feet a couple of times and was a handful. He had to crawl onto the backseat, moaning, where he lay on his right side, still holding his stomach.

"What's your name?" She had to ask him twice.

"Cooger."

"Cooger, I think you need to go to the Med real bad, son."

"Something for the pain."

"That's right, something for the pain. And they'll find out what you did to yourself."

"What's your name?"

"Shay." She looked back at him as she turned around across the bridge. He made gassy sounds of distress. The blood kept coming from one corner of his mouth, slowly. The van bumping across the planks of the bridge brought tears to his eyes. "Do you remember what happened?"

"Right in front of me. Car pulled out. Big one. Maybe a Caddy. I think I hit it. Two guys. Messican, he was trying to help me. The other one, I don't know. Little dude. White cowboy hat. Do you have a phone?"

"Yeah."

"Call Rosalind. Tell her, wasn't my fault. Right in front of me. Tell her I don't know about Sarah. Did she get hurt or not."

Cold shockwave. "Sarah Dubray? She was riding with you?"

"Taking her home. Call Rosalind."

"I'll call her from the hospital. I don't want to waste time now getting you there."

"Don't know if I hit the car or not. Can't remember. Do you work at the Med?"

"No, but I ought to be an investor. Is it Rosalind Dubray you're talking about?"

"Yeah." His voice was weaker. Shay could barely hear him.

"What's the number, Cooger?"

Shay left the emergency room and walked part way down the circular drive to where she had parked the rental van. Four motorcycles came booming in off the street. Rosalind Dubray, without a helmet, in the lead. The guys each with a child-woman mounted behind, candy-colored hair and assaultive makeup. They were probably waking up everybody in the hospital. Chrome flash, studded leathers, thunder-bird denim jackets, dark glasses after midnight. Right out of *Monday Night Biker Flicks* on a cheesy cable channel. Gathering for the sake of a fallen comrade. Hell's Angels *agape*.

Rosalind drove right up to Shay and idled.

"Shay Waco?"

"Yes."

"I thought I told you to wait until I got here."

"So you did. So what? It's late, and I'm sleepy."

"I'll buy you coffee. How's Cooger?"

"Broken ribs, collapsed lung, cracked pelvis, herniated esophagus. He went up to surgery five minutes ago. I don't want any coffee, I want to go to bed."

Rosalind cut her engine and put the kickstand down. The other bikers did the same. Ros swung her right leg back across the saddle with a showboating languor, or could've been her natural style. She had extraordinary long legs, and probably liked exhibiting them. When she stood she was half a foot taller than Shay.

"You're the stunt gal? I know Jack, it's like forever. Thanks for bringing Cooger in."

"What else would I have done?"

"You didn't see it?"

"No. Cooger was by himself on the bridge when I came along. I asked, but Sarah's not here. I don't know if she was hurt in the accident. Maybe it was no accident. Cooger wasn't all that sure."

"How much did he tell you?"

"It hurt him to talk."

"Not what I asked. I want to know everything he said."

When she spoke seriously or angrily, Shay noted that her teeth sort of jumped out at you. Gnash, gnash. A hint of eager spittle on the full lips. Maybe it was the late hour, the sepia, metallic tone of the mercury vapor lights along the drive, but Rosalind's eyes were an odd color: cordovan was as close as Shay could come. An off-red shade of iris. You couldn't easily look away from a face like hers, as if it were the muzzle of a tigress close-up and smothered in eating blood. Shay wasn't fazed by presence, star-quality if you will. But Ros Dubray could make the pulses go like bongos.

"It was a car that jumped in front of him, on Jack's private road. He thinks he hit it."

"Description?"

"Not sure. Caddy, maybe. Two occupants. A Mexican, he said. And another man, with a white cowboy hat."

Ros's shoulders fell a little, her face losing some of its avidity as she pondered this.

Shay said, "He could have been describing this guy I had a run-in with at the Captain's Table where Sarah works. Frenchie something. He thinks they're engaged, but Sarah would rather eat dirt sandwiches the rest of her life."

"Yeah, I know. What did you do to him?"

"Popped him in the chin. With my foot."

"Oh, right. You're good at that shit? Suppose you have to be. What stunts do you do?"

"Climbing, jumping, falling, full burns, Filipino knife fighting, kick-boxing, fencing. I drive, I ride anything you can throw a bridle on."

"Tapioca-and-whipped-cream rassling?"

"Pay me enough. Look, I don't know if anyone in the ER phoned it in, maybe you ought to."

Rosalind shrugged.

"Your friend Cooger was really banged up. So who's supposed to get to the bottom of this?"

After a long but not unfriendly look Rosalind said, "I'm already at the bottom of it. All the way to the slimy bottom." She paused. "Thanks. I'm glad we met. If Sarah hasn't made it back to Jack's place when you get there, I'd appreciate another call."

Shay got out of the van at five minutes to three and walked up the wide steps to the porch, where she found Jack flushed and replete within a haze of fine bourbon, his silver-tooled bullwhip coiled in his lap.

"I hope you waited until Pepper was asleep to get started."

The bottle was between his knees. He hunched his shoulders, as sly and guarded as a dog with a newfound bone.

"I did."

"Is Sarah here?" When he didn't reply after five seconds, Shay repeated, "Sarah Dubray."

"They put her in Frenchie's car. Frenchie took her."

"Took her where?"

"No telling."

"Was she hurt?"

"I think so."

"Did you see it?"

"No."

"Why are you hitting the bottle? You know this is where I get off, Jack. I'd leave right now with Pepper, but I don't think I could drive another twenty feet."

He leaned slowly to one side of his rocking chair, squinting, trying to focus, then looking beyond her as if aware of the lingering curse on their periphery.

"Don't go. Won't happen again. That's my word as a man. It still means something, to some people."

"What's going on with you, then?"

The bottle slipped from between Jack's knees and rattled on the floor of the porch, sounding empty.

"My father, Joe Henry, once lived in a cave on our place for six weeks. He just crawled in there one day with a gunnysack full of canned pork and beans and two jerry cans of water. Didn't say a word to anybody. Have I ever told you that story?"

"No."

"He was well before your time. It's hard to place a value on a man who demonstrates that kind of behavior. Now that I'm a lot older I can understand some of it, although I still have mixed feelings about him. Joe Henry married seven times. He used to say that women were his clear favorites among the near-domesticated animals."

"Good night, Jack."

"He had a flashlight and a copy of the county weekly with him, which he read over and over until the batteries in the flashlight gave out. After that he just sat there in his dirt cave with roots hanging down. Windless nights we'd hear him farting, all the way up to the house, and that was a distance of two hundred yards. Where're you going? Don't you want to hear why Joe Henry finally came out of the cave?"

"Come out yourself, Jack. Then maybe we can talk."

The phone rang when she was in the kitchen having a glass of water. Shay answered.

"No, she's not here. Jack says he last saw her getting into, or being put into, Frenchie's car. She's probably hurt."

"I'll find her," Rosalind Dubray said. "You've done your duty as a concerned citizen. Why don't you come to lunch tomorrow. Jack's old town, where you used to live. How about one o'clock?"

"Why?"

"Girl talk," Ros said, and hung up.

Shay held the receiver for a few seconds, then disconnected at her end and began to punch in Tobin Bonner's home number. Before she finished, she hesitated, remembering what he'd looked like when she'd left him, the face of a man who had been dug out of a cave-in just before breathing his last. Why give him any more problems tonight? On the other hand, Sarah was in trouble. Bonner was a cop, and Shay wasn't his mother.

She heard the creak of Pepper's crutches and turned around.

"Mom? Feeling kind of nauseous again. Why'd you stay out so late?"

"I'm sorry. I'm coming." And she replaced the receiver. Sarah's difficulties would have to keep until daylight, at least.

Along the river, before sunrise, Vida strides. The blunt cliffs above him are not yet capped with light. A few melancholy stars linger in the featureless sky. He sees the blip of an outbound hawk, like the last heartbeat of a vanished universe.

His breath is audible, steady, magnified within the canyon walls, louder than the river's flow, which is only a faint seam of radiance to his glancing eye. His lungs are filled with a different sort of radiance. His body feels strong, blood quicker than the river. Saltcedar and willow living huge around him, breathing in the last of the night. He cuts across the shallows, one low bank to another, splashing, skin cooling where the water tracks down the insides of his thighs. A black-tailed rabbit bounds away from his footfalls, ears like oars aloft. Seven miles from his home, and he is familiar with every step of the way. He has seen mule deer in the canyon, the splayed prints of black bears in sandy places. He has heard, but never seen, the big cat, down from the heights to track the deer. There are few cats in all of the park because each needs its space.

Rare. But not the rarest species now known to him.

Her presence, the sanguine heats of her body, apparent to Vida even before he catches sight of her again.

Vida is overjoyed, but with a mild attack of nerves. Nonetheless his smile flashes as his steps slow in meeting.

She has not roosted on the great bare bow of the tree this time but is on the ground, partly framed by the tree's curvature, as if she is standing inside the time-bleached jawbone of a creature long unknown on this earth. Visitor. Not quite alien. Eyes that circle his head like calm planets warming to life.

"Hello, Vida. Are you glad to see me?"

He understands. He nods.

She takes a great weary breath, smiles back at him. Strips off her flimsy nylon top and turns a little, bare-breasted, hard ripple of ribcage in the mild light. His heartbeat gutters.

"I wanted you to see *my* scars."

He hasn't moved. She didn't expect him to. Drawing another breath, she approaches, places one of his hands on the raggedness scrawled upward from a hipbone and around to the long valley of her back, where it finally ends. Alert to the tremors in his glistening face. One eye slaked, forever uninvolved, the other brimming with fascination. Then, with the impetus of a single fingertip, redirecting his broad hand to one of her breasts. Bending her head to kiss the clasping hand, take the knuckle of a thumb between her lips. Her tongue moving against the rugged knuckle grain. Now feeling the engine of him in motion beneath the dark skin, but not wanting to look at Vida again, not yet. Not just yet.

III.

WHEN ON THE ROAD TO THEBES, OEDIPUS MET THE SPHINX,
WHO ASKED HIM HER RIDDLE, HIS ANSWER WAS: *MAN*. THIS
SIMPLE WORD DESTROYED THE MONSTER. WE HAVE MANY
MONSTERS TO DESTROY. LET US THINK OF OEDIPUS' ANSWER.

—GEORGE SEFERIS,
FROM HIS NOBEL PRIZE SPEECH IN 1963

25 BONNER WAS IN HIS office at eight-fifteen. His stomach was acting up; too much coffee. There was an editorial on the front page of the *Enterprise* that more or less blamed him for the recent crime wave that had shocked the citizenry of Solar County. Bonner glanced at the editorial indifferently, thinking, *If you only knew what else we might be sitting on.* One word about a neutron bomb, presumably in Rhondo Dubray's keeping, and there would be, minimum, a three-state panic.

His stomach felt worse as he went through the computer file on unreturned phone calls from the day before. One was from the chief of police in Spanish Wells, Harville Mayes. Mayes had a fifty-five-man police force to cover a tiny fraction of the territory that Bonner covered with twenty-four deputies—now twenty-three, and four more of the remaining deputies he had assigned to his parents' home. The two law-enforcement agencies shared facilities: the city's communications network, the county's jail.

He gave Mayes a call. The city police had the Hispanic woman who had killed Luz under heavy guard at the Medical Center. She hadn't said anything since coming out of surgery. Bonner had the other one down the hall in his jail. Both were expendable; hired hands who would maintain their silence. Very likely they didn't even know who they were working for.

Bonner explained that he was seriously shorthanded and arranged to borrow some officers from the city for routine patrol work and also the city's chief investigator when he returned from an FBI seminar in a couple of days.

He called his parents.

"She's moody this morning," Willa said. "She wouldn't touch a bite of breakfast, doesn't want her *bebe*. Keeps calling for her mother. Maria Elena's rocking her now. Do you want to talk to your father?"

Hoyt Bonner said, "How much longer is this going to go on?"

"I don't know. Have you talked to Neal lately?"

"A couple of days ago. Why?"

"About money."

"Would that be any of your business, Tobin?"

"The federal district attorney for southern Utah may be making it *his* business."

There was a long silence.

"I never imagined. He's come to me before, of course. Each time I told him, this has to be the last time. What is it?"

"Bank fraud, among other charges."

"Merciful God. Tobin—what can you do?"

"Not a damn thing. I have a shitload of problems myself."

"You sound—resentful."

"You've always coddled him. Now look where it's got him. And you."

"There's no need to be accusatory. Well, then it's a matter for lawyers, I suppose."

"Criminal lawyers. Good ones."

"There'll be publicity. So awful for Poppy and the kids. Who do you recommend?"

Bonner gave his father the names of two criminal lawyers, one in Salt Lake, the other in Phoenix.

"They're expensive. And about all they can do is try to minimize the damage."

"Where's Neal now?"

"Los Angeles, I think. Ask Poppy, he may have called her. She knows, by the way. She needs all the emotional support she can get."

"Merciful God," his father said again, "that it has come to this."

"I'm sorry," Bonner said, looking up as Dale Stearman walked into his office, alone and unannounced.

"Help you?" Bonner asked, hanging up.

Stearman looked uncombed, out of sorts. "Are you taping?"

"Only official interrogations. What's up?"

"Katharine's missing."

Bonner looked at him for a few moments, nodded to a chair, then called Mary Lynn and asked for Alka-Seltzer.

"You don't keep track of your own, Dale?" he said to Stearman, who had declined to take a seat.

"Our procedures are ironclad. In hostile territory we always know where everybody is, at all times."

"Solar County is your idea of hostile territory?"

"Events of the last few days would confirm that. Even if you didn't have the world headquarters of the Brightly Shining."

"So you always know where everybody is, except for Katharine. Maybe she took a personal day. Maybe she met a guy."

"She's relatively new to the team," Stearman said, hedging reluctantly. "She had more latitude in her section at Defense Intelligence. I knew she was used to acting independently, but I—"

"Needed her specialized talents? Was it Katharine who went after Rhondo Dubray?"

"That initiative is cancelled."

"Not where Rosalind is concerned, bet on it. When was the last time any of you communicated with Katharine?"

"Two-thirty yesterday afternoon. She signed out a Ford Tempo, said she was meeting a possible informant who had contacted her. Obviously the contact wasn't made by telephone; we'd have it on tape."

"What kind of communications does Katharine have with her?"

"A personal transponder and a Global Positioning System on the Tempo."

"Then she shouldn't be that hard to find."

"Our tactical satellite hasn't reported her whereabouts since four-oh-five yesterday afternoon. Katharine's transponder has only a ten-mile range. I've had the CM van circulating for the last couple of hours, but we haven't picked up anything."

Mary Lynn brought Bonner a glass of Alka-Seltzer.

"And one for Dale," Bonner suggested. When Mary Lynn had left the office, he said to Stearman, "I don't have the manpower to help you out much, Dale. We'll put it on the net. This is a big county. And there's a hell of a big canyon not far south of us. Big as all eternity."

Stearman had already considered the possibilities.

"It's Rosalind, isn't it."

"You're asking me? She's *your* buddy, Stearman."

"Bring her in," Stearman said, with a sudden show of anger that surfaced a large vein near one of his temples. "Sweat that bitch."

"Rosalind doesn't sweat. I almost admire her for that. I have better things to do with my time this morning. I have five unsolved homicides on my blotter. Maybe Katharine's demonstrating more of that famous independence. She might have decided to go after Rhondo again, even though you cancelled his D and B. I'd say her chances of getting into New Hebron alone could be fifty-fifty, but her chances of getting out again are nonexistent. They're always on a war footing down there."

"I need your cooperation, Tobin."

"You haven't earned it. Give me something. What about Gabriel and his family? Who do you suspect?"

"You know it had to be one of Gabe's brothers. The gunman's a thousand miles away. You'll never solve it."

"Uh-uh. Had to be someone Gabe knew and more or less trusted. That's a small group, headed by Bobby Polikarski. But I've known Bobby since high school, a lot longer than I've known—Dale Stearman. How much personal contact did you have with Gabriel? No, that's not your style. So was it Katharine?"

"We didn't smoke Gabriel. He was valuable to us. You're forgetting about Rosalind. She turns up, doesn't she? Everywhere you look, Rosalind. Even in your own bedroom." Stearman grinned meanly.

Bonner yawned at the implication.

"She told me she didn't do it. I think I believe her."

"Jesus. You're losing it, Tobin. She'll lie to Godalmighty on her deathbed."

"Uh-uh. I don't think she's a liar. But she is a listener. And she doesn't forget what she hears." He leaned back in his squeaky chair. "Speaking of Ros, you're the one who's showing some sweat. Not afraid of her, are you, Dale?"

"For the last time, I'm telling you to bring her in and keep her locked up."

"Just so I can make some pretense of staying within the law, which doesn't seem to be one of your concerns, what do I put on the warrant?"

"There's a steel utility building at that western town where she's living. You'll find a hijacked five-ton in there, with a black jaguar inside the truck."

Bonner didn't look surprised, but he felt disappointed.

"You saw it?"

"She showed the animal to me. Then she stripped and got into his cage with him. Vintage Rosalind. Will that be enough for you?"

Bonner picked up his letter opener, did his balancing act, nodded. He summoned Mary Lynn, who came in with a second glass of Alka-Seltzer for Stearman.

"I want Del to have a search warrant executed this morning. Silverwhip Jack's old town."

"What goes on the warrant?"

"Stolen property. We're naming Rosalind Dubray."

Stearman turned to follow Mary Lynn out of the office.

"Hold it a minute, Dale. Bring me up to date on that body you co-opted."

Stearman hesitated, considered, then acknowledged, "It was Suchary Siamashvili."

"And he left a bomb ticking somewhere."

"Not exactly the way you mean. There's a situation that could get out of hand. I can't say any more."

"Yeah? How do neutrons kill?"

"Silently, aggressively, efficiently. Like a computer virus. Everything in the body shuts down due to massive failure of the chemical-electrical system. A clean, no-fuss kind of death." Stearman looked at the glass he was holding, winced as he drank the Alka-Seltzer.

Bonner watched him, thinking of a no-fuss kind of death. Thinking of his wife, buried without her heart. Forty-two rounds poured into their car in El Paso. As dirty a kill as could be imagined. And the innocent went on suffering. He saw it daily, in the gracious, chopped head of his son. He saw it in his shaving mirror.

Whatever was on his face just then made Dale Stearman uneasy.

"Hey, Dale?"

"What?"

"When was the last time you killed a man? I mean, actually drew the knife across his throat or pulled the trigger yourself?"

"Why?"

"Answer's *never*, isn't it? No wet work for Dale Stearman. Silent, cool, removed. The predator who leaves no tracks."

"What's this about?"

"I'm gonna cooperate with you, Dale. By keeping you alive while you go about finding Siamashvili's little gift to mankind. How do I keep you alive? I'll sit on Rosalind, one way or another. But you can forget about Katharine Harsha. If Ros had reason to believe she was the sniper, then Katharine's a goner. You know what? Compared with everything else that's gone down, I can't bring myself to care. As for Ros, the more I see of her, the more I like her. Hell, I may decide to marry her. She's got a library in her head, and I've been researching your file."

"What kind of bullshit has Ros—"

"The day is coming, and it's coming soon, when I hand you a knife and show you my throat. You'd better seize the opportunity while it's there. Because if you don't, I guarantee you'll be as dead as you've deserved to be all these years."

Stearman leaned forward slightly on the balls of his feet. Not trying to stare Bonner down, just looking through him in an abstract way.

"Careful. You've already said too much."

"What's it going to get me, a one-way trip to the Cube? You could show me the directive that obtains; I'm sure there's one in your back pocket. All you need to do is type in my name. But I'm not going anywhere. You're in hostile territory, remember? *My* territory. You need me right now."

Stearman belched profoundly, wincing as if he'd opened an abscess deep in his stomach.

"And when I don't need you?"

"I'll still be easy to find," Bonner said.

Signe Gehrin walked into the bedroom where Sarah had spent the night and appeared to be sleeping, all but hidden beneath a comforter. The room was cool, almost chilly, but there was perspiration in the blue hollows of Sarah's eyes. Every third or fourth breath was more like a deep gasp.

Signe didn't like the sound of those gasps.

"*Buen dias, señora,*" Conchita said, coming out of the bathroom with a bowl of water and a clean cloth.

"How is she?"

"*No se.* She woke up twice during the night. For a few minutes only. I took her to the bathroom an hour ago. She can't walk by herself."

"Is she talking?"

Conchita sat on the side of the bed to sponge Sarah's face.

"Not really. She says words. But when I speak to her, I don't think she understands."

"Any change at all, find me right away."

Signe went downstairs to the morning room to join Wolfgang. Frenchie Dobie sat in a wicker basket chair in his undershirt, reading the local paper. Lawn sprinklers made lazy arcs over the gorgeous lawn beyond the open windows.

"What do you think?" Wolfgang asked as he helped himself to *huevos rancheros* in a chafing dish. A fat Latino houseman was working in the big kitchen; in another part of the house a vacuum cleaner hummed.

"She will either sleep it off, or she will take a bad turn. Too soon to tell. Needless to say, I can't get any information, the condition she's in."

Frenchie slowly lowered his newspaper and stared at Signe. The swellings beneath his popped eyes were the size and texture of prunes. He had not enjoyed a restful night.

"You can't do anything?" His voice was tight and thin this morning.

Signe selected an herbal tea bag from a rosewood chest on the sideboard and poured hot water.

"It's not a good idea denying her medical attention."

Wolfgang said, "We've made that decision. She has to remain here."

"And if she dies from some neurological trauma? What then?"

Wolfgang looked across the table at Frenchie.

"That would be your problem. Along with the problem of how to deal with the Aum Shinrikyo. Failure to deliver the Dove will be *your* failure. I've acted only as an intermediary. I've always known how to make myself useful to fanatics and madmen without becoming vulnerable should the winds suddenly change. Why don't you start thinking about all that while you go upstairs to bathe? I need to talk privately to my wife about another matter. Oh, and do something about your car, Frenchie. Sooner or later it will attract unwanted attention."

Enough, Katharine thought.

The pain of shattered jaw and jagged teeth was enough. The torment of thirst, the burst lip and aching throat that limited her lament to a dismal croaking. The nausea. The violent spells of trembling as her body tried to adjust to the consequences of a chilly night spent naked and fully exposed on rocky ground. Enough, enough.

She was on her back, a downward pitch to her body. Her head was free. She could raise it a few inches, but the effort required and the edgy movements of pieces of jawbone discouraged her from looking around. It was night, dark where she lay, ringed by cliffs like a crown below heaven. The stars giving light but sharing none of their warmth. She had seen enough to know that her hands, which were numb, had been staked out at right angles to her body. Her feet were lashed together and tied to something immovable between them, gleaming, a mountaineer's piton driven into hard ground. Any muscular contraction or spasm meant pain. After a few hours, with the sky lightening and the stars banked, forgotten, delirium followed the pain.

Rosalind's face in her delirium, like a reflection forming then scattering on the surface of wind-troubled water. The careless shape of her red thatch resembling a poisonous moonflower. Her capricious grin. The steely ring of hammering. Hammering.

Kate, Kate. Perked up in a glist'ring grief and wearing her golden sorrow.

What did that mean?

Enough!

Katherine, out of her drift, in those moments when her body was not jerking involuntarily at her bonds and dissipating much of her strength, tried raising the riot of fear in her breast to the level of a scream. She tried several times during the slow-moving desert hour before daybreak, but heard only weak echoes. Each effort cost more of her voice, until she had no voice left.

Something insectile skittered across a bare breast. It was the last thing she felt until her skin began perceptibly to warm and the heat penetrated to the depths of her heart. She came awake with an explosive start and opened her eyes on a great, glowing sky. It was well past sunrise. Her eyes closed tightly, unable to bear the shock of the light. Instantly, she realized what Rosalind's real purpose had been. Tying her in a lonely place where the sun would find her early and remain with her for most of the day. Heat refracting from the rocks around Katharine, torching her fair skin. Hours and hours of high-desert sun, her golden sorrow.

Shay hadn't taken Rosalind Dubray's luncheon invitation seriously, but when Ros called again at eleven o'clock to cordially confirm it, she decided to go. Pepper had a rebound headache from the shot of Demerol they had given her in the hospital the night before last, and was dozing in the darkened guest room. Jack, sober and well-dressed, had gone into town to see his lawyers, on what business he didn't say. He hadn't been sure when he'd return. And Shay was mildly curious to see Jack's old town again. The past was boiling up in her like a recurring infection whenever she looked at her father. It might not be a bad idea, she thought, to retrace some of her childhood steps and missteps, poke into the old places, stare the memories in the face until they all receded to a bearable distance.

She couldn't deny that she also was curious about Rosalind Dubray. Shay was a child of Hollywood. Living legends had always intrigued her.

At the iron bridge across the Aquiles River Shay found herself behind a flatbed truck carrying a damaged Cadillac; the trunk had been sprung and the back window was in tatters. She thought she recognized the Caddy. Past the bridge she honked politely and pulled up alongside the truck, owned by Sundance Towing and Repairs. The driver was a kid wearing a rancher's straw and a grimy T-shirt. He pulled over on the narrow shoulder, looking at her.

"Morning! Could I ask you a question?"

"Yes, ma'am?"

"Where did you pick up that Caddy?"

He looked at the invoice clothespinned to a sun visor.

"Name was Gehrin."

"Is that his car?"

"No, belongs to Dobie."

"Did you speak to Mr. Dobie this morning?"

"No. I didn't see anybody. I was told I'd find the car in the driveway and bring it on in. Why?"

Shay smiled and waved at him, and drove on.

⬤

"What's it like to have a daughter?" Rosalind asked her.

"Scary. Exasperating. All that hell and valor in her heart. We bicker and contend. Neither of us is the brooding kind. There are no guilt payoffs following a fight. And we have those blissful times when we're quiet together, at each other's best mercies. I can poke a little fun, but you know, eleven, you have to respect the insecurity. She can be as tender and prickly as a baby witch."

"I don't think I'd want another little me," Ros reflected. "Not that I've ever been tempted."

"I may have been lucky. I see just enough of myself in Pepper to be both cautious and protective."

"You didn't get married."

"I wasn't in love with him. I was stuck on him, but it wasn't love. We still see each other, informally. He's Irish, and an artist, and all of his discipline is in his art. Typical of the profession."

"I knew a lot of actors in Vogue-ass. I'm talking about movie stars, but why bore you? Three of them proposed to me before I was eighteen. I guess you could say I had a talent they couldn't resist." She wiggled her long toes a little. The strangeness of her feet gave Shay the skin-crawls. It was hard not to stare at them. "One actually cried when I turned her down, bless her heart." Rosalind shrugged. "How about another beer? Then I'll toss the shrimp in the roux and we'll scarf. You like Cajun?"

"Sure. I gained eight pounds once on a two-week shoot in New Orleans. The gumbos, I mean, *please.*"

Rosalind filled two more Pilsner glasses from a sweating metal keg. The air hadn't stirred for half an hour, but a big floor fan at one end of the Crystal Chandelier's long front porch kept things pleasant. Rosalind wore shorts and a halter top and was barefoot. Her feet were propped on the porch railing. She scratched where she itched, and belched mildly when the beer bubbles rose through her gullet. Shay was far from inhibited, but it was hard to adjust to someone with no barriers, no guile, no facade that needed constant reinforcement and retouching.

A couple of times Shay had been on the verge of telling Rosalind about Frenchie Dobie's Cadillac. Sarah was still missing. But a certain uneasiness made her stay on the surface of things, for now. Taking care with Rosalind, learning the loops and falls, the blinds and hazards of her astonishing mind. An off-hand comment that would sound like neurotic fantasy coming from another woman: *Three of them proposed to me before I was eighteen.* Spoken with a little glint of amusement in her eyes, the aplomb of plain truth. And the catastrophic power of her sexuality needed no further definition.

They were halfway through their lunch when Tobin Bonner showed up with three deputies at the gate of Silverwhip Jack's town.

The warrant soured Rosalind's mood a little. She read it carefully while Bonner loitered on the top step of the porch, looking more or less steadily at Shay but saying nothing to her. The last person he'd expected to find breaking bread with Rosalind Dubray. Shay smiled noncommittally, enjoying the notion that she was a puzzle to him.

Ros waved the folded search warrant like a limp fan beside her face and said, "Who do I have to thank for this?"

"Anonymous tip."

"I'll just bet," Ros said, gazing at a portion of the sky past the brim of Bonner's tired old Stetson hat as if she were about to brew some stormy weather. The day had, in fact, turned hazy. "Can it wait a few minutes?" She grinned. "I may not have another meal as good as this one for a while."

"No. Open that shed, Ros, or we'll do it for you."

Ros glanced at Shay, a shoulder lifting in apology.

"Come on, Shay. I want you to see this. I was going to show you myself after we ate."

She slipped on a pair of sandals crafted for her unusual feet and led them all to the utility building standing at the foot of the small mountain of rubble that had come crashing down from the cliff years ago. She whistled at the clamoring German shepherds inside the fence, and they shut up, retreating watchfully.

Bonner and his deputies, with Shay lagging behind and wondering what it was about, followed Rosalind single file through the unlocked gates of the compound. Bonner's eyes were on the ground, as if he were looking for something. *Tire tracks?* Shay wondered. There were a lot of them, some wide enough for a big truck or a farm tractor.

The outside of the ribbed-steel building simmered in the sun, but two one-ton air conditioners were running, and there were exhaust fans on the roof. Bonner looked up and glanced at Shay again as Rosalind unlocked the single-entry door beside the roll-up garage door. He made a small gesture for her to stay outside.

Shay grimaced and moved over into the short angle of shade cast by the overhung roof, where the shepherds had gone to sit and pant. Bonner put a hand on Rosalind when the door clicked open. Both dogs growled. Ros stepped back and let Bonner go inside first. One of the deputies stayed with her.

"What are they looking for?" Shay asked Rosalind.

"A black cat." To the deputy she said, "Why don't we all go in? It's bloody hot out here. Shay?"

Cool air poured through the doorway. The building was brightly lighted, the air clean and humidified. Bonner stood in the middle of the concrete floor looking around at rows of office-style steel shelving that held books. Nothing but books. There were probably thirty unopened cartons stacked on the floor. Books that hadn't been shelved were piled on one end of a long library table.

At the other end there was a small wire cage with two black kittens in it.

Rosalind opened the cage door and lifted out one of the kittens, held it on a bare shoulder in her cupped palm. She looked benignly at Bonner.

"Want one? I found them up by the KOA campground. Some tourist's cat had an inconvenient litter, I guess. Or isn't this quite what you were looking for?"

Bonner blinked mildly at her, but his jaw was tight.

Rosalind said with hard relish, "I pick up strays where I happen to find them. Can't help myself; it's part of my nature."

Bonner turned to his deputies and said, "Search the rest of the buildings. The saloon, too. Get Bert out here to cast those tracks outside. And all the tire tracks down by the entrance gate. Coy, you and Boone remove the air-conditioning filters and bag them. Then vacuum the floor in here." He turned to Rosalind. "You can finish your lunch now."

"I hate to see you go to so much trouble, Bonner. How about some beers for the guys? Or I could make lemonade."

"Good idea, Ros. We'll be here awhile. Make lemonade."

There was a monotone crackle of thunder when they walked outside again. A gust of wind kicked up a whirl of dust in the yard. Ros looked again at the colorless, glittering sky and predicted rain.

"A real gullywasher," she said. "Maybe fifteen minutes away. Hell on tire tracks, as if that mattered." She hooked an arm companionably inside Shay's elbow. "Mind if I ask what's going on between you two?"

"Funny," Shay said, with a rise of goose bumps from portents and volatile atmospherics, "I was about to ask that question myself."

At the saloon Ros said, "Need to run to the bathroom. You want to send one of your deputies with me, Bonner? No? Back in a minute." She embraced Shay with a gauging eye. "Have a nice chat."

When they were alone, Bonner said to Shay, "I can't tell you how to choose your friends."

"This sort of came about by accident. Used to be my home around here. Ros thought I might like to see it again. By the way, what did you expect to find in that shed?"

"A hundred-eighty-pound feral cat that can be extremely dangerous. Turn on you in a split second. Except for the weight, I'm also describing Rosalind Dubray."

"We're getting along fine."

"Don't press your luck, Shay."

He looked at her for a few moments longer. Shay responded with a shrug, tired of his lingering disfavor, which she didn't feel was justified. He seemed angry about his futile trip out here. Tangential hostility toward her because of Rosalind's calculated bullying. His suit needed a touch-up with an iron. He could have used a new hat. He was just a little shy of presentable, the lack of a woman's influence and attention for many years, sympathies of a loving soul. Shay wondered what the voters thought when they saw him around town.

"Don't worry about me," Shay said finally.

"I don't have time to worry about you."

Bonner turned abruptly and walked down the steps to his car. Clouds were taking charged shape overhead; there was a faint radiance of lightning reflected on his new windshield. He was turning around to drive out of the compound when Shay remembered that she hadn't said anything to him about Sarah. But if time was a problem for Tobin Bonner, maybe he wouldn't be interested. It was no problem for her this afternoon. She decided to stop by the Gehrins on her way back to Jack's ranch, find out if they knew what had happened to Sarah.

26 THE MONEY WAS ROLLED tight and secured by rubber bands, then plugged like corks into the one-inch-diameter length of PVC pipe that ran beneath the floorboards of the deck on the back of Tom Leucadio's house, a shell log home about forty feet square. Glorified cabin, really, but stoutly made. The pipe looked functional to casual scrutiny, but although it ran into the ground near the water meter and was joined to the house by a seal of plumber's putty, it didn't connect to other water lines. A midlength joint was easily removed with a pipe wrench, allowing him fast access to the rolls of bills: U.S. twenties and hundreds and Swiss franc notes. Five years' worth of squirreled-away skimmings from the accounts of Lucky Orchards, and kickbacks from other sources: leasors of heavy equipment; truckers who diverted fruit from the co-op and sold it themselves to roadside markets or grocers looking for a deal; even union officials who organized the *cuadrillas* working the orchards and groves of the Southwest.

The thunderstorm that had rolled into his canyon at three o'clock also shut down the power after a few minutes of pyrotechnics. He retrieved his stash by flashlight, rain sweeping across the deck and dripping down into his face.

In his cubbyhole bedroom, he lit a paraffin lamp and dried off. Two new Samsonite suitcases were open on the bed. He had emptied his wardrobe. His passport was valid. He leased his house from a Nevada holding company no one knew he owned. When things settled down, he would dispose of it anonymously and put the proceeds into a farm in Costa Rica. His unreported and untaxed cash, probably in excess of two hundred thousand U.S. dollars, was something of a liability; but once he was across the border with it, arrangements could be made at almost any Mexican bank to—

"Going somewhere, Tom?"

Leucadio turned in shock to see Rosalind in the doorway of his bedroom, wearing a dripping poncho and a rain-glazed black Resistol.

"Ay! *Dios!* Ros. You scared the—"

"Current's off, so your chimes don't work."

Thunder. The streaming windows overlooking the deck trembled and Ros's elongate image shimmered spectrally. Tom Leucadio's hand dropped toward the gym bag on his bed, an unconscious protective gesture. Then he primed his throat with a swallow of beer to get his voice going again.

"What are you—been awhile since I've seen you, Ros. Yeah, I'm taking a couple of well-deserved weeks, I—"

"Mind if I get myself a beer, Tom?"

"What? Oh, sure. Help yourself. In the kitchen."

Ros sauntered off, lamplight reflecting from her hip-length poncho. He was still on edge, as if she'd popped up from underground, stealthy as an omen. Leucadio glanced at the gym bag, lumpy with hard cylinders of money. Dozens of cylinders, like double-aught shotgun shells. He grabbed the duffel and pushed it into one of the suitcases, closed the lid.

Rosalind was finding her way around his house by flashes from the storm outside.

"Nice place, Tom," he heard her say. "How many bedrooms?"

"Only two. It's small, but I've always been comfortable. Find that beer?"

He started to pack the other suitcase. His heart kept trying to bolt up into his throat. He glanced over his shoulder a couple of times, but Rosalind didn't reappear. Where was she? It occurred to him that it wasn't just coincidence that she'd picked this time to drop by. He went to the door of his bedroom, carrying the lamp.

"Where'd you go? Ros?"

No answer. He ventured into the living room, holding the lamp high, the light grazing hand-adzed ceiling beams, illuminating his collection of Navaho rugs and Indian ceremonial headdresses that hung on the darkly stained walls. He owned only essential pieces of furniture, but they were antiques. Sell everything as is, maybe a hundred-twenty-five tops with the additional acreage, ideal for a retired couple—Tom was suddenly panicked by the intuition that he wouldn't be going anywhere after all, because . . .

"Ros!"

Two steps nearer the kitchen, he saw her boots standing neatly in front of the ornate old Monarch stove. Rosalind wasn't in them.

The door to the deck hadn't been tightly closed. He went to close it, staring at Ros's empty boots, feeling creepy at the neckline. Trying to make an equation from the inconsistent notations of her behavior. Then it struck him with a chill; he returned quickly to his bedroom.

Ros was sitting on the edge of the bed, barefoot, right leg crossed. There was rain on the sill and hardwood floor below the window she had opened from the outside and stepped through. She had taken off her hat and poncho.

The gym bag was out of the suitcase and unzipped.

She drank from a bottle of Carta Blanca, looked at Tom with a thoughtful smile.

"Bring the lamp? I think I picked up a splinter on the deck. Big one. Maybe you can get it out for me."

"Ros—I—that money—belongs to me."

"Of course it does, Tom. What're you looking so worried for?" She put the tip of a finger on the ball of her foot. "Here's the splinter. Sticking out a little. But I don't have long-enough fingernails to get hold of it. Maybe you can pull it with your teeth."

"My teeth?"

"Just nibble out the splinter for me, Tom. I'll hold the lamp."

She set the beer bottle on the floor, zipped the gym bag and tossed it disinterestedly back into the suitcase.

"Come on, Tom. It hurts."

With the air-conditioning off it was close and warm in the bedroom. Ros seemed to be breathing all of the useful air: his lungs were leaden, almost too heavy to lift. Pandemonium beginning at the root of his throat. The sweat he'd raised was rusting the instinct that urged him not to go near her.

"So you're taking a little trip. 'There's good times here, but better on down the road.' Folk wisdom that I've usually found to be true. Tom? I know you're anxious to be on your way. All I need, for a little while, is your full attention. Beginning with my foot. Touch my foot. Lick it where the splinter hurts. Tom, I said I want you to *lick my foot.* This is the price of my mercy. Otherwise, I promise—you will still be here when the wild dogs come."

Tobin Bonner parked his car a dozen feet behind the pickup truck from the county's motor pool. The pickup was off the road opposite a canyon lane with four mailboxes beside it. He got out into the heavy rain and walked to the pickup, opened the door on the passenger side, and climbed in.

The deputy, one of Bonner's criminal investigators, was Charlie Lee Dukes. He was a thin man with a poker face and a gaze so empty of emotion both eyes seemed to be made of glass. Dukes took off his headphones and put aside the guitar with which he had been passing the time.

"She's still up there. It's the last house, one of those shell log homes that fix up real nice."

"Whose house?"

"Deed's in a corporate name. Presco Properties Inc. Nevada. Same for the utilities and phone."

"How long has Rosalind been there?"

Dukes glanced at the dash clock. "Twenty minutes."

"Much of a walk?"

"Quarter mile."

"What is Rosalind driving?"

"Fancypants hopped-up Isuzu shortbed. Maroon and orange."

Bonner went back to his car, opened the trunk, and took out a backpack in summer camouflage colors that matched his rain gear. A couple of cars passed him. When they had gone he crossed the two-lane blacktop and walked up the canyon road, which was awash.

Where the gravel road dwindled to a steep track among tall pines and piñon trees, the log house had been snugly fitted into the hillside. There was a 4WD Ram pickup parked in a carport below the house. Rosalind had left her own ride a hundred feet down the road.

Didn't want anyone to know she was coming?

There were no lights in front, but Bonner saw a glow of lamplight on the evergreens that overhung a deck behind the house.

Instead of taking the steps from the carport to the small porch and front door, Bonner picked his way up the wet bushy hillside beneath swaying trees. He kept going until he was above the deck and looking down into a bedroom, at Rosalind and someone who had his back to the windows.

When Bonner looked at Ros again, through the binoculars he took from his backpack, she was startlingly close. He could see the stray hairs in her bronze eyebrows. But he doubted that she would be able to see him, even if she knew just where he was standing.

A window was open a few inches. Not enough for him to hear what they were saying through the torrent of rain, though he was only about twenty feet away.

Tom Leucadio handed Rosalind the lamp. He kneeled. He took her foot in his shaking hands and pressed the long instep against his perspiring forehead.

"Good, Tom. Now eat out the splinter."

Rosalind leaned back on her hands, face to the ceiling, her eyes up in her head as if she were trafficking in spirits at a seance. After a couple of minutes of his efforts, the long splinter slid out of her flesh.

She sighed, sitting up. "Show it to me."

He raised his perspiring face, the bloody splinter clutched between his teeth. His eyes were big with a need for her approval.

Then Rosalind moved so quickly he had no time to react.

Lifting her left foot from the floor, she seized him around the neck, both feet locking, ankle bones pressing into his throat below the jawline, numbing vital nerves, cutting off the blood flow to his brain.

"What happened to my sister Sarah?"

It wes getting interesting.

Bonner replaced the binoculars in his backpack and took out the audio equipment his brother had given him for Christmas: a bionic ear scout and a bionic booster, useful to hunters for tracking game in deep woods. The headphones and wind-resistant microphones, mounted in a reflector the size of a frying pan, enhanced sound reception by 30 percent. Aiming it at the log house, he could follow, with some gaps, what was going on in the bedroom.

●

When Tom Leucadio struggled, Ros applied more pressure. His hands dropped before they could begin to pry her feet apart.

"Ten seconds, Tom. Those are Dim Mak points in the neck I'm applying pressure to. I can't promise, if you pass out, that you'll make it back. Three seconds. *Two.*"

Leucadio tapped one of her ankles with what remained of his strength, the universal signal for capitulation. Ros released him. He sprawled back on the floor.

"Accident," he gasped, red-faced and writhing.

"Yeah?"

"Frenchie—got in a hurry. Bad timing. Motorcycle hit—his car."

"She was hurt?"

"Unconscious."

"Where is she now?"

"Gehrin."

"*What?* Why is Sarah with the Gehrins?"

"Don't know."

Leucadio sat up slowly. Rosalind planted her right foot against his chest, and he froze.

"Truth," he said.

Ros removed her foot, leaving a little streak of blood on his shirt. She borrowed white boot socks from one of the suitcases and put them on.

"Okay, Tom. I won't ask you what you were doing in Frenchie's company." She glanced at the suitcase that held his stash. "Couldn't be a physical attraction. I've always wondered what it is about money. Everybody needs enough to get along, okay. But the stuff isn't beautiful, and after it's been through enough hands, it smells as bad as garbage. Were you ripping off Jack Waco?"

Leucadio nodded.

"Not hard to figure out. Silverwhip give you that cheek? Sure he did. Will he come looking for you again?"

"I don't think so. I messengered a letter to his lawyers an hour ago. I told them where the accounts are. They'll recover ninety percent." He was momentarily convulsed. "I'm a sorry piece of shit! I had it good there. Jack put me through college. I don't know why I did it."

"Too much coyote blood. So happy trails, hombre. You can go. By the way, do you own this house?"

He looked at her in dismay.

"Give me the keys. I'm gonna borrow it for a few days, that's all. An old friend needs a place to stay where nobody would think to look for him. I'll clean up afterwards."

Charlie Lee Dukes looked up from cleaning his Glock automatic when Bonner tapped on the driver's side window. He put the window down a few inches.

Bonner said, "Rosalind will come rolling out of the canyon any minute. I'm gone. Don't lose her."

"In that pansy pickup? It's even got a neon license-plate holder. Anything going on?"

"I don't know yet. The house is Tom Leucadio's. Rosalind wants it for a few days. If she goes anywhere except back to the Crystal Chandelier, page me."

After her lunch with Rosalind, Shay had met with the claims adjustor for the company that had insured her Tahoe. Total loss. They were cutting her a check. It wouldn't be enough to pay off the loan she had with her bank. She would have to look for something a little older and less expensive to drive to keep the payments within her reach.

It was raining hard when she finished her business with the insurance people, so she occupied a public phone in the small artsy shopping center in downtown Spanish Wells. Time to get back to work. The movie she'd spent a day on in Vegas had wrapped. She placed calls to the various stunt players' associations in Hollywood until she came up with a lead: a picture starting in about a week at Bryce Canyon, requiring climbers and riggers. She was friends with the wife of the second unit director doing the Bryce shoot. It sounded promising. She called Arbor Gower, who wasn't in, left a chatty message on Arbor's answering machine.

All the networking had left her feeling depleted. Blood, sweat, and hustle was the key to her livelihood; the competition was intense.

The rain seemed to be moving on to the north and east. There was a rainbow over the bluff along West Valley Boulevard, a twin-engine prop plane shooting in low to land at the airport on the south end. She made one more stop, picking up a thirty-day supply of disposable contact lenses at a one-hour optical store.

An olive green Jaguar was leaving the gate at the Gehrins' hacienda as Shay approached. Darkly tinted windows; Shay couldn't see who was driving or tell how many were in the car. It went by her fast on the narrow road. Shay slowed down and watched the Jaguar in her rearview until it was out of sight, then turned in and drove to the house.

The front doors were open behind the barred security gate. A houseman was running a floor polisher at the back of a long central hall inside and obviously didn't hear the door chimes. The wrought-iron gates weren't completely closed. Shay hesitated, then opened a gate and stepped inside the house.

"Anybody home?"

The houseman had his back to her, and he was wearing head-phones, doing Salsa steps while he ran the big polisher. It was a spacious house with muted dramatics. Across the gold-veined onyx foyer and to her left a staircase curved up to a second-floor gallery. Sunlight imprinted narrow rectangles of orange light on thickly stuccoed white walls. There were two large El Greco–like paintings on the staircase wall, bronzed faces by candlelight, important solemn faces. Another painting in the style of Diego Rivera. *Hidalgos* and revolutionaries, museum-quality lighting. The broad steps were red quarry tile. Except for the muted noise of the floor polisher, Shay didn't hear anything. The houseman was now out of sight in a plant-filled room at the other end of the house.

"Hello?"

She was looking up the stairs, but movement in a room beyond a Moorish arch caught her eye. A cat strolled into the foyer, looked her over with a frigid blue eye, and continued in a series of bounds up the stairs.

Shay listened to her heartbeat for a few seconds. The floor polisher was turned off. She debated wandering to the back of the house and getting the houseman's attention. She'd come this far, so why not.

She was two-thirds of the way down the hall when a door opened behind her.

Shay turned as Frenchie Dobie walked out of a room with a cell phone to his ear, talking. He didn't look her way as he continued to the front of the house.

"Yeah, I know, time is of the essence, but she just ain't said much yet. Fact is, Sarah's not making a whole lot of sense when she *does* talk. We figure it's a concussion. She'll come out of it soon, then Signe can get to work. If Sarah knows anything about the Dove, Signe will have it out of her in a jiffy. Might not be a bad thing actually, Sarah learning a thing or two about obedience. I'll be in touch, soon as I—now hold on, have a little patience, *compadre*. Is that so? Well, that's your problem. Listen, it's an unavoidable delay. I'm holding up *my* end. You'll get everything you're after, and believe me, it'll be a real pleasure."

As he crossed the foyer and went jauntily up the stairs, Shay stepped behind the door Frenchie had left open in case he looked back. She was hearing her heartbeat again, feeling it in her temples. Not much of Frenchie's conversation made sense to her, but obviously Sarah was in the house, hurt, and virtually a prisoner.

Now what?

"What are you doing here?"

Shay's head jerked around. She saw a Latin girl with an armful of grocery sacks standing in a terrace door space fifteen feet away. A maroon Chevy Suburban was parked on the drive beside the terrace, rear doors open.

"Oh—I, uh, rang: but nobody—I just came to—a social call, I thought—"

The girl turned and put the grocery sacks on a glass-topped table in the terrace room, not taking her eyes off Shay.

"You're a friend of the Gehrins?"

"My name's Shay Waco. My father lives down the road."

"Yes. I know him. Jack Waco."

"What's your name?" Shay asked, with a friendly smile.

"Conchita."

She studied Shay frankly, and Shay found her interesting as well, good body and a somewhat marred but somberly glamorous face imbued with the timeless intricate intelligence of a calendar stone.

"Sorry for walking in. I guess the Gehrins aren't here."

"No. They flew to Las Vegas for the evening. I don't expect them back until after midnight."

"Okay. Well, when you see them, please tell them I stopped by."

Conchita nodded, stared at Shay for a few seconds longer, shrugged slightly and turned to retrieve the groceries from the table. She carried the sacks to the kitchen without looking at Shay again.

Shay let out her breath, decided against leaving by the front door, thinking she might run into Frenchie Dobie, who would not be pleased to see her. As for Sarah—she didn't know what to do yet. But it seemed to be something for Tobin Bonner to handle.

She left by way of the terrace, followed a path around to the front of the house, and got into the Windstar.

Her shoulders jerked in fright when she glimpsed shadowy movement in the rearview mirror, someone leaning toward her.

"Is she in there?" Rosalind Dubray said.

"Oh, my God. Where—? Don't *do* that."

"Sorry," Rosalind said. "I left my ride down the road when I saw your van in front of the house. I asked you about Sarah."

"Yes, she's inside. Upstairs, I think. So is Frenchie Dobie."

"Who else?"

"Couple of employees. One's name is Conchita. She told me the Gehrins went to Vegas, but they'll be back later tonight. Listen, while I was in the house I overheard Frenchie on the phone. I don't know how you'll manage it, but I think you should get Sarah out of there right away."

"Who was he talking to?"

"I don't know."

"What did he say?"

Shay repeated as much of the conversation as she could remember; Frenchie was a fast talker.

Rosalind was watching the house. When Shay finished Ros looked around, her gaze like a knife-edge turning into light.

"I'm going in. I could use your help."

Shay had figured this was coming.

"All right."

"Frenchie carries a little peashooter around with him. But I doubt he has the balls to use it. Anyway, you already know you can handle Frenchie. Let's go. Don't bother to knock."

Conchita was on the stairs when Rosalind came in with Shay behind her. She turned and said to them, "Where are you going?"

Ros said, with her tooth-crammed hungry grin, "Sarah's my sister. Now how bad do you want to try to stop me?"

Conchita glanced from Ros to Shay, then stepped aside.

"Second bedroom on your left."

"Frenchie in there?"

"*Sí.* I try to stay with her, most of the time. Because that one, pop-eye, he likes to put his hands where they don't belong." She shrugged, uneasily. "This whole business, *mala leche,* you know what I mean?"

"Conchita, that your name, Conchita? I'm going to give you some good advice, which is pack your bags and seek employment elsewhere."

Conchita's mouth reformed in a melancholy expression.

"Why? I'm not making trouble for you. Getting my head broke is not what I am paid for, okay? So I don't have anything to worry about."

Rosalind said, "If you stay here much longer, you do," and went on past her.

When the bedroom door banged open, Frenchie jumped out of the chair he'd been in while watching television. Most of a glass of rioja slopped down his shirtfront. He choked on the wine in his mouth, then sprayed the air around him.

Rosalind reached Frenchie in two strides and pushed him back into the antique side chair, tall and Spanish, dark carved wood. It toppled. Frenchie's boot heels arced toward the ceiling; the back of his head smacked the glazed tile floor.

"Keep him there," Ros said to Shay.

She went to the bed. Sarah's small face was sunk into a large pillow. Her eyes had opened during the commotion. She looked terrible.

Shay winced, then turned her attention to Frenchie, who was trying to pull the pistol he carried from a leather shoulder holster. He was still choking, his stunned eyes on Shay. She wagged an index finger warningly at him, but when the pistol cleared the holster she stepped forward and heel-kicked him in the crotch. He gave one more explosive cough and sucked in a vast amount of wind, grabbing where it hurt. The cute pearl-handled revolver rattled on the floor.

The chubby houseman appeared at the door with a Mossberg pump-action and yelled, "Jew two doan move!"

Shay spun and kicked the heavy paneled door into his face. The shotgun went off in the hall. Shay picked up a twin of the antique chair in which Frenchie had spilled, opened the bedroom door with a toe of her boot, and slammed the chair into the houseman, who was on one knee, his nose bleeding, trying to rack the slide of the Mossberg. The chair was a solid piece of furniture, as much as Shay could lift. The curved top of the chair back caught him on the chin and knocked him senseless. Gun-smoked plaster drifted down through sunlight from the vaulted hall ceiling.

Shay had a glimpse of Conchita's face on the stairs; then the girl prudently disappeared.

Shay emptied the shotgun and kept the shells. Frenchie was nearly motionless on the bedroom floor, in a hog-tied position, moaning. She picked up his gun too. Her skin was prickling from a heady flush of adrenaline.

Rosalind, her face bleak with anger, had gathered Sarah up in her bedclothes. She looked at Frenchie and at the prostrate houseman in the hall.

"Damn, you can be impressive."

"I've spent years choreographing this stuff. I even do it in my sleep. How is she?"

Sarah stirred in Ros's arms. "Kill him," she said weakly.

"Hear that, Frenchie? It's your dearly beloved speaking. How do you feel, Sarah?"

"Awful. Sick. Kill him."

"Can't do that right now, Sugarpea. For one thing, I'd like to know what kind of circle jerk Frenchie's participating in. How about it, Mr. Dobie?"

Frenchie said, "Don't touch me. Don't touch me."

Sarah moaned, weeping. Her breath smelled like vomit. There was a goose egg on the right side of her head between the temple and the tip of her ear.

"Rosalind?" Shay said.

"Yeah. You're right. We need to get Sarah to the Med. Can you carry her? I'll just be a minute."

"What are you going to do?" Shay asked. Now with a clear head and adding up the damages, most of it her responsibility. "We're one step over the line already."

Frenchie said, his eyes lifting toward heaven, "Don't let her touch me!"

Ros stared at him for a few seconds, then reconsidered whatever she'd had in mind.

"Aw, it doesn't matter. I'll be able to find him when I want him. Come on."

27

SHAY SAID TO TOBIN Bonner, "There's something I wanted you to hear from me before you hear about it from someone else."

Bonner didn't give the menu at the Short Wolf a glance; he knew it by heart. He'd already told the waitress to bring them a pitcher of iced tea. Brewed fresh. They didn't use the presweetened powder, one of the reasons he liked the Short Wolf. The other being their meat loaf and mashed potatoes—potatoes that hadn't come out of a box. With a place like this, he was thinking, good honest food, reasonable prices, he and Neal could have had a nice steady business and Neal might not be in the trouble he was in today. Or was that just wishful thinking?

Shay realized she didn't have his full attention. She cleared her throat and smiled.

"Sorry," Bonner said.

There was a second mobile TV unit parked on Division Boulevard outside the café, side door open, a cameraman checking his equipment. Another van had followed them the two blocks from his office. They turned on their lights in the parking lot, the video journalist trailing Bonner and Shay to the back door with her microphone. A fast talker. The VJ knew who Shay was, too. So now, Bonner assumed, they were in a relationship worth sixty seconds on *Hard Copy*. Hollywood stunt woman and Utah peace officer. Murder in Canyonland.

"What's on your mind?" he asked Shay.

"Sarah Dubray's at the Med. Concussion, subdural hematoma. She's seeing double. They put her in IC for the night."

"I heard something about a motorcycle accident."

Shay explained, working her way up to her first entry at the Gehrins', the overheard conversation, Frenchie on his cell phone.

Bonner had her go over the conversation a second time.

"You're certain he said " 'Dove.' ""

"Yes. What about it?"

Bonner didn't answer. He closed his eyes briefly, mulling something.

"So Sarah was at the Gehrins with Frenchie, and now she's in the Med. Did we come to the part that's giving you a bad conscience?"

Shay smiled slightly. "How's the chicken fricassee here?"

"You can't go wrong. Biscuits, corn on the cob."

"Great." She folded her hands. "My conscience is clear, but . . . Rosalind Dubray showed up when I was leaving the Gehrins and—"

"*What?*"

Shay looked startled. Bonner reached for his cell phone, scrolled a number, dialed it.

"What was she driving?" he asked Shay.

"I don't know. She popped up in the backseat of my van."

"Charlie Lee?" Bonner said, making a connection. "Where are you? Uh-huh. Well, you can break it off. Rosalind burned us. I think she left Tom Leucadio's place in his Dodge Ram after he drove her pickup to the Crystal Chandelier. Yeah, I know. In the rain you wouldn't have been able to tell who was driving. Don't worry about it. Get yourself some dinner."

Bonner folded his cell phone and looked at Shay. "I don't know how she found out Sarah was there."

"Leucadio told her," Bonner said.

"Anyway, Ros asked for my help. So I went back inside with her."

"I hope you're going to tell me T. Frenchman Dobie is still alive."

A middle-aged waitress took their orders.

"Those TV people out there waitin' on you, Sheriff?"

"I'm becoming famous far and wide, Mattie."

"I sure hope you can solve those murders so we can get back to normal round here."

Bonner smiled confidently, then winced when she left the table. He poured iced tea for Shay and himself.

"Frenchie was carrying a gun," Shay said. "I had to pop him."

"Where?"

"In the nuts."

"Oww."

"Heel kick. It doesn't do a lot of damage, just causes swelling, and sometimes one of the testicles gets lodged in the—"

"That was the extent of the rough stuff?"

"Well, there was a houseman with a shotgun."

Bonner whistled dismally.

"He's okay, though. His nose might be broken."

Bonner's pager vibrated. He glanced at it, took out his cell phone again, dialed.

"Del? I'm having dinner at the Short Wolf, so keep it simple."

"Thought you might want to know. The feds have taken over the entire third floor at the Ramada. That's twenty-two rooms. Real short notice. Ramada had to scramble to find other accommodations for the guests that got evicted. What do you think?"

"Up to our asses in feds is what I think."

"I mean—"

"They're missing one of their own, Del. And Stearman's hot about it. All I had to offer them was Boy Scouts. Let's keep an eye on the airport, see who we have coming in tonight, and from where."

Shay had taken a pair of nail scissors from her purse and was trimming a ragged edge of tape that bound the splinted little finger on her right hand. She looked at Bonner and looked away. The phone call had made him angry.

Bonner said, "What is it with you and Rosalind Dubray?"

"I'm not sure what you mean. We're barely acquainted. I don't get that she's such a horrible person. Ros was very concerned about her sister. So was I. We did it the best way we could. The doctors think Sarah will be okay, but it's too soon to tell. They'll do an MRI in the morning."

"I need to talk to Sarah myself."

"About the Dove? What is that, some kind of code word?"

"Yes. The rest you don't need to hear."

"Does it have anything to do with—"

"The killings? I don't know yet. There's so much going on I don't know which way to look. But I doubt that you have to worry about criminal trespass or assault charges. Frenchie Dobie or Wolfgang Gehrin won't be calling me to demand satisfaction. If there's potential criminal activity on their part, then you might have something to worry about." He thought about this, then said, "Maybe I'll stop by the Gehrins tonight. By the way, thanks for coming to me."

"I might be getting some work on a movie up in Bryce Canyon."

"The Brutal Edge?"

"Is that what they're calling it? How did you know?"

"We process all the permits. That one just happened to cross my desk today. So you'll be staying around for a while."

"It would mean a couple of weeks, at least. I'm still angling for the job. But I like my chances."

"I hope you get it."

Bonner didn't say anything else for a while; he was watching the journalists who had flocked around his waterhole. The last thing he wanted was to hassle with newspeople, but they never knew when to back off. And his silence probably seemed surly on camera. Meanwhile his unworthy opponent for the office, Archer Patterson, was giving interviews as if he knew what he was talking about. TV lighting somehow flattered Arch. He was adept at selling himself, but that was a big part of his business. People didn't just buy cars, they bought the salesman first.

"Want to know how to deal with them?" Shay asked.

"I could use a few hints."

"You treat each of them like a long-lost best friend. Learn their names. Look them straight in the eyes while they're asking questions. Don't slump. Smile sincerely. You have a very nice smile, Tobin. It inspires confidence."

"Sell myself."

"We're all compulsive buyers," Shay said. "We just need a little nudge sometimes."

"I wonder what we're talking about now," he said.

"I'd be amazed if you didn't know."

⬤

A little after 8:00 P.M. Rosalind drives Tom Leucadio's Dodge Ram truck, which she had borrowed along with the keys to his house, through the back gate of the paint-and-body shop owned by the Brightly Shining. Two of the ironheads, Leonardo and his second cousin, whose street name is "the Yuma Kid," ride with her in the truck. The gate rolls shut behind them. She parks alongside the main shop and they go in through a side door. Her brother David is waiting for her in the cluttered office, eating take-out Japanese. The ironheads stay outside on the shop floor, making critical comments on the repair jobs in progress.

"Want some, Ros?"

"Jap food gives me the galloping shits."

Ros sits down and parks her booted feet on the edge of David's desk. He continues to eat.

"How did it turn out?" Ros asks.

"Real nice for a rush job."

"I don't want you to get indigestion, but I've got travel plans."

David reaches across the desk for a key ring hanging on the wall and pitches the ring to Ros.

"The second brass key. Straight on back through the shop."

"How's Marco Polo?"

"Don't ask me. Man, I stay far away. We followed your instructions. He hasn't been fed today. What've you got in mind, Ros?"

"Marco Polo's in show biz. He's what you call a 'leaper.' I'm going to give him a chance to perform at a private party."

David shrugs. "Can't get that animal out of here soon enough to suit me."

"You've been just darling about it. I owe you one, Davey."

Leonardo and the Yuma Kid follow her to the paint shop. Ros turns on the overhead lights. The five-ton truck that had been hijacked from Guy Baker is in the first bay. It has been repainted in the colors of a well-known rental company. All that is missing are the license plates, which Leonardo has with him.

The truck is empty. The Yuma Kid looks around and then at Rosalind.

"Storeroom," she says. "Come on."

Leonardo stays behind to put the stolen license plates on the truck.

Marco Polo, lying in his cage like an ebony sphinx, eyes slitting to the overhead flash of light, recognized Rosalind before the storeroom door opened. His ears are in neutral, a good sign. The rough wind in his throat idles to a warm rasp.

Ros approaches the cage, looking into the molten core of his half-open eyes, lost in rapture.

"Hello, big guy. Miss me?"

Marco Polo yawns, showing off saber canines, and resumes his gruff music.

"Oh, shit," the Yuma Kid murmurs.

"Hear him? That's his hunger drive getting up to speed."

"He's *hungry?*"

"He was meat-trained. Movie cats work for food. When he hasn't eaten, he's eager to please. But with a full belly a big cat can be dangerous, even to his trainer."

"How do we do this?"

"Forklift. Cage slides right in to the back of the truck."

"That part's okay. But when we get to—"

"Nobody's home. Drive the truck around to the back of the house and onto the patio. You toss the little sack with the chicken necks on the floor inside, then back the truck up to the patio doors. The cage door operates by remote; controls are on the dash. Marco Polo will go for the chicken. Then you close the patio doors and leave him in the house. Maybe he'll think it's a movie set. Without a trainer, he'll be uneasy, but still hungry. He'll prowl around looking for somebody familiar. Strangers will make him nervous. Very nervous. When Marco Polo does find some folks, they'd better have a pocketful of raw chicken necks to reward him."

"You ain't coming along?"

"Wish with all my heart I could be there, but I have a prior obligation."

Shay came from the bath of the room they had rented at the Comfort Inn, limping a little, and stretched out on her side beside Bonner again, putting an arm around him, two fingers on the dimpled seam of a healed wound on his broad back. She pressed lightly, as if leaving her fingerprints at the scene of an old crime. The things you think about: Shay thought of the last woman he might have been with, and the death of Luz, which might be the only reason Shay was with him now. Sex as his outlet for grieving. Still, happy to be there, she had her own needs. Their faces were inches apart, rewarming intimacy.

"What's wrong with your leg?" he asked, stroking it, her body still not all that familiar to him. He thought how pretty it was, the inside of a woman's thigh by lamplight.

"It's my knee. Aggravated it in Vegas, and again the other night."

"How long can you keep jumping out of helicopters for a living?"

"Probably not much longer, without permanently crippling myself. Time to grow up, I guess."

She moved the hand on his back. Another scar. The woman he had loved, and couldn't save. But she wasn't superstitious.

"Vegas," he said. "I went up to my room, and I was thinking, Lord, I wish I was going to *her* room. I didn't even know your name."

"Lightning bolt?"

"No. Nothing like that. I just wanted to be near you for a little while."

"Yes, I know. I could tell."

"Kidding me."

"No."

"Well—"

"Listen, I was dead tired and hurt like hell. But—"

"First impression?"

"Strength. Character. Dependability. Not bad-looking. No lightning bolt. But I knew you'd be a good lover."

"I don't know that I was. I mean, I can be better."

"So can I. But it was a better-than-average beginning, Tobin."

He considered that, watching her, and understood she had chosen the word carefully. *Beginning.* There was still tension in his body, but his face had relaxed; it seemed almost youthful to her. The heart, approachable. She put her face in the hollow between his neck and shoulder.

●

When the phone rang, Pepper said, with a hint of fury in her face, "That'd better be Mom."

Silverwhip Jack answered.

"Hey, there, Jack," Rosalind said, "I'm in the mood for a flying lesson."

Jack didn't say anything, but shook his head slightly at Pepper, who turned away in disgust and went off on her crutches to the kitchen for a glass of milk.

Jack said, keeping his voice low, "Tonight? Ros, I—"

"Has to be tonight, Jack. Right away, in fact."

"Where're we going?"

"Tell you when you get here."

"You're at the airport?"

"Just get over here, Jack."

"My li'l gradndaughter's with me. Just can't go off and leave—"

"Thirty minutes. I don't keep my friends waiting, Jack. Don't you keep me waiting."

Shay came out of the Intensive Care room in which she had spent a few minutes with Sarah Dubray. Bonner was waiting for her outside the double glass doors.

"She was happy to see me, but barely able to talk. She doesn't remember the accident."

"Say where she was before it happened?"

"Yes. She was working at the amphitheater, whatever that is."

"Outdoor pageant, the settling of southwest Utah. Big with the tourists."

"Sheriff! I want that woman arrested! She assaulted me twice, without provocation! I'm preferring charges!"

"Uh-oh," Shay said in a subdued voice, as they turned to see T. Frenchman Dobie coming down the hall with a couple of kinfolk bodyguards from the Brightly Shining. Frenchie was walking as if he had barbed wire in his shorts.

Bonner said, "What are you doing here, Frenchie?"

"What am *I* doing here? I've come to take Sarah home where she belongs! She was kidnapped right out from under my nose not more'n six hours ago by this—"

"Hold it, Frenchie. Sarah's in Intensive Care and can't be moved. Now what's this about Ms. Waco assaulting you?"

"Came storming into the room where I was tending to Sarah myself, and the next thing I know—I've got a splittin' headache but my head's not what hurts the worst—she hauled off and kicked me right in the—and *look,* look at this!" Frenchie tilted his head and pulled down his lower lip with a forefinger. "That's a temporary? From when she kicked me in the jaw at the Captain's Table while I was trying to have a private conversation with my little Sarah!" He unhooked his lip and glared at Shay. "I mean, she's some kind of martial arts expert. Don't that make her a lethal weapon? So it's attempted murder, not just assault."

"Hey, hold on now; let's sort this out."

"I want her to stay away from Sarah, even if I need to get a court order! She's a bad influence on my intended. Now I'm telling you, I'm registering a complaint for aggravated assault or whatever you want to call it, and I want her handcuffed here and now!"

Bonner shook his head at Shay and said, "Ms. Waco, these are serious charges."

Shay said, "Well, I think he fell over in his chair when he saw Rosalind with me, then I accidentally stepped on him. Yes, that's what happened."

Bonner looked at Dobie.

"To the best of Ms. Waco's recollection, the alleged assault was purely accidental. I'm sure she's willing to apologize. Eventually. So we'll let it go at that."

"*Wait* a damn minute, Sheriff!"

"You wait. I have some business with you."

Bonner took out his PalmPilot notebook and punched up a file.

"Mr. Dobie, do you own a white 1997 Cadillac Seville, Utah license number—"

"Yeah, I drive a Seville. What—"

"Where is your vehicle now, Mr. Dobie?"

"Now? Well, it's—" Frenchie's outrage was suddenly snuffed by a gust of cold reality. He looked uncertain. "It's at my home in New Hebron. What about it?"

Bonner looked at Shay, who said, "Early this morning I picked up a boy named Cooger on the bridge across the Aquiles River. He said he'd been in a motorcycle accident. Sarah was riding on the back of his bike. Cooger was bleeding from the mouth and had internal injuries. He told me a big car had pulled out in front of him on the road to my father's place. He thought the car might have been a Cadillac. There were two men in the car. Cooger described one of the men as possibly a Mexican. The other, he said, was a 'little dude' who wore a white cowboy hat."

"Mr. Dobie, were you involved in a collision with a motorcycle last night that you failed to report?"

"Bullshit! I don't know what she's talking about!"

Bonner looked at Shay again.

"When I got to my father's ranch after bringing Cooger to the Med—his injuries were very serious—Jack told me he'd heard the accident but hadn't seen it. When I asked him if he'd seen Sarah, he said, and this is a direct quote, 'They put her in Frenchie's car. Frenchie took her.' "

Frenchie's mouth opened and closed, wrathfully.

Shay, staring at him, said, "I think I know where his car is."

"Let's hear it," Bonner said.

"Early this afternoon I was on my way to have lunch with—a friend, when I saw a flatbed truck at the bridge. The truck belonged to Sundance Towing and Repairs. It was carrying a white Cadillac that had been damaged: the truck was crumpled and the rear window partly broken out. I asked the driver if he knew whose car it was. He looked at his manifest and said it belonged to Mr. Dobie."

Bonner said to the men with Frenchie, "You two stand aside. Mr. Dobie, turn around, please, and put your hands behind your back. I'm placing you under arrest."

"You're arresting me?"

"Charges of reckless endangerment and leaving the scene of a vehicular accident resulting in multiple injuries. Those will do for now."

Bonner took his handcuffs from the holder on his belt and put a hand on Frenchie's shoulder. Frenchie was breathing hard. He stiffened as if to resist, then looked at one of the bodyguards and panted, "Get McGill or Hocker on the phone *right now;* I ain't spending a night in jail!"

"You'll be allowed to post bond after you're booked. These are your rights. You have the right to remain silent. If you choose not to remain silent, anything you say can and will be used against you in a court of law. You have the right to be represented by an attorney. If you can't afford an attorney, the court will appoint one to represent you. Do you understand what I have just said to you?"

"Yeah, yeah. Bonner, you're making the worst mistake of your life and that's no lie."

"Are you threatening me, Mr. Dobie?"

"I'm just saying it's a wonder you're still around. You figure it out."

Bonner put the cuffs on Frenchie. The bodyguards took off, looking for a phone. Frenchie called after them, "And get Rhondo over here to take his daughter home! I'm sick of all the trouble she's been to me!"

"That's not gonna happen, Frenchie," Bonner said. "Moving Sarah from IC could endanger her life. I'll have guards standing right here to make sure it doesn't happen. And you ought to reconsider that night in jail. It might be the safest place for you."

"What the hell you talking about?"

"I understand Rosalind's not very happy with you."

●

"Have to admit I enjoyed that," Shay said, when Bonner dropped her at her van.

"There are some compensations for the boring hours and short pay. If you get tired of the movie glitz and your knee goes, you might enjoy the eleven-week course at the Utah Police Academy."

Shay smiled, doubtfully.

"Anyway, thanks for seeing Sarah for me. It was a long shot that she'd be able to say much."

"I'll visit her again tomorrow, if that's okay. Stay close and friendly. I'm really sorry for her. Maybe she'll open up to me. It would help if I knew more about what you want to know."

"I'm not sure yet. But it's obvious Frenchie is anxious to isolate her."

"Does it have anything to do with the mysterious Dove?"

"I don't know. It might be better if you don't mention that to Sarah. Or anybody else."

Shay leaned in to kiss him goodnight.

"Sorry the evening's over so soon. But I have a daughter who's going to be mad at me."

"And I have people to see. One more?"

She kissed him again.

"Tell me the truth now. I'm feeling a little insecure. Do I suck in bed?"

"Yes, you do," Shay said solemnly. "Fortunately that's the part I like the most. See ya."

The chartered Lear jet arrived in Spanish Wells from Las Vegas at 1:25 in the morning. Signe had been drinking while she entertained herself at bacarat, so Wolfgang drove them home, Signe snoozing beside him.

He parked the Jag in the carport and woke Signe up. They crossed the drive and the patio. The motion-detector lights came on. But there were no lights on in the house. The Volvo wagon Conchita drove was missing. Signe wondered about that.

"Did we give Conchita the night off?"

"I don't think so."

The morning room was illuminated by the moon above the Aquiles River as they went in. Signe turned right toward the kitchen, clapping her hands to light up the short hallway.

"I feel like a snack. Want anything?"

"No. I'm going to take a shower. Everyone was smoking at the conference. It gets in my hair, and I wake up with a raw throat."

"See if Conchita is with Sarah. See if there's been any change. I still don't like it that she's here."

"She stays."

"It's a mistake. This thing with the Japanese has seriously dulled your judgment."

They squared off momentarily. Signe said, softly, "You know my hunches are usually right. There will be consequences."

"If the girl dies, it's Frenchie's problem."

Signe raised her eyes. "Trusting him is not the least of *your* problems."

Wolfgang laughed. "The only thing I trust in men is their greed."

"Don't be so sure he hasn't found another trough to wallow in."

"He doesn't have the nerve to cross me."

"But the girl is an unnecessary complication. His '*intended*,' is that what Frenchie calls her? An emotional attachment that may unbalance him if the worst happens. I hope she's not dead already." Her shoulders drew together; her full mouth folded inward in a rictus of distaste. She glanced at something on the tiled floor. "What's that?"

Wolfgang looked too, took a couple of steps and picked up a torn take-out sack from Wendy's.

"It looks like *blood* on that tile. Is that blood?"

"I can't tell. I don't smell anything; my sinuses are clogged."

Signe shuddered. "Well, wake up Jorge and have him clean it. I can't believe this. A mess like that on the floor; he's been so slipshod recently. And Conchita: well, don't get me started, she's entirely *your* fault. I've told you, once you start banging them, they're no good for anything else anymore. They've joined the family. I expect the lights to be *on* when we come in late. And it's too quiet. God! Something *has* happened to that Dubray girl, I feel it in my bones. Wolfie! Are you paying attention to me?"

"I miss Tito. We should get another dog."

Signe shook her head, exasperated.

"A shepherd next time. A *trained* shepherd. Now go find out what's been going on. I'll get Jorge myself."

But Jorge's room off the kitchen was empty—emptied out, it seemed to Signe on closer inspection. His religious relics missing from the top of the dresser, clothes from the wardrobe. All of his shoes and highly polished boots he was so proud of. The TV, for the use of which she had deducted five dollars a week from his pay, also was missing. Signe forgot that she had been hungry.

"Wolfie!"

She found him standing in the doorway of the room Sarah Dubray had occupied.

"Oh, no!"

He shrugged. "Well, they're gone."

"Jorge's gone too; he's left us! What's that smell?"

"I told you, I can't smell a thing."

"Gunpowder. What is it called, cordite?" Signe cast around, saw the white plaster dust on the tiles, a couple of partial footprints, a big paw print. She dragged at Wolfgang's sleeve, suddenly speechless, until he looked too, then raised his eyes to the ceiling, which had been riddled by the blast from Jorge's shotgun.

"Get—" Signe swallowed, choked up again.

"What?"

"A gun, Wolfie. Get—a gun, a big one."

Instead he kneeled to study more closely the paw print in the plaster dust. Signe began backing away toward the stairs.

"No. Wait. Don't go in our bedroom. See? The door's open. It's in there. *It's in there.*"

"What?"

"The thing that made that print. In *there*. Watching us. Run, Wolfie!"

He stood slowly, staring at the lightless bedroom twenty feet away. Signe had retreated to the top of the stairs. Wolfgang looked around at her, then glanced at the print again, bewildered.

Signe turned with a hand on the stair rail, one foot going down.

Out of the corner of his eye Wolfgang saw something large and black spring almost vertically into Signe's face, and she was bowled over backwards with a shriek. His head snapped around and he looked in utter disbelief at jungle-cat eyes and peeled-back ears, a long scythe of jet tail, and the burgeoning blood of Signe's opened throat when her head flopped toward him.

The jaguar's front paws pinned her shoulders as he crouched over Signe. Her hands beat at the thick coal body until his jaws fastened on her head at the temples and his teeth crunched deep. The jaguar gave her head a shake, and blood flew from the rent in her throat. Her eyes never closed. That may have been the most terrible part for Wolfgang, the rest of it beyond immediate assimilation: her eyes stayed wide open while she died.

Wolfgang turned the other way and sprinted toward their bedroom, his mind on his gun cabinet and the cherished firearms he had carried across savannas on three continents in search of elusive big cats like the one that the hand of a malign god seemingly had dropped into his house.

The jaguar pulled him down before he had gone ten feet and broke his neck with a single bite.

This morning, she is not there.

In their usual place, at the tree that curves, bone white in the beginning of dawn, from its exposed lifeless roots across the path by the river.

Vida looks around, not knowing what to think now.

Because she is all he has been thinking about since he left the house.

Not there.

In a fit of gloom he goes down to the river's edge. The water flows clear and cold over stones and a sand bed. On all fours he drinks. His face half-immersed, cooling off. Then he sits back on the bank with his hands on his knees, water dripping from his bearded chin. Listening. Bird calls, and the lulling rush of the river. There is a heaviness in his breast. Disappointment. She may yet come. But he knows he can't wait long—the sun will rise and catch him only part of the way home.

He has her scent before he hears her. She touches his shoulder in passing, which stills the thump of alarm in his breast. Ros goes on down to the river and stretches out full-length to splash cold water in her face. She is wearing Spandex the color of aluminum. After a few moments she rolls over on her back, lies looking up at the sky, and motions listlessly for Vida to come to her.

He kneels beside Rosalind. She raises a hand to cup his face.

"I'm beat. Up all night. But I wanted to see you."

Vida nods.

Ros presses the tips of her fingers against her lips, touches them to his cheek, then draws his face down to hers. Eye to eye. Magpies are waking up in the boughs of a cottonwood nearby.

"I had to give him up. Marco Polo, I mean. It was getting too hot for me. He's probably been shot by now. I'll miss him. But I still have you."

Tobin Bonner got out of his car behind the Gehrin house. Five thirty-six A.M. The sky without a tint of morning yet. He paused to take a long look at the black jaguar lying in a cage on a flatbed truck. Tranquilized, front legs bound, looking totally helpless and not at all lethal. He went on into the house.

Guy and Pam Baker were in the living room, sitting side by side on a sofa with a floral print, huge yellow flowers. Pammy had a wadded handkerchief in one hand. Her eyes were red from crying.

"What time did you get the call?" Bonner asked Guy.

"He woke us up shortly past four."

"Do you know who it was?"

"No. I didn't recognize his voice."

"What did he say?"

"He said if we wanted our jaguar back, we would find him here."

"In the house?"

"Yes. In the house."

"That was it?"

"I didn't have a chance to say anything. The bloke hung up."

"Where are they?"

Pam shuddered. "Upstairs, in the hall."

"I'll be back in a minute," Bonner said.

There was a congealed waterfall of blood on the tiled stairway all the way down to the foyer. Bonner avoided it. Del Cothern and Caswell, the coroner with the tiny head, were waiting for him. Bonner looked over the scene and then looked at each of the bodies. He'd been expecting real carnage, unidentifiable faces, a strew of limbs, but the worst damage had been to Signe Gehrin's throat, accounting for the mess on the tiles.

"Any others?" Bonner asked Del.

"No, sir, that we could find."

Bonner wondered if T. Frenchman Dobie might have been one of the victims, if Bonner hadn't fortuitously locked him up for a few hours earlier. Then he wondered if it was Frenchie who had been Rosalind's principal target.

Which was merely conjecture; he felt right about his conclusion, but he didn't have a thing on her.

"Move 'em?" Caswell asked.

"Do we need any more photos?" Bonner asked, looking up at Del. He was crouched over Wolfgang Gehrin. Neck broken, but scarcely a hair out of place. Bonner admired Gehrin's gold chronometer, enough diamonds to make it worth six figures.

"We're covered."

"Find out who was working for them: the household help, gardeners, I'll want to talk to them."

"Yes, sir," Del said.

Bonner went back downstairs and sat opposite the Bakers.

"How do you see it?" he asked them.

They exchanged looks. Pam did the talking.

"When we got here, no one answered the bell. We went around to the patio. The doors there were closed but not locked. Lights were on in the house. We came in. No one answered us when we called. We wondered if it was some sort of obnoxious telephone prank. We walked through the house anyway, and when we got to the stairs—"

"Where was the jaguar?"

"Marky was lying down in the hall. When he saw us he rolled over on his back to have his belly rubbed. There was some blood on his fur as well as on the steps. Guy went out to the lorry to fetch the CO_2 gun while I—talked to Marky, keeping him calm. I could see—someone lying there, at the top of the stairs. Lying there."

Pam took a deep breath and put her hands over her face.

Guy said, "After we put him in the cage, we called you, then had a look around. There wasn't any scat. So he hadn't been in the house for long. Obviously the Gehrins hadn't been keeping Marky since he was stolen."

"What sort of condition was Marco Polo in before you tranquilized him?"

"No sign of physical abuse, if that's what you mean."

"Does it follow that he would automatically attack anyone he found in the house?"

"I don't think he *did* attack them. Not in the sense of a wild beast stalking prey."

"What do you mean?"

"Whoever took Marco Polo in the first place must have had some knowledge of what he was trained to do. We raise animals to act in films. Marky's forte is pursuit and capture. Either Kit or myself plays the victim. We always wear protective padding. Once the cameras roll, Marky is let off his training leash. His job is to leap and knock me over. Then we do some pretend wrestling, which to the camera appears to be a death struggle. As soon as the director cuts the action, I slip Marky a treat and he's immediately leashed again. We've never had accidents or incidents of any sort on location."

"You give him something to eat."

"A little something. Not enough to satisfy his appetite, of course, because there are always retakes. A hungry cat that is meat-trained continues to perform. A cat with a full belly won't be bothered. He may in fact be dangerous if you bother him."

Bonner looked around. "So Marco Polo is used to bright lights and strange surroundings."

"A movie set? Yes, he might well have thought that's where he was and went prowling around looking for one of us."

"He may have been in the house for a while when the Gehrins

arrived. If he was hungry enough, would he do his act with someone he didn't know?"

Guy thought about it. "I don't know. It's conceivable he was only interested in his treat when he came upon the Gehrins. But once he smelled fear—"

"He would revert to the jungle."

"Very likely that is what happened."

"You can keep Marco Polo for now, because the county doesn't have the facilities. Eventually, after the grand jury meets, he'll have to be destroyed."

"Yes, I know. What a wretched shame. I can't bring myself to hold Marco Polo solely responsible. The true blame lies with whoever was so stupid or callous as to bring Marky here in the first place. What could they have been thinking?"

"Not stupid. It was someone who knew enough about big cats to know what was likely to happen."

"Premeditated murder?" Pam said incredulously.

"Yeah."

"Do you have any idea—"

"I have ideas. But no proof. Because Marco Polo was stolen and you filed a report, you have no liability in this matter. But you found the bodies, so I will need a statement later this morning. You're also going to have problems with the county commission. They'll try to shut down your operation when the hysteria hits the media."

"It won't be the first time," Guy said. "Noise, fecal contamination of ground water, we've heard it all. The facts are we've always exceeded the standards for holding class one wildlife. Of course we make our living raising animals, but we have also taken in many seriously abused big cats from private zoos with appalling facilities. We've always considered it to be a moral obligation."

●

The sun wasn't up when Bonner made it home, but he could feel its presence on the horizon like a rising boil on his neck. He poured a cup of coffee in the kitchen before going to see his son. Mrs. Darke was singing in the shower of her bathroom, as she did most mornings. He leaned against a counter staring out at the river below his property, thinking wistfully about fishing and nodding off until the caffeine took hold.

Vida was sound asleep on his stomach in the charged tropic air of his bedroom. Bonner could have entered with a brass band, and Vida wouldn't have heard. He kissed the back of Vida's neck, wondering if he could grab a couple of hours himself, but he knew he wouldn't be able to fall asleep without medication. Then he'd be walking dead for the rest of what was going to be another brutal day. So shower and get on with it. Fatigue had become a constant presence, which he wore like a hair shirt.

Vida had been sketching when he fell asleep; his box of colored pencils and pad of newsprint lay beneath his dangling fingers. Bonner picked up the pad to see what he'd been drawing.

Unfinished, but there was enough of it for Bonner to recognize the subject. He felt a spasm in his gut, bitterness spurting into his throat.

Vida was working on a portrait of Rosalind Dubray.

28 AT TWENTY MINUTES TO eight Bonner was having a third cup of coffee on his terrace when Shay called.

"I was thinking of taking you fishing," Bonner said. "Sunday's my day off. There's a great little isolated spot on my father's place. Do you like to fish?"

"For marlin."

"Oh, one of those. Let me put it this way. Do you like isolated spots in subalpine meadows with a clear, cold lake, room to park a pickup RV just big enough for two people, and not another living soul within miles?"

"I'd love it. I didn't have a particularly restful night."

"I didn't sleep either. I was in the office until four, catching up on some paperwork. How's Pepper?"

"Cranky. Jack was planning to show her some horses today, but he's totally out of it. Another one who didn't get to bed last night. That's part of the reason why I called, other than just to hear your voice."

"Carousing?"

"No. He was sober. He didn't want to tell me what he was up to, but I was spitting mad because he left Pepper in the care of a teenage Hispanic girl who doesn't speak much English and just took off. Acting out my own guilts, I guess. Eventually I got him to say he was doing a friend a favor, flying said friend down to Arizona and back. Don't know if I should believe him or not."

"Say who he was with?"

"Very evasive." Shay paused, with a slight sigh. "And worried about something. That's when I began thinking about the conversation we had at the hospital a few days ago? You know, about some people he was associated with once upon a time, and *I'm* a little worried."

"I see what you mean."

"He wouldn't still be—in that business, do you think?"

"Not unless he's completely lost his mind. But he might be vulnerable to having his arm twisted. By someone we both know. I'm not on a secure line here, so we won't mention names. I'll check to see if Jack filed a flight plan. I doubt if he did. But it might tell me something to know how much fuel he loaded before taking off and what plane he used. He has two or three, I think."

"You've got so much else to do. The news this morning, my God—"

"Yeah. Shay, I need to cut this short." He was looking past the corner of his house at the driveway. Three cars had pulled in off the road, a government convoy. "Company's coming. I think I'm about to be abducted by the feds."

"*What?* Are you joking?"

"Not hardly. Don't worry about me, Shay. I'm just a county sheriff, but like I keep telling them, it's still *my* county."

Bonner folded his cell phone and put it into the pocket of his suit coat, activated the tape recorder in another coat pocket, put his game face on, and strolled down the driveway to meet the new arrivals.

One of them was Dale Stearman, another citizen who seemed to have been awake all night. He had half a dozen FIAT agents with him, more like legal types than hired guns in their dark suits. Dale wore a sports jacket with a tie that fluttered in the breeze.

"Morning, Dale."

"Morning, Sheriff."

"I heard you ordered up some reinforcements. Sorry to say I haven't had any word about your missing covert."

"We'll find her."

"Coffee? We may have enough left to go around."

"No, thanks. Sheriff Bonner, we're here to take you into custody. Milner?"

One of the dark suits stepped forward with document in hand.

Bonner took the federal warrant but didn't open it. He looked at Stearman and yawned.

"Eyes are a little weak from reading and writing half the night. Why don't you just sum it up for me?"

"The charge is impeding a federal investigation by attempting to conceal facts and suborn witnesses vital to that investigation."

"That's an interesting mix of wholesale bullshit and conjecture. You really give me too much credit, Dale. Suppose I decide to cooperate on the level we've established, that is, B and C; would that make a difference as to the implementation of this warrant?"

"We'll be interested in whatever you have to tell us during formal interrogation, but you will be required to go with us."

"How far?" Bonner said, with a slight smile.

Stearman didn't smile. He looked at another of the suits, who was ready to step forward with handcuffs.

"Hold on, Dale," Bonner said. "Spare me five minutes for a private conversation? Let's you and me walk down toward the river. I promise I won't make a break for it. Your Capitol Hill Irregulars can tag along, out of earshot, if that'll give you a little more confidence."

Stearman smiled then and shook his head.

"Okay, we'll do it here. I assume one of the witnesses you're talking about is Sarah Dubray, whom I've posted off-limits to her family in order to protect her life. So it must have been Frenchie Dobie who came whining to you. Your principal contact inside the Brightly Shining. Apparently Frenchie was willing to double-cross not only Rhondo Dubray but Wolfgang Gehrin—who, as you may already know, met a tragic end last night—and sell you the Dove. If and when the Dove, or the specs, turned up. None of this, I assure you, is wholesale bullshit and conjecture.

"The other witness, if we want to call her that, is Rosalind Dubray. You have personal reasons for wanting to get your hands on her. I'm not hiding Ros. I have no idea of her present whereabouts. I want her as badly as you do." He paused, watching Stearman's face closely, decided he'd made an impression, and concluded, "Private talk now?"

Stearman nodded. They walked down to the river together, two FIAT agents behind them, but not too close.

"That black leopard—"

"Jaguar."

"That was Rosalind's deal, wasn't it?"

"We both know she had the animal," Bonner said.

"Why did she do it?"

"There's no way to figure Rosalind out. She has her own code of honor, and blood atonements are a ruling passion in that family."

Bonner explained about the motorcycle accident, watching Stearman for some indication of how much he already knew; but Stearman's face was impassive. The river glittered as the sun rose. He put on shades and listened with folded arms.

"Do you think the girl knows something about the Dove?"

"I don't know. Sarah is in no condition to talk right now."

"I'm putting her under our protection until she is."

"I can't give you an argument on that. She's probably better off with you than she is with T. Frenchman Dobie."

"Katharine is also Rosalind's doing. I want her, Tobe. You don't have first claim."

Bonner thought it over. "Am I free to go about my business?"

Stearman nodded, reluctantly.

"All right. I'll make Rosalind a priority for both of us. Fair enough?"

He handed the warrant to Stearman, who held it for a few moments, then put it into a memo book.

"You weren't going to let me take you anyway, were you?"

"I had some backup. Might say I was a little concerned that you might have another marksman on call. Or are there limits as to how far you'll go?"

"What do you mean, backup?"

"Cover for my tired old ass. Late last night I wrote out everything I know or can guess about the Santero murders, Suchary Siamashvili's involvement with the Brightly Shining, and the Dove. Headline stuff, when you step back for a look at the big picture."

"Chrissake, Tobin!"

"No, I don't trust journalists. But an hour ago I sent sealed copies by courier to a couple of legal bloodhounds I know. Old hunting buddies. They like action, the high-profile civil liberties cases, and they love being on the tube busting bureaucratic butt. You'd know their names. Another copy went to someone I can trust to post it on the county's Web site, which of course is monitored by the local media people. As long as my friends hear from me once a day, all is secure. If they don't hear from me after twenty-four hours, you will find yourself naked to your armpits in a Vesuvius of shit. So take good care of me. By the way, pal, is my office bugged?"

Stearman's head was tilted back, he was looking at the sky.

"Bugging is old-fashioned. So are wiretaps. We hear what we need to hear. We see through walls."

"I'll do a sweep anyway. We don't have any secrets between us any more, right, Dale?"

The funeral for Lucy Ruiz was on Saturday. It took two and a half hours, including the official procession west on Division Boulevard and north to the cemetery, which was in a pretty green vale between sentinel monoliths of red sandstone. A wind came up, and the burial was completed in a storm of dust.

Bonner went home with a raging headache and drank himself to sleep.

His sister-in-law woke him at eleven o'clock. Poppy was in tears.

"I'm sorry. I'm sorry. Of all nights to bother you like this."

"It's okay, Poppy," Bonner said groggily. He had fallen asleep on a couch in the sunroom. Vida was in the kitchen baking something. The TV was on, sound low. *Saturday Night Live.* "What's up, sweetheart?"

"We haven't heard from Neal. No one's heard from him. Willa said he was supposed to be in Los Angeles. Oh, God! I am totally scared out of my mind. I don't know what to tell the kids."

"He'll turn up. He's scared too, Poppy."

"I want to be with him. I want him to know I still love him. There's a way. There has to be a way. We just have to trust in the Lord and pray real hard."

"I'll come over."

"No, no, don't do that! I know you must be exhausted. It was a beautiful eulogy, Tobin. I could tell your heart was breaking. You rest. It does me good just to hear your voice. There *is* a way, isn't there?"

"Just hold that thought. And don't give up."

"I won't. Tobin—you don't think Neal will do something—no, I don't want to bring this up, don't want to even *think* about it!"

"Have faith, Poppy. He won't hurt himself." Bonner thought, *Because he loves himself too much.*

"That's not what I meant. But he—what if he's—"

"Run away?" Bonner was silent too long, and he heard a sob catch in Poppy's throat.

"Poppy, you keep the household account, don't you?"

"Yes."

"Are there other joint accounts?"

"Y-yes."

"Do you have an account in your name only?"

"No, but my sister and I have a little savings account that we opened years ago; we call it our mad money."

"Get on the computer and transfer everything you and Neal have in the household and money market accounts to that savings account. Do it now; I'll hold on."

"*Why?*"

"I don't know just what state of mind Neal is in right now; it's conceivable he'll decide to—take a little leave of absence to think things through. Transferring the accounts is only a precaution. I'm only thinking of what's in your best interest, you and the kids."

"But I've always trusted Neal!"

"A lot of people have trusted him, and you see the result."

After several seconds Poppy said in a spiritless voice, "I have to put the phone down, I need both hands to do this."

Vida came from the kitchen with a plate of steaming gingerbread, butter melting on the dark brown crust. Bonner helped himself and bolted the gingerbread down. He was ravenous.

He heard Poppy clicking away at the computer keyboard, heard a sharp intake of breath. She came back on the line.

"The money market account is down to twelve hundred dollars! We had nearly ten *thousand* at the beginning of last week—"

"Move that thousand now. How much are you looking at altogether?"

"Well, the mortgage payment was deducted on the twentieth, and the car insurance went through. So all the June bills have been paid, and we still have a balance of $1,576.20 in the household. Look at *this*. Neal must have accessed the account with his debit card. Three hundred dollars today."

"Get the rest of the money out of there."

"But Neal—"

"Look at it this way. The sooner he's broke, the sooner you'll hear from him. Neal's collection of Indian hand gold pieces was still in the safe when I was over there—"

"Yes."

"Sell them, first thing Monday morning." She didn't reply. "Poppy?"

"I'm here. What do you say, after the roof has fallen in? 'Please God, don't let it rain?' "

Bonner rapped softly on Mrs. Darke's door. She appeared, in her bulky corduroy robe and hair curlers. She was holding her Morocco-bound *Book of Mormon*, the leather worn thin and smooth as babyskin from decades of devoted study.

"I have to go to the office for a little while," Bonner said.

"Oh, dear. At this hour of the night?"

"Unfinished business I don't want dragging over into my day off."

"Not to worry. Is that gingerbread I smell?"

"And it's delicious. Alma? In case I'm not back before dawn, I don't want Vida leaving the house."

She looked puzzled by his interference with Vida's routine.

"Have you told him so?"

"I don't have time to argue with him. I'm asking you to hide his running shoes. The back of your closet would be a good place."

"Ohhh. Well, you must have your reasons. It does make me feel rather a sneak."

"What we both care about is Vida's welfare."

"Is there something I should know?"

"I just have a feeling I don't like. Probably nothing to it. Good night, Alma."

The night tour deputy was a rookie named Rowland Tubbs, a former PRCA bronc rider who affected a Wyatt Earp mustache the color of old gold. Not many problems came in the front door on Saturday night; most of the traffic was through the sally port of the jail. Row-land was playing with a Gameboy when Bonner arrived. Rowland covered it with a palm of one huge hand, pushing a pile of mail and folders across the desk. Bonner gathered them up and went into his office.

The FedEx package on top was from the lab in Salt Lake to which Mary Lynn had sent Pam Baker's videotape for enhancement. He tore it open and glanced at the letter from the lab supervisor, then put the cassette into his VCR, shut the office door and settled back in his noisy chair.

Two riders on horseback outside the fence of the Simba Springs compound. The shot was one he'd seen on the Bakers' TV. Guy Baker and Kit Eddington were in the foreground, working with Marco Polo. The man and woman watching from beyond the fence were out of focus.

Then, abruptly, one of them was much closer, and Bonner was jolted by the transition. Still not much in the way of detail. But Bonner easily recognized the young woman he had first seen lying on the dining room floor of her father's house. Prominent cheekbones, deep eye wells, the gravity of her full mouth. She had looked much the same in death, except for the bullet hole like a fungal growth near the center of her forehead.

The man was next, his face large and grainy. But the bone structure was obvious in this enhancement. The definitive shape of brows and nose. The thin mouth that could turn petulant so quickly.

An expression Bonner had often provoked, when his brother Neal was growing up.

●

Bonner went down the hall to the bathroom to splash cold water on his face. He was looking at himself in the mirror when the door opened and Lute Lintree walked in.

"The rook said you wanted to see me, Sheriff."

Lintree was the weekend jailer, ten years past retirement age but still around because Bonner needed him. There were ex-fighters who had cauliflower ears; Lintree had a cauliflower face. He was six-six and weighed 290 pounds. His eyes hated everything they saw. He inspired a lot of terror around the jail, which was what Bonner had in mind.

"Beechman is on his way in to transport a prisoner. Need for you to get him ready."

"This late? Who's the prisoner, Sheriff?"

"I am."

Bonner went out through the sally-port door wearing the jail jumper and shackles. He was doubled over, as if Lute Lintree had given him a farewell fist in the gut. He took only a few shuffling steps to the SUV and climbed into the backseat. Deputy Harry Beechman got in behind the wheel.

"Where we going?" he asked, glancing back through the steel mesh that divided the interior of the vehicle.

"Stop at the Chevron on West Valley for gas," Bonner said, as he was unlocking the shackles.

"Yes, sir." Beechman pulled out of the parking lot behind the jail and made a right. "Sheriff?"

Bonner undid the snaps on the jail jumper and began pulling it off.

"What?"

"Could you let me in on what this is about?"

"No."

"Yes, sir."

By the time they reached the Chevron Mart, Bonner had changed into the dark blue trousers and shirt he had borrowed from one of the officers at Spanish Wells PD, a man nearly his size. With it he wore an in-the-pants holster containing his baby Browning automatic, a Tac Lite, and a steel expandable baton in a sidebreak scabbard. He topped off the outfit with a snag-proof lightweight jacket and a navy baseball cap that had no insignia.

Beechman got out and pumped some gas.

Bonner looked at his watch. Twenty-two minutes after twelve.

A white Windstar minivan pulled into the Chevron and stopped on the other side of the pumps. Bonner watched it. The deputy looked the van over, then looked up and down the intersecting streets.

"Clear," he said.

Bonner got out of the car, crossed between the pumps, and opened the front door of the Windstar, which had tinted windows. He got in.

"Go ahead," he said.

"Where to?" Shay asked him, giving him a look, interested and amused.

"South about half a mile on the interstate to Fir Creek Canyon Road. I'll tell you where to drop me. By the way, thanks for coming."

"Why are you dressed like that?"

"I'm bringing Rosalind in. Somehow I don't think she'll make it convenient for me."

"You're planning to sneak up on her?"

"That's part of the reason why we're going to all this trouble."

"What did Rosalind do?"

"That mess at the Gehrins' last night, for one thing. Although we may have difficulty even getting it to the grand jury. God knows what else she's up to."

Shay didn't say anything, but her lips were tight as she drove down West Valley Boulevard past the airport on the bluff. Bonner was watching behind them for a possible tag team, but traffic was light.

"Are we being followed?"

"I don't think so. The back of my neck tells me I'm clear."

"Is that why you couldn't use your own car?"

"I like the way you drive in a pinch."

"I wouldn't try anything fancy in this," Shay warned. "It handles like a football. Why, Tobin? What did Ros have against the Gehrins?"

"Some complicated grudge they figure into. It could have been Frenchie Dobie she was hoping to turn into cat meat, thinking he might be a house guest. Or maybe she only wanted to throw a scare into everybody by dropping off a wild animal at bedtime. One of these days Rosalind's going to win somebody a Nobel Prize for psychiatric evaluation. Still want to be chums?"

"I guess not."

Shay took the ramp down to the interstate and got off again at Fir Creek.

"With everything else, I guess you haven't found out where Jack took off to last night. I mean, night before last; it's Sunday already."

"Over the border and under the radar in his twin-engine Cessna. He could've put it down on a landing strip in Sonora, but more likely it was the northwest corner of Chihuahua state."

"How would you know *that?*"

"I had a dep search all of Silverwhip's fleet. There was a folded Spanish-language newspaper under one of the seats, *El Diario,* which is published in Chihuahua city. Friday's date."

"Oh, God. I hope this doesn't mean—"

"Want to know what else we found?"

"If you say cocaine—"

"No, the Cessna was clean. We borrowed a dog from SWPD. The other item was a copy of Robert Browning's poems, translated into Spanish."

"I don't know how much Spanish Jack reads, if any."

"The book didn't belong to Jack Waco. It was inscribed to 'Jimmy.' From—your guess."

"How would I know?"

"Rosalind. Quote: 'How sad and bad and mad it was.' I'll bet."

"Who is Jimmy?"

"Jaime Loza, who is to Mexican commerce what Dracula was to blood drives. Pull over here, by that stand of cedar."

"Where do you want me to—"

"I want you to turn around and go home."

"How will you—"

"Rosalind can drive us both back to the lockup. This is as much police business as I care to involve you in."

Shay stopped the van.

"Tobin, I—"

"Get going," he said, opening the door.

"Damn it, call me. *Please.*"

He nodded and closed the door, then jogged into the trees that came down almost to the road, not looking back.

Bonner took the long way uphill through the canyon wood to the log house that Rosalind had told Tom Leucadio she needed for a few days. He now had a good idea of who she'd needed it for. Which called for extreme caution. He didn't know what had prompted Steel Arm Jimmy to cross the border into the United States, certainly not a book of poems or a passion for Ros Dubray. But his presence here would be cause for celebration by the DEA, when they found out.

He used his Tac Lite sparingly, and soon picked up a deer trail. Fir Creek Canyon had no fir trees, at least at this elevation, which was around four thousand feet. The major growth was piñon and juniper, with abundant salt cedar at the creek's edges. Except during big rains there were only trickles of water down stepped and hollowed ledges of sandstone, but it was enough to support a large population of nocturnals from ringtails to spotted skunks. He had shot squirrel, occasionally a turkey, and a lone bobcat in Fir Creek when he was a boy, seen the print of a black bear that had haunted his twelve-year-old dreams; but he had never tracked anything like Rosalind.

Jaime Loza had his own evil cachet, but Bonner no longer was interested in Loza. The feds could have him, for a showcase trial that would boost the stock of all the bureaucrats and politicians who were making black-bag fortunes fronting for the War on Drugs.

Bonner thought about the pelt of the elusive bobcat he had patiently sought for weeks and wondered what had become of it. Mislaid, thrown away, but the dismay he'd felt immediately after shooting the cat he had thought he coveted was newly palpable, brought back by the green spice odors and soft chill of a western wood, a burning, sensuous tension of muscle and nerve arising from the brute feel of the stalk.

He could have rolled up with a troop of deputies and state cops, or he could have told Stearman where to find Rosalind. Instead, Bonner had the sensation of behaving like another moth to her flame, and perhaps risking a bullet from one of Steel Arm Jimmy's bodyguards. But he knew that in Stearman's keeping Rosalind's chances of reaching lockup would be south of infinity. Not that he owed her anything. Maybe she had fed the Gehrins to a jaguar, but that didn't justify his turning Rosalind over to a government headsman who thought he had a score to settle.

And there were questions he wanted answered, now. Good answers might make some difference in how the dice rolled for Ros Dubray.

He heard the hoot of a horned owl, then the soft rush of wings through a stand of Gambel's oak. The hurry-scurry of a night feeder trying to escape into brush. The owl hit its prey and soared, crying out again in triumph. At a distance of perhaps a hundred yards he saw a porch light along the canyon road. A car crunched gravel. Doors opened and closed; there were muted voices. He wasn't sure, but one of the voices could have been Rosalind's.

It got quiet again. Over his shoulder Bonner had a glimpse of the moon behind cloud cover as thin as shredded silk. He took his time, ten minutes or more, moving farther uphill and into position to look down on Tom Leucadio's house. There he settled down beneath a big piñon and took compact binoculars from a jacket pocket.

In Tom Leucadio's bedroom, where Bonner had witnessed Leucadio removing a large splinter from Rosalind's foot, someone was lying faceup in the bed, with a comforter covering him to his chin. The face was emaciated, the color of weathered copper. A woman in black sat next to the bed, spoon-feeding the man soup from a take-out container. The light in the room was provided by three candles in a silver candelabrum on a dresser and votive candles surrounding the candelabrum. The woman wore a heavy-duty silver crucifix that hung on a silver chain almost to her waist.

She was having difficulty getting the man to swallow any of the soup. Bonner saw her lips move pleadingly. There were tear tracks on her seamed cheeks. She put down the spoon and picked up the crucifix, kissing it passionately. Then she pressed the crucifix against the sick man's forehead and mummified lips.

It wouldn't have been much of a surprise to see Jaime Loza writhe in torment as he was reduced to wisps of smoke and a pile of bones by the holy authority of the crucifix. But he was just another man humbled by sickness and helpless at the approach of death. Great or small, Bonner thought, shit's creek was the same for all.

Bonner's attention was diverted by the sound of a blade chunking into wood. He lowered the binoculars and looked at the deck, where a man with slicked-back sable hair, a long ponytail, and diamond rings hanging from the outer edges of his thick eyebrows had thrown a double-bladed ax at a four-by-six sheet of plywood leaning against the deck railing. The outline of a man from the waist up had been drawn on the plywood.

In addition to the ax, the hombre had a couple of tomahawks. He threw those too, overhand, getting his shoulder into each throw, lopping off a phantom arm and taking out a good chunk of indicated rib cage. When he sauntered the length of the deck to retrieve the axes, Bonner saw a gun in the back pocket of his brick-colored jeans. From the shape of the butt, a Sig Sauer.

The hombre was yanking the blades out of the plywood when Rosalind appeared at the other end of the deck, munching a burger, carrying a couple of beers in her other hand. She gave one to the hombre and settled down on a padded glider. Took another bite of her burger, swallowed it with beer, then raised one hand and waved it gaily in the air, looking up and out at the darkness of the canyon slope where Bonner was hunkered down.

"Hey, Bonner!" she called. "Don't be strange! Come on down here and have yourself a cold one. I was gonna call you anyway. Jimmy's kind of anxious to talk to you."

●

When Shay got back to the ranch, there were two rental sedans with men in them parked by the porch. Silverwhip Jack was sitting on the porch railing talking to a tall redheaded man with a countrified cowlick and an air of influence. Jack shot her a worried look as she got out of the Windstar and walked up to the porch.

Shay muffled a yawn, giving the tall man a glance before looking at her father. Trouble was all over his face, making her heart race.

Shay said calmly, "Pepper okay?"

"She's asleep. Where—"

The tall man said, "Ms. Waco, my name is Dale Stearman."

Shay paused and looked at him with no expression. He chewed gum, she noticed. He put a hand inside his jacket and held out a leather folder containing a presidential seal and government credentials.

"I need to find Tobin Bonner right away."

Shay hunched her shoulders slightly and waited for more of an explanation.

"Have you seen him tonight?" His voice was pitched low, the voice of a man whose words cost him vital energy.

"Yes."

"Can you tell me where he is now?"

"No. If you'll excuse me, I'd like to—"

"Can you tell me when you saw him last, and where?"

"I think I'd like to know what this is about."

"It's about a confidential matter of great importance to the United States government."

Shay let out a breath and made a swipe at a hardshell beetle soaring out of the night toward her head.

Stearman had long arms. He was able to grasp her shoulder with one hand without moving toward her. He didn't put any pressure on the shoulder; it was paternal contact, a gesture of communion. His head tilted forward a little as he stared into Shay's eyes. There was nothing hostile in his manner. Yet she suddenly felt cold to the roots of her heart, unwilling to be held by the strictness of his gaze but unable to look away.

"You see, Tobin's apparently gone to some trouble to avoid me tonight. He was in his office, then he *wasn't* there, and nobody seemed to know where he'd gone. Along about that time, a little before midnight according to Jack here, you had a telephone call. As soon as you hung up you left the house. That was"—Stearman looked at his stainless steel chronometer—"an hour and ten minutes ago. Driving time into Spanish Wells is twelve minutes, if you push it. Twelve minutes there, twelve minutes back, hardly leaves enough time for a decent fuck, does it? And you know how us middle-aged guys are. Tobin being, what, fifty-three or so, it must take him awhile to—"

"Quit it," Shay said, as adrenaline spiked to her temples. "What gives you the right to assume a relationship between Tobin Bonner and myself?"

"Well, it might be the tapes of the funeral I reviewed today. He never left your side. And seldom let go of your hand."

"I told you, I don't know where he is."

"Approximately will do," Stearman said, with an appeasing smile.

Shay stood mute.

Stearman shook his head slowly, ruefully. And now she felt the strength of his fingers on her shoulder, while his thumb moved in a slow, stroking motion across her collarbone. Shay fought against shuddering. She felt that it was the most obscene thing anyone had ever done to her.

"Ms. Waco? Shay? Isn't there someone of more importance to

you than Tobin Bonner ever could be? You might want to give that some thought—how much you would miss her if circumstances kept you apart for a number of years."

Shay's eyes widened, but her face felt bloodless and stiff.

"This is *crap*. And I will not be intimidated by you."

Stearman's hand left her shoulder. He settled back on his heels, gently. Past him Silverwhip Jack's face looked taut and drained.

"Of course you won't," Stearman said.

"I never move into new digs without setting up a perimeter first," Rosalind said to Bonner. "Trail timers and a six-pack of these little wireless video cameras." She pulled one from the pocket of her chamois shirt-jac to show him. The camera and transmitter were about the size of Rosalind's little finger. A sensitive gadget to delineate her territory, high-tech substitute for urine and scat. "But you guys use them too, don't you?"

"Too rich for our budget," Bonner said.

"Big question is, how did you know where to look for me?"

"Old-fashioned cop work. Stakeout and a tail day before yesterday. I was here when you visited Tom Leucadio. Where did he go, by the way?"

"Costa Rica, I think. Come on into the kitchen. You hungry? We went out for burgers earlier, but there're pizzas in the freezer."

"No, thanks, Ros. How's Jimmy?"

"Bad. We're set up at the hospital for tomorrow. Seven A.M. Assumed name, of course."

"Rosalind, you might as well try hiding a turd in a glass of milk."

She gave him a look, sharp and sardonic.

"You've probably forgotten how much forgetfulness a gratuity the size of a hay bale can buy. Especially when it comes to the Hippocratic-oath crowd. Anyway, the sooner they get to Jimmy the better, the head neuro told me. But I don't know. I think Jimmy's waited too long."

"Who's with him?"

"His mother. Name's Dolores. You want to handle *her* at the end of a sharp stick. The foot soldier is Cruz. Jimmy doesn't need him, but he felt naked crossing over without some muscle. Down home in Chihuahua there's always about seventy-five of them around the palace. Not that he had to worry about the law, which he owned, just the competition.—Shit, I've got to stop *doing* that. Past tense. The vibes are fucked enough as it is."

Bonner followed her into the kitchen.

"How come you're alone, Sheriff?"

"Maybe I'm not, Ros."

"You're alone. And you're not wired. You would have tripped another alarm coming through that door." Rosalind glanced at a TV security monitor; the screen was blank. The cameras she had planted around the house would be activated only by the breaking of one of the trail-timer laser beams connected to them. "Do you want beer or something highly inflammable?"

"Coffee, actually. I need to stay awake."

Rosalind nodded and set about brewing some coffee, like a devoted housewife. Bonner rubbed his eyes and leaned against a counter. The honcho called Cruz was lurking outside on the deck, arms folded. He had the double-bladed ax in one hand.

"Why were you sneaking up on me?" she asked.

"It's not a social call."

"But you don't have a warrant."

"Probable cause. There was a lot of blood spilled in that house, Ros."

"The Gehrins? Heard about it." She shrugged. "I can account for my time, which I'm sure you already know."

"You didn't have to be there. You had the animal in your possession. Stearman saw it, along with the truck you hijacked."

"Is that all?" Rosalind shook her head in disbelief. "You think Stearman's willing to cook my ass by testifying before a grand jury? *I* don't think so. Remember what I told you at your house? I can blow up Dale Stearman's shit any time it pleases me, and he knows it. Hey, you both know it. That's why he sent you after me the other day. You do the grunt work and he keeps score. That's always been Stearman's routine. Let me ask you something: how long are you going to let him get away with that? Or don't you carry flowers to your wife's grave anymore?"

Bonner was propelled by a surge of blood that felt like a tidal wave smashing through his head. She wasn't quite watching him as she spooned coffee into a filter. He reached Rosalind in two strides, both hands fastening around her neck. He yanked her away from the stove and spun her around, left hand seizing her right wrist. Coffee poured from the overturned can onto the floor. Bonner pushed her hand up hard between her shoulder blades, tightening his fingers on Ros's carotid artery as Cruz came barging in through the screen door, flourishing the black ax in battle mode, showing his teeth.

Bonner released Rosalind's neck, drew his gun, jammed the muzzle against her kidneys.

"Get rid of him or get shot."

Rosalind hacked out a cough and said in Spanish, "It's okay, we're old friends. Pour yourself—a drink, Cruz, and fucking relax."

Bonner said to Cruz, "Also put the chopper down, *'mano.*"

Cruz glared for a few seconds, then slowly reached out and set the ax on a hard maple butcher's block.

"That's good." Bonner looked at the stove, where water had come to a boil.

"Now drop that Sig Sauer in the pan."

"What the fock I do that?"

"Hey, Cruz," Rosalind said in a strained voice, "he's breaking my arm, man. Let's all settle down and be nice here."

"Careful," Bonner said.

Cruz drew the gun from his back pocket, holding it by the butt with thumb and two fingers, moved sideways to the stove, and lowered the Sig Sauer into the water, grimacing as if it were his own flesh he was parboiling.

Bonner figured Cruz had at least one more piece on him, and for sure he had a knife. But this was a good start in establishing who was in charge here—what Guy Baker probably would have described as dominance training.

Dolores, Jaime Loza's mother, appeared wraithlike in another doorway, fury in her face, which was quilted like snakeskin.

"What is going on here? Who is this man? My son lies dying; have you no respect?"

Rosalind said to her, "*Mamacita,* his name is Bonner. The one who Jimmy has asked for."

"Never call me 'mama.' It is an insult to my blood." She looked at Bonner. "So, you have a gun. Shoot her! We would all have been better off if my son had never met this devil-witch, whore of a whore of a whore."

Rosalind said, in English and under her breath, "Thanks a lot. I'm only trying to save his life." To Dolores she said deferentially,

"Permit Sheriff Bonner to speak now with Jimmy. He has told you that it is a matter of honor and duty."

Dolores looked as if she hated the sound of those words coming from Rosalind. Enmity was like a thick film over her dark eyes. She remained rigidly in the doorway for half a minute, one hand clenching and unclenching the silver crucifix. It gleamed from the sweat of her palm. Then she nodded curtly and turned away from them, hearing Jaime Loza call weakly to her from his bed.

Bonner let go of Rosalind, who massaged her strained elbow.

"What's this about, Ros?"

"Let Jimmy say it. Look, Bonner, you know it's not worth your while to book me on what you've got, which is hearsay."

"You're going in, Ros."

"Let it wait then until after Jimmy's surgery." There was a note of pleading in Rosalind's voice.

"If I knew where to find Katharine Harsha, and if she happened to still be alive, maybe that might work in your favor."

"Not much for guarantees, are you? If you take me in, you know I'm as good as dead. But not as a result of due process."

"If you have problems with Stearman, you brought them on yourself. Don't ask me to grieve over your fate."

"Like I said, I know too much about Stearman. And if I get a chance to open my mouth before he pops me, I'll tell him you know what I know."

"Do that. I'll take my chances with Dale. Go ahead and get him primed. It's been a long time coming between us. I'm ready for it, and I want it."

Rosalind grinned. It was almost a simper.

"I could develop a real heartache over you, Bonner."

"Do I look like I have a hard-on? I asked you about Katharine Harsha."

The grin turned sour. "Why waste your time? There are people in this world a whole lot worse than me, beginning with government assassins. We won't bring up Jimmy. Bet you didn't know he's given millions to charity."

"Birdie. Did you kill Katharine?"

Her gaze shifted to the TV monitor. The screen was still blank, the color of the sky on a cloudless summer day. But she moved her shoulders uneasily.

"Stearman taught me a long time ago to take a rational approach to my enemies. Let the scavengers have them; it's all they deserve."

"He does keep popping up in this conversation."

Rosalind rubbed the back of her neck, her eyes losing focus briefly. Bonner sensed uncertainty, an aura of distant worry.

"Yeah."

"Where is she, Ros?"

"Hell, if the sun didn't do it, the coyotes have taken care of sweet Kate by now. First, they smell the fear, you know. From a long way off. They move in cautiously, looking over the situation. They smell her sweat. The next thing they get a whiff of is asshole. And that's where they'd start in, with her asshole. Now that's justice in its purest form."

"Jesus, you make me sick."

"You gotta admit, though, I do have a certain style. Come on, Bonner, let's do this. While Jimmy can still talk at all."

"What's wrong with him?"

"His brain is like a mushroom cellar. The worst of the tumors, so I was told, is a suboccipital glioma. That's the one that's shutting him down."

29

JAIME LOZA WAS BREATHING through his mouth when Bonner followed Rosalind into the candlelit bedroom. He made a drastic sucking sound that was as bad as fingernails scraping a blackboard. His narrow body trembled slightly from the effort of breathing. His eyelids were not quite closed, revealing small new moons of sclera beneath them. Bonner's first impression was that the Mexican drug lord who had caused him so much grief in his career should have been in a hospital already. Maybe he was afraid of hospitals, or of what could happen to him there when word got around.

Bonner flexed his right hand, which still had the feel of the butt of the Browning automatic he had replaced in the holster snug against the small of his back. All the years of frustration had come down to a bust, which, he realized, after a look at Jaime Loza, he would never make—no matter how skillful the neurosurgeon proved to be. The face in the bed was its own tombstone.

He glanced at Rosalind. Her face customarily surged and shone with the electricity of a persona that was like lightning in a bottle, but now her expression was fixed and glum.

Jimmy's mother dipped a cloth into a bowl of water and moistened his dry, cracked lips with it, then used a towel to blot perspiration from his forehead. By candlelight his cheekbones seemed to glow beneath a veneer of darkly blotched skin. The windows were closed. The coils of an electric heater built into one paneled wall resembled rows of fiery teeth in a cartoon face. Another television monitor added a blue cast to the shadowy room.

Dolores looked up wrathfully at Rosalind, then leaned over her son as if she thought she were shielding his soul from a hound of hell. Rosalind kept her distance.

"Jimmy?" Ros said.

He stirred at the sound of her voice, one hand rising from his chest, mouth curving into a smile beneath his graying mustache.

She said in Spanish, "Bonner is here."

Dolores said something to her son, the words crackling with animosity and outrage; he grimaced slightly and waved his hand as if to cut her off.

"I must talk to him," he said. The long dark lashes of his eyes flickered. He moved his head slightly toward them, trying to focus on Bonner's face. He waved his hand again. Long fingers and a wide palm, although the wrist was as thin as a stalk of bleached celery, blue veins in relief. The famous Steel Arm. From what Bonner had heard, he'd thrown a cunning curve and what pitchers nowadays called a slider. But Jaime Loza never had had much size on him, except for his balls and his ego.

Bonner stepped around Rosalind and stood at the foot of the bed, between Jimmy and the blue screen of the television. Loza found his face difficult to make out because of the backlighting.

"Have we met?" he asked finally in Spanish.

Rosalind said, "He wants to know—"

"My Spanish is okay," Bonner said to her. To Loza he said, "No, we never met. I never got that far. But I treated myself to some interesting times with a few of your associates."

"I know about that. And about the source of your anger. You were wrong. I was not involved in the death of your wife."

"I know that now."

"But at the time you had to blame someone. In order to go on living."

"Hate is better than pain. A little better, anyway. What do you want with me?"

"Grant me a favor."

"I can't do you any favors, Loza."

"It is hard for me to talk. To breathe."

"Then save your breath."

"I have turned over to Rosalind a small package. Photographs.

Tape recordings. Many of the faces and voices on the tapes will be familiar to *Norteamericanos.* Very familiar. The talk is of money, always money. The negotiator in every instance is the man who destroyed so much of your life."

Loza sighed harshly, and his eyes closed.

"Are you in pain?" Rosalind asked.

He didn't answer. His chest rose and fell under the comforter.

"Where am I?" he asked, without anxiety. "I can't remember. So many things fall out of my mind now."

"You're in Utah," Ros said.

"Yes. Utah. I have always loved the United States. Truly a great country, until your politicians ruined it."

Bonner said, "You show your love by poisoning a significant percentage of the population. And we were talking about the politicians your trade has corrupted."

"They ask for it. They beg to be corrupted, like children who beg for candy. Yes. The names. They will astound you."

"I may be past the point of caring. Now tell me what you want, Steel Arm."

Loza licked his lips and smiled at his nickname.

"Did you ever see me pitch?"

"No. But I heard you were like Satchel Paige. The change-up, they say, had them swinging like rusty gates."

"Eighteen strikeouts. One game. Eighteen. It was in Matamoros, I believe. Or—"

"Jimmy," Ros prompted.

He opened his eyes. "The child," he said. "I want the child."

Bonner said, "Are you talking about Cymbeline? The child of Graciella Sinaloa?"

"Who is the niece of Jaime Loza. We are blood."

"You can't have her."

"Why not?"

"Fuck you, Loza. It *was* you, wasn't it? You hired it done and they blew the snatch at the hospital and my deputy was shotgunned to death. I buried her two days ago, so *fuck*—"

"You don't understand!"

Rosalind said, "Listen to him, Bonner."

Bonner drew his gun as he saw Cruz appear, slowly, in the doorway, a puzzled look on his face while he slowly grasped the jamb with one hand. One bloody hand. And Rosalind was looking past Bonner at the TV screen behind him. She sucked in her breath as the old woman let out a screech.

Bonner was turning to look at the infrared picture on the screen, the shapes of men moving swiftly through the hillside woods toward the house. Then his attention was caught by the sight of Cruz twisting sideways, falling slowly, with blood streaming from his mouth. There was blood on his shirt in the middle of his back where the bullet had erupted.

"The child!" Jaime Loza cried. "The child has a price on her head! She will only be safe with me!"

Bonner heard footsteps on the deck and a window was smashed. Two men dressed in SWAT-black BDU's and Nomex hoods with goggles jumped in through the shattered window. They were aiming bullpups at Bonner, yelling *Throw it down. Throw the gun down!*

Jaime Loza's mother darted from the bedroom, spry for her age as she jumped across the body of Cruz, lying feet first in the doorway.

Dale Stearman caught her in stride with one arm and, with a little laugh, spun her around and threw her, like a wing-damaged blackbird, ten feet out into the living room.

Two more FIAT agents in full tactical gear jumped in through the breached window. Bonner reached out and laid his Browning at the foot of the bed, then held his hands out from his sides.

He knew they were going to shoot him anyway. Shoot everyone in the room. But not until Stearman had had the full enjoyment of his moment of glory.

"Stearman, you miserable fuck!"

Then Rosalind glanced at Bonner, who shrugged.

"Does it look like I set this up?"

Jimmy said, his head rolling on the pillow, "Who did you say? What is happening?"

Dale Stearman unwrapped a stick of gum and said to his team leader, "Move that body and cruise the house."

The team leader nodded and took two men with him. The other one stayed, covering Bonner and Rosalind Dubray with what looked to Bonner like a British-made SA80, hailstorm weapon that could obliterate everything in the room in two blinks of an eye. Bonner's stomach had turned sour, but his blood was nearing flashpoint as he turned his eyes on Stearman.

Jaime Loza was watching him too.

"Stearman?"

"Hello, Jimmy. You're about the last person, and so forth. Bonner, you and Rosalind move over there. Stick your backs to the wall."

Rosalind didn't move until Bonner nudged her and said, with an effort to keep his voice calm, "Play it his way right now."

They moved together backward to the pickled-pine wall and stood there, elbows not quite touching. Candles burned on a bureau to Bonner's right. Rosalind was two feet from the corner and six feet from the nearest window, which was closed. Bonner measured the diagonal distance between himself and the FIAT agent, better than fifteen feet. *No way,* he thought.

As for Stearman, he probably wasn't carrying a gun, but that wasn't much help.

Jaime Loza made a great effort to raise himself in the bed. His body trembled.

Stearman walked over to him.

"Don't exert yourself, Jimmy. Rosalind told me you haven't been doing so good." He looked at Bonner, thoughtfully. "But I guess you can still waggle your tongue." He put the palm of his hand on Loza's forehead and pushed him flat, held him down, sat on the edge of the bed looking at him.

"What have you guys been talking about, Jimmy?"

Loza was struggling for breath.

Bonner said, "Stearman, don't get stupid this late in your career."

"Well, it's an interesting situation. There's the CYA material you say you dispersed, which I have no reason to doubt, knowing you; but hey, I've thought it over and we can deal with that." Stearman moved the hand that was pinning Loza down, covering his eyes and his nose as well. Loza bucked and snorted air through his mouth. "I'll bet you know how, Tobe. I'm curious. How *do* you see it, I mean right now, from my point of view?"

Rosalind said, "Get your fucking hands off Jimmy; can't you see he's—"

Bonner nudged Ros as Stearman looked at the FIAT agent and said, "Next time, shoot her."

"Sir?"

"Klesko, if she opens her mouth again, shoot her. Wasn't that clear the first time I said it?"

Klesko swallowed something heavy in his throat. "Yes, sir."

Bonner heard the other team members ranging through the house, which offered few hiding places. He knew it wouldn't be long before they returned to carry out the improvisation Stearman was still mulling like a mouthful of fine wine.

"The way I see it, you shoot us, torch the house, and manipulate the media: summit meeting between Mexican drug lord and former DEA agent deeply involved in the traffic north of the border. Federal agents intervene. Rather than surrender, the suspects opt for a Waco-style send-off."

"Former DEA agent desperately in debt because of his son. Let's not forget Rosalind, she makes good copy too, and she's damned photogenic. There should be some darling head shots available from your Vegas days, Ros. You're on the beam, Tobin. With a story like that we can drown out the other noise from your CYAs and go about our business."

Bonner felt Rosalind tensing at his side, as if she were about to spring at Stearman, clawing and spitting. It crossed his mind to let her, but sacrificing Rosalind wasn't likely to improve his own chances. He clamped a hand on her wrist. Loza continued to struggle beneath the weight of Stearman's large hand. Stearman was leaning on him now.

"Help me out here, Jimmy. It would be useful to know which one of your BVI corporations holds the keys to the heavy accounts in Liechtenstein and Mauritius. Just pass me a little sugar, okay, Jimmy? For old times' sake."

Stearman leaned harder, with the beginning of a smile as he chewed a lump of gum. Then he cried out suddenly and tried to jerk his hand away from Loza's face. But Loza had fastened his teeth into the meat of Stearman's thumb and wouldn't let go.

Stearman tried to ream out Loza's eyes with the hooked fingers of his left hand, swearing in pain. Then he balled his fist and pounded on Jimmy's head. He finally yanked himself free with a yowl, but there was bloody muscle and meat between Jimmy's clenched teeth.

Two of the FIAT special ops appeared in the doorway as Stearman pressed his wounded hand against his chest, smearing his tie and jacket with blood. He pounced on Bonner's Browning with the other hand. The Browning was cocked and locked. Stearman awkwardly thumbed the safety down.

Loza spat out the meat of Stearman's thumb and glared at him, still spitting.

"This is how you treat me, Jimmy? After I set you up? Made you billions in this country? Maybe we need to clear your head so you can think straight. Why don't we just do a little brain surgery right here and now?" Stearman raised the Browning and shot Jaime Loza through the middle of his forehead.

The FIAT team leader said from the bedroom doorway, "What the hell is going on here?"

Stearman shot Loza again as Bonner reacted, sweeping the large candelabrum from the top of the bureau. He threw it across the bedroom, not aiming it at anyone, only interested in creating a diversion. With snuffed candles flying everywhere, the light in the bedroom was suddenly reduced to the small flames of the half-dozen votive candles.

Bonner shoved Rosalind hard with his other hand.

Ros took the hint and made for the window, lifting a deer-antler chair and throwing both the chair and her body through the shattered window space. She landed on the deck outside, rolled, and was over the railing without a moment's pause.

Bonner screamed, "HOLD YOUR FIRE!" hoping it just might do some good.

Dale Stearman was between Bonner and the FIAT ops. He jerked his head and then the gun in Bonner's direction.

The two men in the doorway were jostled aside as Jaime Loza's mother came screeching into the bedroom, going straight for Stearman. In her hands was the double-bladed "badaxe" Bonner had last seen on the chopping block in the kitchen. One of the men, off-balance, made a grab for her, too late.

"Dale!" Bonner yelled, but Stearman was already turning in surprise, shocked by the chilling sound he heard behind him.

It had to be a very sharp axe because the old woman couldn't have been that strong. Yet Dolores Loza had fury on her side, the unpredictable strength of the avenger crone.

The blade of the ax split Stearman's face from the freckled bulb of his nose to his chin and sliced lengthwise through his throat. The roof of his mouth and tongue were divided. The blade cut deeply all the way to the notch between his collarbones. The force of the blow threw him backward across the still-trembling body of Jaime Loza on the bed.

Bonner's Browning automatic dropped from Stearman's fingers. He reached for the axe in his head with blood spurting and tried to get to his feet. Managed it, looked around at Bonner in disbelief, looked at the old woman. She raised a clawlike hand and spat at him.

Stearman brushed her aside and started out the door, his left hand clutching the handle of the axe that was canted at an upward angle away from his face. It looked, with his staggered footwork, like a comedy balancing act.

Stearman's eyes had begun to glaze. The other men in the room stared at him and let him go. There didn't seem to be much else that could be done.

They heard Dale Stearman blundering through the living room. A lamp fell over. They heard the front door open. Heard him cross the front porch. They all seemed to be holding their breath.

Stearman must have lost it then, or fainted from trauma. They heard his body tumbling down the steps from the porch. There were a lot of steps.

"Jesus jumping Christ!" one of the men said quietly. Another man flicked some of Stearman's blood off the front of his assault vest, went to a window frame, leaned over the glass-littered sill and vomited on the deck outside.

Dolores Loza crawled up on the bloodied bed and held her son in her arms, weeping, lamenting.

Bonner, feeling a little faint from the pounding of his pulse, said to the FIAT team leader, "You gonna do your deal, or what?"

The team leader shook his head slowly.

"This isn't what was explained to me. You're not what he said you were. This here is a fuckup. After what I heard—" He shrugged. "Sir, I reckon you're in charge now. What do you want us to do?"

Bonner looked around the bedroom. Pressure behind his eyes, the beginning of a headache he knew was going to go on for a week.

"Stand down and notify whoever is second in command to Stearman. I'll get some paramedics out here, although Stearman was probably beyond help before he made it out of the room."

Another agent wearing night-vision goggles on his Kevlar helmet poked his head through the window Rosalind had demolished and said, "The woman got away. She must know these woods. She went by me like a freakin' cat."

Bonner said, "We'll meet again. Fate just doesn't seem to want to leave us apart."

30

T. FRENCHMAN DOBIE WAS waiting in the lobby of the Med Center when Bonner came in through the sliding glass doors. Frenchie was wearing a new pale cream Stetson and a palomino-colored cattleman's suit with a black bolo tie. His boots gleamed from the recessed lighting in the lobby's vaulted ceiling. He was sitting on the edge of a bench seat surrounding the trickling fountain, facing the elevators, holding a giant bouquet in both hands: scarlet paintbrush, bush ocean spray, yellow western wallflower. He looked like a happy man, and even Bonner's unexpected presence didn't do much to darken his mood.

"Happy Fourth of July, Frenchie," Bonner said.

"What are you doing here?"

"Just stopped by to give Sarah my best. Heard she was being discharged today."

"That's right. And she is going home with none other than *yours truly*. Sarah is my intended, and we're gettin' married right away. No argument from Sarah, no sir." A muscle at the corner of Frenchie's left eye began to twitch. "Know what you're thinking, but it's a fact: Sarah decided all by herself it was the right thing for her. I didn't have nothing to do with persuading her. Hell, I ain't been allowed to spend even a minute alone with Sarah, you know that, the feds breathin' on the back of my neck."

"Same here, Frenchie. Did you have a chance to tell Sarah about the accident?"

"I did, and she forgives me."

"So everything's working out okay for you."

"Damn right. I know I still have a court date, but all that'll come of it is a fine and probation."

"Judge Arthur Carson is known to be sympathetic toward the Brightly Shining. Must have something to do with his own marital arrangements a decade or two ago."

"That so?" Frenchie said, too vaguely. He stared at the elevator doors. "Wonder what's keeping her? I know she's anxious to get out of here. What Sarah needs now is the peace and quiet of New Hebron. She's got to rest up for our nuptials. Which is Saturday. Don't look to be there."

"You're a lucky man, Frenchie. Lucky that you didn't end up like your friend Wolfgang."

Frenchie pressed fingertips against the jumpy muscle beside his eye.

"I wouldn't exactly say he was a friend of mine."

"Business associate then. Wolfgang Gehrin, Dale Stearman—you've had the luck of the saints. Double-crossing Wolfie, dealing seconds with a high-stakes player like Stearman. It was only a matter of time until he stripped your hide with a hook knife and dressed you down with rock salt just for having the sheer stupidity of trying to buy into one of his games. So you're getting married and your luck rolls on. Except for what's still out there, waiting on you."

"And I've waited too long for this day. You ain't about to ruin it for me, so why don't you—"

" 'Heaven hides its face when the wild dogs come.' Old Mexican proverb. Something I overheard Rosalind say reminded me."

"Why should I care?"

"Rosalind's nowhere to be found, but I don't think she's skipped the country. Gut feeling I have."

"I'm not afraid of that cock-gobbling freak show."

"Nobody fits into a nutshell anymore, especially the nuts. Sometimes I think Rosalind prefers to find a virtue in her acts of violence; on the other hand, she just may be amused by them. Some hikers way back in Burnt Peak Canyon came upon the remains of a former government employee named Katharine Harsha, who took a long-range shot at Rhondo in Ros's front yard not too long ago. Maybe you heard. Rosalind staked her out naked on the high ground and about all the wild dogs left in one piece was a nice set of teeth in a shattered jawbone."

The elevator doors opened. Frenchie got slowly to his feet, grimacing.

"What I heard was, you had Rosalind and you let her scoot clean away. It'll be a real pleasure seeing you voted out of office next month, you son of a bitch."

Sarah appeared in a wheelchair with a med tech in blue pushing. Shay Waco walked beside them.

Frenchie said under his breath, "Well, goddamn, look who's here." To Bonner he said, "But I told you, it's still *my* day. Sarah and me are leaving here together."

"Nobody's trying to stop you, Frenchie," Bonner said, looking at Sarah.

She was even more pale than usual, but Shay had helped Sarah with some makeup, eye shadow, and lip gloss. She wore her hair in braids instead of a puffy ponytail. She had dressed in Wranglers and a denim vest over a short-sleeved cotton shirt. She looked very young and vulnerable sitting stiffly upright in the wheelchair a little dazed, perhaps. But that wasn't unusual. Her eyes met Bonner's. She looked away immediately, indifferently.

Sarah blinked several times but otherwise nothing moved in her face when Frenchie, making glad sounds of welcome, laid the bouquet of wildflowers in her lap and kissed her cheek.

"What's the matter, darlin'? Can't you walk?"

The med tech said, "Sarah's doing just fine. Hospital regs, sir. I have to take her as far as the driveway."

Frenchie said, with his lips close to Sarah's ear, "Car's waiting right there. Brand-new El Dorado, fully loaded. I just picked it up this morning. Got that beige-honey leather inside, smooth and sweet on the road, you'll love it." He looked up. "Now, if there's nothing else needs attending to, we'll just get ourselves on out of here."

"I'll say good-bye now, Sarah," Shay told her.

Sarah glanced up, catching her lower lip with her teeth.

"Not forever good-bye, I hope," she whispered, closing a hand on Shay's wrist.

"Call me anytime. Love to see you."

"Thank you."

"Well, now, I think Sarah's gonna be plenty busy in the foreseeable future, so don't count on gettin' together for lunch."

Sarah's head was bowed as she let go of Shay, but Bonner saw something in her eyes as Frenchie spoke, a quick dark scurry, that he recalled from another day at the hospital. The undirected look gave him a tingle across the back of his neck, but she was expressionless again, holding tight to her bouquet as the Med tech wheeled her outside to the waiting Cadillac.

Shay joined him and linked an arm with his.

"How was she this morning?" Bonner asked her.

"Still has a headache and she'll need physical therapy for the injury to her neck. I washed her hair for her and she cried a little and asked if we would always be friends. We didn't talk about Frenchie, so I don't know why she's doing it."

Bonner watched as Frenchie hustled around the back end of the Cadillac, jumped, in and screeched away.

"Maybe it's Frenchie who doesn't know what he's getting into."

"What makes you say that?"

"I get these hunches from time to time; they come flying at me from outer space. Nothing I can articulate, but I'm brain dead anyway from all the depositions. Time to kick back, throw a couple of lines in the water, set off a few bottle rockets after dark, drink lake-chilled white wine, and bay at the moon."

"Umm. Does anybody know where we're going?"

"Not a soul. It'll just be the two of us, alone in the universe."

"Take me, Bonner. I'm yours."

●

In the Cadillac, headed south out of town, Frenchie said, "You never did say anything to those FBI, did you, darlin'?"

"No."

"I knew I could count on you."

Sarah's lip curled slightly. "I told them I can't remember much. Since way before my accident."

"That's exactly how you should have handled it. So then you didn't say anything about Suchary Siamashvili."

"I only said he was my friend. He *was* my friend."

"God bless and keep him. And that's all you had to say about Suchary. Just friends."

"Yes."

Frenchie glanced at Sarah as he drove. She had put on dark glasses and was resting her head in the palm of one hand, fingers at her pale blue temple.

"But you and Suchary, I mean, he trusted you and all."

"He told me everything that was in his heart before he died. How he had forsaken Jesus, but found Him again in time."

"Uh-huh. Well, that's good to hear, that he made his peace before hand. What I'm wondering, Sarah, did he ever mention anything about a, what he called 'the Dove.'?"

"Yes."

"Mention maybe where he—"

Sarah said, "Pull over."

"What?"

"I said, Pull over and stop the car."

"You going to be sick?" Frenchie asked, frowning. He hit the brake and slowed down. They were on a residential street near the high school. He stopped in the shade cast by the concrete stands of the football stadium. "Darlin', if you're gonna get the heaves, this's a brand-new—"

"Would you shut up?"

"*What?*"

"Don't say 'what' again. Just turn the engine off and give me the keys."

"Wha—. You lost your *mind,* Sarah?"

"No. There's nothing wrong with my mind. I want the keys. I'm going to take this car. It's mine now."

"Take—? What about me?"

"You're going to walk."

Frenchie pressed a hand on his heart, alert to an early ominous warning of too much stress.

"Sarah, I know you have had a rough time of it, but there is no way you will be allowed to talk to me disrespectful so long as we are—"

"The car, and I also want four thousand dollars."

Frenchie's mouth was ajar. The purple blobs under his hyperthyroid eyes were shiny from perspiration. Sarah watched him as she leaned over and removed the key from the ignition.

"Four thousand dollars a month," she said.

Frenchie grabbed her wrist, but she twisted against his thumb and easily broke his grip, screaming, "IF YOU TOUCH ME AGAIN I WILL TELL THEM *EVERYTHING!*"

Frenchie's hand was poised for a punishing slap, but he froze. "What?"

"You asshole. There's nothing wrong with my memory. When we hit your other car, I don't remember that. Before it happened and after, when I was in the Gehrins' house, yes, I can repeat everything I heard there. And I know what it is you want so bad. But you won't get it. Not the way you think."

Frenchie breathed through his mouth, staring at her.

"You   called   me—an *asshole.*"

"Assholeassholeasshole!" Sarah chanted gaily.

"Oh, my blessed Jesus! I can't believe it. This ain't *you.* This ain't my precious little Sarah Dubray I hear talking. No no no!"

Frenchie twitched and looked around with bulging eyes. His spit dried up. He croaked, "Why did we stop here? *Where is she?*"

"Where is who?"

"Rosalind! It was her, wasn't it? Rosalind put you up to this!"

Sarah sat back, car keys in her right fist, fist in her lap.

"You can get out of my car now. I'm not going any farther with you. I'm certainly not going to New Hebron. *Least* of all, I am not going to put on one of those ticky-tacky old wedding dresses they take out of trunks and be your wife number five, you assholeassholeasshole. I'm going back to school. I'm taking hotel management, and then with the money you give me, I will buy a little place of my own, maybe a bed-and-breakfast or a small ski lodge by the slopes. I'll learn to ski really well. I'll make lots of new friends, and I'll become a *happy* person. Yes, very happy, thank you."

Frenchie's hand was over his heart again, fingers digging at his breastbone. He was turning a bad color.

"When did you see Rosalind? When did that bitch—"

"Oh, it was a few nights ago. Late. Ros came up to my room at the Med."

"She couldn't have got up there; the whole floor was—"

"Rosalind's good at that. The guards were busy with a fire or something in a storage closet. We had time for a nice talk." Sarah tilted her head, as if to catch something only intended for her ears, a distant good-bye, perhaps. "I don't know. Maybe I'm not really her sugarpea and maybe I still don't like her all that much. Rosalind can be *so* obnoxious. But we are sisters after all, and we do have a lot in common. You think?"

"What?"

Sarah hunched her shoulders, suppressing a giggle.

"Rosalind said you'd look just like that, do your oogly-googly eye thing."

"No   fucking   way   you will ever   get a single   *dollar*—"

"Yes, I will. You'll write me a check *now*, and send me a check every month until I say that's enough. Or I will tell the FBI it wasn't Suchary. It was T. Frenchman Dobie who gave me the Dove for safekeeping. And then I'll simply—hand it over to them. What do you think will happen to you then?"

"You   have   ?"

"Yes. It's in a safe place. You shouldn't breathe through your mouth; you'll hyperventilate and black out. They taught us that in PE last year."

Sarah smiled kindly, now willing to bring a little light to the dungeon into which she had cast him.

"Could we hurry this up a little? I don't like to drive fast, but I can make it to Logan before dark. Registration for the summer term doesn't close until after tomorrow. I'm really looking forward to going back to college. But you know something? It was the last thing Rosalind said to me before she left. 'Sugarpea, if you're smart about yourself, you don't need any more education.' "

31

"STEARMAN IS OLD NEWS," Bonner said. "Part of the common dust. He doesn't matter to me any more, and he shouldn't matter to you."

Shay turned more comfortably against his chest and raised her eyes to his face. He had started a cooking fire in a small pit of volcanic rubble, and the smoke from the charcoal briquettes he'd ignited caused her eyes to water a little. The steaks and the fish filets were wrapped in foil, ready to go on the low tripod grill once the charcoal grayed down. Shay had tossed a salad in the miniature kitchen of the piggyback camper mounted on the bed of Bonner's twenty-year-old Chevy pickup.

At dusk on the subalpine meadow a light wind was sweeping down from the westward-running, spruce-clad peaks of the Jasper National Forest, cooling the surface of the small lake, riffling away the crimson light of the setting sun. She rubbed a mosquito bite on the back of one hand. But the meadow wasn't very buggy. About this time every evening, Bonner had said, silver-haired bats common to the area streamed from their mountain labyrinths like smoke from a burning city. One adult bat could pack away a pint jar full of insects every night.

"I need to try to tell you why I gave you up to Stearman."

"You don't have to. I know."

"He was calm. He didn't bully me. It was his detachment that froze my insides. I felt like some powerless, naked soul being checked off in the oven line."

"We'll always have that breed of sociopath. The ones who instinctively stake out the high ground for themselves. Would you like to know how he looked wearing an ax in the center of his face?"

She shuddered. "No."

The meadow was part of his father's land, more than a thousand acres of sunny hillside and outcroppings of old lava beds, compact wooded areas called savannahs, streams that wound through the marshy eastern edge of the lake. A few thick veins of unmelted snow remained in areas that lay in shade for most of the day. It had been a decade since the meadow had been open to livestock grazing, and the wildflowers were nearing midsummer profusion. But inevitably, Bonner thought, land use would change. It was in his father's will. Hoyt Bonner was leaving most of his land to the LDS; and the church would wring as much cash as possible from the bequest. Condominiums and a golf course were a good bet.

Another month and he'd be out of a job.

Bonner looked at the newly risen moon, colored by the setting sun, a blood-red stone in the indigo sky. He felt no anxiety or regret. He'd done what he could for too long. Stearman had been annointed as a dedicated public servant, the smellier aspects of his life and death covered over by one of the PR bulldozers that worked the garbage dumps of Washington politics. A scramble was underway in Mexico for the post of top cocaine trafficker, previously held by Jaime Loza. The most likely candidate disavowed any knowledge of the drug business, saying that he was only a humble, hard-working wholesale grocer. The bodyguard named Cruz, shot in cold blood by FIAT agents, got credit for the axe job on Stearman. Steel Arm Jimmy's mother was allowed to accompany the body back to Mexico for a well-publicized mass and funeral featuring prelates in tall headdresses, politicians and glamorous soap-opera stars. The *New York Times* ran a photo of Jimmy wearing his baseball uniform as a pitcher for the Tampico Seagulls in the old Mexican League. The president of the United States said that the removal of Loza as head of the Juarez cartel was "a major blow to the international drug trade," and with a stern look in his blue eyes promised to spend billions more of the people's tax dollars to keep the heat on. The sun was setting on another day; the moon was up; lies, greed, and expediency would continue to rule the world. It was time to eat and then it would be time to make love.

"I thought you said we'd be alone in the universe," Shay said.

"We are."

"Uh-uh. Someone's coming."

Her ears were obviously sharper than his. He looked around and saw the headlights of a dark blue 4WD pickup bumping its way across the trackless meadow through grasses and tall clumps of orange sneezeweed toward the lake, the last light of the sun glowing like a laser beam on a tinted side window. It looked like the F150 Supercab that his father drove.

Bonner shifted his weight on a stadium cushion, a sense of foreboding rising like a chunk of ice below his heart. The pickup was being driven too fast, almost recklessly.

"What's the matter?" Shay asked, as he got to his feet.

Bonner shook his head slightly, walked to his own truck and opened the driver's door, reached in and took down the Benelli twelve-gauge shotgun clipped to the underside of the roof. He carried it back to where Shay was now standing and leaned the shotgun against a chunk of black basaltic rock. He looked regretfully at the stoneware platter that held their unprepared dinner.

"Maybe we'd better not put those steaks on yet."

Shay rested her body lightly against him, and they waited for the F150 to get there.

The dust-streaked blue pickup stopped a dozen feet from Bonner's camper. The driver's door opened part way. His father sat inside with one hand on the wheel, looking out as if he had no strength to move.

"Tobin."

They went to him. His father fell toward Bonner as Bonner opened the door wider. A livid welt ran diagonally across Hoyt's cheekbone to the right eye, which was partly closed and supperating. There was dried blood on Hoyt's upper lip.

"Need your help," he said.

"What happened? Who did that to you?"

"Neal. I tried to stop him. He hit me with the barrel of his gun."

"Why?"

"He came for the baby. He took her. We couldn't—"

"Cymbeline?" Shay said, after a horrified gasp.

"Is Mother okay?" Bonner asked.

"Yes. In a state of shock, but—"

"What about my deputies?"

"He—shot them, Tobin. Not to kill. Took them by surprise. He was smiling, talking to me, then suddenly he turned around, pulling his pistol, one of his match pistols, from beneath his jacket. A bullet through each knee, so quick. He never intended to kill them.''

Hoyt sounded as if he were trying, feebly, to find something positive in his son's actions. He touched his welted cheek with a trembling hand, brushed away tears.

"You know how well he can shoot."

"I know how well he can shoot. Did you call it in, get medical help for my men?"

"Of course. Then I came to find you."

"How long has Neal been gone?"

"Not even ten minutes."

"Where was he headed?"

"I don't know. He was crying by then. As if he were having a breakdown. He kept saying over and over, sorry, how sorry he was. But he had to finish it."

"My, God," Shay said, staring at Bonner. He stared back.

"Yes."

Hoyt said, "I didn't know him. Didn't know him at all. He never hit me before. Tobin, he was talking like a child, making no sense to me. The look in his eyes—you've got to do something! He wouldn't hurt the baby, would he?"

"It's what he came for. She's the last of the Sinaloas. Otherwise, he can't collect the bounty and disappear. I need your truck. Drive my camper back to your place. Or Shay can drive."

"I'm going with you," Shay said.

"No."

"Tobin—listen. He has Cymbeline with him. She knows me. I can help. Do you have any idea where to look for your brother?"

"Maybe. There's a chance. He may have killed her already. But it's a hard, hard thing to do. No matter how far around the bend he may be. No matter who he's already killed. He has children of his own." Bonner hesitated. "All right. Let's get moving."

He half-pulled his father from the Ford pickup and propped him on his feet.

"Camper keys are in the ignition. If you can't drive, wait here. I'll be back for you."

Hoyt gripped him tightly by one arm.

"Tobin. It's Neal. Whatever he's done. Please. It's *Neal.*"

"I know. What was he driving when he left the house?"

"The Discovery I bought a few weeks ago. He left a rental car behind."

"Get in," Bonner said to Shay. He wheeled and went for his shotgun, ran back to the Ford pickup and climbed in. The engine was running. He handed Shay the shotgun and backed up, took off across the meadow in the direction from which his father had come, then abruptly turned south, toward benchland growing dark against the sky. Shay had buckled herself in, but she wasn't prepared for the ferocity of his driving. She laid the shotgun muzzle-first between the seats and held on with both hands.

"There's one place I can look for him," Bonner said. "If he didn't go there, then I have to turn every law-enforcement agency west of the Rockies loose on him. That's the end of Neal. Right now I'm not sure how much I care."

"All right. Bonner, you're not schooled for this kind of driving. You could flip us over."

He eased up slightly on the gas. "I know the meadow. I know where I'm going. Your idea to come along."

Shay looked at his face, looked away, bit her lip, said nothing more.

Bonner drove for nearly ten minutes without putting the wheels on anything resembling a road. For a while he followed a creekbed through a wooded canyon, then headed uphill along a park service firebreak, at an angle so steep Shay was appalled. Nothing but chasm on her side. As the truck bounced over rock and root on the uneven slope she tried to speak to him, but was jolted and bit her tongue, drawing blood.

He was slowing down. When she could speak, Shay said, "What makes you think your brother—?"

"This is a place we came to when we were kids. We played up here a lot. It was our sanctuary. It's what Neal needs right now. He's here. Those tire tracks are recent."

The break widened into a plateau fifty yards across. The headlights of the pickup illuminated the Discovery Neal Bonner had taken from his father's house. The headlights were on. A door was open. No one appeared to be inside.

Bonner stopped and turned off all but the parking lights. His hands came off the wheel. He sat there for a minute or so, the window down on his side, listening, looking. Shay watched him.

"We'd better look in that Land Rover," he said finally.

He put his hand on the shotgun, hesitated, shook his head, and got out of the pickup. Shay followed him. They walked to the Discovery, coming up on it slowly from both sides.

Shay looked into the backseat, saw a child's stuffed animal, and something else, on the floor. She lifted it out.

"Dirty diaper," she said. "Cymbeline must be with him. We may not be too late."

"Yeah. Wait here."

"Where—?"

Bonner said, "I have to go the rest of the way alone, Shay. I don't know what shape Neal is in. Pretty far gone, I think. If he sees someone he doesn't know, there's no telling what could happen. Stay in the pickup. If you hear a shot, and if Neal comes back alone—"

Shay was trembling. "The truck's in his way. He'll shove me over the side, like he did at the dam."

"This time you have a shotgun."

⬤

There was enough light from a three-quarter moon for Bonner to follow the familiar path to the pools, three stair-step depressions in wide bare outcrops of sandstone. The pools had been made by spring-fed waterfalls and snowmelt on three sides of a natural amphitheater. Two of the pools, studded with boulders that had tumbled down from the wooded cliff above, were broad and deep enough for swimming and, if you picked your spot carefully, for diving. But swimming at this elevation was for the stout-hearted: the year-round temperature of the pools, only in sun for a few hours each day, was about forty degrees.

From the last of the pools the overflow ran across slabs of slippery rock, then fell in silver strands down another, vertical cliff into a small cove thick with spruce and aspen.

Bonner heard a low cough and a stir in scrub pine beside the path. He detoured around a big male porcupine clinging to bare branches, a wild thing with moist, grieving eyes. Porcupines were unaggressive, but you never wanted to get too close to one, as Neal had found out when he was five—

"Don't come any closer."

Bonner stopped immediately. He was at a bend in the trail a few feet above the lowest and biggest of the pools. Moonlight shown on still water through the mountain lilac and juniper clinging like a hedge to the side of the trail. He heard the trickle of a dozen little streams running from the cliff face above. He didn't see his brother.

"It's only me, Neal."

"Oh. Hey," Neal said, sounding glad to hear his voice. "I kind of had a feeling you'd come."

"Yeah. Can't see you." But Bonner knew where to look, getting a fix on his brother's voice, and then he made Neal out, on the other side and between two of the pools, sitting on a low, flat rock. Holding something in his arms. "Been awhile since we had a chance to sit and talk. But we have the time now, if you want some company."

"I don't know. I guess so," Neal said in a melancholy voice.

"I'll come over," Bonner said.

He moved out into the open, stepping onto a ledge above the big pool.

"No. Stay there," Neal said, suddenly aroused.

"Why?"

"You know why. You'll hold my head under water again."

"Neal, that was a long time ago. We were—"

"It wasn't a long time ago. It was *last week.*"

"I—I guess I forgot," Bonner said, his skin clammy, feeling an eerie sense of wonder and terror, talking, once again, to the cut-up, the pesky kid six years his junior, while the shape of the man with the ruined life filled his eye.

"You could say you're sorry."

"Okay. I'm sorry, Neal."

"Why were you so mad?"

"I, uh, think it was because—you were chunking rocks at Suzy Nicholson and me."

"They weren't *big* rocks. I wasn't trying to hit anybody."

"It's over and done with."

"I *like* Suzy. But she likes you better."

"Neal, I'm not mad now. Can I come over there with you?"

"Don't lie! *Everybody's* mad at me. Dad sent you to find me, I bet. But I'm not going home. Ever again."

The remorse and finality in his brother's voice chilled Bonner.

"You know we all love you, Neal. Mom, Dad, they—"

"I'm not going home!"

"Neal, tell me something. Is the baby all right?"

Neal didn't say anything. Bonner crossed his arms tightly to try to control his shudders.

"Neal?"

"I think so. She had boo pants. I didn't have a diaper to put on her. She was crying a lot. Kept on crying. I took my jacket off and wrapped her up in it. She's probably asleep."

"It's getting late, and it'll get colder later on. Why don't you let me take Cymbeline and—"

"No."

"Why not?"

"Everybody will just be more mad. Because I took her. Dad was—did you see Dad?"

"Yes."

"Ohhh," Neal moaned. "Shit. I've *had* it."

"I don't think you meant to hurt him, Neal."

Neal began to sob.

"My head hurts, Tobin. It hurts *so bad*. And I keep thinking— bad things. They're going to blame me, aren't they? Because I was there. But I couldn't stop it from happening. Honest. All I did was watch. *He* made me watch."

"Who?"

"You know who. I never want to grow up and be like *him*."

"Oh, Jesus, Neal. I'm so sorry."

Neal shifted the weight of the bundle on his shoulder.

"I had to put her in the water. To wash her off because she was all stinky. But maybe I put her in the water too long. She's not moving. She's so cold."

"I have to take her, Neal. To a hospital, right away. You understand that, don't you?"

"Please don't come over here," Neal wailed.

"I'm coming."

"I'll have to shoot you!"

"Neal, Neal, now calm down. I just want Cymbeline, that's all. You don't want to hurt anybody else."

"You'll put my head in the water. Choke me!"

Neal stood slowly. Bonner hesitated on the narrow ledge sepa-

rating two pools. Water was seeping into one of his boots through a
sole that needed restitching. He took another step. Neal's right hand
came up, outstretched. Without appearing to take aim Neal shot him,
muzzle flash startling in the night, impact of the bullet high on Bonner's left shoulder, hard enough to cause him to lose his balance. He
fell awkwardly to his knees in the water.

Bonner raised his head and stared at his brother, finding him
unfamiliar, a spectre bristling with harm in the luster of the moon.

"I told you!" Neal screamed.

Bonner raised his left hand cautiously. He didn't know if the
bullet had come out. He hoped not. He didn't feel any blood, but
he felt splintered bone and eased the hand down again, gritting his
teeth.

"Okay, Neal. That's enough shooting for one night. Now, I want
you to put the gun down, okay? Just put it down. I don't like getting
shot. It's happened too many times. I'm bleeding and I feel dizzy.
But I'm still coming. You hear? Getting up and coming over there.
You'll have to kill me to stop me. You want to kill me? Then what?
What're you going to tell them? What will you say to Mom and
Dad?"

"It's your fault! You're making me!"

Bonner rose to his feet.

"Give me the little girl, that's all. Then I'll go away and leave
you alone. That's a promise. Cross my heart, and hope to—*damn
you,* give her to me!"

"I can't let you have her!"

Bonner started toward the other side of the pools, swallowing
hard, trying not to be sick. Searing pain in his shoulder. He felt as if
he had traveled to the end of his strength, come up short for the last
time beneath the white silence of the moon. No wind in his sails.
Just drifting.

Neal jerked his gun hand up again. The sharp stench of powder
from the first shot hung in the still air.

Out of the corner of his eye Bonner had a glimpse of something,
a flash of skin, the white of an eye, bared teeth. Otherwise, Shay Waco
was only a fleet shadow coming down from the level of the highest
pool, with a great athlete's balance and footwork. Keeping to Neal's
side, a few trees between them. She carried the shotgun in both
hands.

God bless, she had followed him.

Neal couldn't have seen Shay and probably he hadn't heard her: his ears ringing, still, from the gunshot. Neal's weapon a .45, Bonner guessed, from the sound of it, the weight he was bearing, the scope of his pain.

But Shay had open space, rock thinly covered with water to cross before she reached Neal. She was now in range but obviously unwilling to stop and shoot, afraid for Cymbeline and maybe not all that handy with a shotgun. It would be useful as a club, but Bonner knew in his gut she couldn't hope to get close before his brother wheeled and killed her. Whatever the distance Neal had traveled in his mind back to the emotional haven of childhood, his adult marksman's skills hadn't deserted him.

Okay, then. Damned if he was going to let anyone else get shot.

Bonner yelled and scrambled toward his brother, alarmed, too late, by weakness, a failure of balance.

Flash, smash, roar.

This bullet hitting him an inch above his left kneecap, off-center, scoring only flesh and muscle but taking him down again, sideways, into three or four feet of water.

As he went under, he heard Shay screaming. A warrior's scream in battle.

●

When he dragged his way out of the pool, choking and trying to focus, it was Shay he saw first. On her feet, holding the howling Cymbeline in one arm, the shotgun in her other hand, butt against her side.

Neal was on his belly, inching along blindly toward Shay, the .45 automatic still in his hand.

"Bonner! God's sake *talk* to him; I don't want to do this!"

Bonner couldn't move, and he made only a strangled noise when he tried to speak.

Neal pulled himself to a sitting position. Shay had laid his head open at the hairline with the barrel of the shotgun, and his face was bloody. He squinted to see, raising his head and the pistol at the same time. He looked up and past Shay at the moon, weeping blood tears.

"Kill me," he said to Shay.

"No!"

Neal's chest heaved. The muzzle of his automatic continued to move, slowly, up and up.

Bonner willed himself to get there.

"I don't want to grow up to be *him!*" Neal said in that childish voice.

Shay cried out in despair, "Bonner!"

He tried, but he was still several feet away when his brother jammed the muzzle of the gun in his mouth and blew the back of his head off.

32

AFTER THEY LET HIM out of the hospital, Bonner took a week off, then two. Then two more. He slept a lot, sometimes fourteen hours a day. The primaries came along, and he won his party's nomination, which amounted to reelection, by 804 votes. Sympathy votes, maybe. But Hoyt Bonner had been busy on his behalf. Markers called in, favors granted. The county commission, Bonner heard, was going to bump his salary by six thousand a year once he was formally reelected. Archer Patterson conceded without demanding a recount, and put his fancily engraved six-shooters away until the next big parade. Bonner's father also had put in a word for him at the bank where he was a director. Bonner was given an unsecured loan, which he'd been denied several weeks earlier, and the matter of the overdue mortgage payments was resolved.

Bonner wondered why his father was suddenly taking such an interest in him. After all, he'd failed and Neal was dead. But Hoyt Bonner may have concluded that the ordeal they were all trying to survive would have been even worse if Neal hadn't killed himself. After the funeral, the media quickly moved on to publicizing current social outrages: depraved teenagers who tortured the mentally incompetent, bomb makers with twisted patriotic sentiments to justify their carnage, disgruntled ex-government employees revisiting and gunning down everything that moved in their former places of employment.

Someday, Bonner thought, he and the old man might have the

opportunity to sort out their relationship. But for now he didn't feel up to it.

Shay stayed on in Solar County after her latest movie gig. Just chilling, she said. But she came nearly every day and they sat and talked past sunset, often well into the night. Those were the times when he drank more than was good for him, to keep his blood from icing, control the trembles and drive the ghosts from his heart. When she brought Cymbeline with her, Vida would be a willing babysitter, entertaining the little girl until her energies flagged and she fell asleep with a bottle, rocking in his lap.

In September, Shay enrolled Pepper in middle school in the Wells and went to work for her father, managing his business. All those college courses in finance she'd taken came in handy. She put her house in North Hollywood on the market and sold it in two days. If she missed show biz, she didn't talk about it.

His move. But time went by, and he didn't feel up to that either. Not as long as the nightmares continued.

"Hey, Bonner, wake up!"

It had been one of the truly bad ones, though it had started innocently enough. He and Neal were kids again, rock climbing. A sunny day in the Cedar Breaks. An uneasy feeling in his breast because he knew Neal was too young, only about six years old, for the cliff they were tackling. He was twelve. Up to him to see that Neal didn't get into trouble . . . but already he was stuck on a sheer face far out of Bonner's reach and crying for help. He had to get over there, even though he was badly frightened himself, the small foot- and hand-holds crumbling as he inched toward Neal. All of Eternity below. And the wind howling around both of them. Neal's face was a study in sheer terror as Bonner reached out for him. Their hands touching. Grasping. Then Bonner had him—but he couldn't hold on, and Neal went hurtling down into a slow-moving river black as tar, disappearing with a terrible sucking sound as Bonner's heart exploded . . .

"Come on, snap out of it!"

He was sitting up in bed, wet with perspiration and shaking, eyelashes matted so that he couldn't see who was in the darkened bedroom with him. But it hadn't been Shay's voice. He turned to the lamp beside his bed and blunderingly knocked it over.

Rosalind Dubray set the lamp upright again and turned it on.

Bonner winced at the glare until she adjusted the dented-in shade. "Hi," she said. "Bad dream?"

"Jesus." Bonner took a couple of deep breaths, wiping his eyes. "Is this going to become a habit with you, Ros?"

"I suppose that means you're not glad to see me."

"What do you think?"

"Still conflicted, huh? What to do about Rosalind? You didn't come looking for me, so I thought I'd drop by. They said you got shot up pretty good by your whacko brother. That one in the shoulder seems to have healed okay."

"I've been taking a little time off from the job. But I'm still sheriff. And I don't have any conflict where you're concerned. I just haven't been looking for you very hard."

"I've mostly been down in New Hebron, looking after Pappy. He hasn't been in a good way since the assassination attempt. Did something to his mind. The Prophet isn't talking to him much anymore. So Brother Jake is in charge of the Brightly Shining. He has a little more practical slant on things. That is to say, he doesn't preach apocalypse and cleansings by fire before the Second Coming. He sold off the equipment in Suchary's lab, and I guess they'll use the caves to store canned goods. Everybody's a lot more relaxed nowadays."

"What are you doing here?"

"Vida invited me to breakfast. The boy's a whiz. You ought to open a restaurant and put him in charge of the kitchen."

"What's your relationship with my son?"

"That would be complicated to explain. We met, we hit it off—"

"Damn you, Ros!"

"Just listen. I like Vida. I'm not using him for anything, although that was my intention once upon a time. I got over that. Believe it or not, I have a decent impulse on occasion."

"I'm going to see to it that you do twenty-five-to-life."

"Now why don't I believe that?"

"Believe it."

"You don't have a warrant for me yet. And you could've just handed my ass over to the feds."

"You've always been *my* business, not theirs."

"You practically pushed me out of Leucadio's house the night Stearman was axed."

"Yeah, I was hoping one of them would shoot you."

"Bonner, you lie like a kid with jam on his face." Rosalind sat on the edge of his bed, smiling aggressively. "You decided to lay off me. Why? I mean, other than the fact that you've always liked me."

"I've always thought you were the devil, Rosalind."

"That's the part you like. So what's the rest of it?"

Bonner looked her over. She was wearing pink, shirt and jeans, with a beaded Navaho vest. He was surprised at the freshness of her face, how young she actually was. But her eyes, as always, were as old as tombs.

"Jimmy leave you well-fixed?" he asked.

"Sure. Are we actually getting around to talking about your price?"

"Just curious. Seems that Guy and Pammy Baker received a letter a couple-three weeks ago from an organization they'd never heard of, dedicated to the preservation of endangered species. The letter commended them for their work. There was a cashier's check enclosed, drawn on a bank in Belize. The check was for two hundred fifty thousand dollars."

"Whoever they are, they should send *me* a check. For sure I'm an endangered species."

"So you don't know anything about it."

Ros shrugged. "If they got some money, I guess they deserved it. Like you said, Jimmy left me okay. Me and the Vatican. Not that I've ever cared much about money. All I've ever wanted is savage delight." She grinned. "Nice phrase. Forget who said it."

"I was wondering if your future plans include a long stay someplace far removed from Solar County."

"I don't make plans. I just keep my eyes open. Do you want to get up now? Vida's gone to bed and I don't know where the old lady is. I could bring you some coffee."

"No, thanks. Just hand me those warm-ups I hung over the back of the rocker."

Rosalind got up and tossed him the clothing. Bonner eased his still weak left leg off the bed and pulled on the warm-up pants. There was a pink scar eight inches long running from above his kneecap, dimpled where the bullet had struck. The .45 slug had done a lot of tearing damage. He had been three pints low on blood when he arrived at the Med Center by helicopter. Shay sitting beside him, holding Cymbeline in one arm, holding his hand.

"You've lost weight," Ros said approvingly. "Need your cane?"

"No."

"So the rest of the deal is, I move on. That sounds familiar. You planning to escort me across the state line again? Did I ever tell you how much fun I had the first time? How many nights I couldn't sleep thinking about getting even? But it wasn't about revenge; that was just girlish pique. It took me a very long time to figure out what I really wanted from you."

"I don't want to hear it."

"You heard it," she said jauntily. "And don't tell me you've never thought about it, too."

Bonner pulled the sweatshirt over his head and limped toward the bathroom.

He said, as he closed the door, "That tightrope you're balancing on is getting awfully frayed, Ros."

When he came out again Rosalind had opened the drapes and cranked two windows to let in the fragrant early morning coolness.

"Now that you mention it, my feet have been getting a little restless. Maybe it's time for new faces. I've been giving some thought to Washout, D.C. Those fabled corridors of power. Now if an old country boy like Dale Stearman could be a player, what do you think of *my* chances?"

"Thinking about it gives me cold chills, Rosalind."

She grinned as if it were a compliment. Maybe it was. With a little toss of her closely cropped red head and a quick wave she was out the door.

"*Hasta la vista*, Bonner. But not good-bye. I'll let myself out."

The door to Vida's room was open. Bonner stood in the doorway for a minute or so, looking at his son. Asleep on his stomach, as always, wearing only running shorts. His head was turned toward Bonner, and there was a slight contented smile on his face as he breathed slowly and deeply.

Bonner knew about the dawn meetings in the canyon by the park. Vida had told him about them, in his fashion. Openly, eagerly. He

liked Rosalind. His friend, the only friend he'd ever had. Bonner's
heart ached. Nineteen years old, and how little Vida really knew about
the world. Whose fault was that? He'd kept his son hidden, telling
himself it was for Vida's protection. But where did protection end
and confinement begin? He needed to think about that. Changes had
to be made, in both their lives.

He tried imagining Rosalind with his son, tried to feel anger. But
it was futile to think about what Rosalind might have done with Vida,
or to him.

It was obvious that Vida's heart had been touched. Only touched,
not damaged.

Rosalind was gone. *Leave it at that,* Bonner thought.

●

A week before Christmas and two days before their wedding, Shay
came by Bonner's office with the dress she had picked up at the shop
of the Mexican seamstress who had made it for her. The wedding
dress was securely wrapped. Couldn't show it to him, Shay explained.
Bad luck or something. Her color was high. Caught up in a whirl of
preparations. Her mother and ten close relatives had flown in from
San Francisco; the Ramada Inn was packed with Shay's buddies from
Movieland. A floating party was in progress from floor to floor.

"But you can let me have a peek," Mary Lynn said to Shay as
she came in carrying a big package, wrapped in what seemed like last
year's Christmas paper. Wrinkled foil with jolly little Santas all over
it. The ribbon somewhat frayed, as if the gift had been a year in the
back of someone's closet.

"What's this?" Bonner asked.

"I dunno. Heavy. Messenger dropped it off. There's a card. No
return address."

Mary Lynn set the package down on his desk, looked at the card
again, frowning.

"I've seen this handwriting before. Can't place it."

Bonner took the Christmas card from her. Modest religious motif. *Joyeux Noel.* He opened the card. Inside, in crabbed feminine
handwriting, he read: *"I won't be needing this anymore. I thought
you'd know what to do with it."*

He looked at the package without touching it. Shay took the card from his hand, curious.

"Uh, Boss?"

"Mary Lynn?"

"Now that I think about it, maybe I should call the bomb disposal guys at SWPD and have them tote it out of here?"

"Bomb?" Shay asked, dismayed.

Bonner shook his head reassuringly and picked up his letter opener. The ribbon was taped to the package in a couple of places, but he didn't see anything sinister when he turned the package to examine it. He left the ribbon alone and slit the foil wrap on one side. He looked up calmly. In spite of his air of imperturbability, Shay and Mary Lynn had backed away from the desk to the door.

There was a big Lego box, which had once contained colorful interlocking building blocks for children, inside the wrapping.

Bonner pried carefully here and there with the point of the letter opener.

Shay said, "We *are* getting married on Saturday. No more excuses, and blowing yourself through the roof doesn't count either."

"Cross my heart," Bonner murmured.

He finished unwrapping the Lego box, studied it, then popped the lid open. He looked inside, looked at the ceiling, looked down into the box again at the polished nickel sphere to which Suchary Siamashvili had dedicated the last years of his tortured life. Fascinating. But in the end just another variation of hell on earth, which a tiny minority of perverse ideologues continue to dream up for the rest of humanity.

He passed a hand between the lamp on his desk and the Dove in the box, casting a swift shadow across its brightness. Outside the December sun was high, the sky without a cloud. The citizens of Solar County went about their business oblivious of the fate that had passed them by. This time.

"Well?" Mary Lynn demanded.

Bonner closed the lid of the box and smiled at them.

"It's a paperweight," he said. "Shay, how about lunch?"